THE SEVENTH MOON

B A N T A M B O O K S

NEW YORK   TORONTO   LONDON   SYDNEY   AUCKLAND

MARIUS GABRIEL

THE SEVENTH MOON

THE SEVENTH MOON

Book design by Susan Yuran.

ISBN 0-553-09654-0

Bantam Books are published by Bantam Books, a division of Random House, Inc. Its trademark, consisting of the words "Bantam Books" and the portrayal of a rooster, is Registered in U.S. Patent and Trademark Office and in other countries. Marca Registrada. Bantam Books, 1540 Broadway, New York, New York 10036.

This book is dedicated to my beloved parents,
Elizabeth and Giovanni.

THE SEVENTH MOON

HONG KONG

It was the fifteenth day of the seventh moon. A storm was sweeping in from China.

Early morning, and the traffic was streaming relentlessly through Kowloon. She gazed, half-mesmerized, at the endless rivers of humanity. Every street, every alley, every inch of space was choked. A city of five million souls was going to work in a brown murk of traffic fumes. The sun had risen, but was already dying bloodily among the storm clouds in the east.

Francine sat alone in the back of the cream Rolls-Royce, cosseted in yards of soft leather. Up front, her driver, Ka Tai, fidgeted and muttered impatiently at the snarled traffic waiting to board the car ferry.

By the side of the road, an old man was carefully piling paper toys on a stall. The models were of desirable possessions—houses, cars, horses, furniture—and were exquisitely made. The driver of the car in front of them darted out to buy some of the models, leaving his car blocking the lane.

Ka Tai hammered the Rolls's horn, sending a blast of indignation into the general ocean of noise.

"Stop that," Francine commanded. "There's no hurry. Let him buy."

"Sorry, Mem," Ka Tai said, easing off the horn. Across half of Southeast Asia, her servants, her employees, even some of her many business partners, called her that.

The Chinese-language press had coined the title *nuhuang* for her, "empress." Among her Asian employees, it was always Mem, the way Asians had addressed European ladies long ago, when the Pacific Rim had been a colonial lake, and not an awesome generator of global wealth. Once, when she had asked one of her managers how the name had come about, he had replied with a smile, "Because you always behave like a British lady." But there was mockery in it, too. There was in most of the names Asians gave Westerners. And she suspected that, no matter what they said, that was what she would always be to them, a *gwailo*, a *gaijin*, a *farang*, a foreign devil.

She was, in fact, half-Chinese, half-British. Her name was Francine Lawrence. Her "Chinese" name, Li Yu Fa, was no more than a vestige, a sad relic that could be neither used nor thrown away.

At fifty she was compact and energetic. Her dark hair was bobbed, so that only part of its natural wave showed. She had a distinctive face, oval, with a full mouth and cloudy green eyes. Once there had been no shortage of men who had desired her for her beauty. These days, though she was an attractive woman, they focused more on her wealth and power. She had found only one who had desired her for her heart and soul. But she had lost both of those commodities long ago, and after they had been torn out of her, there had been nothing more to say to that man.

She had no children. She was still building her empire, and expected to keep building it for another forty years or so. It sometimes occurred to her to wonder whom she would leave it all to when she died. It would be a substantial thing, a conglomerate of money, buildings, land, factories, people, worth many millions of dollars. But that question did not usually trouble her for long. She was alone in this world, and she was not building her empire for anyone else. She was building it for herself. Her achievement, her refuge, her memorial.

The man in front of them was still haggling over the price of the paper models. The things would, in any case, be taken home and burned. It was the Festival of the Hungry Ghosts, a dangerous time. During the seventh moon, the gates of the underworld were opened to allow the dispossessed to roam free, the ghosts of those who had died without the proper ceremonies. The paper replicas of worldly things would be set alight to placate these hungry, wandering spirits.

The Tao meant as little to her as the Bible, yet now, without thinking, she tapped Ka Tai on the shoulder.

"Buy me some spirit money."

"Yes, Mem," he said without surprise. "What else shall I get?"

"An airplane. A horse. Toys. Food. Clothes."

"Yes, Mem."

He got out of the Rolls and hurried over to haggle with the old man who had made the paper models.

The telephone set into the walnut panel beside her began to ring. Francine lifted it, pulling the spiral cord across her lap. "Yes?"

"Good morning, Mem."

Francine checked her wristwatch. The business day that was just beginning here in Hong Kong had already ended in Manhattan. "Good evening, Cecilia. Why are you still in the office? Is anything wrong?"

"Something came up at closing time, Mem."

Cecilia Tan had been with Francine for more than fifteen years, since the early days in Singapore, and there was a bond of trust and understanding between them. "What came up?"

There was a brief pause. "A visitor. A young lady from Borneo."

"What did you say?"

"A young lady called," Cecilia said flatly. "She claimed to know you. She said you last met in Borneo, a long time ago. In Sarawak."

Francine's skin was suddenly cold, colder than anything the air-conditioning could achieve. "Is she there now?"

"No. She left when I told her you were out of the office."

"But you talked to her?"

"We talked for a short while."

"What kind of young lady was this?"

"A young *serani* lady," Cecilia said. She had used the Malay word for a Eurasian.

"Can you describe her?"

"Very pretty. A good figure. She wore a miniskirt and a jacket. Not expensive, but nice."

"What color eyes?"

Cecilia paused. "I don't remember. I'm sorry." Francine could hear the tension in Cecilia's voice. "She was only here a short while."

"What did she call herself?"

"She said her name was Sakura Ueda."

"That is a Japanese name."

"Yes. She said she had lived in Japan for a long time. But she said she once had another name."

"What name?" Francine whispered.

"She said she would tell you when she met you."

"Did she leave a card? An address?"

"No. She said she would call again when you were back in New York. I told her you would be here next Tuesday."

Francine felt that she had been robbed of breath. There was an aching, hollow place in her chest. At the periphery of her vision, the traffic of Hong Kong hurtled past her, silenced by the Rolls's insulation. But she was seeing another road, another time.

"Mem? Are you still there?"

She had been silent for so long that Cecilia was worried. It was an effort to speak. "Yes. I'm here." Mechanically, she checked her watch. "I'll call you later tonight. When I get home."

"Yes, Mem."

The line cut dead in her ear.

Her hands were shaking as she replaced the unit in its cradle. She felt numb. Could it be possible? Could such things happen? She had resigned away hope, in a deliberate act, some years ago. Before then, she had once had dreams something like this. The pain of awakening had been terrible, as terrible as the joy of the dreams. She did not want to awaken now. Yet she knew it was not a dream. She had come so far along the road of life, and had lost so much on the way, that she was no longer afraid of further loss. But she was afraid of the torturer, hope.

"Mem?"

She looked up blankly. Ka Tai had opened the door of the Rolls, wrinkles of distress extending from his forehead over his cropped scalp.

"Are you all right, Mem?"

She raised her hands to her face, and pressed her palms hard into her eyes. "Yes. I'm fine."

He had an armful of papier-mâché miniatures. "I got these things."

He passed the models back to her. He had bought what she'd asked for. Flimsy paper tokens of everything she would have given, everything she would have done.

An airplane. A horse. Toys. Food. Clothes. Money. Everything.

She laid the things on the seat beside her. "Let's go now, please. Quickly."

By evening, Francine had rehearsed Cecilia's few words so many times in her mind that they had started to lose their meaning, and she was almost afraid that she had misinterpreted them, heard in them some meaning that they'd never had.

A young serani *lady. She said you last met in Borneo, a long time ago. In Sarawak.*

During twenty years spent building her business, many people had tried to deceive her. But none had ever tried this particular prank before. Very few people, she supposed, even knew where and how she had passed the war. Like many who had suffered, she did not make a habit of broadcasting her experiences. She had buried them in her own memory, and she had hidden them from others. But those words unleashed a flood of pictures, hideous and gorgeous, terrible and sweet.

Very pretty. A good figure. She wore a miniskirt and a jacket. Not expensive, but nice. She said she had lived in Japan for a long time.

She could not stop thinking of that. Japan. The one explanation she had never considered. The one place she had never searched. Could that one word contain the truth?

She said she once had another name. She said she would tell you when she met you. She said she would call again when you were back in New York.

The storm had raged all day, a monsoon tumult of driving rain. It ran in rivers down the plate-glass windows while she ate, alone in her lacquered dining room.

She had first been based in Tsim Sha Tsui. The relentless pressure on housing had sent property prices spiraling upward in the early 1960s, and in 1966 she had relocated the factory to a new industrial estate at Tai Po, and sold the small original site to a hotel company for a five-million-dollar profit.

Much of that profit had gone straight back into the business. But she had also been lucky enough to buy herself the new apartment on Victoria Peak, using financial muscle to beat the influence-weighted bids from the colonial government and the hongs.

It was an airy nine-room palace, with a spacious balcony commanding a sweeping view of the harbor. The building boasted a pool on the roof, and she had bought parking for five cars in the basement. But Francine loved it most for its natural setting. From the carefully tended communal garden, she could walk straight into forests of bamboo, fern, and wild hibiscus. She could watch kites and hawks gliding on the thermals two thousand feet above the harbor. But now her eyes saw nothing of the luxury around her.

It could not be. Such a thing was impossible. They had found some creature and had prepared her to repeat, parrotlike, what they taught her. No doubt she looked right. No doubt they expected golden results, a rich harvest for the work they had put in.

Or perhaps the woman, whoever she was, had dreamed it up herself. Perhaps she was a cunning and skilled actress, prepared to risk eventual discovery for a brief admittance to the treasury.

The woman had not said that she was Ruth. Of course not. This was a preliminary move, a coat-trailing exercise to lay down the scent. Claim to be Ruth in front of Cecilia Tan? Of course not. She would save that dramatic moment for Francine, not waste it on a secretary.

But Ruth had been dead for nearly three decades. A Japanese bayonet had taken her life. Her body had disintegrated in the jungle, eaten by beasts or covered in a hasty, shallow grave. Nothing remained of her. Not even a photograph.

Tears, for so long strangers to Francine, were perilously close.

It is a lie. It must be a lie.

The servants came in to clear the table, and Francine went to her study. When the storm had quieted to a soft rain, she picked up the telephone and called Cecilia Tan. It would be midmorning in New York.

Cecilia had been waiting for her call. Her voice was excited, and she spoke quickly in Cantonese.

"After I spoke to you last night, I wrote down every single thing I could recall about this person's appearance. I also wrote down everything she said, as exactly as I can remember it. Do you want me to—"

"No," Francine cut in flatly. "I don't want to hear any more about her."

"Mem?" Cecilia said in astonishment.

"She is an impostor."

Cecilia's voice rose. "She did not give that impression. She was a quiet person—"

"Do you think she would come in with a placard around her neck announcing that she was a liar?" Francine retorted. "You told her I would be back in the office next week?"

"I said you would be here Tuesday."

"And she said she would return then?"

"Yes."

"Good. This is what I want you to do. Contact Clay Munro at Munro Security. Tell him about this. When the woman comes back, I want him to follow her back to wherever she comes from. I want Clay to find out who she is, whom she speaks to, where she goes. I want to know everything about her. I want him to keep a daily updated dossier on her. With photographs."

"You want her followed?"

"I want her turned inside out. Naturally, I would prefer that she not be aware of any of this. But it doesn't really matter if she does find out."

"But—but what shall I tell her?"

"Tell her I'm not available."

"Is that all?"

"That's all," Francine said dismissively. "Tell her that I said I was not available."

"I think you should at least see this young lady," Cecilia said. Her voice had changed from that of an efficient secretary to that of someone advising an old friend who is going wrong. "Before you do any of this, you should see her and listen to her."

"No."

"She did not give the impression of being an impostor. She made no claims."

"Of course not. That would come later."

"There is something about this person—"

"Cecilia, do as I ask you, and please do not presume to advise me on my private life." Francine had spoken calmly, but the words were meant to cut. "Tell Clay Munro I'll be in touch with him next week."

"Yes, Mem," Cecilia said without inflection.

"I know what I'm doing, Cecilia," Francine said, more gently. "Good-bye."

She hung up and rose from the desk. She had done the best thing she could have done. She believed that.

Something caught her eye: the pile of paper spirit possessions she had made Ka Tai buy earlier. She stared at them for a moment. Then she took them, beautifully crafted things that weighed nothing, and stacked them in the fireplace. She almost never lit fires, so she had to hunt for matches. She found a box in the kitchen.

She lit the pile. Yellow flames leaped up swiftly. The emblems twisted, shriveled, leaped through ashes into the spirit world. Then they were gone.

Francine was aware, for the first time, of physical weariness. She went to her bedroom and opened the main alarm console, which was close to her bed. She turned the key to arm the system. As always, she stayed to watch the rows of little green lights wink on one by one, signaling that each door, each window, each entrance was secure. When she was sure that she was locked safe within her electronic stockade, she went to bed to face whatever dreams might come.

ONE

BABE IN ARMS

1941

IPOH, MALAYA

Francine looked down into Ruth's face. The child was sleeping peacefully. The morning was sultry, monsoon weather that threatened drenching rain at any moment.

Her mother's sisters squatted on the bamboo mat in a circle, all talking at once. Francine was not listening properly because she was focused on Ruth; but one word kept exploding like a gunshot in the talk: Nippon. The Cantonese phrases rose and fell around it like flocks of birds, fluttering up in sudden fright, settling gingerly, fluttering again. Two nights ago, the Japanese had attacked the American base at Pearl Harbor in Hawaii, doing extensive damage to the Pacific Fleet. America was now at war with Japan.

At the same time, the Japanese had struck much closer: at Kota Bharu, a town on the other side of the Malay Peninsula, a mere 150 miles away. The official British line was that the Japanese had been repulsed. But wild rumors, brought on the monsoon winds, were blowing around the kampong.

"Don't worry, Aunt," one of the younger women said, "the English will make sambal out of the Japanese." She mimed the way *nonya* women pounded chili paste. The others laughed.

But Aunt Yin-ho, who was the undisputed matriarch of the clan, cleared her throat and spat out of the door. "England's day is done."

"Auntie!" several of the women exclaimed in dismay. They were all *peranakan*: born in the Straits, educated in English, loyal to the English crown.

Yin-ho lifted a finger. "The Japanese are coming, Yu Fa." That was Francine's Chinese name. "They are the new lords of Asia. Tell your husband. You and he should go away. Tell him."

Francine nodded. The aunties were all much older than she was. And the details of her birth and marriage (English father, English husband) gave her a low status here, even though she was now mistress of the handsome general manager's bungalow at the Imperial Tin Mine. "Yes, Auntie."

Francine came in to Ipoh every week, bringing little Ruth. She left with baskets of fruit and food prepared by the older women. For the past few weeks, she had also been entrusted with dire warnings about the Japanese to carry to Abe. Abe had laughed and asked, what did a load of nonyas know about war and international politics? But Francine had been born in the kampong, and she knew the kampong voices were wise.

She touched the face of the child sleeping in her lap. Francine had married Abe at seventeen, and Ruth had been born nine months later. She was just four years old.

Ruth was a baptized Methodist. But on all the important occasions of her life, Francine had taken Ruth to the Buddhist temple where the devout burned joss sticks and pasted gold leaf to statues already thick with gold. Abe disapproved of the idea of Ruth being taken into "heathen temples." If, when he took Ruth in his arms when he came home in the evening, he caught a snatch of incense in her dark hair, or found a flake of gold leaf on her little fingertips, he would be angry.

The eyelids of the child in her arms fluttered. "Mama?"

"Mama's here," she said softly. Ruth was arrestingly beautiful. Her skin was pale gold. Her hair was thick and gleaming brown. She had inherited Francine's oval face and full mouth. Her eyes were almond-shaped and dark-lashed, set over high cheekbones, yet their color was not brown but silver-gray.

Even at her tender years, Ruth could pass neither as fully Chinese nor as fully European. Like Francine, Ruth would stand uneasily between two races, despised by the British, only tolerated by the Chinese. She would be enriched by two cultures and yet she would be excluded by both.

What hurt Francine most was when the aunts predicted that she was no more than a temporary wife, that one day Abe would marry a European woman and have European children and that they would never see him again.

That was what Francine's father had done to her mother. She remembered her father as an affectionate, generous man. Yet when his contract had ended, he had gone back to England, and apart from the twenty Straits dollars a month that always came, they had never seen or heard of him again. Once, when she had asked her mother for the thousandth time where her father was, her mother had banged her fist on the box where she kept the receipts, and had replied bitterly, "He is in here," and Francine had known that the twenty dollars a month was all she would ever know of him from then on.

And that was the unspoken theme that underlay almost all the aunts' nagging. Since the death of Francine's mother, they were her moral and spiritual guardians. Though Francine knew there could not possibly be any truth in what they said about Abe, it filled her with terror nonetheless.

She heard a car engine and checked the pretty little gold wristwatch, Swiss and expensive, that Abe had bought her when Ruth had been born. It was time to go back. The taxi threaded its way through the trees toward the house. In its wake ran a throng of naked children, to whom a car was still a marvel.

The aunts came down the rickety steps to say good-bye, five middle-aged Chinese women in creased pantsuits, puffing on small metal pipes or rolled cigarettes. The chatter did not cease. It was Chin Yin-ho's voice that rose above the others: "Yu Fa, tell your husband to send you away." She pinched Ruth's flushed cheek. "Let him take you and the child to England, to stay with his family." Her lined face took on a hard cast. "But of course, he is too ashamed to show you to them!"

For once, either because she was nervous or because she was exasperated, Francine was impatient with an older relative. "Abe isn't ashamed of anything!"

Yin-ho sniffed. "Then let him take you. You know what the Japanese do to Chinese women who marry white men?"

They crammed the baskets into the taxi and waved from the back window as it drove away. Ruth nestled up against her mother. "Are we going away, Mama?"

"Auntie sees bad people behind every bush," Francine said irritably.

"Are the Japanese bad people?"

"Don't worry, my darling. Mama will look after you. Perhaps we'll all take a holiday in England."

Not understanding, the child smiled her beautiful smile.

Abe came home early. The food was still on the stove, the table unlaid, the servants chattering.

As soon as he got out of the car, and walked up the drive, she knew something was terribly wrong. She knew his face. She hurried to meet him as he came in.

"What is it?" she asked urgently.

"Bad news, darling," he said, kissing her.

Abraham Lawrence was a tall, rangy man in his late thirties. He looked older because his face was weather-beaten. His eyes were a deep blue, the whites slightly yellowed by the chronic malaria from which he, like so many other mining engineers, suffered. Squinting against the sun had etched deep crow's-feet at his temples and had bracketed his wide mouth with two curving lines.

"What's the bad news?" she asked in dread.

"The *Prince of Wales* and the *Repulse* are gone. Sunk by Japanese torpedo bombers."

Francine's hand went to her mouth. "It can't be." She felt a sinking in the heart. "It must be Japanese propaganda."

"Afraid not. It's been announced on the radio. Turn it on."

She obeyed. As the valves warmed up, announcers' voices faded in from the ether, drawling in that strange idiom known as MBC English, after the Malayan Broadcasting Corporation. Her eyes were wide and anxious as she tried to follow the commentary.

Ruth was clamoring for her father's attention, calling, "Dadda! Dadda!" Abe picked up the child and hugged her. "Have you come home to play with me, Daddy?" Ruth asked.

"That's right, honey," Abe said, kissing her.

Francine listened to the handsome teak-boxed radio, stunned. Two great ships, indeed, the whole Royal Navy presence in Malaya, had gone. The news had the impact of a vast natural disaster, a flood, a chasm opening in the earth.

Francine could feel the pounding of her heart. "The aunties say the Japanese are coming."

"Yes," Abe said, looking at her over Ruth's shoulder. "That much is true. The MBC says they're being driven back into the sea. But I've heard other stories."

The voices on the radio, like Abe's, sounded calm, but vibrated with tension. "What stories?"

"They've established a beachhead."

"What does that mean?"

"It means the landing was a success. They're pouring troops into the country." The Malay kitchen staff had stopped clattering around the stove, and were standing in silence. They were listening intently to what the tuan was saying. Becoming aware of this, Abe took Francine's arm and led her away from the kitchen door. "We're going to have to do something, old girl," he said in a low voice.

"What?" Francine asked in dread.

"You and Ruth will go down to Singapore. Find an amah to help you there, of course."

"And you?"

"I have things to do here."

"What things?" she demanded.

"I can't just drop everything."

"You could shut down the mine," she said. "Give the workers a couple of weeks' wages and let them go to their homes for a while. That way, everybody would be out of danger."

"And what would the owners say about that?" he snorted.

"The way things are going, the owners are going to lose the mine anyway," she said bluntly.

"Is that what your old nonyas are saying in the kampong?" he said scornfully. "I wish you wouldn't listen to those silly old fools. We all know they can't wait to see the Japanese crowing on the dunghill."

"How can you say that, after what the Japanese have been doing in China?" she exclaimed.

"In any case," he said shortly, "I can't come down with you, and that's that. My first duty is to the owners."

"A bunch of fat businessmen in Manchester?" she said incredulously.

"You haven't joined the Kuomintang, have you, old girl?" he said dryly. "You sound like a bloody Communist!"

Little Ruth piped up, her face alarmed. "Don't shout at Mama, Daddy!"

"Don't you turn against me, too, Ruthie," Abe said. "I'm not shouting at Mama. Just trying to reason with her."

"We won't leave you," Francine said quietly.

Abe pinched her cheek. "Now, don't be silly, darling. There's no danger at all. I just want you and Ruth out of the way of any panic. You'll be better off down there. As soon as the situation gets back to normal again, you can both come back home."

"And if the situation doesn't get back to normal?"

Abe paused, glancing at Ruth. "Then of course I'll come and join you in Singapore," he said. "But it won't come to that."

"It might well come to that, and it might well be too late by then! We have to go together, Abe. All three of us."

"Don't be silly," he repeated, trying to be patient.

"We need you, Abe," she pleaded.

"So does the mine," he said, smiling. "So do the owners."

"Don't we count for more than the mine and the owners?"

He cocked his head at her. "What's that old poem? 'I could not love thee, dear, so much, loved I not honor more.' Know it?"

"There's no honor in a mine, Abe. Don't be a fool!"

Abe stiffened. He was not used to having her argue with him in this way. She had joined the mine at seventeen, as a humble clerk. Abe had been dazzled by her, and she had not worked for very long. But Abe had given up a lot for his infatuation with a Eurasian woman. Many of his former friends and colleagues regarded it as an unpardonable offense to marry what their terminology called a half-caste, and now they ostracized her. Even the ones he called his real friends had not accepted her. They had both had to put up with slights, snubs, and worse. People said the marriage had crippled his career.

"If it comes to the worst, I will need to disable the machinery so that the Japs can't use it for their own war effort. Tin is a strategic metal, you know, and—"

She interrupted angrily. "I know what tin is, Abe. And you can't disable the machinery badly enough so the Japanese can't repair it."

"If you'll pardon me for saying so," he retorted coldly, "I think I know rather more about the subject than you do. You'll go on down to Singapore, Francine. And I will follow you if necessary."

"If necessary! So Ruth and I come second to the mine?"

His gaze was frosty. "In this situation, yes."

Francine was wearing a blue *cheongsam*, high at the throat and clingy at the hips. Suddenly, it felt chokingly tight. "I have to change for dinner," she said. She hurried to her room to change into a skirt and blouse and change her little black slippers for leather shoes with a heel.

Her family upbringing had instilled in her that a wife never contradicted her husband to his face. But she knew Abe was terribly, terribly wrong now.

When she came back, Abe was lying on the floor, playing with Ruth. " 'And this little piggy went *wee, wee, wee,* all the way home!' "

"Daddy," Ruth squealed in delight, "stop tickling!"

Francine was trembling with nerves. Her voice trembled, too. "They point the wrong way," she said.

"What?"

"The guns of Singapore. I've seen them. They point out to sea, Abe. The Japanese are coming from the north. From the land."

He stared at her for a while, thinking. Then she saw the dismissal in his eyes. "The Japs have worn themselves out in China," he said. "They haven't the resources for an invasion of Malaya. They're just trying it on. It'll fizzle out soon. Then everything will be back to normal. They'll never get to Singapore. It's impossible."

"You said they're pouring troops into the country," she said, her voice rising.

"Keep your voice down, for God's sake," he commanded, nodding toward the servants.

"The servants know what's happening. Do you think it's a big secret?"

"I've never seen you like this before," he snapped, "and I don't like it much. What the hell has got into you?"

"I just want us all to stay together in the middle of a war, not split up!"

"Mohammed will drive you down in the Ford," he said obstinately. "You can stay at Raffles. You love Raffles. Remember our honeymoon?"

"I won't leave you!"

"Don't worry about going in on your own," he said, ignoring her. "Any trouble, refer them to me. All right?"

"I'm not going!"

"Don't argue," he said, raising his voice, taking on the tone he used at the mine, when he needed to get his way. "I know better than you, Francine. Get that into your thick Chinese head, for heaven's sake."

She stared at him incredulously for a moment. He had never spoken to her like that before, or in that tone. Then she looked from him to the child sprawled on the silk rug. Ruth's safety was more important than either of their wishes. She knew now that Abe would not go with them, in which case, she had to get Ruth out of the way of any harm. "Very well, Abe," she said quietly. "I'll do as you say."

"Well, thank God for that," he said, still cross with her. "Now go and pack."

Ruth chattered nonstop as Francine wept during the long drive down to Singapore.

"But why isn't Daddy coming with us?" she asked for the hundredth time.

"Because he wants to stay at work."

"But the bad people are coming!"

"I know, darling."

"What will the bad people do to Daddy?"

"They won't hurt Daddy. Daddy will run away before they arrive."

"Daddy says he won't run away from anybody," Ruth said proudly. "He said the Japanese are just silly people. Why are you so frightened of them, Mama?"

Francine shook her head without replying. Abe had paid little attention to what the Japanese had done in Nanking. To him, it had been one bunch of Asiatics squabbling with another. But in the kampong, the ghastly tales of slaughter, rape, and looting had had a profound impact.

Abe had been wrong. The Japanese had gotten to Singapore even before Francine arrived. Or at least, their planes had. As the car crossed over the Strait of Johore at dawn, greasy pillars of smoke were climbing from the city, ominous in the humid air.

But the city wore an air of studied unconcern. No more than a handful of bombs had fallen. Impassive workers were sweeping rubble and shattered glass off the pavement. The Europeans picked their way through the debris with the air of people determined to ignore a display of boorishness.

"Did the Japanese do that?" Ruth asked, staring at the bombed buildings with wide eyes.

"Yes, Ruth."

"That was bad," Ruth conceded thoughtfully.

Raffles Hotel, like the rest of Singapore, wore a slightly detached air. There was an unnatural quiet in the foyer, very different from the bustle she had enjoyed so much during their honeymoon five years earlier. On that occasion, with her British husband at her side, she had been too happy to pay much attention to the staring and muttering. This time, she was alone with her child, and it was evident that the staff were disagreeably surprised to discover that "Mrs. Abraham Lawrence" was Eurasian. The old Sikh jaga, stiff in his white whiskers and cream turban, stood at her shoulder as though ready to throw her out at a word from the reception staff.

"I do hope there hasn't been any confusion," fluted the receptionist. She pretended to scrutinize the ledger. "I'll just check that your booking has in fact been made."

"If there is any confusion," Francine replied in a quavering voice, "you may take it up with my husband." She placed the card on the polished mahogany desk. "This is his telephone number."

The receptionist's eyes slid away from Francine's, saw the words *General Manager* on the card. "Excuse me." She took the card and melted into a back office. Francine heard the rattle of a telephone handset being wound.

Ruth was clinging to Francine's skirt, her head resting on her mother's hip, her silvery eyes wandering. The grand hotel seemed deserted.

She glanced over her shoulder. The bellboys had already brought in her trunk. Outside the portico, Mohammed stood beside Abe's big, mustard-yellow Ford, waiting patiently to see her installed before returning up-country.

"And there's worse." The voice was clipped, military. It belonged to an elderly, gray-mustached man in a white flannel suit and a panama hat. He was talking to a wattled woman in a floral print dress as they emerged from the elevator. "A damned sight worse."

They came up to the desk. The man smacked the brass bell sharply to summon attention. The receptionist's glossy head poked out of the back office. "Oh, good morning, Brigadier."

"Key," the brigadier said, rapping the heavy steel thing on the desk. She glided out to take it from him. The old man reached out and chucked Ruth under the chin. "Hello there, young lady."

"Hello, Mr. Man," Ruth said. "You've got a nice hat."

"I like it, too." He smiled at the child with watery eyes that Francine assumed were too faded to see that she was Eurasian. His companion's wattled elbow jabbed him briskly in the ribs. He ignored her, and tipped his hat to Francine. "Just come down from up-country?" he asked.

"Yes," she replied, embarrassed at the attention. "That's right."

He nodded. "Good show. Get the small fry out of the way, what? Doesn't do to have them frightened."

"No."

"I'm not frightened," Ruth informed him.

"Good show." He rose and fell on his bootheels. "Ill-mannered brutes, the Japs," he said, as though the just-begun invasion were a show of bad form, no more. "Soon teach them a lesson, don't worry about that." He glared at the receptionist. "Can't you see this lady is tired? Let her get up to her room with the child. Chop-chop!"

"Of course, Brigadier," the receptionist said, evidently intimidated.

The brigadier and his companion walked out, the old man swinging his cane grandly. "Devil of a show going on," Francine heard him saying. "Heard it from my nephew half an hour ago. Devil of a show." His companion glared over her floral-printed shoulder at Francine.

"They will show you up to your room, now," the receptionist said to Francine. "Fourth floor. I do hope everything is to your complete satisfaction."

Francine went out to say good-bye to Mohammed, the Malay driver. He gave her a smart salute before getting into the car. Watching the Ford drive away, Francine felt the tears perilously close to returning.

The room, for which she was paying the princely sum of twenty-two Straits dollars a day, had a balcony and a bathroom and two double beds.

She walked to the balcony. The lush square below was quiet. Palm trees rustled in the humid breeze. Beyond, the sea sparkled. Overhead, the sky was sultry. There was a faint smell of burning on the wind, though that might have been her imagination.

"Let's go and swim!" Ruth exclaimed.

"Perhaps later." Despite her vivacity, there were shadows under Ruth's eyes. She had not slept well during the night drive. Francine carried her to the bed, where she was soon asleep.

She unpacked her trunk. She had brought all her smartest European clothes. Hanging the dresses in the wardrobe, she wondered how long she would be staying.

They went down for lunch at one. The cavernous dining room was almost empty, rows upon rows of vacant tables stretching out around them among the cream pillars. The Malay table "boy" brought her the menu. She ordered, and the food arrived shortly, gray in color and taste and barely lukewarm. Her appetite disappeared. They both ate little, Ruth kicking her legs wearily against the rungs of her chair.

"I'm bored, Mama. There aren't any children here."

Francine had noticed that fact, too. "We'll find some children," she promised.

While she was sipping the brackish coffee that followed, the mustached brigadier marched into the dining room, his panama squarely on his head, swinging his cane. He was alone. He stopped by their table with a smart click of bootheels and peered down at them.

"Settling in all right?"

"Oh, yes, thank you," Francine said.

"We all have to put up with some inconveniences, I'm afraid. Might be another raid tonight. Brownouts. Blackouts. Same thing, really. You'll see. Just thought I'd warn you. Prepare the little one. In case she gets frightened."

"I'm not frightened," Ruth piped up. "I'm bored. There's nobody to play with me."

"Oh, there'll be some children, you'll see. No problems about getting your billet, I take it, Mrs. Lawrence?"

Francine met his eyes. She noted that he had learned her name. "No problems, thanks."

"Good. Last week, one of our chaps took a native woman onto the dance floor. Band stopped playing. Wouldn't start again till they left. Turned out she was an Indonesian princess on an official visit. Damned disgrace. I've been in this country forty years, and I never held with any of that rubbish."

Francine smiled awkwardly. "Everybody's being very kind."

"Good. Good. Got to stoke up the old boiler." He touched the brim of his hat and walked on as abruptly as he had stopped. Francine realized he had been showing his support for her as publicly as he could.

"Is there a real princess here?" Ruth asked in awe.

"So it seems."

"With a crown?"

"Perhaps."

"I want to see her!"

"We'll keep an eye out for her," Francine replied. She smiled brightly at Ruth. But the brigadier's talk of further raids had made her queasy.

The people at reception obtained an amah to help her with Ruth. She was an experienced, fifty-year-old Malay woman, to whom Ruth took an immediate liking. They arranged that the amah would sleep in the servants' quarters on the same floor. Francine would have preferred to do without the amah, but she knew Abe would be outraged at the thought of her looking after Ruth on her own. There were certain standards, he had impressed on her. And having the amah would bolster her status as an honorary European, until Abe came.

When darkness fell, she understood the brigadier's warning.

The "brownout" meant that, after dark, lights in the hotel were turned so low that people blundered into one another in the corridors, cursing and apologizing. Ruth, who was afraid of the dark, complained unhappily about "monsters." Only in the dining room, where the windows had been shuttered, were the lights turned up.

The same listless couples as at lunchtime were picking in the same lethargic way at the same gray dishes. There were only two newcomers, a preoccupied middle-aged man and his teenage daughter, who ate in complete silence a few tables away. Several times, Francine caught the girl's eyes on her or Ruth. She was a pretty girl, with curly, dark hair and a gentle expression. When the pair left, the father ignored them, but the girl gave Ruth a shy smile.

Francine went upstairs and lay in bed, listening to the dance band playing Victor Sylvester tunes on the veranda downstairs, Ruth sleeping at her side. She longed to telephone Abe, but he had forbidden it until the weekend. She remembered her honeymoon. Ruth had probably been conceived in this hotel. She remembered the nights, Abe's body heavy on hers, the new rituals, so intimate, so strange.

She and the amah played with Ruth on the lawn, watching the hotel staff lugging sandbags to stack around the rather insubstantial-looking air-raid shelter in the garden.

In the early hours of the next morning, the alert began to moan like a large, wounded animal, waking her from confused dreams.

Clutching Ruth in her arms, Francine joined the panic in the corridors, which intensified when, after a moment, the dimmed lights went out completely. She was jostled and bruised on the way down the stairs. The shelter was already crammed when she got there, kitchen boys and waiters hunkering down beside European guests, the distinctions of race suddenly lost. She made herself a place as best she could, pressing the child's face to her breast. There was little talk.

They all knew, either from experience or from the news that had been coming out of Europe for two years, what to expect. In silence, they waited for the drone of planes and the thudding of antiaircraft guns. Neither came.

"Are the Japanese coming, Mama?" Ruth demanded in a stage whisper.

"I think so."

"I can't hear them," Ruth said practically.

And after a quarter of an hour had dragged by, the all clear sounded to a chorus of groans and complaints.

They filed out tiredly. Brigadier Napier was in the foyer, imposing in a red silk dressing gown, speaking angrily to an assistant manager named Mr. Mankin.

"It's a damned bad show, I tell you," he barked. "In future, kindly leave the lights on until everyone is in the shelter. Then turn the bally things off. Otherwise you'll have more people killing themselves by falling down the stairs than will ever be hurt by Jap bombs. Understand?"

The other man, looking fretful, made some soothing reply.

A large crowd of irritable guests had already gathered at the elevator doors. The brownout made the machinery very slow. There was some jostling and arguing going on. Francine decided to use the stairs. Her arms were tired after holding Ruth for so long. She put the child down now, but Ruth cried to be picked up again, her face woebegone.

"Walk, Ruth," Francine commanded.

"No," the child wailed. "I'm tired, Mama!"

"Mama's tired, too."

"May I carry her for you?" It was the girl who had smiled at her in the dining room. She waited politely for an answer.

"Thank you, I can manage," Francine said, stooping to hoist Ruth in her arms.

"It's a long walk up to the fourth floor," the girl said. Francine guessed she was around fifteen or sixteen. "My father and I have a room just down the corridor from yours." She reached out. "Let me take her. It's no trouble."

She found herself passing Ruth to the girl, grateful for the assistance. "Thank you."

"You're awfully good," the girl said to Ruth as they began to climb the stairs. "You didn't cry once in the shelter."

"I'm brave," Ruth said complacently. "Only, my legs were tired."

"I'm Edwina Davenport. What's your name?"

"Ruth Lawrence."

"Hello, Ruth," she said gravely. Ruth, not normally sociable with strangers, smiled up at the girl. "You've got curly hair," she announced.

"That's right. I wish I didn't have."

"Why not?"

"It's very hard to manage."

"What's 'manage'?"

"Get it to look right. Not like your hair. You're very pretty. Like your mama."

"Yes," Ruth said, nodding, "we're very pretty."

"Where's your father?" Francine asked the girl.

"He stayed in his room. He didn't want to come down to the shelter." She was looking down at the child in her arms. "Has her daddy stayed behind?"

"He's general manger of a tin mine. He has to look after it."

They reached the fourth floor. The girl, who was a little plump, was slightly out of breath, her pink cheeks more flushed than ever. Her bare arms were mottled. She passed a dozing Ruth back to Francine. "There. She's almost asleep now."

"You were very kind," she said.

"Not at all. I can help you with her anytime, you know. I'm good with children."

Francine did not smile, though Edwina was little more than a child herself. She had a low, musical voice, like the note of a woodwind instrument, which pleased the ear. "Thank you," she said at her door. "Good night."

"Good night, Mrs. Lawrence."

Francine's room looked dim and dingy. "Brownout" was a good name for this dirty-looking light. She undressed Ruth and lay down beside her. The child began to rock back and forth, humming.

Francine felt desperately alone. She missed Abe terribly, and was worrying about him more and more. But she knew that Abe would do as he wished. As he always did.

She telephoned Abe on Saturday night. The line was bad, full of scratches and whistles. His voice sounded faint and remote. She had to shout.

"You have to come down, Abe. Soon."

"What's that?"

"They say the Japanese are moving very fast. You shouldn't delay in coming down to Singapore!"

His reply faded into the static. "Alarmist talk never did any . . ."

"Everybody says they're at Kalantan. That's only a few miles from you!"

"Don't worry about that."

"How can I not worry?"

"Everything's fine here. Perfectly normal. Even if I wanted to . . . couldn't suddenly close the mine without instructions. What would the owners say?"

"Damn the owners!" she yelled.

He did not seem to hear that. "Besides, no point in spreading despondency and alarm among the . . . so don't worry. How's Ruth?"

"She misses you. Every day she asks me when you'll come."

". . . all be together again soon. Hotel okay?"

"Fine."

"Staff treating you properly?"

"Yes, they treat me well. Abe, I'm so worried about you."

". . . don't be." Suddenly, his voice swelled on the line, close and reassuring. "I'm doing my job. Let the army do theirs. Damned if I'll run from a bunch of yellow monkeys." Just as abruptly, he faded away. "Take care. Got to go . . . awful line . . . waste of money."

"Please. It's so good to hear you!"

"Not worth it. Buck up, darling. Keep . . . very soon. Okay?"

"When will you come?" she shouted.

". . . no hurry . . ."

"I'll call you again tomorrow," she said wretchedly.

"No. Too expensive. Wait . . . weekend."

"Ruth wants to speak to you. Good night, darling. Please take care."

Ruth grabbed the phone. "Daddy! Daddy!"

Francine got up and went to the window while the child chattered gaily into the instrument. The square outside was no livelier on a Saturday evening than it had been when she'd arrived. The usually languid air of the city seemed to have atrophied into something else, something stagnant. A gust of warm rain swept down, bringing a smell of the jungle, blotting out the elegant white buildings.

"Daddy's not there anymore," Ruth said, holding out the silent receiver with a stricken face.

"I'm sorry, sweetheart." Francine sighed. "We'll speak to him again soon."

She closed the shutters.

During the subdued dinner the next night, the unmistakable thud of guns began, though the air-raid sirens had not sounded. Heads lifted in the dining room, which was fuller than Francine had yet seen it.

"Ack-ack batteries," someone said in a clipped voice. "There's a raid on."

For a stiff moment, no one moved. Then there was a loud scraping of chairs as the diners rose. As she took Ruth out of the high chair the waiters had brought her, Francine saw that the brigadier had not moved. He continued eating, not even looking at the guests who were leaving. A few tables away, she saw that Edwina's father, too, was still seated, staring at his plate in a fixed way. The girl, however, was making her way toward them.

"We have to hurry," she said, her plump face pale. "Let's go!"

The child clung to Francine as they followed the throng hurrying out of the dining room. This time, perhaps because of the brigadier, the lights remained at brownout level until they were all crammed in the shelter. Once again, the hotel staff were cheek by jowl with the guests.

"I must say, it's a bit bloody thick," someone said angrily, though whether at the presence of the waiters and kitchen boys or at the interruption to the meal, Francine could not tell. The alert began to wail. "Bit bloody late," the same voice said. Several other voices burst into speech after that, as though to shut out what was happening.

Francine crouched beside Edwina.

"I'm frightened," Ruth whimpered.

"Don't be frightened," Edwina said to her. "We'll be all right in here, Ruth."

The antiaircraft guns were firing continuously now, a barrage that was reassuring until deeper thuds began to shake the ground, the sound of bombs falling on the city. Francine had a sudden vision of the night sky filled with bombers, the eyes of the pilots focused greedily on the naked city below.

"Is that the Japanese?" Ruth asked in dread.

"Yes, little bird."

"What are they doing?"

"Dropping bombs."

"Why are they dropping bombs?"

"To break the buildings," Francine said.

"But if there are people in the buildings?" Ruth demanded, her face anxious.

There was no point in hiding the truth from Ruth. "Then the people will be killed."

Ruth digested that silently, clinging to her mother.

"Might have expected this." It was the brigadier, who had finally found his way into the shelter. "Bomber's moon, don't you know. Raids all this week, I should think."

"Won't your father come down?" she asked Edwina in a low voice.

"No."

"But it's dangerous! Can't you persuade him?"

The girl shook her head slightly. "He'll probably go up to his room and wait until it's over." Ruth had started to cry in fright. Edwina pressed her cheek to the child's glossy head. "Don't cry," she whispered. "Don't cry, Ruth."

The booming of the bombs was swelling in a crescendo, shaking the ground beneath their feet. The chatter grew louder, people talking animatedly; there was even some laughter.

"Where's your mother, Edwina?"

The woodwind voice faltered, an oboe playing a tragic passage. "She died. A couple of months ago."

"Oh, I'm so sorry!" Francine exclaimed.

"It's all right. She'd been ill for a long time. Almost as long as I can remember. The climate didn't suit her."

"That's very sad."

"My father should have taken her back home. The doctors all said so. He wouldn't. He said he couldn't face going back." She spoke detachedly, without rancor. "We moved up to the Cameron Highlands a few years ago to get away from the heat."

"Oh," Francine said, "that's close to where I was born. I was born in Ipoh."

"Really?" Edwina brightened. "That is close. I love the Cameron Highlands. People say they look like Scotland, but I've been to the Scottish Highlands, and they don't look a bit alike. Anyway, it didn't make any difference to Mother. She got a fever and died."

"I'm sorry," Francine said.

"Father's a tea planter. We came down here when the Japanese landed. I don't know what's happening to the plantation. It's been rather dull, here." She glanced up. "At least, until you and Ruth came along."

"What about school?"

"I was at boarding school in Kuala Lumpur until the invasion," Edwina said. "Father tutors me now."

"He must be a very clever man."

"Oh, yes." There was something sad in the girl's voice. "He's a very clever man."

The bombs had ceased quite abruptly, all at once. The ack-ack batteries continued firing for a few minutes longer. Then they, too, fell silent. The conversation in the shelter stopped as people listened expectantly.

"Have they gone, Mama?" Ruth whispered.

The all clear began to groan. People sat up stiffly, rubbing themselves. "Do you know," someone said, "those bally sirens sound just the same here as they did in London?"

"Why haven't we got any fighter cover?" someone else asked in an aggrieved tone. "It's shocking."

The raid had not been particularly dramatic, but the pains in Francine's stomach told her how frightened she had been. She felt weak and slightly nauseated. They went back to the dining room, where their meals still lay, now congealed, on their plates. The waiters filed back to their stations along the wall, muttering inaudibly to each other. Some of the guests sat back down, as though to resume dinner.

She saw that Edwina's father had not moved from his place. He sat slightly slumped in his chair, staring at his plate. The bald spot on the top of his head gleamed in the dim light.

"He must be very brave," she said to Edwina.

"He doesn't care whether he lives or dies."

She was taken aback by the words. "And you?"

"I don't want to die." Edwina looked at Francine. There was an adult quality in the glance. Perhaps that came of having no mother and a father who did not care whether he lived or died.

"I think I'll take Ruth up to bed now," she said. "I don't want any more food."

"Shall I carry her for you?"

"It's all right. The elevators will be free. Thank you, Edwina."

"Let's meet tomorrow," Edwina said eagerly. "We can talk about home."

" 'Home'?" Francine repeated. When the English used that word, they generally meant England.

"Perak," Edwina said firmly. "I was born there. I miss it awfully. We can talk about tea farming. Or if that's too boring," she added hastily, "about the beautiful hills and the mists and the ferns and everything."

"All right, Edwina," Francine said, "we'll do that."

At the door of the dining room she looked over her shoulder. Edwina had sat down opposite her motionless father. Neither was speaking. Perhaps Edwina had taken to her because, as a girl, she did not feel she was lowering herself in befriending a "native," as an adult would have done. But then there was that obvious love for her highland home, the pride in having been born in Malaya.

Certainly, apart from Edwina and Brigadier Napier, the white residents of the hotel ignored her utterly. They neither spoke to her nor looked at her as she passed. It was as if she were invisible to these tuans and memsahibs who donned full evening dress in the tropical heat, and sweated through the conventions of "home."

To fill the emptiness of her days, she found war work at a Red Cross center in the town, winding bandages for several hours a day with a group of other women of all ages and races. It offered her company, as well as activity. They called themselves, cheerfully, the WWW, which stood for War Work Women. Though it was a mixed group, here there were no barriers of class or race; sitting at their long tables, deftly looping yards of lint and gauze that would soak up the blood of men, white women chatted with brown, shared the same jokes, the same fears, the same fragile hopes. The women were inquisitive about Francine, and once they knew her situation, were sympathetic.

The Red Cross organizer, an older woman named Lucy Conyngham, made something of a pet of her, and soon the others—Chinese, Indian, and Malay—followed suit. Their friendliness helped her deal with the studied rudeness of the guests at Raffles, which was making her stay increasingly wearisome.

The war work and Ruth filled her days. Her nights dragged interminably. The great dining room, which reminded her oddly of a Hindu temple that had been whitewashed and adorned with parlor palms, was a special purgatory, in which she sometimes felt almost intolerably lonely and excluded.

She read Margaret Mitchell's *Gone With the Wind* in great gulps, losing herself in that exotic world. It made her ache with longing for Abe. But the scenes of war were unsettling.

By now the hotel was starting to fill. Singapore was becoming congested with exiles; already there were few vacancies at Raffles or any of the other big hotels. The deserted air had gone. In its place was a feverish yet uneasy air of bustle.

At least there were now several children for Ruth to play with. Under the guidance of amahs, the children of the hotel played all day on the lawns or along the shady verandas.

At night, Raffles became a different, much more glamorous place. Candles glimmered on the tables in the garden, where people ate in the darkness under the whispering palms. There was dancing on Wednesdays and

Saturdays. Swirling fans created at least an illusion of coolness for the dancers.

She had been able to speak to Abe only twice more. On both occasions, the line had been wretched. The last call had been more than a week ago. Since then, the switchboard had been unable to get her a line. Real concern for his safety gripped her. She worried, too, about the aunts in Perak. It was likely the Japanese would behave with particular viciousness toward the Chinese population, official enemies for four and a half years.

A few days before the end of the year, the receptionist waved to her as she crossed the lobby.

"Mrs. Lawrence! Mrs. Lawrence! Wire for you!"

Her heart palpitating, Francine hurried to snatch the little gray slip. She unfolded it with trembling fingers. It contained just two lines:

FINISHING UP HERE. COMING DOWN 3RD JAN.
LOVE ABE.

"Thank God," she whispered. She hoisted Ruth in her arms. "Daddy's coming at last, my little one!"

"Good news?"

It was Brigadier Napier, who had come up beside her. She beamed at him. "My husband, Brigadier. He'll be coming to join me after the New Year."

"Jolly good show. Had some news of my own about my nephew, Clive."

"Good, I hope?"

"Good and bad. Good news is he's coming home as well. Bad news is he's on the casualty list."

"Has he been wounded?" she asked in concern.

"Bit of a cut on the head." He cupped a hand around his lips and silently mouthed the word *Machang*. There had been rumors of a big engagement there, though the radio had been studiously silent about it. "Unconscious for a couple of days."

"Oh, my goodness."

"He says it's not too bad. But they're sending him back here. For observation. I'll be glad to see him. Fond of the boy. No children of my own, you see."

The receptionist, who had been listening, leaned forward to Francine. "So glad to hear about your husband, Mrs. Lawrence. As a matter of fact we were going to ask you if you'd mind terribly moving to a single room. To make way for some of the families. But that's all right now, isn't it?"

"Is Daddy really coming?" Ruth asked with a touch of skepticism.

Francine knelt and hugged Ruth. "Yes, Daddy's really coming," she whispered to the child.

"Will he bring me my other toys? And my teddies?"

"Yes! I promise!" Her legs felt wobbly as she walked to the dining room for breakfast, Brigadier Napier at her side.

"Can anyone kindly tell me," she heard a woman's voice say loudly behind her, "why that bloody stengah and her brat have a room while Europeans are sleeping in cellars?"

Ruth turned, looking back in childish wonder. Burning anger rose in Francine. *Stengah* was the contemptuous British word for Eurasians. She, too, almost turned to face the venomous voice. The brigadier's hand closed around her arm, steadying her silently.

"Who's that woman?" Ruth asked.

"A silly woman," the brigadier said. "Never mind her. Come along."

Francine swallowed her anger and walked on without a backward glance, talking to the old man about his nephew. Abe was coming. That was all that mattered.

The next day, she allowed Edwina to talk her into going to the pictures, not for the feature film, a British comedy that had already been showing for weeks, but to see the newsreels.

The first newsreel was American. It showed the results of the attack on Pearl Harbor three weeks earlier. The scenes of destruction were appalling: the *Arizona* blazing, the *California* wallowing brokenly, the *Oklahoma* bottom-up in the oily water; the wreckage of nearly two hundred aircraft destroyed on the ground. Francine felt that for the first time she was seeing the true power of the Japanese, the full violence of their intentions. It shook her badly.

Still stunned, they sat through the much more guarded British newsreel that followed, with its reassuring footage of His Majesty's troops filing through the jungle. There were even shots of Japanese prisoners of war, bewildered men in unflattering uniforms, many wearing the round spectacles familiar from the caricatures in the *Straits Times*. According to the commentator, the invaders were already being driven back.

They emerged from the darkness to find a heavy afternoon shower in progress. Taxis were becoming ever more elusive, disappearing completely during air raids. All private motorcars had been requisitioned by the authorities and it was becoming difficult to move around the crowded city.

As they huddled on the swarming pavement, a bedraggled group of European evacuees filed by, women herding children under umbrellas. Their faces wore expressions of bewildered resentment. Francine knew that the Asian eyes that observed these whites were seeing something new. The dignity, the supreme arrogance of the European in Malaya, was quite gone. They looked defeated.

The Japanese bombers had now started coming during daylight, unafraid of the antiaircraft guns. A direct hit scored on an oil tank produced a cloud of smoke that hung in the sky like a gigantic black cauliflower for hours before slowly drifting away. Francine stared at godowns charred to the foundations, Chinese shop-houses demolished, lives shattered. The continued raids prevented repair work. In the heat, the shattered sewers had started to stink.

By now, tales of Japanese atrocities were arriving with the daily flood of new evacuees: women raped and slaughtered en masse, prisoners of war bayoneted without mercy, Chinese civilians tortured and publicly executed. Malaya was receiving the same savage treatment meted out to Nanking. By now, everyone in Singapore suspected what was really happening to the British army—a rout followed by a chaotic retreat.

In the taxi back to Raffles, Edwina tried to sound cheerful. "It's New Year's Eve in two days. Nineteen forty-two!" She rubbed the condensation on the window and peered out. Teeming traffic of pedestrians and rickshaws swirled around the taxi. Beyond, the rain beat down on smashed roofs and blackened walls.

Raffles was crowded on the last night of 1941. The atmosphere in the ballroom, where a dinner-dance was in progress, was at once feverish and melancholy. Feverish because everyone wanted to forget the war, melancholy because almost everyone present was an evacuee, celebrating the New Year a long way from home and family.

Francine had intended to see in the New Year quietly in her room with Ruth; but something, perhaps a desire for human warmth, kept her sitting at the table after the meal was over, listening to the band. Dancers began to glide across the polished floor. She was wishing sadly that Abe were here.

"Excuse me."

She looked up. A man in the uniform of a major was standing at her table. A neat white bandage had been wound around his forehead. Beneath it, his face was darkly handsome. The bandage, together with his hawked nose and clipped mustache, lent him a piratical, almost Errol Flynn air.

"We haven't been introduced," he said in a confident way, "but my uncle's told me about you. I'm Clive Napier, Brigadier Napier's nephew."

"Oh, yes! How do you do?" she said.

"Sorry to just introduce myself and all that. But I guessed who you were, of course. My card." He passed her a crisp little piece of pasteboard, on which was printed his name and address. She put it in her bag dutifully. He was studying her with the bold eyes of a man used to success with women.

"Isn't your uncle here, Major Napier?"

"He's lying down. Touch of malaria."

"I'm sorry to hear that. He's been very kind to me."

"May I have the pleasure?" he asked, holding out his hand.

She rose somewhat reluctantly and allowed him to lead her into a waltz. His arms were strong and confident, but she could not take her eyes off the bandage around his head. He was the first wounded soldier she had seen. He noticed her glance. "Don't mind the turban," he said. "I still have what little brain I was born with."

"Doesn't it hurt?" Francine asked.

"Japanese grenade. Killed the man next to me. My best friend, as it happens. It hurt when I woke up, I can tell you."

"Oh!" She was horrified. "I'm so sorry."

"Don't apologize, for God's sake. The worst of it is, I'm missing the rest of the show. Six weeks' forced rest." His dark eyes were fixed on her face, a slightly mocking smile on his mouth. "No wonder Uncle likes you. You're the only pretty girl in the room," he said. "Matter of fact, you're the prettiest girl in Singapore tonight."

She did not answer, torn between indignation at the crude flirtation and concern at the thought of his losing his best friend.

"Do you like strawberries?" he asked.

"I've only had them once. Why?"

"I'll get you a couple of baskets. I know a chap who flies them in fresh every day from Australia."

"That sounds very extravagant," she commented.

"Strawberries, fresh oysters, sirloin steaks, grapes, whatever you want. All comes in from Sydney. The smart clubs buy them. Amazing, isn't it? We may as well have some fun before Yamashita gets here. He's a clever little devil, our friend General Yamashita. Cleverer than we gave him credit for. Taken to calling himself the Tiger of Malaya. Stylish, eh?"

"Do you think Singapore is going to fall?" she asked, looking up at him.

"Oh, no," he said, arching his brows in exaggerated surprise. "Oh, dear me, no. Singapore fall? Not bloody likely. I'm privy to our illustrious leaders' intimate plans for the defense of the island, my sweet." He was slurring his words. She realized he was very drunk. "They have a foolproof plan. Even if Yamashita drives every British soldier out of Malaya, when he gets to the causeway, we'll simply blow it up. That ought to do the trick, oughtn't it?"

"I suppose so," she said, troubled.

"Only one snag," he said. "The causeway's just four feet deep at low tide. The Japs'll just wade across with their baggage on their heads. I've seen 'em do it. Saw 'em cross a raging river in about five minutes flat. Didn't even take their uniforms off. Just put their rifles on their heads and paddled over."

"Then Singapore can't be defended," she said, staring up at him.

"Our leaders have a final plan. Operation Jellyfish."

"Operation Jellyfish?" she repeated.

"It's top secret. Hush-hush, my sweet. May I call you Francine, by the way?"

"If you want."

"Beautiful name. Beautiful girl."

"But what is Operation Jellyfish?" she asked, insisting.

"It's an entirely new concept in modern warfare. The way it works is as follows. Yamashita lands on Singapore in force. He orders his men to fix bayonets, preparatory to disemboweling us all. We take one look at him and start shaking and wobbling. Just like jellyfish. Hence the name. We shake and wobble so violently that Yamashita gets alarmed. He turns around and runs all the way back to Tokyo. Brilliant, isn't it?"

"You're making fun of me," she said angrily.

"Nothing funny about the Japanese," he said. His eyes were glazed, his handsome face set. "I know, my sweet. I've fought them. Seen their little tricks. When they get to a village, they round up all the women and rape them in front of the men. Children, too. If they're feeling jolly, they bayonet them afterward." His right hand, which held hers, suddenly gripped her fingers brutally tight. His eyes burned. "Look," he said, "don't take this wrong, but shall we leave? I know a place where we can have a damned sight better time than this morgue."

"Of course I can't go anywhere with you," she retorted indignantly.

"Why not?"

"I'm a married woman. My little girl is asleep upstairs."

"There must be an amah with her?"

"Yes. But I can't leave her. I think I'd like to sit down now, Major Napier."

He ignored her request, holding her body tight against his. "Where's your husband? Safely out of the way, so I hear." He grinned. "I won't tell him if you don't."

"He's coming down from Ipoh," she said angrily. "He'll be here any-time!"

Clive Napier lifted a dark eyebrow. "Ipoh? Nobody's coming down from Ipoh, my sweet. As of this morning, it's in the tender hands of General Tomoyuki Yamashita."

Francine went pale. "I didn't hear the announcement!"

"There won't be an announcement. Think the censors want us to know how badly we're doing?"

"My husband's disabling the mine," she said, trying to hide her sicken-ing dismay. "He'll be here soon. In three days."

"Whatever you say. The important thing is, he's not here now. But I am."

"I want to sit down!" she exclaimed in disgust, trying to wrench herself away from him. He held her tight, his body hard and strong against hers.

"He's a lucky man," he said. "He'll be luckier still if he gets out of Yamashita's clutches."

"I want to sit down now," she said, feeling nauseated.

"Good idea. We'll order a bottle of champers."

Desperate to shake the man off, she broke away from him and headed to the table where Edwina Davenport and her father were sitting. The major followed her.

"May I join you?" she asked. Mr. Davenport raised his empty blue eyes to her, then rose slowly to his feet. "Of course."

But Clive Napier had followed her determinedly. He ushered Francine into her chair, snapped his fingers for the waiter, and ordered a magnum of Dom Perignon. Reluctantly, she introduced him to the Davenports. Edwina held out her hand, and Clive Napier made a great show of kissing it, which delighted the girl. The major now looked very feverish, his face sallow under the tropical tan, dusky, hectic spots over each cheekbone. "It's true about Ipoh, my sweet," he said to Francine as he sat. "Quite true, I assure you."

"What about Ipoh?" Edwina wanted to know.

"Major Napier says Ipoh has fallen to the Japanese," Francine said tightly.

"I don't believe it," Edwina replied. But she looked stricken. If Ipoh had fallen, then her own beloved Cameron Highlands, and her father's tea plantation, were also in Japanese hands.

Clive Napier shrugged. "I'm afraid there's no doubt about it." He drank his champagne in one long swallow, then dug the heel of one hand into his left eye. "Oh, Christ, my head hurts."

"You shouldn't be drinking so much," Francine snapped.

"I shouldn't even be out of bed, according to the quacks," he said with a wolflike smile. "Don't cut it too fine, my sweet Francine. Don't miss the last boat home."

"She has to wait for her husband," Edwina said.

"Ah, but will he come? Or has Yamashita already used him for samurai sword practice?"

"That is not funny," the girl replied sternly. "She's had messages. He's safe and on his way to Singapore."

"Well, I hope he can move faster than Yamashita. Don't wait until the Japanese are at the door. They don't like Eurasians."

"Why are you so defeatist?" Edwina was cross, her plump cheeks flushed, her normally musical voice flat. "The army will thrash the Japanese."

"It isn't an army, old girl. It's a constabulary. It was only designed to keep law and order. Not to fight tanks and Zeros." He laid his hand over Francine's. His palm was burning hot. "Ever been to England?"

"No." She tried to pull her hand out from under his, but he grasped her fingers possessively.

"You won't like it."

"Major Napier!" She finally got her hand back.

He refilled their glasses. "But you'll like Singapore under the Japs even less. Look, I meant it about the strawberries and the oysters. Or anything else you want. Need any help, you come to me, my sweet. I'm a useful sort of chap."

The room was filling steadily now. Mingling with the uniformed or mess-jacketed Europeans were a sprinkling of Malays and Chinese, admitted for the New Year's Eve festivities. The Asian women, for the most part, wore dazzling jewels, far superior to anything the European women boasted—a "native" had to be very rich to qualify for admittance. It was fiercely hot. Mess jackets were creasing and blotching with sweat, gowns were crumpling, powder had started to fade from shiny noses.

A Chinese photographer was doing the rounds, and the major summoned him with a snap of his fingers. "Here. Take a picture of the two of us. Handsomest couple in the room."

He put an arm around Francine's shoulders, pulling her close. Francine frowned, and the flashbulb exploded, dazzling her. "Handsomest couple for sure," the photographer chuckled. Disconcertingly, the hotel suddenly shook like a house of cards.

"Operation Jellyfish," the major said. "Told you, my sweet. It's started already." Over the syrupy music, the unearthly warbling of the air-raid sirens could be heard starting up.

Francine had risen to her feet, uncertain whether to rouse Ruth and take her to the shelter. The child had been sleeping badly of late, suffering from a constant and debilitating diarrhea that was making her lose weight. She decided that unless the bombs drew closer, it was better for Ruth to sleep on.

"Sit down, sweet one," Clive Napier growled, pulling her back into her chair. "We have to see the New Year in together."

Francine realized that nobody was bothering to leave for the shelter. The table boys were hurrying to and fro with bottles of Scotch, champagne, and brandy. A lot of alcohol was being consumed. She thought of her own family's New Year's rituals, the little red envelopes of *lai see* for the children, the sweets, the branches of peach blossom, the dragon rampaging through the streets. The Chinese New Year was not for some time, yet, but she doubted whether her family or anyone else would be celebrating it this year.

A middle-aged Chinese couple approached their table, escorted by the maître d'hôtel. The man, who was short and rotund and whose face was puffy, bowed to them.

"K.K. Cheung," he said. "Member of legislative council. This is my wife, Poppy."

"Room for all," Clive Napier said, rising. "Boy! More champagne and more glasses!"

The newcomers were both encrusted with precious stones. The man wore a gold watch set with diamonds, as well as several diamond rings. He also wore brilliants at his cuffs, fastening the points of his collar, even on the gold buckles of his shoes. The woman wore even more spectacular baubles.

Her jacket was fastened with huge diamond buttons. She wore an emerald-and-diamond choker around her throat, a matching bracelet at her wrist. A deep, blood-colored ruby glowed on one of her fingers.

The towkays of Singapore were legendary for the wealth they had amassed. But K.K. Cheung had not been born rich; on his left wrist Francine saw the triangular mark of a tong tattoo. He had made his money, Francine guessed, in the boom in rubber, tin, and other metals, which had started in 1939. He was even drunker than Clive Napier, and not holding it as well. He swayed in his chair, his mouth slack. "Member of legislative council," he repeated. "Defense of Singapore. Priority case. Confidence, resolution, enterprise, and devotion to the cause." His blurred eyes settled on Francine. "My concubine is dead," he said. Clive snorted loudly. The Chinese went on, oblivious. "Japanese bombed her house. House I made for her."

"Keep quiet, K.K.," his wife said briskly.

"Beautiful house," the man said, ignoring the command. "The best of everything. Silk sheets. Crystal chandelier. Thousands of dollars."

"Cheh!" His wife's feline eyes gleamed for a moment.

"Brilliant girl. Studying all day. Innocent. Why do they kill so many innocent people?"

"It's the very model of a modern war," Clive said, grinning hollowly. "She's better off, old boy. I've seen what the Japs do to beautiful Chinese girls."

K.K. Cheung reached out a stubby hand and touched Francine's wrist. He was not crying outwardly, but Francine saw that behind his puffy lids he was weeping without cease. "You have a pure and gentle face, child. Where are you from?" he asked in patois.

"From Perak, Ah Peh," she replied.

"You left your family?"

She nodded. "I left everyone."

"Your husband, too?"

"Yes."

"You should have stayed together. Man and wife should not be separated."

"I hope he will find me soon."

"Terrible things are coming, child."

"No Chinese, that's not fair," Clive protested. "Speak English!"

The hotel shook again, more violently, as another bomb landed a mile or so away. There were shrieks and laughter. Francine checked her little gold wristwatch. It was eleven-thirty. She rose nervously. "I'd better go to my daughter," she said. "Excuse me. Good night, everyone."

"Don't go yet," Clive said. "There's only half an hour to 1942." He rose with her, but stumbled, clutching his head. Francine had to grab his arm to stop him from falling.

"Drunk," the towkay's wife said in disgust.

But Francine was concerned for Clive Napier. His face had gone ashen, and he was leaning heavily on her for support.

"Sorry about this," he said to Francine, enunciating carefully. "Think I need a bit of fresh air. Could you help me outside? I'll sit on the veranda for a moment or two."

Neither Mr. Davenport nor K.K. Cheung made any move, but Edwina rose to help. Between them, they supported the major, and made their unsteady way out of the sweltering, overcrowded room to the veranda.

"Don't be upset by what he says," Edwina whispered to Francine. "He's a defeatist."

Together, they got Clive Napier onto a bench. He seemed in danger of slumping, so Francine sat beside him, propping him up. He sighed, resting his bandaged head on her shoulder. The veranda was deserted. Everybody was in the ballroom. "I think he's very drunk," Edwina said censoriously, studying Clive. "He's not very nice, is he?"

"He's been wounded. He's probably a bit off his head."

"I'd better go back to Father," Edwina said. "Are you staying with him?"

"I'll just make sure he's all right," Francine said. "You go back and see the New Year in with your father."

"Are you sure?"

"Yes. And don't worry about your Camerons. You'll be back there sniffing the mist and brewing tea in no time."

Edwina smiled sadly. "I hope you're right."

"Happy New Year, then, Edwina." She extracted an arm from behind the heavy body of the major, and they shook hands formally. Then Francine pulled her close on an impulse and kissed her plump cheek. She watched the girl hurry away.

"Sorry about this," Clive repeated, his mouth close to her ear. "Too much champagne on top of a fractured skull."

"You've got a fracture?" Francine said in horror.

"So they tell me."

"You shouldn't even be out of bed, let alone drinking and dancing. You're going to kill yourself like this!"

"No such luck."

"You should be in hospital."

"I'd rather be here, in your arms." She felt his lips touch her neck, hot and breathy.

"I think I'll go and find the jaga," she said firmly. "He'll call a taxi to take you home."

"Please don't leave me," he said quietly. "Christ, look at the sky. Quite a fireworks show for New Year's Eve." The bombers had moved farther away, in the direction of the naval dockyard. The explosions had dwindled to thuds, which floated ominously on the humid air, no louder than the rustle of palm trees along the veranda. But the night sky was brilliant with the deadly fireworks of war. A scarlet glow marked where godowns had been set alight. Crimson tracer spiraled sluggishly upward from the ack-ack batteries, following the waving beams of the searchlights, disappearing into the darkness without any apparent effect.

Please come, Abe, she begged silently. *Come on Saturday.*

Clive straightened himself with an effort, and groped in his pocket. "Got it in here somewhere," he said. "Ah. Here it is." He produced a small silver flask, which he unscrewed. He held it out to her. "You first."

She was about to make some retort, but thought better of it. The world was on fire all around them, and common sense seemed a futile virtue right now. She took the flask, and drank. The whiskey was fiery, smoky. It tasted of sin. She wiped her mouth and gave the flask back to Clive.

"Good girl." His eyes gleamed in the darkness. "You're special. I knew you would be, by the way my uncle described you." He swigged at the flask in turn. "Know why Uncle took such a shine to you?"

"No," she replied truthfully.

"After my aunt died, he married a Eurasian. They were together for nearly twenty years. She looked a bit like you. He never rose above brigadier, though. Should have retired a full general."

"What happened to her?"

"She died. He's never got over it."

"He must have loved her very much."

He tilted his head back, watching Francine. He didn't seem so drunk now. "Oh, yes. He loved her to distraction. Maybe it runs in the family."

"What?"

"Falling in love with beautiful Eurasians. Career suicide for a soldier, of course. Worst thing you could do, short of shooting the C.O. But then, I don't need to tell you what nauseatingly hypocritical bastards we British are, do I?"

He offered her the flask again, and she drank automatically. The burning liquor made her gasp. "My husband—" She broke off. She didn't know what to say.

"You don't have to explain," Clive said dryly. "Shunned by the gang. Not invited to any decent home. Children not allowed to play with clean white children. It's a hard road. I'm sure he doesn't give a toss, though. Marrying a girl like you is worth a hundred times all that."

She wondered if that was how Abe felt, how he would always feel. In the distance, she heard the sonorous drone of the bombers returning north. It reminded her of the drone of the lawnmower on the cricket pitch on a summer afternoon, before the horror began, before the gates of Eden had shut. "I'd better go to my little girl," she sighed.

"Wait," he said. He turned to her, putting his arms around her. Before she guessed what he meant to do, he was kissing her on the mouth. Francine had been brought up strictly. The only man who had ever kissed her in that way had been Abe, and then only after they had become engaged. This was very different, this hungry pressure of an alien male mouth. She felt astonishment for a second. Then a hot weakness flooded her lower body, as though her legs were melting. Without knowing why, she put her arms around Clive's shoulders and clung to him. Perhaps it was the loneliness and the fear.

His lips forced hers apart, and she felt his tongue, hot and wet, try to enter her mouth. Confusion rose in her heart. She twisted her head away. They grappled awkwardly on the bench, Francine half-resisting him, half-complying.

"Francine," he whispered huskily. "Francine, kiss me again."

"No. Let me go."

His mouth covered hers again. She was bewildered by her own response. He kissed expertly, not like Abe, but with a skill that was meant to arouse. She felt his hand cup her breast for a moment. Then his hand slid down to her knees and pushed between her thighs.

Casual lust, she thought. Her mother had warned her about casual lust time and time again. Not to let boys do this to her. Not to give in to those feelings that would come, those instincts that would press. It had been easy to resist. She had never encountered those feelings, not even with Abe. But now she felt them, darkly thrilling, intoxicating. She felt as though her heart were a wild horse, galloping inside her.

Clive was kissing her with almost savage passion, one hand cupped behind her neck, the other grappling with her underwear. She squirmed in maidenly panic. His fingers slid past the elastic and penetrated to her privates, where she was already dishonorably, shamefully wet.

The pleasure of his caress was so intense that she clamped her thighs shut on his arm. She put her hands on his chest and shoved as hard as she could. "Stop!" she hissed shakily. "Stop, or I'll scream!"

"Then let my hand go," he said.

She had effectively trapped his hand, and she had to open her thighs to let him go. She pulled her dress straight frantically. She was burning with humiliation and self-reproach. But the pleasure remained, turning her bones to water. "How dare you?" she gasped, knowing she sounded like the amateur heroine of a bad play.

He smiled at her slowly. He lifted his fingers to his mouth and licked them. She realized he was tasting her on his fingertips. She would have jumped up and run away, but she was truly afraid that her wobbly legs would not support her. "Some other time," he said softly. "Some other place."

"You're not a gentleman," she said, trapped in the vein of cheap melodrama. She did not, however, know any other way of expressing her outrage.

"No," he agreed. "But I like you very much. I'm glad we're together for the New Year."

Passion had deafened her, but now she became aware of the chorus of shouts and whistles from the ballroom that heralded midnight. Bells were ringing across the city. "Oh, God," she muttered.

"A kiss," Clive said, leaning forward. "A chaste one this time. Happy New Year, my sweet."

Numbly, she let him touch her lips with his. "Happy New Year," she whispered.

"What year is 1942 in the Chinese calendar?" he asked.

"The Year of the Horse," she remembered.

"A wild horse this year, with glaring eyes and thundering hooves. Look, Francine, I want to say something—"

But he did not get it said. English voices were raised in a chorus of "Auld Lang Syne." Francine shuddered. The sentimental Scottish tune was almost identical to the music played at Chinese funerals. She thought of her mother's death, and burst into sobs. Without another word to Clive, she jumped to her feet and fled.

Upstairs, the raid had awakened Ruth and she was wailing bitterly. The amah was trying in vain to comfort her. Francine grabbed the child from the amah and, consumed by guilt, rocked her in tight arms.

"Hush, little bird," she crooned. "Hush, my little bird."

It was all falling apart. All order, all dignity, all morality, the whole thing crumbling into ruins. *What if they're right?* she asked herself. *What if Abe is already dead, and the Japanese will soon be here, slaughtering and burning? I should have stayed with that drunken man and let him take me on the grass. I should have given in to casual lust, and at least tried to snatch a few moments of pleasure before the end. What else is there, in the face of nothingness?*

It had been a disgusting encounter, she decided the next day, born out of her tension and her fear that the world was coming to an end. She resolved to forget it, and Clive Napier, immediately and permanently.

The morning of the third of January was unbearably sultry. In the early hours of the morning, another group of Japanese bombers came and went, leaving parts of the city blazing once more, an ugly red glow in the sky, an ugly smell of burning rubber in the humid dawn.

Abe had not come by lunchtime.

Infected by Francine's tension, Ruth grew increasingly restless and boisterous, eventually breaking a jar of face cream. Francine slapped the child, something she almost never did. Ruth started to cry in shock. Heartbroken, Francine cradled the sobbing child, who eventually fell quiet. Then she set to work cleaning up the sticky mess with its treacherous, jagged blades of glass.

They stayed in their room all afternoon, waiting for Abe. Francine gazed out of her window at the endless stream of refugees in Raffles Square. Where were all these homeless thousands to go? There was hardly room in Singapore to hold today's arrivals, let alone tomorrow's, or the next day's.

By the next evening, Abe had still not come. Nor had he sent any word. While she lay with Ruth on the bed, it occurred to her for the first time that "Coming down 3rd Jan." might mean he was leaving on the third and thus would not be here for a few more days yet. Nothing was certain. She had to control her emotions.

She was awakened in the early hours by the sound of a door slamming loudly. She roused herself, feeling dazed. It was past midnight. A restless monsoon wind was rattling the palm leaves, spattering rain in long shudders.

He'll come tomorrow, she told herself. *He'll come tomorrow.* She felt almost cold. She rose to undress and get into her nightclothes.

When she heard the knock at her door, she thought it was Abe and joy surged in her, making her cry out. She ran to the door and flung it open. It was Edwina, wearing nightclothes. The girl's round face was pale as ice.

"Edwina," Francine said in concern. "What's the matter?"

"It's Father," she whispered. "Please come."

Francine checked that Ruth was asleep, then followed the girl down the corridor. She was unprepared for what greeted her when Edwina opened the door of her room.

The first thing she saw was the red spray across the wall and ceiling. The second was the crumpled figure that lay on the floor, a revolver clutched in one still hand. She almost fainted, but fought the giddiness. She knelt by the dead man, reaching out.

Mr. Davenport had shot himself under the chin. Most of his head was gone.

"He's dead," she heard Edwina say. The girl was trembling violently, and yet in the unreal calm of deep shock. "I thought he was cleaning it."

Francine rose unsteadily and pulled Edwina away from the corpse. "Don't look at him," she pleaded, though it was far too late for that. "Come away. Don't touch anything." There was a dreadful amount of blood. It was still pouring slowly from the corpse, like an emptying bottle.

"I thought he was cleaning it. He often cleaned it late at night. I was in bed—" Francine grabbed Edwina as she sagged to the ground. Somehow she supported the half-unconscious girl.

The doorway was filled with guests in dressing gowns, peering in.

"He's shot himself!" a young man with blond hair and horn-rims called out. "It's Davenport. Blown his brains out!"

"Please," Francine said, holding Edwina to her breast. "Please call a doctor. Please."

They were torn out of bed at dawn by the heaviest raids so far. The hotel was shaking as though giant fists were pounding into the belly of the city. The deep drone of the bombers was everywhere, a sound that vibrated below the sternum, drowning out the thin complaint of the alert sirens.

She got Ruth and hurried downstairs with her. A thick smell of burning was in the air. With each detonation, she felt the ground tremble beneath her feet. The clatter of a fire engine rushed by outside. She ran to the shelter, but it was crammed to capacity. As she tried to push her way in, a hand thrust her back with such force that she staggered.

"No more room," a man's voice said roughly. She had a blurred impression of hostile eyes glaring at her before she turned and ran back to the dining room, which was the second-best refuge, having been shuttered and sandbagged.

It, too, was crowded. Service of a sort was even being offered; a few harassed waiters were scurrying to and fro with trays of bacon and eggs, or bowls of congee. She found a table jammed up against a pillar and sat holding Ruth on her lap. The child stared around with wide silver eyes.

The bombs were louder and nearer than she had ever heard them; she watched, hypnotized, as the glasses shivered on the table, so fragile, so brittle. She had last seen Edwina Davenport being taken away by the doctor, stumbling and retching. She could not imagine what would become of Edwina now. She had to find her this morning, somehow. She and Abe would try to take Edwina under their wing. Edwina had no one else now. She had once told Francine that her nearest relations were two maiden aunts in Cornwall. She would need help.

Abdul, the aged "boy" who always served her, came up to her table.

"Breakfast, Mem?"

"Just toast, please, Abdul. And some mee for the little one. Do you know what's happened to Mr. Davenport's daughter?"

"Queen Alexandra Hospital, Mem." The man looked at her from the corners of his eyes and lowered his voice. *"Jaga baik-baik."*

She was about to ask him what was wrong, why she should be careful, but he was already scurrying away, his headdress falling loose down his back.

The raid ended with the usual abruptness while she sat drinking her coffee. A flood of guests from the shelter started pouring into the dining room, demanding food. She left with Ruth. People were staring at her as she passed, not bothering to conceal the hostility in their eyes. "Bloody niggers," she heard someone mutter. She felt her skin crawl. She pulled Ruth close and hurried out.

She was stopped in the lobby by Mr. Mankin, a tall, obsequious man with a permanent smile stitched on his lipless mouth.

"Mrs. Lawrence, if I may—a word?"

She followed him unhappily into his office.

He sat with his thin legs elegantly crossed and gave her his wide, empty smile.

"Your husband, madam. He has not yet arrived?"

"No."

Mankin clicked his tongue sympathetically. "No message?"

"None. There are no communications with Perak anymore."

"Have you considered the possibility of alternative accommodation?"

"No, of course not! Why should I?"

His smile widened a fraction. "Perhaps you have relations in Singapore."

"No. I have nobody."

"Friends, then. People of your own . . ."

He let the sentence trail off deliberately. She could hear the blood pounding in her ears. She held Ruth tightly on her lap. "My own what?" she asked.

"Many of our guests are complaining."

"About what?"

"About having to share the hotel with a native woman."

"But my account is up-to-date," she stammered.

The man's eyes were hard. "Besides which, you are occupying a room in which we can fit a whole family." He did not need to add *a white family.* "The situation is not one I or my staff enjoy, Mrs. Lawrence. If your husband does not join you by tonight, I am afraid we will no longer have a vacancy for you here."

"But where will we go? I have a child! There's hardly a room in Singapore!"

Mankin rose and bowed. "Good morning, Mrs. Lawrence."

She walked out into the lobby in a daze. The angry, hostile eyes followed her. She saw mouths muttering, but she shut out the words.

Where was she to go? If she had to leave Raffles, how would Abe ever find her? Her privileged little bubble had been ruptured. Somewhere within herself a Cantonese voice taunted her: *You've played the memsahib long enough, Yu Fa. Now you have to face the real world, as what you really are.*

Her first thought was to try another hotel. She called in the amah to look after Ruth and hurried out.

She tried the Goodwood Park, the Cathay, the Hotel de l'Europe, and then a round of lesser hotels. All rejected her instantly, whether because they were truly full or not she could not tell. The bombers came again at eleven o'clock, pounding the city mercilessly, forcing her into a crowded shelter on Bukit Timah Road, where she crouched with two hundred others, deafened by the destruction. When she emerged, Indiatown was burning, yellow-brown smoke billowing up over the rooftops. She continued searching, by taxi when she could find one, but mostly on foot.

The bombers came again at noon. This time she was over on Cavenagh Road. A man dragged her down to the cellar of a shop-house where his family was preparing a meal. They offered her food and she ate a little with them. The bombs were like a giant stamping around the city, making the earth shake, crushing whatever was in his path.

As she continued searching, the sky darkened with the smoke of burning buildings until a menacing twilight fell. The reply was an endless "No vacancy." She was exhausted and starting to despair by afternoon, when the bombers returned for the fourth time. Such a rapid turnaround could mean only one thing: The Japanese now had bases only an hour's flying time from Singapore. Soon the city would be within the range of guns as well as planes. And then it would be in range of tanks. Of bullets and swords, rape and bayonets.

She went back to Raffles and rested in her room with Ruth, eating fruit and drinking jasmine tea. Through her window, she could see a column of smoke rising from the island of Blakang Mati, where the bombers were blasting the batteries of naval guns. She had never yet seen a bomber shot down, or even hit, by the antiaircraft fire. Nor had she ever seen British aircraft oppose the bombers. She had heard that the RAF Wildebeests, capable of ninety knots against the Zeros' three hundred, had been destroyed in the first days of the war, with the loss of all the brave, helpless pilots.

There was a knock at the door. She went to open it, without any real hope that it could be news of Abe. Edwina Davenport, very pale, with shadows under her eyes, stood in the doorway. Behind her stood a smiling, snub-nosed nurse with a broad hand on her shoulder.

"Edwina!" she exclaimed, drawing them in. "How are you?"

"I'm all right," the girl said tonelessly.

Francine put her arms around Edwina. She stood passively, her cheek resting on Francine's shoulder.

"She's been discharged," the nurse said in a cheerful Australian accent, "but she needs someone to keep an eye on her. Just until they can get her a passage to Australia or England. She said you would do it."

"But I have to leave the hotel tomorrow!" Francine said.

"Oh, take her with you," the Australian said cheerfully. "Doesn't matter where you are, as long as she's got a shoulder to cry on."

"But I don't even know where I'm going!"

The nurse gave her a piece of paper. "Here's our number. Alexandra Hospital, Ward Fifty-three. Call Dr. Wilkes or Sister Carter. They're usually there. We don't go off-duty much these days. They'll tell you what to do." Without giving Francine time to reply, she passed over a little parcel. "Doctor's put her on these. Give her one of the pills every four hours. She's due her next at six. The powders are to help her sleep. Just mix one in a glass of water at bedtime. All righty?" She patted Edwina's arm. "Try not to think about it," she urged, not without compassion. "It wasn't your fault. All righty?"

She left with a cheerful wave. As soon as she was gone, Francine turned to Edwina. "I'm so sorry, Edwina," Francine said uselessly, "but it's true. I have to leave Raffles tomorrow."

"Why?"

"The management won't let me stay here any longer unless Abe comes. And I don't know when he'll come."

Edwina looked up, her face haggard. "They're kicking you out?"

"Tomorrow morning."

"Why?"

"Because I'm not white."

"The rotten swine!"

"They need the room for European families," she said, shrugging.

"Tell them you're not going!"

Francine picked up the telephone and called the number the nurse had left her. Dr. Wilkes answered in a tired, hoarse voice.

"The girl's had a severe shock," he told her. "She's only fifteen. She needs a maternal presence."

"Yes," Francine said. "The problem is, I have to leave by tomorrow morning."

"Leaving Singapore?"

"No. Just the hotel. I'm looking for somewhere else."

"That's all right then. You can take her with you, can't you?"

"For how long?"

"It's all in hand. Her name has been passed to the evacuation committee. She'll be sent back home on the next available boat."

"Oh," Francine said. It was the first she had heard of an evacuation committee. "When will that be?"

"It might take a week or two to arrange. Three weeks at the most. They're giving priority to the women and children, of course."

"I have a child of my own," she said.

"Then get your name on the list as soon as possible."

"But I'm waiting for my husband!"

The man grew impatient. "Look, I have patients to attend to. Make sure she takes the powders. They'll stop any nightmares." She thought he would hang up, but then he grunted. "Ah, yes. One more thing. The burial."

"I'm sorry?"

"The girl's father. The body. The sooner it's buried, the better. Will you take care of it?"

"But I've no idea—"

"It's in the morgue, here. I had to perform an autopsy, of course. As if I didn't have better things to do. The police have released it now. I've prepared the death certificate. Pick it up as soon as you can, please, we're very full." This time, he did hang up.

Francine put the telephone down and looked at Edwina, who seemed calmer now. "It's all right," Edwina said quietly. "I'm coming with you."

"Edwina," Francine said tiredly, "that's impossible."

"I haven't anyone else," Edwina said matter-of-factly. "I've got all Father's cash. And I can help with Ruth. With everything. We're better off together."

She stared at Edwina, knowing there was no way out. "They've asked me to arrange the burial. I don't even know where to start."

"Ask Brigadier Napier," Edwina said in a low voice.

"He's sick in bed with malaria."

"Then ask his nephew, that major. He's horrible, but he's probably used to doing things like this."

Francine suddenly remembered that Clive Napier had given her his card. She searched in her bag, and found the thing. She tried not to think of Clive's fingers reaching hungrily between her thighs. There was no one else. She called the number.

"Clive Napier," she heard his voice crackle.

She took a deep breath. "Major Napier? It's Francine Lawrence. I don't know if you remember me—"

"Hello, my sweet," he said, his voice changing. "This is a delightful surprise."

"I need your help," she said brusquely. "There's been a tragedy here. Mr. Davenport is dead."

"Davenport?" he asked.

"He was at our table on New Year's Eve."

"The gloomy old bird with the rosy daughter?"

"Yes."

"Shot himself, has he?" Clive asked crisply.

She had no idea how Clive had guessed that, but she was grateful that his brutal assessment meant she didn't need to go into details with Edwina present. "Yes," she said simply.

"He looked the type," Clive said calmly. "What can I do for you? Bury the old chap?"

"Yes," she said again. "Edwina, his daughter, is staying with me for the time being, and—"

"You don't need to explain," Clive cut in. "Where's the stiff?"

"At the Alexandra Hospital."

"Good. Buddhist, Christian, Jew?"

Francine turned to Edwina. "I'm sorry, Edwina. What religion do you belong to?"

"Church of England," Edwina replied, eyes reddening.

Francine relayed the information to Clive. "I'll get onto it straight-away," Clive promised. "Be in touch tonight."

"You're being very kind," Francine said awkwardly.

"Not at all," Clive replied briskly. "I told you, anything you want, my sweet. Strawberries, oysters, funerals. All part of the service."

"If you need any funds—"

"We'll work out the payment later," he said. He rang off, leaving her with a throaty chuckle to think about.

Francine looked at Edwina. "He says he'll do it. Right now, I have to keep on looking for somewhere to stay. I need to go out."

Edwina nodded. "If you like, I'll look after Ruth. You can send the amah away."

That was true. She was going to have to dispense with the amah, in any case. She made up her mind. "All right. There isn't much chance of finding another hotel room, Edwina. We may have to go to a very different area."

"You mean Chinatown."

"Or Indiatown. Or a Malay kampong."

The girl smiled slightly. "I don't have any prejudices. As long as I'm with you."

Francine nodded and started getting ready to go out.

The evening brought death closer to her than it had ever come.

She had boarded a tiny yellow eight-horsepower taxi, whose driver had promised to take her to see a flat in Popiah Street, in Chinatown. They were just entering the maze of Chinese shops when the taxi suddenly lurched to a halt. The driver flung open his door, screamed, "Get under the car!" and vanished.

Tired and confused, Francine got out. The driver was scrambling under his car, but the ground was filthy, and she couldn't possibly get down beside him in her smart clothes. The street was crowded with running people, their faces distorted with fear. A street vendor on a tricycle was careering down the pavement, bananas and mangosteens spilling from his baskets. She tried to see where people were running to, but each seemed to have his own hiding place, in shop doorways or down alleys.

Suddenly, the street vendor exploded in a crimson shower, as though he had become his own overripe fruit. She stared, transfixed by the astounding event. A woman near him leaped in the air like a dried leaf, the same crimson stuff spooling from holes in her body, and a man arched with arms flung high, shrieking.

Then she saw the Zero, silvery-gray like a shark, hurtling toward her. Its stubby wings seemed to brush the rooftops. The machine guns were gouting fire. She screamed in terror, but the huge snarl of the engine drowned her voice. She ran wildly down the street, arms flailing, feet pounding the slippery pavement. The noise of the Zero's engine exploded overhead, the fighter's wings tilting as it hosed the street with fire.

It swooped high against the sun, turning, wheeling in the bright air. She crouched by a street corner, gasping with raw lungs, watching it. For a moment it was a black cross, motionless in the glare. The roar of the engine rolled from one corner of heaven to the other, like a boulder on the roof of a house. It disappeared from view, and she thought it must have gone away. Then the noise was descending, growing, coming again.

She turned on her heel and ran the other way, down another street. It was still crowded with men, women, and children. Incredibly, despite the repeated raids, fruit stalls were still set up, lacquered ducks glistening in shop windows, racks of clothes fluttering; a man crouched behind his sewing machine, a pair of trousers clutched in his hands.

She heard the machine guns start firing, the bullets making a shrill whipping sound, like bamboo in a gale. Her foot hooked on something and she went sprawling in the street, her hands bruising on the tarmac. She rolled frantically into the gutter and curled up among the filth, covering her head with her arms.

The Zero howled overhead. She felt the bullets tearing into the structures around her. Her soul cringed in a gigantic fear, not just for herself, but for Ruth. *Who will look after her if I'm killed?* she thought in panic.

Then she was lifted in the air and tossed against a wall with casual, brutal force. Her head cracked cement so sharply she almost passed out. At first she thought she had been hit. Her ears were ringing. She opened her eyes and saw the fireball rising from the rooftops. The Zero had launched a torpedo directly into the crowded, swarming tenements. For a moment she had a hellish vision of flimsy wooden roofs sinking into matchwood, walls toppling outward, human figures spilling from dollhouse rooms. Then black smoke billowed around the ruined buildings, obliterating everything.

A stink of explosives and brick dust choked the air. All around her were scenes of carnage. The street was painted red, as if for the New Year. Blood had spattered, poured, splashed. Figures lay broken among scattered cabbages and melons, human beings turned into bundles of bloodstained rags in the matter of a few seconds. The tailor lay dead by his overturned machine. Beyond him, a child was spread-eagled among the rubbish. His mother had sunk to her knees beside the corpse, plucking at his clothes.

As her ears cleared, she could hear a gramophone still playing a popular Chinese song in some shop-front, the singer's shrill voice mingling with the screams of the wounded.

"Come! Come!" It was her taxi driver, tugging her sleeve. He had reappeared, astonishingly, out of the smoke and dust. "Come this way!"

The all clear was wailing. The Japanese had gone as suddenly as they had come. Her mind still paralyzed, she allowed him to drag her down an alley and into the next street. The little yellow Ford was where they had left it, doors still open like a butterfly poised for flight. The driver thrust Francine into the car, hands heaving at her buttocks as though she were a reluctant cow. He jumped behind the wheel and started up.

"We go to Popiah Street now," he said.

"What?" she asked stupidly.

"Popiah Street." He pointed with a brown finger at the dash. "Meter still running. We go see flat now?"

He had promised to take her to a vacant flat. Francine burst into tears, her whole body beginning to tremble in reaction. "Yes, Popiah Street," she managed to say.

"Okay." He set off, steering briskly around the wreckage of a shop that had been blown into the street. "You hurt?"

"No." She curled up on the backseat, sobbing helplessly.

"When Zeros come, better not run round like chicken without head. Find somewhere safe and just lie still." The driver hurtled on, ignoring her hysterics. The Japanese fighter had turned her from a human being with dignity into an abject animal, cowering in the slime. She saw the limp figure of the dead child in her mind's eye. What if that had been Ruth? What if that mother had been her?

A few minutes later, the driver pulled up outside a small block of flats. "This is it," he told her. "Second floor. Mrs. D'Oliveira. I'll wait."

Somehow, she was sitting up and looking around. Popiah Street ran parallel to Hongkong Street, near the river. The area lay on the edge of Chinatown, forming a triangle with the slums of Boat Quay and the imposing white complex of government buildings. The building, grandly called Union Mansions, was pretty, the street tidy.

She found herself checking her face in her pocket mirror, wiping away the tears, brushing her hair, dabbing powder on the dark shadows under her eyes. She wanted to make a good impression. The strafing had blended into the unreality of all the other unreal things that had happened to her this day. A weird calm possessed her as she got out of the taxi. There was blood in her hair and exploration revealed an exquisitely painful lump on the back of her head. She examined her dress. It was covered with filth. She brushed herself clean as best she could and walked up the stairs.

From one of the flats drifted the smoky sound of Duke Ellington's band playing "Mood Indigo." The air stank of raw sewage from broken drains. At least the building was clean and well maintained. Glossy potted palms flourished on the landings. Her heart lifted.

Mrs. D'Oliveira was an olive-skinned, birdlike woman who rubbed her hands together in distress when she saw Francine.

"Oh! I was expecting a European person! We only have Europeans here!"

"I'm married to an Englishman," Francine said, not knowing what else to say. "He's a mine manager. He's coming down from Perak to join me soon. We have a little girl, aged four."

"And Eurasians, of course," the woman said, peering closer at Francine. "My father-in-law was Portuguese, you know. We welcome Eurasians, of course."

Francine gestured at her dress. "I'm sorry about this. I got caught in the street."

"Poor thing! You can clean yourself up in the bathroom."

She let Francine into the flat. Like the rest of the building, it was clean and neat. There were three bedrooms and a small kitchen. It was fully furnished; indeed, the whole place gave off a strange impression that the inhabitants had just popped out to do some shopping. The living room had a variety of easy chairs, a gleaming gramophone with records, a cabinet full of the brass-and-silver "Eastern curios" that European tourists liked to buy. Plants flowered on the windowsills.

"It was a Captain Edmondson," the woman said, rubbing her thin hands with the sound of dry paper. "Lovely man. Bachelor. Killed in a raid. I miss him so much!" She wiped a sudden tear from her cheek. "You can use his things. He had no family. Ten dollars a week. Two weeks in advance, two weeks' notice."

Francine walked to the window and pushed the heavy blackout drape aside to look out. There was a lush little back garden with a handsome pipal tree. A perfect place for Ruth to play. The whole place was perfect. But she could see why this outwardly desirable flat had not been rented in two weeks. Three blocks away, the Chinese quarter was billowing smoke from the recent attack. A little farther on, a deeper, denser cloud marked where godowns were burning on the pier. Less than half a mile across the river, which was still packed with sampans, Fort Canning had been badly damaged. The bombing had come frighteningly close to Popiah Street. Between the green hill of Fort Canning and the crowded alleys of Chinatown, it was not in a good spot.

As though divining her thoughts, the woman spoke with sudden sharpness. "You could search Singapore and not find a better flat! Furnished! We don't usually consider non-Europeans!"

"Where is the nearest shelter?" Francine asked.

"Oh, we have such a safe shelter, Mrs. Lawrence! Built by Mr. Carmody. Just at the end of the street. Room for everybody. You may inspect it yourself."

The woman was right. She could search the whole of Singapore and not find a better place. Her mind was made up.

"Five dollars," Francine heard herself say. "Ten is far too much."

"Eight."

"I'll go as high as seven. No higher."

"Yes," the other woman said. "Yes, yes. All right. Seven."

"All right. We'll move in tomorrow." She tore her eyes away from the burning buildings of Chinatown and turned to Mrs. D'Oliveira, who was beaming at her. She took the purse out of her bag and counted out fourteen dollars. "There are three of us. I'm taking care of a girl who's lost her father. She's fifteen."

"A European girl?" the woman asked, reaching for the money.

"A European girl."

"She is most welcome," Mrs. D'Oliveira said graciously, folding the money into her pocket. She hopped forward in her birdlike way and clasped Francine's wrists in her little claws. "Welcome to Popiah Street, my dear!"

They buried Edwina's father at noon the next day, in the Protestant cemetery on Monk's Hill. Several other funerals were in progress; theirs was the smallest. The only mourner to turn up apart from Francine and Edwina was Clive Napier. He was in uniform, his head still bandaged.

"Wish you'd told us about those swine at Raffles," he said to Francine, watching the Tamil gravediggers still busy in the grave. "I'd have talked the management around. At gunpoint, if necessary."

"It's done, now. How is Brigadier Napier?"

"Not very well. Wanted to come, but he's too weak, of course."

"Please give him my best wishes."

"I will. Is your new place all right? Clean and all that, I mean?"

It was difficult to ignore the memory of their feverish grapple on New Year's Eve, but Francine tried hard. "Oh, yes, thank you. I should have done it weeks ago. Not waited to be thrown out like a dog."

"You're going to be a lot closer to the bombing."

"I know. There's a good shelter nearby. Better than the shelter at Raffles. We'll be all right."

"I'll drop in on you," he promised. "Bring you some of those strawberries and oysters."

"There's no need," she said hurriedly. He just winked at her.

They had spent the morning moving into Union Mansions. Edwina had helped tirelessly. They had just had time to get their bags unpacked before they had had to hurry back across the city to Raffles, where they met the car Clive had sent to take them to the cemetery.

The Tamil gravediggers clambered out, dusting the red earth from their clothes. They hauled the coffin into place, securing it with straps over the raw hole. It was a handsome thing with silver handles. Silently, she blessed Clive for his mastery in handling all this. The vicar had been talking in a low voice to Edwina. Now he stepped to the edge of the grave and opened his prayer book. His voice was thin and reedy on the wind.

" 'Not unto us, O Lord, not unto us, but unto thy name give the praise: for thy loving mercy and for thy truth's sake.' "

Francine felt Clive stiffen beside her. "Hold on a moment, Padre," he said. "You've got the wrong service, I think."

The vicar looked at him irritably. "There is a different service for suicides, Major."

"You mean you won't read the pukka service for a suicide?" Clive demanded in disgust. At the same time, the air-raid sirens started to wail, rising up from the city below, momentarily submerging the faint words of the psalm.

The laborers immediately let the straps slip through their fingers, and took to their heels. Francine flinched as the coffin crashed down into the grave, wedging with one square wooden shoulder upward. People were streaming from other gravesides, heading for the Roman Catholic chapel, which was the nearest building.

A neat row of black dots had appeared on the horizon, surrounded by a halo of exhaust fumes. The dots swiftly became crosses.

"We'll have to adjourn until later, I'm afraid," the priest said, closing his prayer book. "Their path lies directly over the burial ground. They have shot at funerals before now. I'm sorry." He gathered his skirts and hurried off toward the chapel.

Francine looked at Clive helplessly. He grinned at her, showing white teeth. "Think they'll waste a bomb or a bullet on us three?" He took Francine's prayer book from her. He began to read, this time from the orthodox service. " 'I am the resurrection and the life, saith the Lord: He that believeth in me, though he were dead, yet shall live.' "

He kept reading, even when the roar drowned out his words.

Strangely unafraid despite the terrors of yesterday, Francine looked up. The formation, perhaps fifty planes, was no more than a few thousand feet up. She could see the bomb-bay doors already gaping open in the bellies of the Mitsubishi bombers. The crimson disk of the rising sun was bold against the paintwork. She could even see the silhouettes of some of the crew peering down at them through the glass canopies. The sustained thunder of the engines was overwhelming, shaking the ground, hurting the ears. Puffs of ack-ack fire opened around the airplanes, looking like thistledown and seeming to do about as much damage.

The terrible procession passed overhead and began banking over the city, heading toward Tanjong Ru. Clive nodded toward a shovel abandoned by the gravediggers. "You ought to do the honors, old girl," he said to Edwina.

Edwina stooped, sobbing, and scraped up a handful of red earth. It thudded onto the coffin. Francine knelt to pick up a few clods and let them fall into the grave. Then she took Edwina in her arms. A barrage of explosions rolled over them. The bombers were attacking the gasoline-storage depots on Tanjong Ru. Crimson flowers opened among black foliage, cruel and evil. She could hear the distant howl of the Zeros dive-bombing, the busy chatter of ack-ack fire from the ground, firing with mad, useless bravery at the bombers.

Clive reached out and stroked Edwina's curly hair briefly. "She's lucky to have found you. She'll have to be sent off home."

"I know. Someone's taking care of that."

"You and your daughter should go with her."

"How can I go without my husband?"

"He can follow you. This place hasn't long to go, Francine. You know that. It hasn't a hope in hell." He pointed at the fires that were blazing on Tanjong Ru.

"I'd better get Edwina home," Francine said. Edwina was crying as though her heart would break.

They started to walk toward Cemetery Road, where their car was parked, a dignified black Humber that Clive Napier had somehow managed to obtain for the occasion. None of them looked back at the abandoned, unfinished grave.

"How much is all this going to cost?" Francine murmured to Clive.

"Forget about that."

"What do you mean?"

"It's all been taken care of."

"Who's taken care of it?"

"I have, of course."

Francine was dismayed. "Oh, no! Edwina has money, and so do I."

"I don't think we'll make the kid pay for burying her father," Clive said dryly. "And it's nothing to do with you."

"It's nothing to do with you, either! I wouldn't have asked you to help if I'd thought you were going to pay for it!"

"Forget about it," he repeated. "I'm not exactly poor. Glad to help."

"Thank you, Major."

"Oh, please. Clive."

On the way back along Orchard Road, they passed a stream of several hundred wounded troops making their way into the city.

"Just arrived from the ulu," Clive commented briefly. "They look about done in."

Francine looked at them as the Humber edged past. They stared ahead of them grimly, like men freshly returned from hell. This, too, was something new and ominous, this spectacle of the European soldier so clearly defeated.

Something was happening to Francine. It must have begun a long time ago, but she had first become aware of it yesterday, when she had conquered her hysteria to go and inspect Mrs. D'Oliveira's flat. She was becoming a different person. It was as if the softness of her former life was being burned away by the horrors she was going through, leaving something enduring in its place, some core of strength.

She wondered how Abe was going to like her new self. She did not care: He would have to live with it. The terrible misjudgment of not coming down to Singapore with them had forever dented her esteem for him. She no longer worshiped unthinkingly at the shrine of Abe's male, British superiority. She would not let him bully her again, not ever again, no matter what he said about her thick Chinese head.

When they reached Popiah Street, she felt obliged to invite Clive Napier in for a cup of tea. He accepted readily.

Ruth, who had been in the care of an amah all morning, was delighted to see them. She was also much taken with Clive, his officer's uniform, and the bandage around his head.

"Did the Japanese do that to you?" she demanded immediately on meeting him.

"They did indeed," Clive said, smiling.

"How, with a sword?"

"Hush, Ruth," Francine warned sternly.

"It's only a scratch," Clive assured Ruth. He was carrying a briefcase of the type officers used, and now he opened it and started looking inside. "Now, I believe I've got something for you, young lady, if I can only find it."

"What is it?" Ruth demanded, excited.

"Ah. Here it is." He produced a package, and presented it to Ruth.

Francine, watching from the kitchen door, saw Ruth tear off the paper to reveal a wooden model of a fighter plane, proudly painted with RAF roundels.

"A Spitfire!" Ruth squealed in delight.

"That'll look after you when the Japanese bombers come around next time."

Francine was touched that he had thought of a present for Ruth. The child had few toys in Singapore. It was not exactly what she would have chosen herself, but Ruth was captivated with the thing.

"Look, Edwina! *Weee-ow, vrooom, weee-ow,*" Ruth crooned, waving the Spitfire and imitating the noise of airplane engines. "Take that, take that, take that, you nasty Japanese!"

"I suppose I should have got her a doll," Clive said, catching Francine's eye. "But I thought that might be more in vogue these days."

"It was very thoughtful of you. Thank you."

"My pleasure."

"I think I'll go and lie down," Edwina said tiredly.

"I'll bring some tea to you in bed," Francine promised.

"Thanks." The girl reached a plump hand out to Clive. "Thanks, Clive. You've been marvelous."

Clive kissed her hand gently. "No problem, old girl. I'm always here."

Francine made the tea and took a cup into Edwina's room. The girl was crying quietly, propped up on pillows.

"I'm so sorry," Francine said, stroking Edwina's curly hair.

"How could he do it?" Edwina raised her face, which was haggard. "How could he?"

"I don't know," Francine replied helplessly. "I suppose he just couldn't face it anymore, Edwina."

"I'm facing it! Everyone else is facing it!"

"We're not all the same, dear. We all have different capacities to suffer and endure. Some less than others. Your father's inability to endure has meant that you have to endure more. But you have that capacity."

"It's all right," Edwina replied, after a silence. "I'll be all right. When the war's over, I'll go back and take over the plantation. I'll go to agricultural college, and learn how to do it properly."

Francine was touched by the firm declaration. "Good for you."

"He's nice, isn't he? Clive, I mean. I thought he was awful at first, but he's been a pillar of strength."

Francine nodded. "He certainly has."

"You need a man like that, Francine," Edwina said. "You should grab on to him."

She laughed, despite herself. "Men aren't like buses, dear. You don't just relinquish one and catch another."

"Your husband's relinquished you," Edwina said meaningfully.

"He'll be along, by and by," Francine replied lightly.

"Like a bus?" Edwina sipped tea, the cup quivering in her shaky fingers. "Just promise you won't chase Clive away, that's all. He's too good to lose."

"I promise." Francine smiled.

When she was sure Edwina was composed, she went back to Clive and Ruth. The child was by now nestled in Clive's lap, looking very much at home there. She was interrogating him minutely, evidently relying on Clive's army rank, and experience of fighting the Japanese, to give the answers nobody else could.

"But why doesn't God just *stop* the Japanese?" Ruth demanded. She looked up at Clive. "God could stop the Japanese, couldn't he, Clive?"

"Yes," Clive said, "but I rather think God's relying on us to stop them on our own. To show what we're made of, if you see what I mean."

"To show how brave we are?"

"That's it."

"What if God's wrong, and they beat us?"

"They won't beat us."

Francine poured the tea while Ruth studied her Spitfire, lying comfortably on Clive's strong chest. "Have you got children of your own?" Francine asked Clive casually.

"Oh, I'm not married. Footloose and fancy-free, as they say." There was an unmistakable message in his laughing eyes. Francine rose, smoothing her dress nervously over her thighs. "Well, it's getting toward lunchtime," she said. "I'd better get busy."

Clive could not ignore the broad hint. He kissed Ruth and put her down. "Good-bye, Ruthie. Next time I come, I'll bring you another present."

"When will you come?" Ruth demanded eagerly.

"Soon," Clive promised, eyes glinting at Francine.

And though at the door she offered him a cool hand, he leaned forward and kissed her quickly on the mouth, leaving her with an impression of warm lips. "I'm in love with your daughter, Francine. She's very special. So are you. I'll be back," he promised meaningfully.

As she lay in the narrow, sagging bed that night, her new, hardened self asked her whether she really had any hope of seeing her husband ever again.

The remains of her old soft self began to cry. And in the next room, despite the bitter powder she had mixed in the girl's bedtime drink, she heard Edwina Davenport's quiet sobbing.

The mood among the war-work women had changed since the end of the year. There was less laughter around the long tables, less gossip, more frightened whispering. Everyone complained bitterly about the rains that had begun, and the impossibility of keeping clothing dry.

As yet, there did not seem to have been any exodus of memsahibs; indeed, as Lucy Conyngham said at the Red Cross, nobody had yet told them to go.

"The *Narkunda* sailed yesterday morning," she said, snipping through gauze and deftly turning the dressing around her fingers. "Half-empty, so they say."

"But that's terrible," Francine said, looking up. Her first thought had been of Edwina. "They should at least have sent the children."

"Of course, she's bound for Australia," Mrs. Conyngham said. "Most people would rather go straight home, wouldn't they? What's the use of being stuck in Australia for the duration?"

"Wish I'd known she was half-empty," one of the younger European women, Violet Maudling, said bitterly. "I'd have got out." She leaned forward, lowering her voice and widening her big blue eyes. "Have you heard what the Japanese do to any white woman they capture? They—" Her eyes widened even farther as she sought a genteel word for an ungenteel act. "They debase them."

A Chinese woman named Mrs. Chen retorted grimly, "Tens of thousands of Chinese women have already suffered that fate, Mrs. Maudling."

"Oh, but it's different for you," the Englishwoman retorted, bridling.

"Of course it isn't different," Mrs. Conyngham said fiercely. "It's the same for any woman, Mrs. Maudling."

"It depends how you've been brought up," Mrs. Maudling said, snapping thread briskly.

"Chinese ladies are not brought up to be violated with indifference, Mrs. Maudling," the woman named Chen said dryly.

"Nor Tamil ladies," piped up a little wizened woman in a gold sari.

"It's different," Mrs. Maudling sniffed obstinately. "They're more your own kind, aren't they?"

A squabble broke out, several women talking at once, some very angry.

Francine herself was aware of a burning indignation inside; not at the crassness of Violet Maudling, but that the *Narkunda* had sailed without Edwina.

She was so glad of Edwina's company. The girl seemed to have endless patience to amuse Ruth, who would otherwise have been driven mad by being enclosed all day. Edwina seemed to have grown to love the child, bestowing on her the smiles and tenderness of her fifteen short years. Her devotion to Ruth had freed Francine to do so much. But it was her duty to get Edwina out of Singapore as soon as possible.

Without telling Edwina where she was going, she left Popiah Street after lunch and found a taxi to take her to the offices of the Director General of Civil Defense, who she knew was responsible for the evacuation of civilians.

She was seen at once by a tall, spare major named King, with weary blue eyes and a thin mouth, who heard her out with his hands clasped on the blotter in front of him. The walls of his office were covered in lists and maps on which someone had pinned hundreds of red and blue thumbtacks.

"It's perfectly true, I'm afraid," he said apologetically when she had finished. "The *Narkunda* sailed yesterday morning, with only half her berths taken up."

"But that's disgraceful," Francine said, horrified. "They should at least have sent the children."

"Oh, yes. Your young friend should certainly have been on her. But you know, Mrs. Lawrence, liners have been leaving Singapore half-empty since October. You see, we have rather a delicate situation on our hands. Sir Shenton has already decreed that anyone who wants to leave may do so, regardless of color. But we've stopped short of a compulsory evacuation order. We can't order people to go, d'you see?"

"Edwina Davenport is a child," she said. "She was promised a berth on the next boat!"

"There's been an unforgivable mistake," he said soothingly, making a note. "You may rest assured that Edwina will be evacuated as soon as possible. I'll be in touch shortly." The tired blue eyes surveyed her. "May I ask what plans you have for your own good self?"

"I'm waiting for my husband. He's coming down from Perak."

She had repeated the phrase so many times that it had begun to sound wooden and unconvincing even to herself.

"Perak?"

"He's general manager of the Imperial Tin Mine."

"Ah." She saw the inevitable change taking place in the major's expression. "When did he set off?"

"At the beginning of this month."

"I see. He's English, of course?"

"Yes. We have a little girl. She's with me in Singapore."

"Ah." He drummed his blunt fingertips momentarily on his blotter, running his tongue round the inside of his cheeks. She could smell the man's starched uniform, his skin, the coppery smell so many ginger-haired Englishmen seemed to give off. "Non-Europeans who have been associated with Europeans in any way are one of our priorities, Mrs. Lawrence. My advice to you is to start making plans for your own evacuation and that of your child. As the wife of an Englishman, you have automatic British citizenship. Do you hold a British passport?"

"Yes."

"Got it with you?"

"Yes."

"And the child is inscribed on it?"

"Yes."

"Excellent," he said, brightening. "Then we can get you a place on one of the P and O boats without any problem at all."

"I can't think of going without my husband," she said. "Or at least," she amended, "without having news of him."

"You know," he said gently, "he may not be allowed to leave. Our orders are to facilitate the evacuation of women and children. Not able-bodied men. At the moment, they're all being ordered to stay. Civilians as well as soldiers."

"I didn't know that," she said, feeling cold.

He studied her for a while. "The situation may change," he said at last. "We're always here. Just don't leave it too late. There might be a stampede at—" She was certain he was about to say *at the last minute,* but he did not finish the sentence. "As for young Edwina, we'll sort her out in no time. Leave it to me."

She left the DGCD offices with turbulent emotions. *What am I to do?* she asked Abe angrily in her mind. *Go without you? Wait for you until the Japanese are wading across the Strait of Johore, even though you may never come? Damn you!*

She cried a little, tears more of frustration than grief, in the glaring heat of the street. Then the sky began to cloud over and the shattering thunder of a squall drove her to hunt for a taxi.

She returned home to find that Clive Napier had arrived while she was out. He was sprawled on the floor beside Ruth, in shirtsleeves, strong brown arms bare. A pile of children's books were spread out around them.

"Look, Mama," Ruth squealed. "Look what Clive brought me. Picture books!"

Francine could not but bless him for the thoughtful gift. God knew how he had procured them; books of all kinds had vanished from the shops for some reason, and Ruth had been stuck in the flat, unable to play outside because of the monsoon.

"That was very kind of you," she said sincerely.

He grinned up at her, unmistakably a man on the make. "No tea this time, for God's sake. I brought something better."

Edwina, who had spread his soaked jacket on a chair to dry, was wide-eyed as she took Francine to the kitchen and showed her the princely gifts Clive had brought: fresh strawberries, juicy Australian sirloin steaks, a bottle of whiskey.

"I think he must fancy you," Edwina whispered excitedly.

"At least somebody's still living in luxury," Francine commented wryly. "Does he expect us to cook these for him?"

"Don't be like that," Edwina pleaded. "No, he doesn't want to eat here. He has to take somebody out for lunch."

"Some powdered memsahib, no doubt," Francine said tartly.

"You're jealous!"

"Of course I am not jealous," Francine snapped. But it was too late. Her unwise remark had set off Edwina, who began dancing, and singing teasingly, "He fancies you, and you fancy him!"

Impatiently, Francine walked out of the kitchen with the bottle, and poured Clive a drink. He was reading Ruth a story about a character called Chicken-Licken, and she was entranced. They ignored her completely, wrapped up in each other and the books. Clive knew how to make the simple tales come alive, putting on funny voices and screwing up his handsome face.

Clive Napier was one of the most vividly alive men, Francine realized, that she had ever met. She had long since decided that he was a scoundrel, but his very vividness was what made him attractive. His uniform fitted him perfectly, evidently made by the best tailor in Singapore, and all his leather gleamed as brightly as his batman could shine it. The bandage on his head only emphasized his piratical air. His brown eyes were perpetually alight with ironic merriment, as though everything around him were a wry joke.

She passed him the whiskey. "Have you been discharged fit yet?"

He nodded, looking up at her. "I've been seconded to the censor's office. We get all the bad news first. Our job is to turn it into musical comedy for mass consumption. Funny sort of job, but ours not to question why. Any news from your husband?"

"None," she said flatly.

He grunted, and rose. "Not having any whiskey?"

"No, thanks," she replied primly.

Edwina came in with a tray on which she had carefully set out a bowl of stuffed olives and another of pickled onions.

"My word," Clive exclaimed gratefully. "This is service. Much as I adore you, young Edwina, may I ask why you haven't been sent home yet?"

"She's on the list," Francine said, explaining what she had found out that morning. "We're just waiting for them to call her."

"Good." Clive put an arm around Edwina and hugged her. "I say," he said, lifting one eyebrow suggestively, "you'll be breaking hearts back in Blighty, old girl. You're like June, bursting out all over."

Edwina flushed, squirming. "Please don't pinch me, Clive. I'm not a farm animal."

"No, you're an English pippin."

"What's that?" Edwina asked suspiciously. "Some breed of prize pig, I suppose?"

"If you hadn't been born in the savage jungles, you'd know that an English pippin is a crisp and juicy apple."

"Thank you for the steaks," Francine forced herself to say. "Meat is so rare now. I don't know how you got them," she couldn't help adding suspiciously.

"Luxury is still to be had at a price," he said. "People are still raking in fortunes. Profiteers, hardheaded businessmen, merchants, squeezing gold from the panic of others. So why shouldn't you three have a steak? Besides, it'll put some color in Ruth's cheeks. She's looking peaky."

Francine had noticed Ruth's pallor, too. "Yes, she is."

"Well," Clive said, finishing the whiskey, "I'd better be trotting along. Got a luncheon date." He pulled on his damp jacket before meeting Francine's eyes with a wicked gleam. "A powdered memsahib, as a matter of fact."

Damn his sharp hearing, Francine thought. "Good. Do have fun."

"She won't be very pleased. She thinks I'm going to bring her those steaks. But I've donated them to a worthier cause. Aren't you going to invite me for a meal one of these days, my sweet?"

"Of course," she replied woodenly. "Any time you choose."

"Well, I'll just drop in, shall I? So long, Chicken-Licken," Clive said, sweeping up Ruth and kissing her.

"Will you come again?" she pleaded.

"Soon," he promised.

"And bring more presents."

"Ruth!" Francine exclaimed.

"Don't scold her. She's got the right idea. Ask and ye shall receive." He landed a good kiss on Edwina's mouth, too, but Francine managed to keep out of range. His kisses on the lips were a lot too casual for her liking. As he left, the heavens opened again, and the monsoon rain thundered down on him, drenching him. She closed the door with satisfaction.

They ate the steaks and the strawberries, but Francine traded the nearly full bottle of whiskey for a sack of rice. And the raids resumed, despite the monsoon.

By now, the people who used Mr. Carmody's shelter had formed a sort of community and Francine knew the names of most of them, who they were, and what they did. It was a group of prostitutes from Lower Shanghai Street who were the dominant characters, with their raucous laughter and gaudy presence. They were of all races, including a group of Hakka Chinese, their cheeks and lips bright with paint at any hour of the day, and four or five Eurasians who were more discreet.

One of the Eurasians had taken a particular interest in Ruth. Francine had heard the soldiers call her Battling Bertha. She was in her mid-thirties, a big woman with slab hips, her bosom straining her embroidered cheongsam, her fingers sparkling with cheap rings.

During one of the heaviest raids, she left the card game and sauntered over, arms akimbo.

"You not getting much sleep these days, hmmm?" she said to Ruth, who was fretful in the arms of a suspicious-looking Edwina. "Give her to me, girl." She gathered the child to her bosom and settled down at Francine's side with Ruth in her enveloping arms, bringing a wave of perfume. "I got four kids of my own," she said in a singsong lilt. "Sent them all off to the Dutch East Indies when the Japs invaded. You should do the same. Don't wait until they get here."

"I have nowhere else to go."

"They'll rape you and then kill you," Bertha said unemotionally. "Get out now, while the going is good." She stroked Ruth's cheek with a red-nailed forefinger. "So you brought another little stengah into the world."

"Yes."

"Good. Bring more." She laughed. "Bring plenty stengahs into the world. The world needs more. Where's your man, honey?"

"Coming down from Perak," she said for what felt like the thousandth time.

"He stayed there?"

"Yes."

"What for?"

"To take care of business."

"Stupid British tuan, eh?"

"Yes." Francine nodded. "A stupid British tuan."

"Life's hard without a man, even a stupid one." Bombs shook the shelter violently. Dust and talcum showered down on them. Bertha casually cupped her broad hand over Ruth's face to keep the dirt off. "Who's the other girl?" she asked.

"The daughter of a man who was killed in the bombing," Francine replied.

Bertha peered at Edwina with tawny-green cat's eyes. "You got a lot of responsibilities, honey. Too many, ah?"

"Maybe." Francine sighed.

"You take my advice," Bertha said. "Get yourself a man, honey. You understand me? Never mind your husband. Get a flesh-and-blood man, not a man made out of smoke."

The all clear was sounding. People rose to make their weary way back to bed. One grew almost accustomed to the fear, but Francine thought it was impossible to grow used to the sheer inconvenience of the raids, of having to tear oneself out of bed in one's nightclothes, or leave food to spoil on the stove, or washing in the sink, or any one of a thousand jobs unfinished.

Ruth was asleep in Battling Bertha's arms now. She passed the child over to Francine. "I miss my kids," she said. "Any time you feel like a drink, come over to our club. The Golden Slipper, on Shanghai Street. We have a good time there."

"Thank you," Francine said.

"It's not as bad as you think," Bertha said. "Might fill in some gaps in your education."

"Is she a prostitute?" Edwina asked, watching Bertha's rolling buttocks.

"What do you think?" Francine replied tartly. Edwina was certainly getting an education very different from her sheltered upbringing thus far in life.

Bertha's brutal advice about getting herself a "flesh-and-blood man" echoed in her mind. She was talking to Abe in her mind less and less these days, even to berate him. There had been a time when she had consulted "what Abe would want" before almost every action. Now, for good or for bad, that point of reference was gone. Though Battling Bertha was everything her own upbringing had taught her to fear and despise, Francine envied her. She envied Bertha her street wisdom, her courage and strength. Francine wanted to be more like Bertha, with her driving will to survive, less like the well-brought-up Eurasian lady she had always striven to be.

Ruth seemed unable to shake off her diarrhea and she often vomited during or just after raids. She was losing weight; the little bones of her hips were beginning to show. She was growing listless. When Francine took her to Robinson's to be weighed one morning, she found to her dismay that the child had lost over ten pounds since leaving Perak. She showed her to the chemist, who probed the thin stomach gently with his fingertips.

"It's dysentery," he said, and Francine's heart sank painfully at the dread word.

"Dysentery!"

"Sonne dysentery, probably, not Shiga. Maybe even no more than an infestation of lamblia. That's lucky. Watch out for any blood in the stools. If you see any, bring her in at once. The organisms usually die out of their own accord after a week or so. I haven't got any drugs for you, I'm afraid. Keep her rested and make sure she gets plenty of fluids. And of course, be scrupulous about hygiene. Boil everything. Keep her hands clean. Yours, too. Don't worry too much."

But she did worry. As she dressed Ruth, she thought seriously for the first time about the possibility of leaving Singapore without Abe. If it came to a choice between Abe and Ruth, she would have to choose Ruth. Abe could, at least, fend for himself. Ruth could not.

She got home just in time for another raid, and had to run down to the shelter with Edwina and Ruth.

Mr. Carmody's shelter looked less impressive now. The godown had been ripped to shreds, and hung raggedly around the inner structure. Blasts had shifted some of the bales of rubber; shrapnel had ripped many of the sandbags, which were only prevented from leaking their contents by having been soaked by the monsoon rains.

The shelter was crowded with new faces from the outlying streets, every inch of space crammed. The Shanghai Street prostitutes were crowded around a Chinese woman who squatted, clinging to one of the iron pillars that supported the roof. She was rocking to and fro. Francine realized that the woman was in labor. What hope could there be for new life brought into this? Someone had produced the shelter first-aid kit. It stood next to the pregnant woman, its lid opened, its rows of bottles and bandages looking pathetically ineffective.

She and Edwina settled themselves where they could. Ruth fell instantly back to sleep in Edwina's arms. The heavy thudding of bombs began somewhere to the south. Edwina was watching the pregnant woman in fascination, her eyes wide. Bertha seemed to have taken charge, now and then wiping the woman's face with a bandage, murmuring into her ear.

Three huge explosions in quick succession shook the shelter. Everything seemed to become jelly, a brief and dreadful sensation that the world was dissolving. A shower of filth rained down. The pregnant woman clung to the swaying iron pillar, still completely silent.

A fourth explosion, even closer, caused mutters of dismay. The blast crushed the air momentarily, squeezing Francine's chest, hurting her ears despite her protecting fingers. She looked at Ruth in concern. The child's eyes were open now. She looked dazed. A gout of thin vomit spilled from her lips over Edwina's chest. Francine reached for the child anxiously.

Another explosion turned the air and the solid world into a palpitating mass. Francine found herself wondering whether they would have a home to return to when this was over. One thing she had learned, at least, was to take things as they came. For the moment, she needed to concentrate on survival, nothing else.

"Push," Francine heard Bertha urge the woman in labor. "Push!"

The woman's body convulsed. She cried out something in a hoarse voice. She pulled her skirt up and peered down. The baby's head had emerged. Bertha reached down in a businesslike way and cleared mucus from the baby's mouth. Then she nodded to the mother.

The maroon body of the infant exploded from her. Bertha's big, sure palms were ready to catch it. Suddenly, the shelter, which had been tensely silent, was full of voices, people laughing, crying, calling congratulations. Francine was choking back tears.

"It's a boy," Bertha said cheerfully, holding it up. The crumpled face emitted a scratchy wail from a huge mouth, tiny fists waving. Francine glanced at Edwina. She was staring in awe. It was a brutal but effective education, she thought.

More explosions shook the shelter, but nobody seemed to care. Bertha wrapped the child and put it into the mother's arms. Weakly, the woman produced a swollen breast. The seeking mouth found the nipple, fumbled blindly, then began to suck.

Francine closed her eyes, feeling the warm tears trickle down her cheeks. Damn Abe. Damn him for what he had done to them. He had chosen some sterile sense of duty above his wife and child. She remembered the words he had quoted, a lifetime ago: "I could not love thee, dear, so much, loved I not honor more."

What stupid, empty words!

For the sake of those Manchester businessmen, those greedy white towkays who never even came to see where their money was earned in sweat and mud, Abe had sacrificed her and Ruth. He had abandoned them to face this horror alone. And he had probably sentenced himself to death or capture by the army he'd contemptuously referred to as a bunch of yellow monkeys.

She was angry and despairing.

Why had she let herself be overruled? If she'd had her own way, they would all have been safe in England by now. From now on, she vowed, she was going to do things her own way.

A man made out of smoke, Bertha had said. That was what Abe had turned out to be. A man made of smoke, who had been blown away with the wind. She would never forgive him for that, she realized suddenly. Even if he came, she would never forgive him. And she would never again let him make her do something she knew to be wrong.

I can't wait forever, she told him silently. *Come, or I will live my life without you.*

Clive Napier arrived at Union Mansions the next evening.

Francine opened the door to his knock, and he stood there with a package under one arm, looking smart in his uniform. The bandage around his head had been reduced to a square pad of gauze, held on with strips of tape. He grinned at her. "Hello, my sweet. I thought I'd drop in for dinner."

Francine was flustered. "You'll have to take potluck, I'm afraid," she said awkwardly.

He came in, closing the door behind him. He unwrapped the parcel, revealing a tray of strawberries, three dozen oysters in a wicker basket, and two bottles of French champagne. "Got any glasses?" he asked. "All alcohol has to be destroyed before the Japs get here. Let's do our bit."

She went to get glasses and ice to pack the bottles in. He picked up Ruth and tossed her in the air, making her squeal with pleasure. "How's my Chicken-Licken?" he growled, tickling her. Ruth wriggled with delight.

"Are you going to read to me?" she begged.

"Yes, darling," he said. "You and I will look at books after we've eaten Mama's potluck."

"What's potluck?" Ruth wanted to know.

"What I always take." He met Francine's eyes. "Get out of this town, Francine. We haven't got long."

"How long?" she asked simply.

"Three weeks or a month," Clive said.

She was appalled. "Is that all?"

"Churchill hasn't given up Singapore," Edwina said stoutly.

"Everyone's given up on Singapore, old girl."

"You're a defeatist, Clive," Edwina said sternly. "You're spreading despondency and gloom."

"That will be enough impertinence from one of your youthful years, child."

"Child? I'm nearly sixteen," Edwina said indignantly.

"In which case, Francine, make that three glasses of champagne. Young Edwina is joining us in a tipple. I'm not a defeatist, Edwina, I'm a realist," he explained. "Your very good health, ladies." He raised his glass. Francine and Edwina, to whom Francine had given a small glass of champagne, raised theirs in return. Clive gulped most of his down in one go. "Your best bet's the *Wakefield*, Edwina. She sails next week. Uncle's going on the *Duchess of Bedford*." Clive emptied the glass in a second gulp. "Aah. That's better. Being a realist, I need more alcohol than others. It dulls the discomfort. Let's have another." He took the bottle and filled all their glasses generously.

"I've never had so much champagne before," Edwina said, sipping cautiously at the bubbling liquid.

"Well, go steady," Clive advised, "or you might become a realist, too."

"I think that's enough champagne for Edwina," Francine said. "I'll go and cook."

"I'll open the oysters," Clive offered.

They went into the kitchen. While Clive, with considerable expertise, opened the oysters using a screwdriver, she set rice to boil. Then she chopped ginger, onion, and garlic and fried them in an iron pan, the closest thing to a wok she could find in Captain Edmondson's kitchen. She had bought a fish on Boat Quay, a nonya favorite. She filleted it, dressed it with *taucheong* paste and some sticks of lemongrass. She put the fragrant parcel in the hot oven to bake. The rich smell flooded the flat. *Where are you, Abe?* she demanded in her mind, as she did so many times each day. *Why don't you come?*

"I say." Edwina was laying the table. "That smells good."

"I hope you like Chinese cooking," she said to Clive.

"Love it," Clive said simply.

They ate around the table, the windows thrown open to let in the cool evening air. The oysters were delicious with Tabasco and lemon juice. They vanished swiftly, after which they started on the fish. Ruth ate with a spoon, pushing the succulent fish into her mouth, humming with pleasure. Francine ate with chopsticks, a habit she had fallen back into recently. Clive watched her handle the slender sticks with unthinking dexterity.

"Did your husband eat with chopsticks?" he asked.

"Sometimes. When I forced him to. He wasn't very good at it. He didn't really like Chinese food."

"Foolish fellow," Clive said lightly. His eyes were on Francine constantly. "You're a wonderful cook."

They finished the meal with the strawberries Clive had brought. Then Clive, as he had promised, read to Ruth for half an hour, including the Chicken-Licken book, which she adored. It got late, and became time for Francine to put Ruth to bed. Clive offered to help Edwina with the dishes. While she put Ruth into her pajamas and rocked her to sleep, Francine heard Edwina's high-pitched squeal of laughter from the kitchen. She had not heard her laugh like that for days.

When Ruth was asleep, Francine slipped silently out of Ruth's room, closing the door. Edwina was kneeling on the floor beside Clive, sorting through Captain Edmondson's collection of records. "We're going to dance," she told Francine eagerly. Her plump face was flushed and pretty, the way it had used to be. Clive Napier certainly had his uses, Francine thought. "Come and choose some records!"

Luckily, the late captain had been a dance fan, and they managed to find a sheaf of suitable records. The tunes had been specially recorded for dancing in the tropics; that was to say, at three-quarter tempo, the sedate pace that the heat dictated.

They put them on the gramophone. Edwina only knew how to waltz, so Clive taught her to foxtrot. Her adolescent body moved eagerly in Clive's arms. The dance tunes were already sickly-sweet with repetition—"The Way You Look Tonight," "I Only Have Eyes for You" and, "Have You Ever Been Lonely?" in melancholy succession. Francine felt her throat swelling with tears as she remembered other times, other places.

"Your turn," Edwina panted. "I'll put on the records."

She did not feel like dancing, but she rose, and let Clive take her. Her head was swimming. The first bottle of champagne was already empty and the second had somehow been half-emptied, and Clive had not been responsible for all of it. Francine knew that Edwina had been taking surreptitious gulps. *So what?* Francine thought. *Poor child, if it cheers her up, then let her.*

Clive was a good dancer, smooth and fluid. He was very strong. "Come here often?" he asked, looking down at her.

"Only during invasions," she replied.

"Speaking of which," he said in a low voice, so Edwina could not overhear, "it's time you faced the facts of life, Francine. First fact of life: The boats home are leaving every week, but there isn't an unlimited supply of them. Soon there won't be any. We're already getting reports that some of them have been torpedoed. You understand? As the Japs tighten their grip, it'll get harder and harder to get out."

"I understand," she said quietly. She was floating in his arms, serene in the movement, not wanting her blissful bubble to be punctured.

"Second fact of life: There isn't much hope that your husband will arrive, now."

"That's nonsense."

"The whole of Malaya is in Japanese hands, my sweet. The causeway will be blown up any day. If he's not dead, he's in a prison camp. The best you can hope for is that you'll see him again when the war's over."

"I'm going to wait for him," Francine said.

Clive frowned. "Third fact of life: If you don't get yourself and Ruth out, you'll be captured by the Japanese. You're going to be a target, not just because you're a despised Eurasian, but also because you're married to an even-worse-despised European. You can expect to be summarily beheaded. Ruth, too."

"Stop," Francine said, feeling physically sick. Her bubble was punctured now, and she was falling to earth.

"All right. I hope you've understood me. Our little friend is out for the count." She looked. He was right. Edwina was sprawled on the chair, fast asleep, her rosy mouth open. The champagne and the dancing had proved too much for her.

"Shall I carry her to her bed?" Clive suggested.

Francine nodded. He picked up Edwina without effort and followed Francine to the girl's room. They laid her on her bed. She snored softly as Francine covered her. Then they went back to the gramophone, where "Smoke Gets in Your Eyes" was just coming to an end. In the silence, Clive walked to the open window. "The monsoon's coming tomorrow," he remarked.

"How do you know?"

"I can feel it. I can always feel it." He picked up the bottle and poured them both another glass of champagne. She felt she had long since had enough, but she took the glass nonetheless, and sat down. She drank, then looked up at him.

"Thank you for tonight," Francine said quietly, meaning what he had done to cheer Edwina up.

"My pleasure, Francine." He smiled. "One more dance?"

"All right, if you want."

"This one's especially for you." He put "Sophisticated Lady" on the turntable, and they danced to the amorous, elegant melody. "How did you come by a name like Francine?" he asked.

"Don't you like it?"

"It suits you. It's just unusual."

"My mother chose it. After France, the country. My elder cousin is called Sidney, after the city in Australia. My younger cousin is called Frank, after San Francisco in America."

He smiled. "Really? And Ruth? Was she named after a city, too?"

"No. Abe chose Ruth. It was his mother's name."

"And your father? British, I take it?"

"He was Welsh." The champagne had loosened her tongue, or she would never have spoken about such things to Clive. "My mother called him her husband, but he wasn't, really. He always said he would marry her, but when his contract ended, he just went home and left us."

"Ah," Clive said gently. "That must have been rough on both of you."

"It broke my mother's heart," she said simply. "But that's the way it happens, isn't it, Clive? That's what native women are for. For the benefit of lonely white bachelors. Sleeping dictionary, isn't that what they call them? It's a pity about the stengah children, but what can you expect? My father sent twenty dollars a month until I was married, and that was noble of him, wasn't it?"

Clive did not say anything for a while. He was holding her close, swinging her pleasantly in time to the music. "I don't feel that way about you, you know," he said at last.

"Of course not," she said mockingly.

"Do you have any idea how much I like you?" he asked. Something in the tone of his voice made a soft heat flood her belly.

"I hope you don't like me too much, Major Napier," she said. "I'm a married woman. What about you? I bet you were lying to me about being a bachelor. I bet you have a devoted wife waiting at home for you in the officers' quarters. Or do you have a pretty little native girl tucked away somewhere?" She slitted her eyes at him wickedly. "Which way do your tastes run? Stengah? Malay? Chinese?"

Clive's eyebrows lifted. "I didn't know you had such sharp claws," he commented.

"No claws, Major Napier," she said, putting on the flirtatious chee-chee accent she had heard Battling Bertha use, "I soft as the rising moon, almos' a virgin, you be generous with me!"

Her caricature had been accurate enough to make him smile wryly. "Don't be like that. I'm not married, and I don't have a mistress of any color."

"Are you looking for one here, then?"

His smile faded. "Francine, stop. I'm not trying to take advantage of you."

"Then you must be foolish," she said.

"Perhaps you make me foolish."

They danced in silence for a while. "Sophisticated Lady" turned into "Caravan," and they changed pace for the sinuous, exotic tune.

"You must have two names," Clive said, swinging her adeptly in his arms. "You must have a Chinese name, too."

"Yes."

"What's your Chinese name?"

She hesitated. "Yu Fa. Li Yu Fa. Li was my mother's family name."

"Yu Fa," he said gravely. "I like that very much. Does it mean anything?"

"I suppose it means something like 'fragrant bud,'" she said, embarrassed.

"Fragrant bud, ripe for the plucking," he said. He bent down and kissed her on the lips. It was unexpected and it silenced them both. She saw his eyes change. "Francine," he said quietly, "you're so perfect. I've wanted you from the minute I set eyes on you."

"It's no good, Clive," she said unhappily.

"So gentle," he said. "So sensitive. Delicate. You make other women look like oxen."

"You shouldn't be talking like this."

"But I want to say it." He stroked her cheek. "You're an angel."

"Do you always woo in clichés?"

"I'm sorry," he said, drawing her closer. "Clichés are what come to the hopelessly infatuated."

The music was sensuous, dreamy, and the sculpted presence of his body was the only real thing, a rock in a twilight sea. His thighs pressed between hers in time with the rhythm. He stroked the tender skin of her cheek and neck with his lips, his breath warm and intoxicating against her ear. Molten honey seemed to be spreading through her veins, bringing with it a desire for him that possessed her in a sharp ache.

His fingers tugged at the buttons of her dress. She did not stop him, anticipating the feel of his hand on her flesh. She wore no slip, because of the heat, and he cupped her naked breast in his palm. She sighed, melting against him. He took the nipple gently between his finger and thumb, and an electric current spread down into her loins. She became aware that it was now or never; if she did not send him home, all would be lost.

She stopped dancing and pushed his hand firmly away. She fastened her buttons. "I think it's time you left."

"I'm in love with you." He said the words matter-of-factly, but they made her heart twist inside her. She went to the gramophone, and took the record off.

"No more dancing. You'd better go home."

"All right." He pulled her around to face him. "But give me one more kiss before I go."

She lifted her cheek to his, expecting a chaste peck. But Clive took her gently in his arms and kissed her on the lips. He was warm against her. She could feel his hard body under the stiff uniform, and though his formidable strength was restrained, she felt as though he were crushing her.

But his kiss was so tender, as though he had a legitimate right to kiss her this way, as though he expected her to do no less than respond. And her lips parted gently. She felt his tongue probe the sweetness of her inner moistness, an erotic invasion that she ought to have resisted, but didn't.

Instead, she clung to him, desperately wanting the reassurance of his strength, the reassurance of being desired.

"The moment I saw you, I knew I was going to fall in love with you," he whispered.

He kissed her again, holding her tighter. The texture of his kiss, warm and thrusting, sent her mind into turmoil, a frightening maelstrom. Suddenly, she was not thinking of Abe anymore. Her body arched without her volition, betraying her. Clive caressed her slim shape under the light summer dress. Their tongues met, touched, caressed. Shuddering, she drew back and looked into his eyes. "Clive . . ."

"Is there a room we can lock?" he asked quietly.

"No, Clive," she said. But he had awakened need in her, urgent and fierce.

"Where can we go?" he whispered. "Francine, for God's sake!"

"I'm a married woman."

"It has nothing to do with your husband. Just us."

"I should not do this!"

"For Christ's sake. The world's collapsing around our ears. We need each other. I can take care of you, Francine, of you and little Ruth. Don't you understand? I love you. I love Ruth, too. I want to be a father to her. You can't live for a husband who isn't here!"

She pushed him away. Her legs were shaking. A husband made out of smoke, she thought. Why was she arguing? In that moment, she knew that she wanted Clive. She wanted this to happen. It was her decision, and taking it suddenly filled her with calm.

She felt her body relax. "My room has a lock," she heard herself say. Clive was pale, now. He nodded.

She led him there, locking the door behind them. He slipped the dress from her shoulders. Her breasts were exposed, neat and pale, with erect peaks. "God, you're beautiful," he said in a husky voice. He gave her a rough kiss that tasted of champagne.

Francine put her arms around him and drew him to her. "Kiss me again," she said softly. They kissed, at first tenderly, then with an igniting passion. She thrust her body against Clive's. There was a kind of desperation in her. He pulled off her dress. They sank onto the bed together.

She was a little drunk, but it was not the alcohol that was fueling this desire. He pulled her panties down and she kicked them off. She fumbled at the buttons of his uniform, her fingers clumsy.

"I'll do it," he whispered. He stripped swiftly, fingers tugging at the leather and brass that fastened his uniform. His body was unexpectedly beautiful, the sinewed body of an athlete. Dark hair spread across his chest and down his muscular belly, to his loins, where his desire was thrusting out, hard and ready. Her eyes were half-closed to slits. She had taken her lower lip between her teeth and was biting it hard. She was breathing swiftly. "Clive, Clive. Hurry."

She pulled him to her, pressing her naked skin to his. The contact was electric. He cupped the silken mound of her sex possessively, fingers reaching in to caress the wetness. She wanted him desperately. "Hurry," she said, "hurry, my love. Come to me."

She parted her thighs as he mounted her. He sank into her, and she lost all sense of herself. Their inner heat was searing, fierce. They did not speak anymore. Her own panting breaths became cries as her desire mounted. She watched Clive's eyes glaze, his lips part, his pirate's face become a primitive mask. His breath rasped in his throat. She, too, was possessed by something savage. It had been years since she had experienced anything like this. Perhaps she had never experienced it.

The end came swiftly. She cried out, arching back in his arms, a pleasure so intense it was almost a pain rushing through her body. There was no regret or fear to spoil the moment, only a wild fulfillment.

Afterward, they clung together.

"I love you," he whispered, his mouth close to her ear. "You're wonderful. Why are you crying?"

"I'm just happy," she said, pressing against him. But the truth was much more complicated than that. She was crying for many, many things. But happiness was among them.

They made love again, again without words, and this time much more slowly, and with greater abandon. Clive was expert at love, as at other things, but she did not want to think about how he had gained his expertise. She had been aroused by Abe, had discovered feelings of tenderness and desire within herself. But this was very different. Clive Napier was not only physically beautiful; he was a lover more tender and more skilled than Abe would ever be. He had the power to make her feel sensations beyond her dreaming.

She was deeply grateful for the physical fulfillment their lovemaking brought her. Somehow, it canceled out the shame and guilt that would otherwise have destroyed her. Had it been no more than a rough-and-tumble rutting, something hurried and trivial, she would never have forgiven herself. That it was something sublime made it, in some way, legitimate.

He left much later, at almost three o'clock in the morning. She kissed him at the top of the stairs, a long, lingering kiss, with lips that were soft and bruised. "I'll come back tomorrow night," he whispered. "Tell me you love me, then. All right?"

She watched him walk down the stairs. He did not look back. Then she went back inside. She closed the door and leaned back against it. She felt wonderful, yet she felt terrible. She felt exalted, yet knew she was a thing to be despised.

"Damn," she whispered to herself painfully. "Damn it all to hell." She checked on Ruth, then undressed and went to bed. Exhausted as she was, it was a long time before sleep came.

The next day, ferocious rain awoke Francine very early, after no more than an hour or two of sleep. Remembering that she had left a window open, she dragged herself out of bed, feeling shaky and bruised.

It was dark outside. The rain had flooded the floor under the open window, and she waded through it in bare feet to get the mop. All she could think of was Clive, and what she had done. He had said he would return the next night, and she already ached to see him again. But she sternly told herself to expect nothing. Perhaps, having conquered, he would be satisfied, and she would never see him again. And that would be the best thing. She could not sleep any longer. She cleaned the house silently while the two girls slept, and at eight o'clock, though the rain had not abated and it was barely light, she went out to shop for food. If you did not start early, you had no chance.

Clive's instincts had been right. This was the northeast monsoon, blowing with unprecedented ferocity. It would last for days, perhaps weeks. Driven by the wild wind, the rain pounded human faces, drenched clothing in seconds, slashed palm leaves to ribbons, flattened vegetation back to the earth. It turned the narrow streets into furious torrents, extinguishing the sun, forcing people to fly for shelter where they could.

Food was scarcer than ever, and she had to walk miles afield, every inch of her soaked. She bought a copy of the *Tribune*. Her little plea for news of Abe had appeared each morning that week, without response. She was certain now that there would never be a response.

The squalls were short-lived, followed by soaring heat as the wind hurled the clouds far out to sea. Choking, noxious steam rose from the flooded gutters. But the next downpour was close behind, disgorging thunder, wind, and water.

She got back to Popiah Street at midmorning, to find Edwina feeding

Ruth. Edwina looked up at her and grinned. "Hello! What happened last night?"

"You fell asleep," Francine said, taking over from Edwina, "so we put you to bed."

"I know that," Edwina said. "I mean, what happened with Clive? Did you snog?"

"Edwina!" Francine said, looking quickly at Ruth.

The swift, guilty glance answered Edwina's question, and her eyes and mouth opened very wide. "You did! You snogged with him!"

"What does 'snogged' mean?" Ruth asked, eyes wide in her pale face.

"Nothing, little bird. Just that Clive kissed me good night," Francine said, aware that her face was flaming.

"Then what was all that laughing and music I heard?" Edwina demanded.

"You had a dream," Francine said shortly. "That was all."

"I think he's a dish," Edwina said, her eyes dreamy. "If I was older, I'd have him. If he'd have me."

"I think Clive would have anybody," she replied dryly.

"Oh, no. It's you he wants. And look how lovely he is with Ruth. He's not a Don Juan. I've seen another side of him." She giggled. "I bet you did, last night, too. Is he a good snogger? I bet he is."

Edwina, in her innocence, imagined that she and Clive had done no more than kiss and cuddle, "snogging," in her schoolgirl slang.

"Is Clive going to be my new daddy?" Ruth asked innocently, with a child's instinctive grasp of the real meaning of things.

Francine stared at her for a long moment. "Your daddy's in Ipoh," she said haltingly.

"Daddy's dead," Ruth said matter-of-factly. "The Japanese have killed him. He would have come by now if he wasn't dead. I want Clive to be my new daddy."

Francine felt short of breath. It was time to be honest with the child. She took Ruth's small hands in her own. "Listen to me, my darling," she said gravely. "This is very important."

"I'm listening," Ruth said solemnly.

"It may be that your daddy is dead. If that is so, then we will never see him again. But it's possible that the Japanese have captured him, and put him in a prison."

"A prison for bad people?"

"No, a special prison for their enemies. If that has happened, then one day we might see him again. But for now, you don't have a daddy. And I don't have a husband."

"What about Clive?" Ruth demanded.

"Clive wants to take Daddy's place in our lives. He wants to be a daddy to you, and he wants to be a husband to me."

"Hooray!" Ruth exclaimed, clapping her hands. "I love Clive!"

Francine knew that Ruth was not being callous about the fate of her real father. It was just a child's simple way of dealing with terrifying necessity.

"But sweetheart, one day Daddy might come back."

"And then what will we do?" the child asked, her alabaster forehead creasing at the possible dilemma.

"I don't know," Francine said tiredly, "and that's the truth."

There was a knock at the door, and Mrs. D'Oliveira's sallow face peered in at them. "The Golden Slipper was hit last night," she said. "Did you hear?"

Francine's heart sank. She immediately thought of Bertha, and of the mother and her new baby.

"You stay here with Ruth," she commanded Edwina. "I'll go and see if I can help."

The air was thick with choking smoke in Shanghai Street. Francine made her way down the steep cobblestones, jostled by running figures, forced into doorways by the honking trucks that lumbered up from time to time, their wheels barely clearing the buildings on either side. Some of the close-packed side streets were blocked with fallen timber and piles of rubble.

One block seemed to have taken the brunt of the bombing. She headed toward it. Men were milling around furiously.

She pushed her way among the crowds, squinting through the smoke. She saw something lying in the street: a yellow neon sign representing a woman's shoe. She looked up. The Golden Slipper had once been a three-story building consisting of a nightclub on the ground floor and a "short-stay" hotel above. The top two floors had now gone. Piles of rubble had disgorged into the street through the remaining doors and windows. Smoke poured upward from still-smoldering beams.

Khaki-clad figures worked in the smoke, dragging bodies out of the building. A row of corpses had already been laid on the pavement outside. All were women. Beneath the blood and filth, she recognized the faces of the Golden Slipper girls. Some were in their nightclothes, drab garments differ-ent from their garish work-wear. Among them lay Bertha, her battling over, her broad face peaceful. Someone had folded her hands on her breast. She stared at Francine with half-closed eyes, her gold teeth showing in a faint smile. Not far away lay the Chinese woman who had given birth in the shelter. A small bundle lay at her side.

Despairing, Francine turned to go home.

Clive arrived at six. He, too, had been caught up in the bombing. His uniform was torn and singed, and he smelled of smoke. He held her close. "Sorry I'm late," he said in a husky voice. "Been pulling people out of the rubble all day. Seemed more to the point than censoring the news." He looked at her with red-rimmed eyes. "Francine, tell me you love me."

"I love you," she said automatically, not knowing whether it was the truth or not.

Ruth came running up to him, her arms outstretched. "You're going to be my new daddy," she informed him, radiant with happiness.

"Oh, my precious," he said, picking her up and crushing her in his arms. "Yes, I'm going to try and be a good daddy to you, my own one."

"Will you look after us?"

"Your mama and I will look after you between us."

"Do I have to call you Daddy?" Ruth asked practically.

"What do you want to call me?"

"I like calling you Clive."

"Then Clive it is."

"Let's read books and play."

"In a little while," Francine said firmly, taking her from Clive's arms. "Clive has to get clean and rest." She led him to the bathroom and gave him a clean towel and soap. Leaving him to wash, Francine went to the kitchen to begin preparing a meal.

They ate in silence. After the meal, Francine and Clive went out onto the balcony, leaving Edwina playing with little Ruth.

"There are two big ships preparing to leave, the *Duchess of Bedford* and the *Empress of Japan*. The *Empress of Japan*'s bigger and more comfortable. Ghastly choice of name, I know. There are also two troopships, which will be pretty spartan. Nobody can say whether there'll be any more departures after then. Do you understand what I'm saying, darling?"

"Yes," Francine said quietly. She felt surprisingly little emotion now. Perhaps she was numb.

"We have to get you all out to the P and O agency house at Cluny to get your berths. We have to do it tomorrow."

"All right," she said.

"You don't need money. The government's paying. There'll be room for a single trunk between the three of you. Not more. I'll come round with a driver and pick you up at seven. There'll be queues."

She looked up at him. "And you, Clive?"

"I have to stay," he said matter-of-factly. "We'll meet again somewhere else."

"I don't believe that!"

"You must believe it," he said.

"Oh, God," she said, starting to cry again. The prospect of losing Clive, after already having lost Abe, was too much. "I love you, Clive," she managed to gasp, and this time it felt like the truth.

Nobody spoke during the drive out to Cluny Hill the next morning. It was another monsoon day, the rain lashing down pitilessly on the gangs of laborers struggling to repair the shell damage to Orchard Road. Ruth had had more diarrhea and vomiting just before leaving. She sat, pale and listless, between Edwina and Francine on the backseat. Clive sat in front, beside the Malay driver, staring glumly out of the window.

Agency House was on a hill overlooking the Johore Road. The streets around were already jammed with traffic. Sweating policemen were directing the cars along alternative routes in the shimmering heat. A long procession of women and childen wound up the drive, disappearing behind the lush shrubbery of the garden.

"Christ," Clive muttered. "The whole of Singapore's here."

"There won't be any places left for us," Francine said in despair, looking at the flood of cars that were streaming up from Singapore.

"Yes, there will," Clive vowed. "Abu-Bakr, drive round the back."

The Malay driver nodded. "Okay, tuan," he said.

They skirted the traffic jams, driving along the back roads. Others had had the same idea. They passed a group of workmen pushing cars off the road; Francine saw their windshields had been shattered, their bodywork punctured by bullet holes. The Zeros had been busy here already this morning.

"I've made such a mess of things," she said.

"Everything's a mess, darling," Clive said. "The important thing is—"

His words were ruptured brutally by the sudden howl of Japanese planes overhead. The cars scattered, leaving the road helter-skelter. The

Humber swerved violently to avoid a fountain of earth that had erupted in front of them. The big car tumbled into a ditch, coming to rest at a wild angle. The driver flung the door open. "Take cover!"

"Come on!" Clive yelled. "Move!"

Francine heard the mounting scream of a dive-bomber overhead. She looked up, but could see nothing against the dazzling sun.

"Move!" Clive screamed, grabbing Ruth.

There was a concrete culvert a little way down the ditch. Edwina had already reached it, and was calling to them to follow. Out of the chaos came the wailing note of a dive-bomber. Francine ran along the ditch, undergrowth tearing at her legs, Clive clutching her hand and dragging her on. The scream of the Zero swelled to bursting point, splitting the eardrums. With a strange, calm certainty, she knew it was coming for her. She threw herself flat at the last minute.

Then a huge hand plucked her off the earth and swatted her into the darkness.

Consciousness returned with a scream.

"Ruth! Ruth!"

It had come out as a wordless croak. Francine knew that a dreadful danger loomed, but could not remember what it was. Something cool brushed her face. "Ruth's all right," she heard Clive say.

The darkness swirled, a black river in flood, her mind rippling and dimpling like the surface of water. She tried to open her eyes, which seemed glued shut. Through a dim crack in the blackness, she saw Clive leaning over the bed. He sponged at her eyes. Water stung her lids cruelly, but freed the glue that cemented them. In little painful jerks, she turned her head on the pillow to face him.

"Ruth!" she whispered.

"She's all right," he repeated. "Not a scratch, I promise."

"Where?"

"I'll bring her to you. Wait."

"No!" She tried to grasp at him, prevent him from leaving her in this swirling terror, but her body would not obey. The darkness returned, rushing around her, tumbling her body in its currents. Ruth's small hands drew her back, touching her face, pulling at her hair.

"Mama! Mama! Wake up, Mama!"

Francine clung to the little body with all the strength she could muster, too weak even to cry. When she slid into the dark waters again, she did not resist.

She awoke again, later, with frightful nausea, choking on her own vomit. Hands helped her roll over, held a cool metal basin to her chin for her to spew into. The violent retching of her stomach produced a frothy slime that tasted of lime paste. Her body was wet with sweat, some shroudlike garment clinging to her skin. She slid back wretchedly into the dark.

The third time she awoke, she was feeling stronger, more curious about her surroundings. She turned her head, forcing her eyes open. Clive was asleep at her bedside, slumped in a chair with his chin on his chest. She was in a crowded hospital ward. An eerie silence hung over the dimly lit room. All the other patients were women, most of them Malay or Chinese. Bandaged or plastered limbs jutted from the motionless figures. Their relatives slept like Clive, in chairs, or sitting on the floor, propped against the lime-green walls. It was suffocatingly hot. The windows had all been shuttered, a lamp giving the only bleak light. She was soaked in sweat.

She must have made some sound, because Clive jerked into wakefulness. He leaned forward. "Francine! Oh, darling, thank God! How long have you been awake?"

She grasped at his hands. "Did I dream that Ruth was here?"

"No. She's fine. She's sleeping in the nurses' room."

"I want to see her!"

"Shhh," he said, sponging her face gently. "Don't wake the others. It's only five A.M."

Panic filled her as memory returned, for the first time, of the ditch at Cluny. "Clive! Where's Edwina?"

"Gone," he said flatly.

She stared at him numbly.

"Not dead," he said. "Gone on the *Wakefield*. She'll be on her way to Southampton by now, please God." He dipped the sponge into the water and mopped her face.

"Clive, our berths! The boat!"

His face was weary. "The last boats sailed yesterday."

She was confused. "What do you mean?"

"They've gone."

"All the boats?"

"All of them," he said. "*West Point* and *Wakefield* left on Wednesday. *Empress of Japan* and *Duchess of Bedford* left on Thursday."

The sweltering heat was suddenly gone. A freezing draft blew across her skin. "Clive, how long have I been here?"

"A week. They didn't know if you would wake up. You're very badly concussed."

She touched her fingers to her heart, wondering if it had stopped beating. "Aren't there any boats left?"

"Not troopships or P and O ships. There might be smaller boats, if they haven't been requisitioned."

Exhaustion was wearing away her horror. She was too weak to take in the magnitude of the tragedy, the scale of the disaster. "I have to sleep," she said fretfully, closing her eyes. "Let me sleep, Clive."

"Sleep," he said gently.

She was jarred out of the darkness by an explosion. It rumbled across the sky like monsoon thunder for a full minute before fading away. It sounded to her like the crack of doom. Other women had been awakened by the detonation. The ward was filled with whimpering and rustling as bodies stirred stiffly into consciousness.

Clive, too, had awakened. He rubbed his face and rose. "I'll go and see what that is."

He went out. She remembered, with a sinking despair. The boats were gone. She and Ruth would never leave Singapore.

A Malay nurse came in, carrying Ruth in her arms. The child was half-asleep. The nurse laid her in Francine's arms and Francine clung to her, crying.

"Don't cry," the nurse said cheerfully. "You want to look pretty for your nice major, don't you?" She lifted one of Francine's lids and peered at her eye. "I think you going to be fine," she said. "You know your little girl got dysentery?"

She nodded.

"Maybe the doctor give her something, too." Another nurse arrived and they began preparing for the ward round.

Clive returned, his face expressionless. "It was the causeway," he said. "They've blown it up. You can see the column of smoke from here. We've lost the battle for Johore. We've lost the whole of Malaya. Now there's only Singapore left."

Francine was discharged the next day. The concussion had made her weak and confused. She had difficulty walking in a straight line, as though she were drunk. A blinding headache hovered behind her eyes.

"We have to get out of Singapore, Clive," she said when they got to Union Mansions.

He shrugged. "There are no more boats. Someone told me on the quayside that a Free French boat sailed two nights ago from Keppel Harbor, with civilians on board. If only I'd known."

"It doesn't matter. There must be other boats."

"They've all been requisitioned. Or sunk."

"A prau, then. Even a sampan. Anything. We've got money. We could pay someone to sail us to somewhere safe."

"Such as where?"

"Java. Maybe even Ceylon."

He raised one eyebrow. "That's a journey of thousands of miles. Too far for a prau or a sampan."

"You'd be with us." She met his eyes. "You will come with us? You can leave now, can't you?"

"Technically, no," he replied. "It would be desertion."

"Soldiers are leaving all the time," she said urgently.

"Yes." He nodded. "Soldiers are leaving all the time. Anybody who can leave is leaving. It's finished."

"We need you, Clive," she said quietly.

His lips twitched in a smile. "I'm not like Abe, if that's what you're asking. I love you much more than I love honor. Of course I'll come with you."

Her eyes were wet. She'd told him about Abe's empty little quotation. "Thank you, Clive."

His voice was gentle. "The only thing is, my sweet, that we've left it too late to go anywhere."

"There must be something," she said, holding her aching head.

He was silent for a while. Then he nodded. "Yes," he said. "You're right. There must be something."

She took his hands. "Clive, this is all my fault. We should have gone weeks ago. I didn't listen to you. I should have done. I'm sorry, so very sorry."

He smiled, kissing her. "It's all right," he said. "As you say, there must be something. We'll find it."

Over the next days, they searched through the chaotic city for news of a reliable boat out of Singapore. The markets and quaysides were abuzz with rumors of ships sailing or preparing to sail. But each time, they found that the vessel in question was already crammed to capacity, or had left the night before, or was no more than a figment of gossip.

As the Japanese closed in on Singapore, too, bleak news came in that thousands of those who had already left would never be seen again. The Japanese showed no mercy to even the smallest boat leaving the beleaguered city. Untold numbers of civilian boats and ships had been sunk by torpedo-bombers in the South China Sea, with dreadful loss of life. Others had been blown up in the minefield that the Japanese had sown around the harbor. The way out was perilous, and growing more perilous as the noose tightened.

A Japanese artillery-spotting balloon had been flown into place over the Strait. Guided by observers, the Japanese guns rained shells on the city at a range of under fifteen miles. Whole sections of the old town were now destroyed forever. Orchard Road, with its shops and lovely old houses, had been devastated. Chinatown was a smoldering ruin. The Elgin Bridge was hit and burned for days, making progress across the city more difficult than ever.

Clive was in a permanent state of exhaustion. The work of pulling the dead and mangled from the ruins was never-ending. There was barely enough water to drink, let alone to put out the flames. Electricity came and went erratically as the lines were cut, mended, cut again.

Thirty thousand more soldiers, the remnants of the British army in Malaya, had poured onto the island in the last hours before the breaching of the causeway. The city was now filled with troops, many seemingly without leaders or orders. They were everywhere in Singapore, dirty and disheveled, milling in the squares or wandering aimlessly down the streets. With the tacit agreement of the authorities, all who could find a way out of Singapore were taking it. Though the fact remained unspoken, imminent defeat by the Japanese was accepted by everyone.

The nights were suffocating, presided over by a huge, golden moon. Francine and Clive took to lying in each other's arms on their little balcony in the evening, listening to the record player. They did not talk much, she and Clive, though they made love with tender passion under the stars. There seemed little to say.

For days the three of them had lived on rice flavored with whatever scraps of fish they could find. One day, Francine returned from her wearying, largely futile shopping trip to find that Clive had news.

"They say there's a Chinese skipper at Telok Blangah," he told her.

"Sailing for Batavia tomorrow with a group of civilians. He's charging eight hundred Straits dollars for each passenger."

"What's his name?" she demanded.

"I don't know. But the boat's called the *Whampoa.*"

Francine turned wearily. "I'm the only one who speaks Chinese. We'll go down to Blangah now."

"The whole harbor's burning," Clive warned.

"What if he sails tonight?" Francine said. "We have to try. We'll leave Ruth with Mrs. D'Oliveira. Let's go."

They made their way along the railway line, walking because they could find no rickshaw willing to take them into the inferno of the harbor, still burning from yesterday's incendiaries. As they hurried past the godowns that lined the railway on West Wharf, some of them burning violently with no one to douse the flames, a truck roared out of one of the excise sheds. Two or three dozen soldiers were mounted precariously on the back, shouting and singing. As it wheeled past her, the soldiers' attention was caught by the sight of Francine. A man began screaming obscenities at her. The others cheered and laughed. Something flew through the air toward them. It smashed in the road, a large beer bottle, spattering Francine with froth. She shrank against Clive. He put his arms around her tightly, covering her face as more bottles followed, splintering on the pavement.

The truck squealed to a halt. The cab door opened, and a soldier jumped out. Terrified that they would rape her, she grasped Clive's wrist. "Clive!"

"Don't worry," he said, his face tight. "I'll deal with this." He opened his holster and drew his pistol.

The soldier approached cautiously. "Blokes go' carried away, sir. Shouldn't have thrown bottles. Drunk and disorderly." He himself was very drunk, his eyes bloodshot, swaying on his feet. "Here." He waved a bottle of gin at Clive. "You have this."

"No," Clive said shortly.

He peered at them blearily. "Then take this." He unclipped a hand grenade from his belt and held it out to Clive. "Here. Best thing a lady can carry. If the Japs catch you, miss, just pull the pin. Won't know a thing." He turned and staggered back to the truck. It drove off to a chorus of hoots and whistles.

"Throw it away," she begged Clive, who was holding the grenade.

"No. He's right. It might come in useful. You take it."

She stared at the bomb in his hand, a dull steel egg with a curving lever. It represented power, of a brutal and very final sort. It might do to end her life if that ever became necessary. She took the thing reluctantly.

"Let's go," Clive said.

Telok Blangah was covered by a pall of greasy black smoke. The naval installations on Sentosa Island opposite had been relentlessly targeted by the Japanese for weeks. In the little harbor at Blangah, an ancient Chinese riverboat had been struck by a bomb. It listed sullenly, somehow still afloat in a ring of fire that blazed on the surface of the water around it. Smaller wooden craft shrank away from the catastrophe, huddling at the outer edges of the harbor.

The wharf was almost deserted. They walked toward Jardine's Steps, the smoke burning her eyes and throat. At last, they found a knot of Chinese sailors and fishermen squatting in the doorway of a godown, playing fan-tan. Francine went over to them.

"I'm looking for the skipper of the *Whampoa*," she said in Cantonese. "Can you tell me where to find him?"

One of the men looked up at her, squinting through the smoke that curled up from the cigarette in his mouth. "Who wants him?" he asked.

"I do."

"What for?"

"I want to buy a passage for myself and two others on the *Whampoa*."

The man threw down the cards in his hand with a slap. There was a roar from the others. Among a gabble of oaths, sinewy hands reached out to shuffle the piles of money that surrounded the cards and dice. The man swigged from a bottle and rose, thrusting his winnings into his pocket. His face bore the deep scars of smallpox. He studied them for a moment, then jerked his head at the riverboat that blazed in the harbor. "That's the *Whampoa*," he said tersely.

Cruel disappointment made her sag as though she'd been punched in the stomach.

The man was studying her and Clive, rubbing his tattoos thoughtfully. "Where do you want to go, missy?"

"Anywhere," she said wearily. "Anywhere safe." She stared at the burning riverboat.

"He was going to Batavia," the man said, following her eyes. "He would never have got there. That thing was too old. It would have sunk ten miles from land, if the Japanese hadn't bombed her first."

"Where is the captain?"

The man grinned and jerked his head at the *Whampoa* again. "Counting his money in hell. I have a boat that will get you to Batavia in two weeks."

Hope flickered in her. "Where is it?"

He pointed. A black junk with patched sails bobbed at anchor near the steps. As Francine stared at it, an old woman emerged from below and slung a bucket of slops over the side into the water. "That?"

"She's a good boat," he said, flicking his cigarette away. "I've taken her to Java and beyond hundreds of times. She's got a six-horsepower American diesel engine." He spoke Cantonese, but with a thick accent that placed him at once as a Tanka, one of the clannish fishing community who lived on board their junks and were known disparagingly as boat people. His eyes were slitted as he watched her face, as if guessing at her thoughts. "I'll take the three of you for two thousand dollars each."

"Five hundred each," she said, without thinking.

He laughed in derision. "Don't be a fool. Who would take the risk for so little? I'll knock off two hundred and fifty dollars each."

"I could buy a whole junk for less than that!"

"Go buy one," he said. "Then sail it to Java yourselves."

"What is he saying?" Clive demanded impatiently.

"He says he'll take us to Batavia for one thousand seven hundred and fifty dollars each."

Clive's face was flinty. "The *Whampoa* was charging only eight hundred," he said to the man.

"Eight hundred dollar to be eaten by shark," the man scoffed at Clive in English. "To get to Batavia in one piece, at least fifteen hundred each. You rich man, army officer." He turned to Francine and went on in Cantonese. "Less, and I would be risking my life for nothing. I have a family too, missy."

It occurred to her in an ironic flash that they were haggling for their lives on this sordid quayside. But instinct made her keep arguing. If she did not, the man would perceive them as fools, and perhaps betray them. "Twelve hundred," she said. "No more than that."

He jerked his head at Clive. "He's a major, a rich man."

"I assure you he's not rich. None of us are. Twelve hundred dollars each and that's it. What's your name?"

"Lai Chong. And yours?"

"Li Yu Fa. This is Clive Davenport. Twelve hundred dollars for a one-week trip," she pressed. "It's almost four thousand dollars altogether."

Lai lit another cigarette, considering them. His eyes were like slits cut in the puffy flesh. "Okay. Twelve hundred dollar each, I take you to Batavia. You bring own food."

She glanced at the black junk. Its rigging was a ramshackle mess, yet its familiar outline was somehow reassuring, sturdy. It bobbed in the filthy water with something like jauntiness. She did not know whether hope or fear was uppermost in her mind.

"You know your way through the minefields?" Clive demanded.

Lai laughed. "Of course."

"We want to look around the boat," Clive said.

"Okay," Lai said, shrugging. "Come."

They followed him. He walked with the bandy-legged gait of the Tanka. His belly stuck out, but his back and arms were strong, and his calves bulged with muscle.

The junk bore the name *Lotus Flower* in tarnished gold characters on her bows. She had a tiny foredeck with a cooking stove lashed to the planks, and an even tinier afterdeck where the wheel stood in a sort of decaying shanty. The hold gaped open, covered by an atap roof, smelling of belacan, molasses, vinegar, excrement, urine, black-bean paste, and rot in equal proportions. A little old woman was squatting in a corner, sucking at a bowl of soup she held to her toothless lips.

"This is my aunt," Lai said. "She does the cooking."

Francine peered down. Three or four chickens scratched around in a bamboo cage, pecking at insects between the planking. In one corner was a shabby little shrine to Tin Hau, the protective Tanka goddess. Francine paid silent respects to her, remembering the merciful Tin Hau's reputation for rescuing those in deadly peril.

"All of us in there?"

Lai chuckled. "All of us. In there."

"Show us the engine," Clive demanded.

"Engine is here." Lai hoisted up three planks. They crouched to look into the hole. A smell of diesel rushed out hotly. The pipes and engine block of a large motor gleamed in the dark, startlingly clean in contrast to the filth of the rest of the junk.

"It looks new," Clive said.

He winked at them. "New. And fast. Faster than coast guard, lah."

"Have you got fuel?" Clive demanded.

"Plenty."

"Show us."

The man's eyes slitted. "You trust nobody, aaah?" He showed Clive the filler pipe of the tank, lowering a graduated steel rod into it to prove that it was almost full. "Okay? We go?"

"We'll let you know."

"When?"

"Tomorrow."

"Maybe I not be here." He smirked. "Plenty other nice women not want to be raped by Japanese."

"Tomorrow," Clive repeated.

They trudged back toward the railway line. "What do you think?" she asked Clive.

"I think he's a crook and a smuggler. But I also think his boat can make the voyage easily. I think we should accept, Francine. We'll pay him half up front, half when we get to Java."

"You really think we should go?"

"I think we should go as soon as we can," he said tersely.

She fell silent. Thoughts were tumbling through her head. The little black boat had filled her with excitement. But what did either of them know of boats? Could they trust their lives to the *Lotus Flower*? Could they trust Lai himself, with his tong tattoos and insolent eyes? There were a thousand Lais along the shoreline. But they could not interview each one of them until they found a face they liked. It was a way out, the only one that opened.

As if to underline that thought, a barrage of explosions came rolling down from Tanglin Hill. Bombers and fighters had returned after less than an hour's break to attack the barracks. From the more distant city center came the scream and thunder of shells, followed by the boom of British artillery responding.

They made their way along the tracks, hoping they would find a rickshaw at Spottiswoode Park to take them back to Popiah Street. She had entered a strange state of mind. Sometime during the past days, she seemed to have begun a completely new life. Everything that had happened to her in the previous years seemed unreal, events that had taken place around another person in another world.

Her consciousness had focused with blazing clarity on this small, ever-decreasing space that surrounded her and Clive and Ruth. All her senses were heightened. She felt almost unwilling to leave this brilliant pocket; the thought of departing from Singapore gave her a kind of regret, as though she knew that nothing in her life could ever be quite as intense, quite as vivid, as these past weeks.

Here, days seemed to fill the space that years had filled in her previous life. Each was filled with momentous emotions, momentous events, birth, death, fire, beauty. She felt that she and Clive were living through history, riding on the crest of the huge wave that was changing the fate of peoples and nations.

"All right," she heard herself say. "Let's go."

They had their last sight of Singapore two nights later, on Friday the thirteenth of February.

Lai had insisted on waiting until nightfall before weighing anchor, wanting to get at least a hundred miles from Singapore by the next dawn, to reduce the danger of being spotted by Japanese aircraft. The four of them huddled on the small, rocking foredeck of the *Lotus Flower,* waiting, watching the sun go down on Singapore. They had been unable to bear the stinking confines of their cabin, even with the danger of shrapnel above. None of them spoke. There were no words, in any case. All had some idea of the bloodbath that awaited the doomed city.

Singapore was a terrible spectacle, bracketed in sheets of flame; dozens of huge fires poured columns of black smoke thousands of feet into the sky. The drone of enemy aircraft and the thudding of bombs were incessant now. In the past days, the Japanese army had reached the very outskirts of the city and hand-to-hand fighting had begun.

It was another exquisitely beautiful evening. As the light faded into purple and then indigo, an ocean of stars came out, icy-white against the velvet. A waning moon, the color of Indian gold, rose out of the sea. High above the tortured land, millions of other worlds were indifferent, serene.

Darkness fell swiftly. Explosions drifted through the night air. The myriad conflagrations of the city glowed crimson in the darkness, illuminating the windows of dying buildings, running along the streets, so that Singapore seemed a city made of fire, peopled by fiery creatures with fiery limbs that writhed and fluttered.

Francine had changed into Chinese clothes for the first time since her arrival in Singapore. She wore a comfortable pantsuit called a *sam fu,* a scarf wrapped around her head. She had brought little else for herself; all the rest was Ruth's. They had all reduced their clothing to fit the one trunk that Lai had permitted. Against their arrival in Batavia, she had only the little bag of gold sovereigns the aunts had given her in Perak. Her eyes were burning, her throat raw with the smoke she had inhaled. She and Clive clung to each other, Ruth's small body between them. She was unable to tear her eyes away from the flaming vision.

"We go," Lai said.

Francine nodded.

Clive rose and helped Lai cast off, pulling the gangplank aboard as the junk bobbed away from the quayside. The throbbing of the diesels accelerated. With a jerky thrust, the *Lotus Flower* was under way, plowing through the dark water. Ruth started to cry weakly at the new motion. Clive held her close.

Francine had no tears. The well had run dry long ago. She watched the fires of Singapore recede in the tropical night, saying her own silent farewells to this city of the living and the dying.

She thought of Abe. Perhaps she would meet him again, in some other life, in some other world. But she was Clive's woman now, and nothing could change that.

I have the most important thing with me, she thought. *I have Ruth. I have Clive. And I have myself.*

I have lost the past. I still have the future.

Lai steered the *Lotus Flower* through the minefields in the darkness. He had evidently done it many times before, and knew the way.

The next morning, when Francine awakened, they had left Singapore far behind. The horizon was almost completely clear; the only sign of land was a few small islands, which slipped beneath the horizon while Francine tied up her hair on the foredeck. Clive was already up on deck.

He kissed her. "Lai says we'll be at Bangka in two days. After Bangka, another week to Batavia."

"How far are we from Singapore?"

"Almost seventy miles."

"So the planes can't reach us?"

"I wouldn't count on that," he said.

She climbed up beside him and put her arms around his supple waist. "I want us to be safe, Clive."

"We will be, darling," he promised.

Cooling land breezes no longer blew. The sky became white-hot by midmorning and the boat turned into an oven. There was nowhere cool, no refuge from the dreadful sun. With Ruth exhausted and limp, and Clive steering patiently while Lai slept, Francine felt pressure crush her like a physical force. She felt she could jump into the choppy blue water, not just to escape the heat, but to break free of the cramped atmosphere on board.

By noon, Francine's face and body dripped with sweat. She sat cross-legged beside Ruth, pouring a little water onto the child's skin from time to time.

"I'm hot, Mama," Ruth whimpered. "Too hot!"

The throbbing of the engine seemed to be growing unnaturally loud, filling her head like the pounding of overheated blood. She realized that the diesel sounded so loud because all other noises had ceased. There was no whistle of wind through the ramshackle rigging. The battened lugsail hung limp, its flapping silenced. Even the interminable rush of waves against the hull had ceased. Raising her weary head, she saw that the sea had turned to molten glass, smooth and green as far as the eye could see. The *Lotus Flower*'s brisk progress had become a tired stagger. The horizon all around them had vanished into a dark, hazy ring.

Lai came up from the hold. He hauled himself halfway up the mast and peered around, shading his eyes with his palm. When he came down, he was sucking his teeth.

"Maybe storm coming," he said to Clive. "You help me."

The heat seemed to intensify as the atmosphere grew steadily more oppressive. Francine sat cradling Ruth in her lap while Lai and Clive went about the junk, fastening anything loose.

A distant rumble of thunder drifted across the sea. The storm was coming from Sumatra; away to the west of them, the horizon had darkened to black. Francine felt her heart sinking. The *Lotus Flower* was such a cockleshell, its mast so flimsy looking, despite the impressive new American engine. Lai himself did not look unduly worried. But the thought of cowering in the dark, stinking hold through a storm was not appetizing.

When the hatches were all battened, they settled down to wait for the coming storm. The sea remained glassy smooth, but darkened steadily. There were more rumbles of thunder, closer now. The sound spread out across the sea ominously, lingering on the air. Clive squatted beside her, sweat dripping from his forehead.

"Shall I take Ruth?" he asked.

She gave her to him. "I'm hot, Clive," the child moaned.

"You'll soon be cool, Chicken-Licken," Clive said tenderly, stroking her face. "It's always like this. After the storm passes, it'll be cool and fresh. You'll see."

"It's suffocating," Francine said. "Are we going to be safe?"

Clive nodded. "Of course. I've been through a storm in the Straits. We saw the most broken-down-looking junks ride out the worst gales."

"That's reassuring," she said dryly.

Another rattle of thunder rolled across the sea and the rigging gave a single sharp rap. "Time to go below," Clive said. The sound of the thunder lingered on the air, a hum that grew to a rumble. Abruptly, she recognized that the sound was not thunder but something else. It was the drone of approaching aircraft engines. She searched the darkening air, tasting the coppery fear in her mouth. Her eyes caught it at last, the all-too-familiar cross in the sky.

"It might be British or Dutch," Clive called to Lai, who was staring in the same direction. Lai turned from the wheel, his face taut.

"Not British," he shouted. "Japanese seaplane. Go below!"

Clive thrust Ruth into Francine's arms. She stumbled down the companionway, clutching Ruth. The old woman looked up from some chore she was doing, her wrinkled eyes widening. Clive came tumbling down after her into the darkness.

"I think they saw us!" he gasped.

"Perhaps they didn't," she said. It was a prayer. She shrank down beside Clive. Their arms went protectively around Ruth. The Japanese plane blasted overhead, its shadow flitting across the atap awning. They heard it soar up into the sky, the note of its engine fading. For a moment she thought a miracle had happened and that it was flying on. Then she heard the sound of the plane turning.

The junk lurched violently, breaking their tight embrace. Her back thudded agonizingly into something sharp. A storm of machine-gun bullets drove through the ancient timbers. Splinters howled around them. The junk shuddered under the onslaught. The seaplane roared overhead.

Francine lifted herself on her elbows and looked down at Ruth. There was blood everywhere, but when Francine hunted frantically for wounds on Ruth, she could find none. Most of the blood seemed to be coming from cuts on her own body, though she could feel no pain. Clive had been thrown against the shrine of Tin Hau and lay motionless. Several of the heavy water-drums had broken loose and were rolling around. Seawater was swirling into the hold. The *Lotus Flower* was wallowing heavily. Francine realized that the engine was now silent. The throbbing heart of their existence had been stilled.

Lai's aunt had been killed, and lay in a crumpled heap, half-submerged. The water was already ankle deep. A panic at being drowned like a rat in a cage seized Francine. She grabbed Ruth and splashed over to Clive. "Get up!" she screamed at him. "Get up! We'll drown!"

He dragged himself slowly to his feet. Like her, he had been cut in dozens of places by flying splinters, and he was streaked with blood. Clinging to each other, they made their way toward the companionway. "How is she?" he asked, peering at Ruth from under his blood-matted fringe.

"All right." Ruth was dazed-looking, as she had been during raids in Singapore.

They pulled themselves up the steps, emerging cautiously into the harsh light. The drone of the seaplane was still audible. But it was far away now. It seemed to be circling the junk at a distance of a quarter of a mile.

"He's wondering whether it's worth coming back for another go," Francine said, her voice unnaturally calm.

"He probably won't bother. He'll want to get back to base before the storm comes. He'll reckon we'll sink anyway."

"Are we going to sink?"

"I don't know."

"We haven't got a lifeboat. Not even a raft."

The drone of the Japanese plane was starting to fade now. It was heading steadily west, away from them, climbing to avoid the black clouds of the storm.

"He's going!" she said.

Clive nodded grimly. "We have to find Lai."

Keeping a wary eye on the distant plane, they crept onto the deck. It had been devastated. The sail had collapsed in a heap like a huge, dilapidated accordion. The deck was strewn with debris and fallen rigging. The primitive wheelhouse, where Lai had been standing, had been hit. Clive ran to the splintered structure. Leaving Ruth curled up in a safe corner, Francine followed him. He dragged timbers out of the wheelhouse. There was a welter of blood in there, but no sign of Lai.

They ran from one side of the junk to the other, peering over, hunting the dark surface of the sea, searching for a waving arm, a bobbing head. The sea was as flat and empty as ink. "Nothing," Clive said hollowly, turning to her. "He's gone."

Lai, their skipper and protector, was gone. "Can we get the engine to start again?" she asked Clive.

"It's underwater. It would need to dry out for days before it had a chance of working."

"We've got the sails." Francine looked down at the ruined things. "We haven't got a hope if we don't set some sail. We'll be bowled over in the first five minutes."

Thunder muttered, like a grim chuckle. An oppressive silence fell. The *Lotus Flower* hunkered deeper into the water, making no progress at all now.

"You're right." Clive's trousers were flapping open, torn from knee to hip. He pulled them off impatiently and, completely naked, began to gather up the fallen rigging.

Between them, they hoisted the sail, but it was a heavy task. It weighed at least a ton, perhaps more. The complex rigging, with its wooden blocks and tackles, was in a tangle. As she hauled on the coarse ropes, she became aware for the first time of the injuries she had suffered. Her whole body ached. The splinter cuts on her legs and back hurt sharply with the strain. But the thunder of the approaching storm was at her back, ever closer.

Clive shinned up the mast several times to try and untangle the rigging, sometimes slashing ferociously through the twisted ropes with his knife. The main sheet, with its huge treble block, was still intact. The sail rose by painful inches, slowly taking some kind of shape. As each batten filled out, the weight grew a little more, the task got a little heavier. By the time the sail was almost set, the first puffs of wind were making it snap and shudder. Francine was pouring sweat as she ran to the remaining deck anchorages, pulling the sail as taut as she could. About half of the rigging was gone, and the sail was torn badly, but it towered over them protectively like a ragged brown wing. The sky had by now grown almost black.

"We don't seem to have sunk any more," she said.

Clive nodded. "Maybe we've reached level."

"I'm going below with Ruth."

"Are you all right?" he asked, reaching out his hand.

"Yes."

"I'll come down in a while." Their fingers knotted briefly. They were both probably filled with the same despair, she thought, neither wanting the other to know.

She gathered Ruth in her arms and clambered back down into the hold. The sea was rising, and the *Lotus Flower* was starting to roll heavily. The water in the hold slopped like soup in a huge basin, a soup made up of the shattered objects of their everyday life. There was a poisonous stink of diesel. The tanks must have been holed. The old woman's corpse floated in the scum.

"Is she dead?" Ruth asked.

"Hush, darling." Gingerly avoiding the rolling fifty-gallon drums, she reached the engine compartment. It was flooded with oily water, the engine completely submerged.

There was a narrow space, not much bigger than a cupboard, over the engine, where Lai had stored a jumble of things to do with the engine, boxes of tools and cans of oil. She raked out what she could and clambered into the relatively dry space with Ruth. She pulled the child close to her chest. "We'll be all right, now," she whispered.

Thunder boomed. The rolling was worse with each minute that passed. The wind had started to blow; she could hear the shrill whistle of the rigging, could feel the shuddering of the hull as the sail filled. She had a sudden strange, external vision of their position; hundreds of miles from their destination, their engine dead, their hull filled with water, facing a storm with their single ragged sail. She wondered whether they had the faintest hope of survival.

The first assault of the storm was furious. The filthy water in the hold crashed over them as the junk rocked, flooding their tiny compartment. Francine rolled out of the compartment and dragged Ruth after her. She could feel the child's thin body racked with coughs. "Can you breathe?" she asked. It had become so dark that she could see almost nothing; nor could she hear whether Ruth answered her.

The ancient beams of the *Lotus Flower* thrummed wildly. She snatched at Ruth, but Ruth slipped through her arms. Another surge of water swept her off her feet, bowling her among the wreckage. She felt herself swirling in the blackness, her head sometimes above water, sometimes below it. Inanimate things battered her. Choking, she clawed to find Ruth. A body swept into her arms and she clutched at it. But it was not her daughter's body. She was clutching the body of Lai's aunt.

Francine pushed herself to her feet, exhausted. Something soft swept against her shins and she groped down. Her fingers knotted around Ruth's long, wet hair. She drew the child up into her arms. She could scarcely tell whether Ruth was alive or dead. She only knew that they could not survive the storm down in the hold. She had to get back up on deck before the next descent.

She dragged herself and Ruth up the companionway. The wind battered them. It was as dark above as it had been below. There were no stars, only a swirling, inky blackness. She clung to the top rung of the ladder, buffeted one way and the other, hunched against the chaos. In her arms she felt the faint marvel of Ruth's survival, a movement, a weak clinging.

A sudden glare of lightning revealed the world to her; an apocalyptic world, changed beyond recognition. The image was burned on her mind as the darkness returned: the ragged sail straining the mast like a bow above her; higher than the mast, an incredible wall of water that towered, foam-flecked and glistening, with a jagged-toothed top fifty or sixty feet high; above that, a whirling mass of baneful cloud that discharged rain in driving sheets. There had been no trace of Clive in that glaring moment.

Then she felt strong hands grasp her arm. Clive's slippery, naked body tumbled down beside her. He dragged her close, thrusting his mouth against her ear. She heard the words faintly, as though across a great distance.

"Can't—stay—below," she screamed at him. "Full—of—water."

"Ruth?"

"Here."

She felt his hand grasp at Ruth, touching her face in the blackness. He pushed his mouth to her ear again. "Might—not—last—long."

The *Lotus Flower* was plummeting again, nose down, her stern rearing high. Another glare of lightning scurried across the sky, revealing that they were sliding down the back of a cataract into a well of darkness.

"Typhoon—I—think," she heard Clive's faint scream. "Wait—here—get—ropes."

He slithered away from her into the dark. She sensed, rather than saw, a wall of water rushing toward her across the deck. She hunched herself around Ruth, bowing her head. The weight of water crushed her, sweeping her back down into the hold again. She flailed helplessly, half-drowning, groping for the body of her child. Again, by some miracle, she found her once more. She hauled herself painfully back up the companionway. More water, this time sweet, lashed into her face. She stretched out her free hand and clutched at a cold, wet, muscular arm. She had found Clive.

"Lifeline!" he shouted. "Hold—on—tight!" Clive had pulled a rope taut from the column to a nearby stanchion. She grasped it.

"What—if—we—sink?"

"Won't—sink!" The rope jerked tight as the junk rolled. She clung to it, its roughness biting into her flesh. In the next blaze of lightning, she saw that he had vanished.

The junk bottomed out in a trough and staggered drunkenly. She turned Ruth's face to her breast and pressed her close. Another flood of water exploded over the wheelhouse. Clinging to the rope, she could only bow her head and shelter Ruth. As the water departed, it dragged at her, trying to take her as it sank back into the dark.

The lightning leaped through the clouds. These seas were more than mountains; they were mountain ranges, endlessly sinking and rising as the wind lashed them; and the *Lotus Flower* was no more than a walnut shell. She hunched over Ruth, afraid to open her eyes again.

The storm blew with an unrelenting hostility that soon beat her into a daze. She retreated into some inner place. Her sense of herself, of being the mother of a little creature who clung to her for safety, was sublimated in the elemental fury of the weather. She lost all conception of time. It was a quite literal loss; she could not have told whether she had been roped to that post for three hours or thirty. She simply became aware, after a time, that the storm had changed character.

It was still pitch-black, and the wind and sea were still raging; but she sensed a note of weariness in the bellowing voices. The wind was no longer omnipotent. She could hear the crash of the sea. She could hear the flap of the sail; so their mast was still standing. And when she looked up, she even saw a few trembling stars. The extreme conditions of the typhoon had faded into a mere storm. To her, it was like an oasis of peace.

She lowered her head again to nuzzle Ruth. The child seemed to be asleep, or in a daze. Her hair was pasted in a dark, wet fan across Francine's arms.

Francine turned to look back, waiting for the next flash of lightning to show her Clive. It was a long time in coming. When at last it flickered, she saw that Clive's post at the deck anchorage was empty. He was gone, whether swept overboard hours or days ago, or somewhere else on the boat, she could not tell. Perhaps they were all alone in the midst of the sea.

Pain was everywhere. The salt had bitten into the multitude of cuts she had received. Her strength was spent. She let her head droop, and sank slowly back into the inner dark.

She awoke to feel a hand shaking her shoulder. She looked up stupidly. There was light, dim and lurid, but enough to see that Clive was crouching in front of her. "Oh, thank God you're alive!" she said, clutching at him. "Where have you been?"

"Down below. Stopping some of the leaks."

His hair had been swept down to frame his face in two dark wings. She could feel the junk surging on a big swell. "Are you and Ruth all right?"

"Yes. Are we going to sink?"

"Not just yet. I got the hand-pump working. Pumped about a million gallons out of the hold." Clive lifted Ruth, who was as limp as a storm-battered sparrow. "It's all right, now," he crooned. "All right, Chicken-Licken."

Francine tried to roll out of her cramped position. Her body seemed to have frozen solid. It was an agonizing effort to get to her feet. Livid welts on her arms showed where the ropes had bitten into her, time and time again.

She emerged from the wheelhouse and looked up. The sail was an incredible sight; against a dim gray sky she could see that every panel of sailcloth had been fantastically shredded. The bamboo battens were splayed like the skeletal bones of a dead gull's wing.

Everything, including their own bodies, was coated in a rime of salt. It glittered dully on the deck, the rigging, their hair. The *Lotus Flower* looked like a ship crewed by ghosts. Mountainous, drab waves rose and fell around them. The wind was still blowing hard.

"What time is it?" she asked.

"Early evening, I think," he said.

"Where are we?"

"I don't know. A long way from where we started."

"Typhoons are circular," she said. "We could be halfway back to Singapore."

He groaned and shook his head. White salt crystals matted his hair and streaked his body. Francine examined the child carefully. She was exhausted and almost certainly dehydrated. Her lips were cracked. There were livid bruises on the pale skin. No bones had been broken, but Francine knew with an inner note like a leaden bell that this frail sparrow's body could not take much more punishment. "Is there any fresh water, Clive?"

"Yes. I'll bring you some. There's nothing to eat, though. All the food's been ruined." He went below and came up shortly with a cooking-pot full of water, which he laid beside her. She began gently rinsing Ruth's face. The child stirred, opening dull eyes.

"Mama?"

"Mama's here, darling."

"Are we there, yet?"

"Almost," she promised. She heard the grating clank of the hand-pump start up. Clive was heaving at the ancient mechanism, his efforts rewarded by a stream of oily water that spewed across the decks and over the side. It began to rain, a sudden, steady downpour. The rainwater was infinitely sweeter than the oil-contaminated stuff in the basin. "Drink, Ruth," she commanded. She lifted her own face and opened her mouth to it, gulping with her salt-parched throat. The relief was marvelous; she felt the salt sluicing from her body, releasing her skin as though from a straitjacket. She scrubbed Ruth's hair and then her own.

The wind had freshened, driving the rain in silvery sheets. She retreated back into the wheelhouse and watched Clive working the pump, the rain streaming down his back. He, too, had been washed clean. He had found an old rag that he had twisted, coolie-fashion, around his loins.

It rained and blew all through the night. From time to time she slept, to wake within a few minutes with vivid, hallucinationlike dreams of being back in Singapore or at home in Perak. Ruth lay motionless in her arms. She did not know how many hours or days it had been since they had eaten. Were Lai's nets still on the junk? Could Clive, who had piloted them through a typhoon, conjure fish from the sea, somehow?

The rain began to settle around dawn. The wind dropped. Aware of a dull gray rim of light to the world, Francine felt that the worst was over now.

When she awoke again, she felt like death. She dragged herself upright and crawled out of the wheelhouse. It was early morning. The sky overhead was a clear, milky blue. Away to the west, a long smudge of cloud, like the battlements of some fortress, showed the storm from which they had emerged. The sun was drawing mist from the smoothly rolling surface of the sea. Through the mist, she saw that they were passing between two islands, a large one to the north, round and domed, a smaller one to the south, low and flat.

"Land," she whispered in wonder, as though she had never expected to see rock and green jungle again. "Clive! Land!"

Clive had been sleeping, but her scream awoke him. He crawled out from under the gunwale and followed her pointing finger with bloodshot eyes.

"Oh my God, you're right. Land."

She threw her arms around him. They pressed their chapped lips together in the semblance of a kiss. "Steer toward the big island!" she commanded.

"We don't have a rudder," he said.

"There might be fresh water and food on the islands! There may even be people who'll help us!"

"We can't do anything. And there may also be Japanese," he pointed out.

The remains of their sail carried them forward in the breeze at a steady pace. But to where? If it was an onshore wind, it was taking them to land. If it was offshore, it was carrying them out to sea, to death. Ruth lay with her swollen eyes closed, her thin arms folded across her breast. For the first time, Francine felt a sharp hunger-pang gripe at her stomach. If they did not eat soon, they would begin to grow too weak to survive.

She curled up beside Ruth, hunching in on her own hunger, and drifted back into a kind of doze.

She was summoned back to life, hours later, by Clive's call.

"There!"

She went to the mast. Dead ahead, a long rim of land had emerged over the horizon. She moved to stand beside Clive, staring at it in disbelief. "It's just cloud," she said, as if wanting reassurance.

"No." He laughed. "It's land, real land. Java. We've done it."

Over the next hour, the dark ripple grew, forming peaks and folds, revealing hills clothed in green jungle, spikes of gray rock emerging from the greenery. "I told you," he repeated. "We've done it." They clung to each other, lips too sore to kiss.

The sweltering heat had returned. As they neared land, the breeze faded, then dropped altogether. The *Lotus Flower* wallowed in the swell, made heavy by the water she had taken on board, a frustrating mile from the shore. They could even see the white line of the beach and the fringe of palm trees. There was no sign of humanity, but that did not matter to Francine. If she could just feel dry land beneath the soles of her feet, she would know they were going to live. She stared at the distant beach with hungry eyes.

"Too far to swim," Clive said laconically. "The current will probably pull us closer. As long as we don't sink, first."

"Sink?"

"The pump's broken. The thing was about a hundred years old. I can't fix it."

She sat down on the deck. To sink now, within sight of land! But the swell brought them steadily toward the land. By early afternoon, she felt they could almost wade to shore. She could see that mangroves lined the muddy beach, fantastical roots making arches and buttresses. Beyond, some ragged casuarina trees marked the edge of the jungle. The *Lotus Flower* was taking on water constantly. She had by now sunk deep in the water. Soon, the sea would be slopping over the gunwales, or what was left of them.

"Can't we swim?" she begged Clive.

"We could. Ruth couldn't."

"I'll carry her in my arms!"

"You wouldn't make it. In another hour, we'll be a lot closer."

"But we're sinking!"

"Well, there's no point in jumping off the boat until it does sink," he said practically. "We'll leave it to the end. At least there's no coral. We've been lucky. I've got everything that's worth salvaging. Look." He unwrapped a strip of cloth and showed her his haul—a heavy parang, a few knives and cooking utensils, some rope. Incongruously, the hand grenade that the soldier had given her in Singapore lay among the domestic things. He touched it with his forefinger. "That may save our lives if it still works." He wrapped the things up again.

They sat silently on the deck as the *Lotus Flower* floated sluggishly toward the shore. With every half hour that passed, the boat lay deeper. Muddy water gurgled and slapped in the hold. On it bobbed the few floating things that had been left by the storm. Ruth had emerged from her stupor enough to sit upright, gazing vacantly ahead. Francine stroked her dank hair mechanically. They could smell the land now, a rain-forest smell of decay and growth.

Three hundred yards from the beach, something thudded against the hull, jolting them. Then, with a prolonged shudder, the rocking motion ceased. Francine staggered a little, her legs adjusting to the strange fact that, after so many days at sea, the deck was still.

"We've run aground," Clive said. "We should be able to wade to shore from here."

She looked at the dark mass of jungle, searching for some sign of humanity, an atap hut, a wisp of smoke. There was nothing. The green jungle rolled over hills toward the hinterland. In the distance, heaps of cloud marked what might be a mountain range.

The *Lotus Flower* was tilting over on one beam. They hauled themselves over the lowest side, sliding down into the sea, Clive taking Ruth in his arms.

The water was warm, brown, and shallow. At first, Francine flailed for a footing. Then her feet touched firm sand on the bottom. The water was up to her chin. Half-paddling, half-wading, she made her way behind Clive, who had hoisted the child onto his shoulder.

Halfway to the beach, when the water was waist high, she turned and looked back at the *Lotus Flower*. The junk was on her side, her black hull exposed, her tattered sail drooping almost to the water. She looked like a dead thing.

"Next high tide'll carry her off," Clive said unemotionally. He waded on. A wave slapped into Francine's back, as though urging her impatiently to shore. She staggered on. The sand squirmed between her toes. Exhaustion was making her head swim. She drove her weightless body onward, until she was plodding in the footmarks Clive had made in the sand, and could at last collapse to her knees on the shore of refuge.

Trees had been uprooted all along the shoreline. The palms had survived for the most part, but their coconuts lay strewn among the wreckage, manna from heaven. While Francine rested on the beach with Ruth, Clive collected a dozen of the largest green coconuts, hacking the tops off with the parang. They gulped avidly at the sweet, slightly fizzy water the fruit contained. As soon as she had drunk enough, Ruth fell into a swift sleep, her head pillowed on her arms. Feeling bloated, Francine lifted her head and stared wearily at their landfall.

They had come to shore on a small crescent of beach, composed half of mud, half of sand, fringed with mangroves, whose leathery leaves glittered with salt crystals in the afternoon light. The beach was strewn with debris from the storm. Leaning forward, she saw what looked like the feathery fronds of a nipa palm, growing beyond some rocks at the far end of the beach.

"We're near the mouth of a river," she said. "Or at least a stream."

Clive looked up from the parang, which he had been sharpening on a stone. "How do you know?"

"I know this sort of place," she said simply. "Stay here with Ruth."

She took a small knife and walked down the beach toward the rocks. The sun was hot on her back. It was so strange to feel the earth beneath her feet that she wondered whether this was a dream from which she would soon awake to a reality of raging sea and howling gale. But the black hulk of the *Lotus Flower* told her it was no dream. Wherever their voyage had taken them, it was over, at least temporarily.

Her whole body was sore. Her legs, in particular, ached fiercely. Salt had chafed raw places at all her joints, making her walk with careful slowness so as not to inflame the furious pain. She longed hopelessly for a freshwater bath.

She looked down at herself for the first time in days. She had been wearing a cotton sam fu and sandals when the storm had struck. The pantsuit had been reduced to tattered brown rags that clung to her body, barely preserving her modesty. The sandals had gone long ago. The clothing hardly mattered. The sandals were a serious loss.

She had made sure that Ruth, at least, had shorts and a stout shirt. Clive, with only his loincloth, was much worse off. He would be burned, bitten, and torn within hours unless he covered himself.

Her left wrist was bare. Her beloved gold watch, Abe's present to her on the day Ruth was born, had gone. It had become unclipped and had washed away, she had no recollection of where or when. It was like the last remnant of Abe being stripped away from her.

She clambered over the rocks, trying not to cut her bare feet. It had been a long time since she had walked barefoot over rocks. Shoes had softened her soles. Beyond the rocks, there was only mud, no more sand. A cluster of nipa palms grew almost at the water's edge. Carefully avoiding the daggerlike roots of the mangroves, she waded to the palms and peered into the rain forest beyond. As she had suspected, there was a small creek running inland, its brackish water motionless between the tides. She felt a prickle of hope.

The nipa were in flower, spectacular orange bracts emerging from the muddy water beneath the fringed leaves. She groped down, avoiding the razor-edged leaves, hoping to find the floating fruits. She was rewarded. She gathered several large, pineapple-sized fruits and waded back toward Clive and Ruth.

"Sand flies are stinging Ruth," he greeted her. Ruth's legs were covered in swollen red bites.

"We'll have to rub coconut water on them. Look. Nipa fruit."

"You're a genius," he said.

"There's a creek just past those rocks, Clive. Where there's fresh water there are always people. If we followed it up into the forest, we'd be sure to find a village, eventually. Or at least a fisherman."

He was squatting, breaking open one of the nipa fruits for Ruth. The child bit into the gelatinous flesh with delight. "We can't walk barefoot through the jungle. We'll have to make shoes of some kind. Out of bark or leaves. Is that good, Chicken-Licken?"

Francine searched through the bundle and rolled the hand grenade out. "I've seen fish being dynamited. We could pull the pin and throw this into the water."

"Good idea." He took the grenade and walked to the edge of the water. Almost casually, he pulled the pin and hurled the grenade out into the sea. After a moment, there was a muffled thump, and the water boiled up turbulently. Clive swam out to the place. When he came back, he was clutching three small, limp fish.

"Better than nothing," he said. "We'll have to eat them raw, I'm afraid."

They dined off the slimy, bony fish and jelly-sweet nipa flesh. The sun was now low, dipping toward the horizon in a flare of scarlet. They collected fronds and pulled together a bed of sorts as high up on the beach as possible. Then they sat in silence, clinging together, watching the sun go down into the sea. As darkness settled, the murmur of the waves seemed to grow louder. The forest behind them, too, began to sing. A million insects, frogs, and birds were tuning up for the evening chorale. The sound soon swelled to a shrill roar. Some large creature crashed through the branches, making Ruth wail in fright.

"Just monkeys, Chicken-Licken," Clive said reassuringly. Francine imagined the bright round eyes peering at them through the dark, the simian fingers clutching, the sharp teeth bared. How long could they possibly survive without meeting other humans? Her only consolation was the thought of that creek, the hope that somewhere along it lay their salvation.

Francine awoke to a white, silent world. A heavy mist had closed in, blotting out the sea and the land. The air was suffocatingly hot. There was a rotting marine stench of low tide.

She dragged herself upright, running her fingers through her grit-clogged hair. Clive was cradling Ruth in his arms. He managed to smile at her tiredly. They were all coated in sand and covered in bites. She rose and walked to the water's edge. She stripped off her clothes and waded into the warm water. She floated for a while in the disorienting whiteness, rinsing her hair. Her body felt thin under her palms, her hipbones poking sharply through the skin, her breasts little more than hard nipples on bony ribs. The salt stung her raw places viciously, but it at least got rid of the sand, which would have made walking unbearable.

She washed her clothes. She must look like a wild woman, she thought wryly. She wrung out the things as best she could and put them on, still wet. She could not see the *Lotus Flower* through the mist. Perhaps she had already drifted away during the night.

Ruth was already breakfasting off nipa fruit, chattering quite cheerfully to Clive. She had moments of animation, for a while becoming the old Ruth, before she slipped back into apathy.

"I'm going to live in a big, big house with Clive," she told Francine.

"Can I come and stay?"

"Of course," Ruth said. "And we're going to buy a new car."

"What kind?"

"A fancy car," she said emphatically. "And Clive's going to be my daddy."

"Ah. That sounds like a good solution," Francine said solemnly. Clive's eyes were warm as they met hers. *We're becoming a family,* she thought. *Please God, let us always be a family.*

She showed Clive how to make an impromptu cloak out of dried atap leaves. Slung over his shoulders, the garment made him look like a human scarecrow. Impatient, he wanted to throw it off. She persuaded him not to; it would make some kind of cover against sun, insects, and thorns.

She threaded a twist of atap through the "monkey eyes" of coconuts so they could be carried. Clive slung six of the large, green fruits over his shoulder. With that as their only provision, they set off to the creek.

The brackish water was now flowing sluggishly, following the tide. Scraps of foam and leaves drifted on the surface of the brown water. Further up, she hoped, it would become pure enough to drink. With Clive at the front and Ruth in the middle, they waded up the creek, into the rain forest.

The mist persisted, limiting their visibility severely. They could see no more than a few yards of brown water ahead, overhung with plants. As they penetrated deeper, the invisible trees began to tower over them, closing, making a shadowy darkness.

The creek was for the most part little more than knee deep. Underfoot, the soft mud of the creek bottom was kind on their soles. But the resistance of the mud and water was tiring, and Ruth's feeble strength soon gave out. She whimpered to be carried. Francine picked her up and walked for a painful half hour, until her arms could no longer bear the strain. Then Clive hoisted the child over his shoulders in a fireman's lift. She seemed to go to sleep at once, her long dark hair hanging down in a ribbon.

The heavy mist was somehow hypnotic. It obliterated all sensation of forward motion, so it seemed they were on an endless conveyor belt, always trudging, never moving from the same spot. Before them always was the same creek, the same branches drooping from white nothingness.

From time to time, the fog thickened into drenching rain that lasted up to half an hour. She had promised Clive she could find food in the jungle. But how would she discern fruits in this impenetrable fog? It obliterated sound itself, so that they moved through a cathedral-like hush.

Slowly, however, the water grew a little colder and a little deeper. The squelching mud bottom began to give way to smooth pebbles and outcrops of stone. The mist thinned slightly as it grew hotter.

After four or five hours' walk, they reached a place of noisy water. Rapids spouted and rumbled. They had come to the main body of the river. From here, various creeks snaked in different directions toward the sea. Upstream, the river broadened and deepened.

"We have to follow the main branch," Francine said wearily.

The river was now so wide and deep that they had to wade along one of the banks. Past the rapids, gigantic trees overhung the river, their tops sometimes almost meeting over the wide stream, so that it was like wading through a cavern at times. A few birds had begun to sing. From time to time, brilliant kingfishers, disturbed by their progress, darted from holes in the bank and swept across their path. Huge butterflies flitted in the fog, sky-blue or butter-yellow.

They reached a sandy shoal where they rested and drank a coconut each and then scraped out the melting flesh. By now, their legs were covered in tiny black leeches, which had burrowed imperceptibly into the flesh, and were already starting to engorge with blood. Francine, shuddering, tried to scrape the parasites off, but Clive stopped her.

"You'll get a bad infection. Leave them. They'll fall off when we're dry again."

She made a face of disgust. Ruth, too, had the creatures embedded in her skinny legs.

They dozed in the white silence for an hour, then set off again.

At first she thought it was a waking dream or hallucination. Then she caught it again: a sour smell composed of dung, decay, and woodsmoke. The unmistakable smell of humanity.

"People!" she called.

Clive half-turned, his face weary. "Where?"

"I can smell people."

He sniffed the foggy air. "I can't smell anything."

"I can!" She was elated. "I told you! There must be a kampong up ahead."

He looked skeptical. But the scent grew stronger as they plodded upstream, until even Clive could smell it. Francine felt like singing. The smell of smoke predominated, made more acrid by the humid air.

At last they reached another shoal, this time at least fifty yards long. Dimly through the mist, she made out the shapes of three or four dugout canoes drawn up out of the water. There was also a pile of cut bamboo tubes. They had reached a settlement of some kind.

"We're here," she said joyfully. "*Selamat!*" she called in Malay into the mist. "Is anybody there?"

Her shouts brought only a more intense silence. Clive put down his bundle. "I'll go on ahead."

"No. Let me."

"Why?"

"Don't forget, I'm a native," she said with a smile. She was buoyed up by triumphant excitement. "I'm better at this than you are. You stay here and look after Ruth."

"All right," he said reluctantly. He stepped aside to let her pass. "Shout if you need help."

She walked into the mist, straining her eyes to make out shapes. The smell of burning was strong. It was a ghost world made out of infinitesimal shades of gray. She found she was walking through a cultivated patch; bananas and sago extended broad fronds out of the murk, dangling clusters of fruit. The sweet smell of the ripe bananas made saliva rush into her mouth. She fought down the impulse to reach up and pluck some. Stealing fruit would not be a good way to open relations. She reached an atap fence and clambered over, calling. There was no reply.

A grunt made her stop in her tracks. The bushes rustled. Her heart pounded as she waited. A small pig emerged from the undergrowth, rooting in the earth with its snout, pausing to glance at her with small, sad eyes.

Then she saw a human figure. But it was not on the ground; it floated impossibly in midair above the pig, as though by some sorcery. She walked closer, feeling the sweat freeze on her skin. The man had been hanged from a tree branch.

Farther ahead in the mist, more hanged men loomed, two of them lynched from the same tree. Lying on the ground was a fourth figure, barely recognizable as a naked woman. She had been bayoneted or shot, it was impossible to tell which from this distance, and Francine could not bring herself to approach. The heavy smell of putrefaction was in the air. All she would find here would be more death, more savagery. There could be no question who had done this.

Francine turned and ran back blindly the way she had come. Wet leaves clutched at her face. She stumbled painfully over something and recoiled. It was only a heap of husked coconuts.

As she dragged herself to her feet, she saw a huge barnlike shape hulking in the mist. She knew what it was, though she had never seen one before. It was a longhouse, a primitive communal home raised on stilts. Its atap roof was blackened and gaping in one place. It had been set on fire and partially burned. She dared not investigate further.

She reached Clive, gasping.

"What's wrong?" he said sharply.

"The Japanese have been here!"

"When?"

"I don't know. There's a longhouse up ahead. It's been burned. They've hanged people from the trees. And I saw a dead woman on the ground—"

He put his arms around her as tears welled up, choking her. "No sign of any soldiers?" he asked. She shook her head dumbly. "We can't be in Java, then," he said heavily.

"Perhaps we were blown back to Sumatra."

"God knows where we are. We have to get out of here."

"Where are we going to go? We might walk straight into them." She drew back, wiping her wet eyes. "They might not come back here. The place is deserted. There's food here, Clive. Bananas and sago. Maybe rice, too. And the longhouse hasn't been completely burned. We should stay. There's no point going on."

He thought. "All right," he said at last. "Let's go and check it out."

Francine nodded at Ruth, who was listlessly throwing pebbles into the stream. "I don't want her to see what's up there, Clive. Can you do something before we come?"

"Don't worry about it. Wait here until I call." He set off cautiously into the mist, his parang in one hand. The mist now seemed threatening, full of invisible menace. She was so sickened of bloodshed. They had lost so much, traveled so much, been through so much. Had it all been to end in capture or death at the hands of the Japanese, after all?

She felt a kind of superstitious dread of them now, these implacable enemies who seemed to be everywhere, from the clouds to the heart of the jungle. How disastrously they had all underrated the Japanese. For years, they had laughed at the cheap glass bangles, the tinny cameras, the gimcrack imitations of real things, without ever realizing how ruthlessly efficient those "imitations" were. Even when they had invaded China, only a partial recognition had dawned of their real power, their real intentions. And now that the shadow of their bombers and tanks had covered the world, it was too late.

"Are we going to stay here?" Ruth asked.

"Perhaps."

"Where's Clive gone?" Ruth asked.

"To get things ready for us."

"What's he doing?"

"Tidying up."

"Tidying up what?"

"It's dirty."

"How, dirty?"

"Hush!" The child had not been so alert or talkative for weeks. Francine touched her forehead. For once, it was cool and dry. She wondered whether the long fast had improved Ruth's condition somehow.

"Mama," Ruth whispered suddenly, clutching at Francine's clothing. "Look. A man."

She looked up. Across the stream, a naked savage was standing motionless, watching them.

Shock froze her heart for a moment. She could not move. She had no idea how he had materialized so silently out of the mist without her noticing.

The word *savage* had entered her mind instantly and without qualification. A cloth was wrapped around his waist, a flap hanging before his loins. She glanced swiftly at his hands. They hung empty at his side. His face was as impassive as a mask. They stared at each other in a tense silence.

At last, she spoke in a shaky voice. "Is this your place?" she asked in Malay.

He made no reply.

"Is this your place?" she asked again. "We didn't mean to trespass." Ruth was hiding her face against Francine's side.

A shorter man materialized behind the first. He was dressed in the same kind of loincloth, but with a cloth headdress. Strips of the same red cloth were tied around his elbows and calves. They spoke to each other in a language she did not recognize. Then they waded across the river toward Francine and Ruth.

She sat, frozen. When they reached her, the taller man spoke in Malay. "What is the tuan doing?" he asked.

"He went to cut down the dead," she replied.

"Why?"

"I didn't want the child to see. She's very young." Francine's mouth was dry. "We were going to stay here for a while. We have nowhere to go."

He studied her. His naked skin was tattooed with black designs, ornate rosettes on each sinewy shoulder, another design on his throat. "Who are you running from?"

"The Japanese," she said, knowing that if it was the wrong answer, it would take nothing for him to pull the parang from his waist and cut her down with a blow.

He nodded. "They are our enemies, too." Ruth was still hiding, her mouth muffled against her mother's skin. "My name is Nendak," he said. "Come with me."

Her knees were weak as she rose. They walked toward the longhouse in silence, Francine carrying Ruth. Chopping sounds came faintly through the mist. Taking her elbow in a firm grasp, the man guided her toward the sound. Beyond the sago patch, they came upon Clive, covered in sweat, digging a trench with a hoe he had found. Nearby, laid out in a neat row, lay five bodies. One of them, Francine saw, belonged to a child.

Clive turned as they approached, his eyes widening. He had already dug some way into the soggy earth and stood knee deep in the trench. He gave Francine a quick, interrogative look. She shook her head infinitesimally.

"What is he doing?" Nendak asked.

"He's digging a grave," she replied.

"That is not the place or the manner. Tell him to stop."

"He wants you to put down the hoe, Clive," she said quietly in English.

Clive laid the tool down and climbed out of the trench, his legs covered in red mud. "Are they hostile?" he asked Francine in a low voice.

"I don't know."

Nendak studied each corpse somberly. When he came to the bodies of the woman and the child, he lifted them in his arms and pressed them to his chest, his head bowed silently. The second man, showing more emotion, covered his mouth with one hand and sobbed huskily.

Francine and Clive watched without speaking. These poor, murdered corpses had been their kin. They had, at least, a common enemy.

The tall man turned to look at them. "Wait there," he said grimly to Francine in Malay. "Do not move."

"He says to keep still," she told Clive.

"Ask him about the Japanese," Clive said. "Ask him where we are."

But the two men, ignoring Francine and Clive, began carrying the bodies up into the longhouse, one by one. A sense of resignation closed in on her. They had come this far. Here lay some kind of halt, at least, to the journey. Whether death or salvation lay here, their traveling was over for a while. She held Ruth against her breast, crooning to her softly, waiting to find out their fate.

The third man to arrive was older, his headdress decorated with hornbill feathers, which nodded as he moved. His silver hair hung down to his shoulders, framing a fierce, patriarchal face.

After staring at the three of them, he took a basin of water and began to wash the dirt and blood off the corpses in silence.

A shaft of sunlight slowly penetrated into the clearing. Francine saw the longhouse more clearly. It was a large structure, built on belian posts, walled and roofed with bamboo, across which atap matting had been stretched. It extended almost fifty yards. To one side was a row of rickety bamboo verandas. On the other side were several small huts raised on posts. Around the longhouse was a straggling plantation of papaya, sago, taro, and other jungle fruits. Somewhere nearby, she imagined, would be hillside paddy fields. It was a village more primitive than any kampong she had ever seen. She did not think people had lived this way in mainland Malaya for a hundred years or more.

More people began to arrive, men and women, old and young, a community returning to what had been their home. Each carried something precious that he or she had snatched up as they fled: women with babies and children in their arms, the elderly with baskets of rice on their backs, the young carrying piglets or chickens. Dogs and adult pigs followed at their heels.

Francine, Clive, and Ruth sat on the earth beside the half-dug grave, watching and waiting. The clearing began to ring with voices, though nobody spoke to them except the youngest children, who chattered at them inquisitively. Francine could recognize isolated words of Malay, but could not follow the rest. She was almost certain now that their landfall was neither Java nor Sumatra. They were on one of the thousands of large and small islands that scattered the South China Sea. "We're still in the Malay States," she said quietly to Clive.

"How do you know?" he asked, staring at the tribesmen in fascination.

"Their language contains a lot of Malay words. And that tall man speaks good Malay."

"So where are we?"

"I don't know."

Each group of new arrivals climbed up into the longhouse to see the row of corpses, which had been laid out on the veranda. A few screamed or sobbed, the rest stared gravely. The old man with the hornbill feathers presided silently, black eyes watching. Having paid their respects to the dead, nearly everyone came to stare in curiosity at the strangers, a curiosity that was somehow not intrusive.

All were bare from the waist up, the men wearing loincloths, the women skirts, their breasts exposed in a way that would never have been permitted in Muslim Malaya. The men were equally handsome and well made. Almost all of the men wore at least some tattoos on chest, arms, buttocks, and thighs.

Smoke began to wreathe among the banana and sago fronds. A party of women went down to the river's edge, and standing in line, began packing rice into cut bamboo tubes. The fog was lifting now, and the sun made dappled patterns on their honey-colored skin. They laid the bamboo tubes on racks over the flames to steam. The smell of cooking rice filled the air. Francine felt saliva fill her mouth.

Dogs and pigs began to charge around, unchecked. Roosters, splendid creatures evidently more pets than livestock, crowed fiercely. The empty green jungle had been filled with chattering, smoky, untidy humanity. Four or five young men climbed into the roof beams of the longhouse. As if motivated by a single will, they began to repair the burned roof, hacking bamboo beams to fit, roping them in place, working in a concerted team.

The last of the fog melted away. As she had suspected, paddy fields were now visible, extending beyond the longhouse. The forest had been cleared for several hundred yards around, after which it suddenly resumed, an almost impenetrable green barrier that protected this place. The shoal where the tall man had found them was littered with praus and canoes. The river provided the only easy access.

The women had started preparing a meal, shoveling the cooked rice into bowls with some fragments of small, grilled fish. Francine could feel her stomach twisting violently. Ruth was whimpering with hunger.

"Hush, darling," she murmured. "Perhaps they'll give us something to eat in a little while."

There must be, Francine estimated, at least 120 people in all. Nendak led them to a small group sitting cross-legged around a woven blanket on which stood communal bowls of rice, eggs, fish, and vegetables. The family invited them to eat with gestures, offering the food. She thanked them, and filled the battered plate they offered.

None of Nendak's family, she noticed, had touched the food. Some of the women were crying bitterly, rocking with their hands pressed to their mouths. "Aren't you going to eat?" she asked, a handful of rice halfway to her mouth.

He shook his head slightly. "We cannot. The dead woman was my youngest sister. The child was hers. Two of the men were my brothers-in-law."

Francine lowered her eyes in compassion, astounded at his composure. "I didn't know." She turned to Clive and explained.

He winced. "Then we won't eat, either," he said, putting the rice back.

"You have no reason to grieve with us," Nendak said.

"I lost my husband to the Japanese," she said, trying to show him she understood the tragedy that had overtaken his family. "And many friends."

"So you're a widow?"

"Yes."

He nodded at Ruth. "Yours?"

"Yes."

He indicated Clive. "And the tuan?"

"He is my new man."

"He was kind to try and bury our dead. He did not know that it was not the way." He pushed the food back toward them. "Eat. You're all weak. It gives us no consolation to see you starve."

She explained to Clive, and after a moment's consultation, they obeyed. The food was bland and simple, but it tasted like heaven.

"Ask him where we are," Clive said.

"What is this place called?" she asked the man.

He jerked his head. "This is Rumah Nendak."

That meant simply "Nendak's home," the name of the longhouse. He was the chief of the village then. She nodded politely. "Thank you. We were caught in the storm," she added apologetically. "We don't know where we are."

"This is Sarawak."

She felt suddenly weary. She had half-suspected that. "And what people are you?"

"We are Iban."

"Who is your king?" she asked.

"King George the Sixth," he said proudly.

"I am called Yu Fa," she said, knowing that would be easier for them than *Francine*, "and the tuan is called Napier."

Nendak nodded his understanding.

She turned to Clive. "We're in Sarawak, Clive. Borneo. These people are Ibans."

He groaned. "We've been blown more than a hundred miles off course."

"At least they're loyal to the crown," she said. "That means they probably won't eat us."

"Is that supposed to be funny?" he asked dryly.

The rest of the community were observing them with unabashed curiosity as they ate, making loud remarks that were almost certainly comments on the appearance of the three strangers.

Nendak, too, was staring at them intently. "Where do you come from?" he asked.

"Singapore. We were sailing in a boat, hoping to reach Java. A Japanese plane attacked us. Our captain died. Then the storm brought us here."

He nodded. "It was a sacred storm. It saved us. The Japanese tried to burn down our longhouse and our rice paddy. The rain put out the fires."

"Is there fighting in this land?"

"Much fighting. They came with many airplanes. All the tuans are in prison camp now."

"They've taken the whole of Sarawak?" she said in dismay.

"And Brunei," he said dryly, "and Sabah, and Kalimantan. Singapore is also theirs?" he asked.

She nodded. "Yes. We were going to Batavia, Nendak. Do you know what has happened there?"

He shook his head briefly. "Batavia is theirs, too."

Feeling sick, she explained to Clive. "The whole of Borneo has been captured. And he says Batavia has fallen to the Japanese, too."

"Right, then," Clive said, sounding unconcerned. But she knew he was hiding the same despair she felt. "Ask them why the Japs did this to them," he said, gesturing at the burned longhouse.

"To make us afraid of them," Nendak replied. "They know we hate them and are loyal to the British."

"Are the Japanese near here?"

He gestured. "In the town."

"How far?"

"One day's walk."

That sounded horribly close. "Will they come back?"

"Yes," he replied simply. "You and the tuan cannot stay here. You must go from here. I will take you."

"Where to?"

"We have to go from here into Kalimantan. Many days' walk through the forest. We know people there, friends of Dutch missionaries, who have a big prau. With the prau they will take you to the islands. From there, the guerillas will take you to Australia. Tell the tuan this. And eat, Yu Fa."

As she ate, she translated tersely for Clive's benefit. "They say we can't stay here for long. Nendak says he'll help us get out."

Clive nodded. "If the Japs found us here, they would kill the whole community." He reached out his hand to Nendak. "*Sama sama*, Nendak."

Nendak smiled gravely as he shook Clive's hand.

"We have to keep going, then?" Francine asked.

Clive nodded. "We'll do what we have to," he said flatly. He stroked Francine's face, knowing how weary she felt. For the moment, she was just glad of the gifts of food, companionship, and life.

"All right," she said.

Clive smiled at her. He took a glowing stick from the fire and began to burn off the leeches that still hung in their flesh.

It rained again in the night, beginning with a tremendous thunderstorm, then settling into a prolonged, steady downpour that rattled on the palm-matting roof and among the forest leaves.

Everyone slept in the long, covered veranda. Francine huddled with Ruth and Clive under a woven blanket that someone had given them. The darkness fell swiftly and was absolute; no light burned in the longhouse. People shuffled to their places, murmuring to one another. Within an hour of darkfall, the whole tribe was asleep.

Francine lay in Clive's arms. But sleep came slowly. Her mind filled with images of what they had been through. So much that was hideous; and yet, looking back over the past weeks, she was surprised, suddenly, by the terrible beauty of so much she had witnessed. She remembered the armada of Japanese bombers thundering over Mr. Davenport's grave on Monk's Hill. She remembered the child born in the air-raid shelter. She remembered making love with Clive that first time, the growing power of love in her heart. Even the red gout of exploding bombs, burned onto her memory forever, had its own dreadful brilliance. The anger of the sea and sky. The temple gloom of the rain forest. Birth, love, death. The savage beauty of nature, the savage darkness of the human heart.

Beneath the longhouse, pigs rooted for the food scraps that fell through the gaps in the floor. Roosters crowed all night long, a triumphant screech that jangled the nerves.

All the dogs of the community had come up onto the *ruai*. They charged up and down the gallery in wild games, their paws drumming on the loose bamboo floor. Nobody seemed to be disturbed by the cacophony, nor by the earsplitting thunderstorm that broke sometime after midnight. Francine lay with her eyes open, watching as the blue glare of lightning illuminated the ironwood posts, thinking of the strange fate that had brought her here, to this place called Rumah Nendak.

She was awakened by a hand shaking her shoulder. She dragged herself from the depths, scarcely knowing where she was. A dim gray light suffused the ruai. Clive was leaning over her. "The women want you to go with them," he said. She sat up. A woman was waiting, her face dimpling in a smile. She pointed to Ruth and beckoned.

Wearily, Francine rose, picking Ruth up in her arms. All the men were still sleeping, sprawled out on the floor among the finally recumbent dogs, but all the women were awake. She followed them as they quietly made their way down to the river with their children, each carrying three or four gourds. The river was swollen with the night's rain, rippling briskly toward the sea.

The early morning was both misty and smoky. The remains of yesterday's fires smoldered sulkily by the riverside. It was mercifully cool. The green gloom was silent but for the occasional squawk of a bird high up among the branches of the great trees.

Out of earshot of the sleeping men, they formed a chattering line in the shallows, washing themselves and their babies, then dressing for the day. The young woman who had woken her, and whom she now recognized as one of Nendak's family with whom she had eaten the day before, held out a dark blue sarong, smiling broadly.

At first Francine shook her head, but the woman nodded encouragingly. She pointed to Francine's clothes. "Finished," she said in Malay. "No good now."

She had to agree. Suddenly envying them their clean, bare-breasted decency, she made up her mind and took the gift.

"Thank you so much," she said gratefully.

"*Sama sama,*" the women all replied, beaming. They watched with interest as Francine stripped off her clothes. There were exclamations of sympathy at the injuries that covered her body. She had been cut by splinters, burned by ropes, battered and bruised by a hundred things. It looked as though every inch of her journey had been written on her skin. And while she had not yet reached the point of emaciation, she was thin. She immersed herself in the river water. It was cool and sweet. It enveloped her with a sense of peace.

She washed Ruth, then put on the sarong. It seemed foolish to cover her top when no other woman did, so she fastened the thing around her waist in the Iban way, leaving herself naked from the waist up. They nodded approval. One of them looped a string of shells around her neck, which provoked more approval and laughter. Now she was not only properly dressed, but even adorned. Francine laughed at herself and her abject poverty. Then sudden tears filled her eyes, tears at the simple kindness, tears at being in the sweet company of women after so much hardship. Her benefactor consoled her with little fluttering pats on the shoulder.

"Don't cry, Yu Fa."

"What is your name?" she asked the young woman.

"Segura," she replied. Segura took Ruth from Francine's arms. "Your daughter is very sick, Yu Fa," she said, looking at the child's thin body. "She has parasites in her stomach. Dysentery. She is weak."

"I know." Francine nodded. "Do you have any medicine that will cure her?"

"Yes," one of the older women said. "You must take her to the *tuai burong.*"

"Who is the tuai burong?"

"The doctor. He will heal her."

The women had gathered round, examining Ruth in concern.

"What is his name?" Francine asked.

"Jah," several of the women replied. "His name is Jah."

"But medicine is not enough," Segura said. "To cure the dysentery, the child needs rest, much rest, and good food."

There was a chorus of assent from the other women.

The older woman patted Francine on the shoulder. "You must leave her here, or she will die, Yu Fa. We will take good care of the child until you come back."

"Until I come back?" she repeated stupidly.

"You cannot stay here," Segura said gently. "And you cannot take the child with you, or she will die. Your journey is a long and hard one. The little one cannot survive it."

Francine snatched Ruth from the woman's arms and clung to her in dread. The women clicked their tongues in sympathy.

"It is true, Yu Fa," Segura said, compassion softening her face. "The Japanese will come back at any time. If they find you and the tuan, they will kill you, and everyone in the village. We will all die."

"Nendak will take you and the tuan," the older woman said. "He knows the path through the forest to a place where the Dutch built a school. There you will find our friends with a prau. You will begin your journey to Australia."

"But it is a journey of many weeks," Segura said. "Much walking, much hunger, much hardship. Sleeping in the forest, swimming. The little one will die. You must leave her here. We will hide her from the Japanese. When the Japanese are gone from Sarawak, you will come back for her."

Francine was too stunned to reply. She clung tightly to Ruth and looked around for Clive.

The men had finally begun to emerge, stretching and yawning as they walked down the notched-log ladder from the longhouse. Clive was following them. Like her, he was wearing Iban dress. Someone had given him a woven cloth to wrap around his loins.

"Clive! They say we can't stay here. They say we have to go. They want me to leave Ruth here with them!"

He took her in his arms while she told him what the women had said. His dark eyes grew sad. "They're right, Francine. I didn't want to say it yet, but it's obvious. She would never survive a journey like that."

"No, Clive," she said. "I'm not leaving Ruth!"

"Look at her, darling," Clive said gently. Ruth was apathetic, so weak that she had not even understood what her mother and Clive were talking about. She lay in Francine's arms, light as a feather. "She needs to rest, and to eat properly. She needs to be cared for. We have to keep going. We can't take her with us."

"I can't," she said, shaking her head. "Don't ask me to do this, Clive. I can't. This is what Abe did to us."

"They can hide Ruth. But they can't hide us. If we stay here, the Japs will soon get to hear of it, and they'll come. They will kill Ruth, my darling. They will kill you, they will kill me, they will kill everyone in this tribe."

She turned blindly to watch the men of the village. Unlike the women, with their dainty morning toilet, the men threw themselves bodily into the river like otters, splashing and shouting.

"We have no choice," Clive went on. "I love Ruth. I only want what's best for her. This way she will survive. If we try to take her with us, she will die. And if we try to stay here, either the Iban will kill the three of us, or the Japanese will massacre the whole lot."

"How can we trust them?" she demanded.

"How can we not? We're going to have to trust them with our lives, darling. The moment we set off with Nendak, we're in his hands. Leaving Ruth with the women makes no difference."

She walked away from Clive, heartsick.

As soon as they had washed, the whole tribe began preparations for a feast of some kind. Segura came to Francine and knelt beside her.

"Are you sad, Yu Fa?"

"I cannot leave my child, Segura," Francine said, looking up into the sweet face of the other woman.

"You cannot watch her die, Yu Fa," Segura replied simply. "You will understand, when you think about it." She pointed to the old man who had washed the corpses yesterday. "That is Jah, the tuai burong."

Francine glanced obliquely at the savage face, the tattooed hands and forearms. "Is he a doctor? He's frightening," she said.

"Yes," Segura agreed simply. "But he will cure your child."

There was no question the man radiated power. She glanced at Ruth's skinny body and knew she had no choice. "I'll take her to him," she decided.

"Not today, Yu Fa. After the *gawai*." She began plaiting flowers into Francine's hair. "You must be beautiful for the gawai."

"What is the gawai?"

"The festival to prepare the dead for the journey to Sabayon."

"Where is Sabayon?"

She smiled at Francine's ignorance. "Sabayon is the land of the dead, Yu Fa. Don't you know anything?"

"I'm ignorant," she said emptily.

The festival gathered pace over the day. Though they had not the remotest conception of what it all meant, Francine and Clive watched from the fringes. The old man led the ceremony, waving a live chicken in his hands, which squawked in protest. At length he slaughtered the fowl and spattered the blood over the offerings. Music and dancing began, at first slow and stately, becoming progressively more exuberant.

More food was prepared, this time for the community, including bottles of rice wine. The men downed ritual tumblers of the stuff, becoming more elated, dancing more energetically. The sweat streaked their bronzed bodies as they whirled in mock battle, swinging their parangs. Their smoothly muscled bodies were perfectly set off by the crimson cloth and by the silver bangles they carefully fitted to their arms and calves.

The women, too, knew how to accentuate their beauty, though their dress was simpler and more delicate than the men's, consisting mainly of intricately woven blankets wrapped tight around their slim waists. Almost all wore bright, clattering rows of silver dollars.

In the early part of the afternoon, the brilliant white clouds that were never far away gathered overhead and discharged a brief, drenching downpour. Shortly afterward the tribe gathered in a milling group.

The dead had lain in state on the ruai all this time, screened with woven hangings. Various things, perhaps their personal possessions, had been arranged around the corpses. Now the bodies were wrapped in blankets and brought ceremoniously out of the longhouse. Singing and clapping, the whole community set off along the riverbank, following the corpses.

"We're going to the graveyard," Segura told Francine, her eyes bright with the rice wine she had drunk. "You must wait here."

Francine nodded. The sound of voices faded into the jungle, along with the clanking of weapons and the tinkling of silver dollars. The whole tribe had gone except for three old people too infirm to walk, who sat staring with filmy, unseeing eyes. Ruth had fallen asleep, curled up in Clive's arms.

"It's a terrible thing to ask a mother to do," Clive said softly, gazing down tenderly into Ruth's sleeping face. "But less terrible than letting her die."

The Ibans returned from the burial in small groups. Some of them beat sticks on the ground as they came. Francine knew they were scaring away the spirits of the dead to stop them coming to haunt the longhouse; she had seen superstitious people do the same thing in the kampong as a child.

Nendak was among the first to return, his face somber. Segura walked beside him, tears still streaking her plump cheeks. They came to squat beside her and Clive.

"You and the tuan are well, Yu Fa?" Nendak asked.

"Yes, thank you. I'm very sorry for your loss," she added formally.

He nodded. "The Japanese are coming, Yu Fa."

Her heart seemed to stop. "How do you know?"

"They are coming to all the longhouses. They are looking for white people. They will come in two, three days. They will search everywhere. Tell the tuan."

She turned to Clive, pale-faced, and explained. "When will they be here?" Clive asked.

"They may come tomorrow," Nendak said. "You and the tuan must go tonight. I will take you."

She translated that, too. Clive nodded slowly.

"Well, my sweet," he said in a gentle voice, "looks like we're on the move again."

She got up without speaking and walked away from the men. She looked up. The sky was a deep blue overhead. Mountains of dazzling white cloud climbed high, a promised land in the sky.

Those are the hills of heaven, where I shall never reach.

After a while, she stopped her tears, and prepared for her own next journey, into Sabayon, the land of the dead.

TWO

A CHILD OF
THE DUST

1970

NEW YORK

The young woman called Sakura Ueda was tense. Her mouth was so dry that she could hardly thank the driver. She paid him and got out of the taxi. Before going in, she stood in front of the building, nervously smoothing her dress over her thighs. The checked miniskirt was very short, and gave her long legs a coltish look that she did not like. She was over thirty, or so she believed, much too old to look like a gawky schoolgirl. But she had few clothes to choose from, and certainly no money to purchase a new wardrobe for this encounter.

In fact, she was wearing exactly the same clothes as the last time she had come here, the same tan pumps, the same beige blouse and light jacket. The light tropical clothes were too thin for the winter cold, and the bag slung over her shoulder contained little money. She was getting right down to zero. She would eat today and tomorrow. After that, she did not know. Taxis were expensive, but in case anybody was watching, she had chosen to arrive in style, rather than emerge from the subway entrance only fifty yards from the building, or get off the bus that stopped nearby.

She looked upward. Francine Lawrence's Manhattan office gave little outward indication of the woman's global wealth. The block was an old one on the outskirts of Chinatown. Sakura knew that when she was in town, Francine would lunch daily at one of the many cheap Cantonese or Szechuan restaurants farther down the street. That showed both a loyalty to her roots and a dislike of wasting money.

Francine's New York residence, farther uptown, on Park Avenue, was also unostentatious, but only on the outside. That building, too, was an older one, but the apartment was filled with wonderful European antiques. Sakura had glimpsed something of it when she had delivered flowers there a week earlier. The housekeeper who had answered the door had been flustered by the sight of such a huge bouquet, and had allowed her in, telling her to put the flowers in the kitchen. It was obvious that large bouquets of flowers were not regular arrivals in Francine Lawrence's life, which had surprised Sakura, who had been counting on the reverse.

She had paid for the flowers herself, of course, another reason why her dollars had run out so frighteningly fast. She had tried to extend her visit by making the housekeeper sign a spurious receipt for the flowers. Her heart beating wildly, she had tried to drink in the atmosphere of the place while the old woman fumbled shortsightedly for a pen. The furniture had been like nothing she had seen before, gleaming masterpieces out of French and Italian palaces, glowing oil paintings, Persian carpets, all of it (as far as Sakura could tell) of extraordinary value.

Right now, on the sidewalk, her heart was beating even more wildly than on that occasion. She closed her eyes for a moment, reaching for inner calm. She had rehearsed this moment so many times, and in so many ways. Yet now, all her prepared words had vanished, and her mind was empty. Perhaps it was better that way. She always did her best at improvisation, rather than rehearsed pieces.

The stream of pedestrians passing around her paid her little attention, though she was a striking young woman. Her face, with its discernible Asian lines, had the dewy freshness of an orchid. Her body was slender and graceful, so her clothes, cheap as they were, hung well on her. Her hair, a rich chestnut, tumbled down her back in shiny waves. With a little more skill, and when you got right down to it, a little more money, she would easily make the transition from striking to exquisite. Yet in her gaucheness there was also a kind of charm that the very beautiful seldom have, and that usually does not survive wealth.

She walked into the foyer and took the antiquated elevator up to the third floor, where she emerged to face a glass door bearing a plain sign reading Lawrence Enterprises. The thought that Francine Lawrence was behind that door made Sakura's legs turn to water. She tried to control her breathing, but she was panting as if she had run up the stairs.

Last time she had spoken to an elderly secretary. The memory of her kind manner helped steady Sakura's nerves now. She took a deep breath, and pushed the door open.

Last time, the reception area had been quiet. This time it was crowded.

Sakura's tension increased. That must mean Francine Lawrence was in. There were seven or eight people waiting patiently on the row of chairs, some clutching bulky briefcases, others leafing through magazines listlessly. Nobody paid her very much attention as she walked to the desk. The gray-haired woman behind the sign reading MRS. TAN looked up.

"Hello," Sakura said, leaning on the counter, her voice little more than a whisper.

"Oh, hello there," the woman answered. There was a vase with a few pink carnations on her desk. She had evidently been arranging the flowers, for now she picked up the vase and put it on the counter next to Sakura. She smiled at Sakura, but it was not the warm smile of the last interview. It was a tight little grimace, and the eyes behind the horn-rimmed glasses were watchful. "Miss Ueda, isn't it?"

"Yes," Sakura said. "Could I see Mrs. Lawrence this morning?"

"I'm afraid that's impossible."

Sakura thought she had misheard. "I beg your pardon?"

"Mrs. Lawrence asked me to tell you that she is not available."

"Not available? Did you tell her about me? What I said?"

"Of course, Miss Ueda. She specifically asked me to tell you she was not available to see you."

Sakura clung to the counter to keep upright. She felt she might fall, otherwise. "I don't understand!"

"There is nothing to understand. She does not wish to see you."

"Why not?"

"I really cannot say."

Sakura stared at Mrs. Tan blindly, her gray eyes wide. "What am I going to do?" she asked quietly.

She must have looked so ghastly that there was a flicker of something like pity in the secretary's eyes for a moment. She lowered her voice. "You could try again some other time," she murmured. "Maybe in two or three weeks. But I cannot promise anything."

"It will be too late by then," Sakura said.

"Can I give Mrs. Lawrence any message from you?" Mrs. Tan asked.

Sakura was silent for a moment. "Tell her I—" She stopped to think. "Tell her I won't ever come to her again," she said in a flat voice. "Thanks for your time."

She turned and walked out of the office.

Out in the street, the world was spinning around her dizzily. She did not know which way to walk. It hardly mattered. Her sense of failure was overwhelming. She needed time and space to consider what to do next. Yet that hardly mattered, either. Given her absolute poverty, she would be starving within a day or two. Panic caught her by the throat, and she had to fight it down.

She walked slowly toward the subway entrance. For now, she needed to go back where she had come from, and rest. She checked her purse, counting out the few coins she would need for her token. She found the New York subway system complex and difficult to understand, and down in the echoing concourse, she spent a long time staring at the map, figuring out the route she should take and where she should change trains.

She boarded her train, and sat staring at her reflection in the opposite window. Why? Why had Francine Lawrence rejected her like this? Had she done or said something wrong, made some tiny slip that had raised doubt? Did Francine Lawrence think she was a fraud? But what could possibly have aroused her suspicions? Sakura could not imagine.

She felt stiflingly hot, barely able to breathe. Awkwardly, she shuffled out of her jacket and laid it on her lap. She pushed up her sleeves and closed her eyes, her body rocking passively to the beat of the train. Her mind searched for something to console the pain.

As always, she thought of Japan, of cherry-blossom time. That was what her name meant in Japanese, "cherry blossom." She had been called that because it was at that time that she had first been brought to Japan. She remembered it so clearly. Among the dark, turbulent, and sometimes wildly confused memories she had of her childhood, that stood out like a beacon: the wonder of those acres of pink-and-white froth, the way the petals had carpeted the ground. It was the first vision she'd been given of pure beauty, and it had stayed with her, just as her name had.

She was not Japanese, though she had been given a Japanese name, and had lived in Japan for a time; she could not say what nationality she belonged to. Concepts like nationality were alien to her way of thinking. But those syllables, *Sakura Ueda,* were among the very few things in this wide world that were truly hers, and she would cling to them until the day she died.

She opened her eyes with a jolt, feeling that she was drifting into sleep. She had to change trains here. She gathered up her jacket and her bag, and got off the train.

She pushed her way through the crowds, found the platform she needed, and got on the train. She picked listlessly at her nails as she rocked in her seat. The polish was chipped and flaking off. She could not even afford a bottle of polish remover to clean her nails. She looked up sadly. The car was half-empty. Opposite her, a tall black man was sitting in a coiled slouch. The plump white woman next to him had drawn herself, consciously or unconsciously, as far away from him as she could. The man was a symphony in black. He wore wraparound sunglasses that looked as though they had been carved out of the same material as the rest of his face, a glossy hardwood. He wore a black T-shirt and jacket, black pants, and black snakeskin boots. Even the elegant briefcase that lay negligently in the man's lap was black alligator.

The buckle of the briefcase pointed at her like the muzzle of a gun. Then Sakura looked closer, struck by something. Within the brass of the buckle, something gleamed at her. Convex optical glass. Not the muzzle of a gun. The eye of a camera. The briefcase contained a camera. And the camera was filming her.

Sakura froze. Her apathy evaporated at once, to be replaced by the sharp, clear fright of a creature that had been hunted many times before. She looked away.

She thought back to the office in Chinatown. Why had so many people been lounging on the waiting-room chairs? One of them had even come down in the elevator with her, and she had not paused to ask herself why he might be leaving, without keeping his appointment.

Her eyes slid back to the tall black man. His lean body radiated arrogant boredom. His face was like a mask, his head lolling to the beat of the train. But behind the wraparound dark glasses, she knew that his eyes were watching her.

Terror seized her. But she could not afford to panic now. The danger was far too imminent, far too urgent. She let her gaze drift away from the black man, to take in the others in the compartment. There would be more watchers, more followers. Professionals always carried out such work in teams, never alone. But if they were professionals, she knew it would be hard to detect them. The others in the team could be anybody, young or old, black, brown, or white.

Her only hope was to let them think she hadn't seen them. She rose as the next station approached, and prepared to get off the train. As she waited by the doors, looking out, she sensed the black man get up behind her and join a handful of others waiting to get off. Her heart was pounding in her throat.

The train slowed to a halt. The doors rattled open. She stepped out onto the platform, and began walking toward the far exit. She let her head hang down in a torpid way, her body language radiating weary disappointment. But she kept close to the train. The black man was behind her. Though he wore boots, his tread was silent. Beyond the black man was a young woman, looking in her shopping bag. Something about her too-relaxed gait told Sakura that she, too, was a member of the team.

The public-address system boomed out a warning to stay clear of the train doors. They started to hiss closed. When barely six inches of open space remained, Sakura unleased the clenched muscles of her stomach and legs. She sprang to the nearest door, thrusting her hands between the rubber seals, and wrenching them apart. She had underestimated the strength it would take: It was almost impossible. Somehow, she forced herself frantically through the tiny opening, hearing her clothes catch and tear. A shoe was twisted off, and she lost it.

"Are you crazy?" a voice squawked irritably from within the train. An elderly man helped pull her in, turning his face away from her as he did so, as if wearied by the endless foolishness of the young.

Her purse was trapped outside the doors. She turned and saw it fall to the platform. The last of her money was in there. And her cigarettes. And she only had one shoe. She took it off and stood in her stockinged feet, panting.

The black man had run up to the doors, and was trying to pry them open from the outside. Sakura shrank back in horror as the doors opened a few inches. He grimaced with the effort, his teeth gleaming.

Then the train jolted, and began moving out of the station. The black man fell back, defeated. Sakura sagged weakly, all her strength gone now. She had done it. Nobody else had got on the train with her, and now nobody else could. Sakura peered out of the window. The last thing she saw before the tunnel blacked it all out was her pursuer, stooping to pick up her fallen bag.

"Why wasn't she picked up at the next stop?"

Clay Munro's face showed no emotion. "We got to the next stop in a couple of minutes and got straight on the first train that came in. But she wasn't on it."

"She vanished into thin air?"

"It was a busy time, Mrs. Lawrence. Lots of people, lots of trains. Maybe we got the wrong train."

"How did she discover she was being followed?"

"I think she made the camera in my briefcase. I was sitting opposite her."

Francine was grim. "You sat opposite her? Clay, are you under the impression that you're inconspicuous?"

Munro toyed with the wraparound dark glasses he had worn while following Sakura Ueda. "When Mrs. Tan gave me the brief, she told me it didn't really matter if the subject became aware she was being investigated. She said that came from you."

"I didn't mean that you should lose her in the first five minutes," Francine snapped.

There was a yellow light in Munro's eyes. He did not enjoy failure, and he did not enjoy Francine's displeasure. "She's done this kind of thing before," he said in his deep rumble.

"What do you mean?"

"The way she made our tail, the way she lost us. Taking flowers to your apartment and getting inside. She's been around."

Francine had arrived from Hong Kong the day before to hear the bad news from Clay Munro. That Sakura Ueda had actually penetrated her apartment had added insult to injury. There was no doubt the mysterious flowers had been brought by her for the purpose of gaining entry. Everyone who knew Francine well knew that she disliked cut flowers. No friend would have sent them. And her housekeeper's description of the delivery girl coincided exactly with Cecilia Tan's description of Sakura. The insolence of that act was disturbing. Last night Francine had prowled her apartment uneasily, ostensibly checking that nothing was missing, but really casting about for some trace of the intruder's psychic scent. She had picked the bouquet apart, flower by flower, looking in vain for some further evidence of treachery. There had been nothing, just a heap of flowers and petals that she'd angrily thrown in the trash. Francine studied him for a moment. "Yes," she said. "I think you're right. I think she must be a professional of some kind. You must not underestimate her again."

"I won't." Clay Munro had been providing security and detective work for Francine Lawrence for two years. He was a former army officer who had been badly wounded in Vietnam. Discharged from the army, he had set up a small but effective security agency. He had been recommended to her when she'd needed help, and she had been impressed by him. He had worked well for her. The fact that he was black had appealed to her. Like her, he belonged to a marginalized community. Like her, he was a formidable fighter.

He was a powerful man in his mid-thirties, with a taste for expensive conservative suits. His office was a stark place; all the man's many secrets were securely locked behind the impregnable gray steel cabinets that lined three walls. At Francine's behest, he had rooted out spies, dug up secrets, protected her business, and even, on occasion, her person. Though he was a grim, almost forbidding man, she continued to prefer his services to those of bigger, less personal agencies, and she had never been disappointed in him. Until today.

"But I wouldn't necessarily say she was a pro. That trick of jumping trains—it was crude."

"It fooled you."

Munro accepted the rebuke with the merest inclination of his head. "She could have fallen under the train, or busted her arms. It took courage to do that. Or desperation."

"What do you mean?"

"She didn't just run like a thief. She ran like her life depended on it. Like all hell was behind her. She's a very frightened bunny."

Francine swung in her chair. "She *should* be frightened," she said.

"Another thing. She's not Japanese. Take a look at the pictures."

Munro passed her the file. It was thick; if nothing else, he had reaped a rich harvest of photographs. The young woman standing at the counter in the office, her short skirt revealing good legs, her clean profile set off by the long hair. The young woman out in the street, head down, the sunlight patterning her blouse. The young woman waiting in the subway, her shadowed and melancholy eyes gazing down the tunnel as if staring at her own fate.

"She's five foot seven," Munro said. "A hundred and twelve pounds, brown hair midway down the back, gray eyes, fair complexion. Approximately thirty years old. Pretty. She's got some Asian features, but I'd guess at least one parent was white."

Francine leafed through the pictures, pausing only at those that offered a glimpse of the woman's face. Her throat tightened. Why was this young woman so familiar to her? Why did she keep seeing flashes of other faces in these black-and-white images, of her own mother, her own father, her husband? *Of course,* a voice inside said angrily; *that's why they chose her—because she looks as Ruth might have looked.*

"The best picture is at the bottom," Munro said. "It was the last one I took, on the subway, just before she got off."

In this picture, Sakura Ueda had taken off her jacket and laid it on her lap. She wore a simple blouse, and she had pushed the sleeves up to reveal slim, pretty arms. She was staring straight into the lens, her eyes wide. Her face was oval, with a full mouth and a short, slightly snub nose. The eyes were large and almond-shaped, and in this shot, at least, wore a haunting expression of anxiety.

"There's something interesting about that particular shot," Munro said. He passed a magnifying glass across the desk to her. "Take a look at the left arm."

Francine held the picture closer, studying it through the glass. Then her heart seemed to stop inside her. Goose bumps washed across her skin.

There was no question about it. The tattoo circled the forearm just below the elbow, like a bracelet. The sleeve almost covered it, but it was there in the grain of the print. A geometric pattern of three parallel zigzag lines, with spaced dots. It was black, or some very dark color.

"I've never seen a tattoo quite like that before," Munro said. "It's rare for women to get tattoos anyway, but this is not your run-of-the-mill tattoo-parlor stuff. It looks kind of primitive."

"It is primitive," Francine said.

Munro noted the tone of her voice. "You've seen tattoos like this before?"

She nodded. "In Borneo."

She had given Munro a brief explanation of the background to this inquiry, and now his eyes narrowed. "Does that mean this is your daughter, after all?"

"No, it doesn't mean that," Francine replied.

"Hold on," Munro said. "Did your daughter get a tattoo like this in Borneo?"

"Not while I was with her."

"But it might have been done later on, when she was older?"

"The people I was with, the Ibans, tattoo themselves like that. But only the men do it, Clay. Not the women. Certainly not a girl-child. In all the years I visited there, I never saw a woman or a girl tattooed in this way."

"So this thing on her arm is a fake?" Munro looked more closely at the photograph with the magnifier.

"It's probably a real tattoo. But that does not make it genuine. A person who was ignorant about the Ibans might have a tattoo like that done, to try and fool me, if the stakes were high enough." She paused. "Or it could be a rare exception, and genuine."

Munro's piercing eyes were hooded again. "What do *you* believe?"

She was silent for a long time. When she spoke again, her voice was strained. "Not long after I left Ruth at that Iban village, the Japanese came.

They slaughtered men, women, and children. Then they burned down the longhouses. Only a handful survived. Of that handful, the most reliable witness clearly remembered seeing Ruth bayoneted by a soldier. I don't believe my daughter is alive."

Her face was pale and taut, but she showed no sign of tears. Munro tapped the photograph. "But you still want to talk to this girl, right?"

"Yes, Clay. I want to talk to her," Francine said quietly.

"You want me to find her again?"

"I want you to find her. I don't care what it costs, or how you do it. But find her."

Clay Munro's eyes glittered. "I'll find her."

"I felt sure it was her, right from the start."

Cecilia Tan, not given to expressions of emotion, was trembling. They were sitting at the very back of the Dragon Pearl, a Cantonese restaurant down the street from the office. Its crude facade put off all but its regular customers, mostly drawn from the people who lived or worked on the street. Francine nodded for the waiter to pull the carved screen farther across.

"Don't be a fool, Cecilia," she said flatly. "You never knew her."

"I know this," Cecilia replied obstinately. "There is something about her. Some special quality."

The waiter adjusted the screen to shelter them, shielding their table from eavesdroppers or lip-readers. It also blocked off the light from the street, so she could take off her dark glasses. "Repeat what she said," she commanded Cecilia. Though Munro had placed a man with recording equipment close to the reception desk, the young woman's voice had been unusually soft, and only a dim murmur had been recorded.

"It was no more than a few words. She asked for you, and I told her what you instructed me to say. She seemed very shocked, and I thought she was going to faint. I hinted she might try again in a couple of weeks. She said it would be too late." Cecilia glanced at Francine. "She said, 'It will be too late by then.' "

Francine grunted. "You didn't ask *why* it would be too late?"

"You did not authorize me to interrogate her. Francine," Cecilia said, with a rare use of her first name, "how many serani girls are running around New York with longhouse tattoos on their arms? What are the odds?" She had tried to advise Francine against this brutal and foolish course of action, and now her whole small, neat person radiated reproach. "She was you, exactly."

Francine was contemptuous. "She was *me*?"

"Like you used to be. When I first knew you."

"How was that?"

"She was innocent."

Francine smiled ironically. "And now have I lost my innocence, Cecilia?"

Cecilia shot her a look. "We all lose certain qualities."

"I used to be very different," Francine said quietly. "I used to be a soft, yielding, frightened girl-woman who did as I was told. I worshiped my husband. I believed that without a man to protect me, I was nothing. But the war changed me." The carved dragons of the screen cast baroque shadows on their faces, snarling fangs, grasping claws, twisting tails. "I learned to rely on myself and to trust nobody. I learned to survive alone." Francine arranged the chopsticks beside her bowl. "What else about the woman struck you?"

"She was pathetic."

"Then she played her part well."

Cecilia's cheeks colored. "I'm too old to fall for hard-luck stories," she said. "I felt sorry for her because she was defenseless and unwell."

"She looked sick?"

"No, she didn't look sick. But there was something about her. She isn't well."

Francine's eyes narrowed. "Explain."

"I can't. There was something about her."

Francine was exasperated. "Cecilia, that must be the hundredth time you've repeated, 'There was something about her.' Can't you think of something better to say?"

Cecilia turned back to her food sulkily. "You asked me to tell you in my own words."

Francine sighed. "Yes, I did." Beyond the dragon screen, the restaurant was bustling. No English was being spoken. For Francine, it was an indulgence to be here, wrapped in the sights, sounds, and tastes of the East, in the midst of Manhattan. Though half of her was Western, she always went for refuge to her Chinese side.

"You still don't believe it, do you?" Cecilia said. "Not even now!"

"Belief without proof is faith. I don't have very much faith anymore."

"What makes you think she's a fraud?"

"Cecilia," Francine said patiently, "I am a very rich woman. And I am not getting any younger. If some credible young woman could persuade me that she was my long-lost daughter, what couldn't she get out of me? She would be able to take millions, Cecilia." Francine's face was tight. "What do you think I would do, if Ruth were really alive, and came to me again? My joy would be without equal. She would live as a queen. She would take anything she wanted from me, have anything she desired."

"And what if this woman *is* Ruth?"

"That remains to be seen," Francine said, reverting to her usual composure.

The waiter eased the screen aside to put more bowls on their table, pork and shrimp dumplings, stir-fried clams, steamed scallops. He also brought fresh pots of green tea. "Try and remember all you can, Cecilia."

"She was fragile," Cecilia said. "She was vulnerable. She was deeply hurt when I told her you would not see her. I could see the pain in her eyes. Like an animal when you strike it. And what's more," Cecilia went on firmly, "I could tell she had had a hard life. She had suffered. People had hurt her, a lot of people. But she had survived. And now she came to you for help."

"You could tell all this?" Francine could not help saying, with mild irony. "At first, all you told me was that she was a smart young woman."

"That was the first time I saw her. The second time, I saw that she had a soul. A suffering soul."

Francine sighed again, wondering if she would ever get anything more sensible than this kind of drivel from Cecilia. "Cecilia, remember that this woman got herself into my apartment under false pretenses. No honest person, no person with good intentions, would have done that."

"She came to the office on the Festival of the Hungry Ghosts." Cecilia's eyes were sly, as though she'd made a telling point.

They ate in silence for a while. "Well," Francine said at last, "we'll just have to wait until Clay Munro finds her again. Then we will see what this hungry ghost has to say for herself."

Clay Munro had woken up early on this winter morning. He sat by the window, picking through Sakura Ueda's possessions. He had already been through all her stuff a dozen times, but he couldn't stop going over it yet again.

She didn't have a thing worth more than five dollars. He picked up the tan leather shoe and studied it. It was old, but had been regularly polished, and it had a new heel. The shoe of a woman who didn't have much money, and who had to make her things last. Not exactly the profile of a master criminal. He tossed it aside.

He counted the money. Fifteen dollars and sixty cents. No checkbook. If this was all she had, she was going to be hungry when she woke up this morning. He raked through the other things. A pack of cigarettes, nearly empty. A book of matches. A map of New York, which he pulled open. There was a ballpoint circle around Francine Lawrence's office address, but no other notes.

Impatiently, he held the bag upside down and shook it. A few loose items clattered onto his desk.

The woman in the bed stirred into wakefulness. She blinked at him over a smooth, naked shoulder. "Whatcha doing?" she asked drowsily.

"Go back to sleep," Munro growled. He picked through Sakura Ueda's makeup, his powerful hands surprisingly precise. Cheap stuff. None of it revealing anything about the owner except her poverty. A compact with a cracked mirror. She didn't carry, probably couldn't afford, perfume; but a faint trace of something sweet lingered on the plastic brush. He inhaled, holding it to his nose. Jasmine, maybe. There were a couple of long, glossy hairs caught in the bristles. He pulled them loose and held them up to the wintry light. They glinted tantalizingly. He let them fall onto his desk.

He swiveled the lipstick out of its tube. A nice-nice, neutral color, worn right down. He licked the pink button. It tasted the way lipstick always tasted, and he snorted the smell out of his nose with distaste.

The girl in the bed giggled. "Kinky, man." She had rolled onto her side, and was watching him with her chin cupped in her hand. "You wanna go through my bag, too?"

"No," Munro said.

"I carry much better stuff than that."

"Shit," he said quietly, tossing the bag away. He'd managed to get just about everything Sakura carried, and there wasn't even an address book in it. Bitch.

"Who is she?" the woman asked. "Your ex?"

"Work," Munro said tersely.

She laughed. "Boy, are you thorough in your work. Come back to bed, sweetie pie, and I'll let you lick my lipstick, too."

He glanced at her. She was a cocktail waitress. He'd wound up in a club late last night, where his search for Sakura Ueda had developed into three double bourbons. Although the girl's skin was coffee-colored, she'd had her hair straightened and dyed blond. Last night, while she'd flirted with him over her tray, that platinum hair had seemed awfully cute to him. This morning, it didn't anymore. "I have to go out in a half hour," he said, dropping a big, fat hint. "Why don't you get dressed?"

"What about breakfast?" she asked, swinging her legs.

"I don't eat breakfast. Let's get moving, huh?"

He went to shower.

Munro rented an enormous loft in a building that had yet to be zoned for residences. Because nobody had even thought of living in it, except Munro, it was still a huge space by Manhattan standards, and he hadn't cluttered it up with too much furniture. He was a big man, and he liked space to move around in. He kept the place scrupulously clean and barrack-room neat. Now and then he bought a sofa or a table he liked, and he had even bought one piece of art, an African carving in some dark wood, which had cost him an obscene amount of money, in his opinion. The rest of the furnishing was air. Nothing detracted from the spectacular view of the Hudson.

He turned the shower as hot as he could take it and soaped himself vigorously, rinsing away the smell of the platinum blond and her expensive perfume. The water exploded off his hard muscles. He'd always worked mercilessly on his fitness. Growing up in a Brooklyn neighborhood filled mainly with Italians and Poles, he'd needed to be strong. He'd had no older brothers, though his five sisters were each and every one a piece of work, and he'd had to defend himself and his baby brother, Lou, on the street from four years old. Luckily, he'd grown fast and big.

He glanced down at the scar that crossed his broad chest, where the shrapnel had ripped him open.

Munro had faced the battle injury with the same fierce determination with which he had faced all the other challenges in his life, starting with birth into an overlarge, impoverished family, governed by a brutal police-patrolman father and run by domineering older sisters. He'd clenched his teeth and gotten himself fit again. As the army doctors had predicted, he didn't really miss the spleen that they had removed. He was making a good recovery. He couldn't run the eight hundred meters in under two minutes anymore, but he was getting too old for the track, anyway.

He was getting stronger daily. He was winning back his physical confidence. A hole had been blown through him, but he was rebuilding steadily.

He'd been sent to Vietnam in 1963, hard on the heels of the Communist takeover. He had been one of the first Americans in the country, and the whole thing had seemed like a big adventure. While in Alabama and Mississippi people of his color had faced police dogs and fire hoses, beatings, shootings, and bombings, he'd been an ambitious young officer intent on proving that the army had made a sweet deal for itself promoting him to captain.

America had been a world away. The day of Martin Luther King's Lincoln Memorial rally, he'd been wading armpit deep in the Mekong. They'd heard snatches of the "I have a dream" speech on VOA, and though Munro had never taken part in a civil-rights march in his life, he'd cried, picking leeches off his legs.

He'd cried again the day JFK had been assassinated. He'd been under heavy fire that day, his face pressed into the weeds, machine-gun rounds battering the jungle all around him. He'd felt a long, long way from home.

Despite the way his head had been slowly ballooning, heading for the point of final explosion, he had fallen deeply and irrevocably in love with the green marvel that was Vietnam. Munro had been an urban child, unused to gentleness or natural beauty. Vietnam had entered his veins like a drug. In his tours there, he had seen Vietnam crisscrossed by lines of trenches, concertina, and razor wire, disemboweled by B-52s, defoliated with dioxin, defaced, degraded, and raped on every side. He had felt as though the same had been done to him.

He had been sent home in a body cast in December 1967, by which time the adventure had been long over, and he'd been through the acid bath of several kinds of disillusionment.

His first and last glimpses of Vietnam had been through the open door of a chopper. On the last occasion, antiaircraft fire from a Chinese 37-millimeter cannon had been ripping through the fuselage. As they went down, it had been Munro who had given their coordinates on the radio, and set off the emergency locator beacon. Then searing metal had punched a hole in his chest, and his lungs had filled with blood.

A search team backed by Skyraiders had been deployed to find them. Clay Munro had been the only one left alive, and so little alive that the men who found him had begun zipping him into a body bag before loading him on. He had just managed to move his hands to get their attention, and that had saved him.

When he'd gotten back home, his father had wanted him to join the police force. He'd started nagging him, the way he'd done when Munro was seventeen. Munro's younger brother, Lou, had already graduated from cop school near the top of his class. But Munro hadn't wanted to put on another uniform. Mentally, Vietnam had scarred him more deeply than any bullet. In tranquil jungle villages, he had seen and done things that haunted him, and would haunt him for years.

He knew with razor sharpness what the army had done to him. He knew the tracks where the rage monster roamed in his heart now. He knew that he had forever lost those frail bonds that kept other men civilized.

If he had not been wounded in the army, he sometimes felt he might have ended up really badly, the way he had seen other burned-out veterans go. Jail, or addiction, or maybe stabbed in some whorehouse brawl. If he joined the police force, he could see himself, somewhere down the line, kicking bums to death in alleyways, beating confessions out of punks, winding up swallowing the bottle, or a bullet. Winding up like his father. The way his brother was headed.

That was why he had started his own business, so that he would never become someone else's weapon again. The first time he saw, or was asked to do, something he despised, he could turn around and walk away. He needed that. He needed to be in control over the strange, dangerous animal that Clay Munro had become.

He turned off the shower and emerged, toweling himself dry. He'd been fully hoping that the cocktail waitress would be dressed and gone, but she was in the kitchen, wearing one of his handmade shirts, fixing breakfast. She'd done a lightning repair job with her makeup. "How do you like your eggs?" she asked him.

"Over easy," he grunted, displeased at the invasion.

"Coming up." She bent to throw eggshells in the trash, and her rounded buttocks peeked out from under the tails of his shirt. He glowered at her, trying to remember her name. It came to him hazily. Chantal.

He dressed, meticulous about the fit of his clothes and the way they matched. Ties were a particular problem. He had to buy them where the fat guys bought their clothes, for his towering height made normal ties look silly, and fat guys seemed to have poor taste in ties. He chose a red-and-yellow silk stripe, and knotted it scrupulously.

Chantal laid breakfast on the table. "I love this place," she told him eagerly. "You have wonderful taste." She came to him, and draped her arms around his neck. She looked up at him, her eyelids drooping. "And I want to tell you something else," she said softly. "You are the best, best lover I ever had in my life. You took me to heaven and back." She tried to pull his head down so she could kiss his mouth, but his neck was as unyielding as a tree trunk.

He was itching to get back on the trail of Sakura Ueda. She had made a monkey out of him, and he wanted to get his hands on her again, soon. "I'm in a hurry."

"It's not even seven, Clay."

He pushed her away impatiently. "I have to go. Get dressed."

She looked hurt. "What about your eggs?"

"I don't want them."

"You said you liked them over easy!"

"That's the way I like them, but I never eat breakfast. I told you. Get dressed, Chantal. I want to lock up."

"It's Chiffon, not Chantal!"

He shrugged.

Her face tightened. "So last night didn't mean a thing to you?" she asked incredulously.

His mouth curled. "Are you kidding?"

"All that stuff you did—it was just routine?"

"It's called sex."

"Where I come from, you only do that stuff if you really care about someone!"

"Chiffon," he said, his temper rising, "let's move, huh? And take my shirt off. Those cost me thirty dollars each."

She hauled off his shirt and flung it at him, her breasts bouncing. "Screw you."

"Screw you, too."

She started snatching up her clothes. "You don't have to be like this."

"These are yours," he said, throwing her lace panties at her. He picked up the plates she had set out and shook the eggs and bacon into the trash.

"You put out some really bad vibes, man," she said stiffly. "You're really fucked up, you know that?"

"You named that tune in one." He washed the plates and put them on the rack. "Are we ready?"

She pulled on her clothes in silence, her eyes puffy. He held the door open for her. There was always something poignant to Munro about a woman in evening clothes and slingbacks at seven in the morning. Also, now that he looked at her, she was very young, despite the makeup and the golden beehive. He felt a moment of pity for her. "Look, I'm really busy . . . uh . . ." He groped for her name, but he'd forgotten it again. ". . . uh, honey. It's nothing personal."

"I worked that part out, uh, honey."

"How long you worked in that club?"

"Two months," she said sullenly.

"You have to learn something. You work in a club, guys take you home at closing time, chances are high they're not looking for a permanent relationship. You know what I mean?"

"Chances are high they'll remember my name next morning."

"I remember the fun we had," he said, trying to be kind.

"Oh, get fucked," she said. She walked away from him, her high heels snapping on the flooring. At least he didn't have to offer her a lift anywhere. He shut his door and locked the two dead bolts carefully, by which time she was out of the building and out of his mind. He was ready to get back on the trail.

Sakura was shivering. She felt ill, so ill that it was displacing her anger. She had lost her purse, her last few dollars, and one of her only two pairs of good shoes. She felt the loss with the acute anguish that only people who own very few possessions can know. She mourned the shoe more than the purse. She could get by with a plastic bag, if it came to that, but her only other shoes were sneakers, unsuitable for walking in winter. And walking was what she did. She had walked a long way in those tan shoes, and she had relied on them to carry her a lot farther.

The loss of the money was also painful, even though it would have run out tomorrow, anyway. It brought hunger a day closer than necessary. She felt as though a huge chunk of her tight little world had been ripped away. She felt more helpless than ever. *I hate you,* she thought bitterly. *I didn't ask you for anything, and you sold me to my enemies.*

She huddled against the window, hugging herself tightly. It made her flesh creep to think of how close she had come to capture. All those people in the waiting room, all of them had been enemies. Their idle conversation had been the meaningless murmuring of stage extras, waiting for the action to begin. Their briefcases had concealed cameras, recording equipment, walkie-talkies. The vase of carnations lifted onto the counter had been a signal to the dogs that this was their quarry. They had followed her out, and had been tracking her to her home when she'd spotted them.

They had reckoned without her razor instincts. They did not know that she had survived in cities beside which New York was a kindergarten. They could not even begin to imagine the places she had been, or the things she had done.

And she, for her part, had misjudged the woman. She had not expected open arms, but she had expected that the woman would at least let her in and give her a fair hearing. She had not dreamed of this betrayal.

She recalled the face of the black devil on the train, and shuddered. It had been pitiless. Francine Lawrence had thrown her to the dogs, knowing they would tear her to pieces. Knowing that her fate would be the torture chamber and a brutal death.

What had she done to the woman to merit this? She thought of the flowers she had taken to the apartment. Had the woman guessed that had been her? But she had stolen nothing, damaged nothing. She had simply left an anonymous gift. It had been a stupid, risky thing to do, but her nerves had been taut, and she had needed something to stop herself from going crazy. She had not deserved this.

She rested her head on the glass. She had to get out of New York. She needed money urgently.

The tiny second floor room looked out at a vista of drab buildings just like this one. Between the buildings, she could see glimpses of the river and the George Washington Bridge. Planes roared overhead every few minutes. There was a railway line nearby, too, and trains rattled past all night long.

The man she rented it from, Stefan, was an Albanian, a street artist. He went out each morning, carrying his chalks and his portfolio. He sat on the sidewalk, drawing the portraits of tourists for five dollars a throw. That was how she had met him. He'd had a little paper attached to his fold-up easel, reading ROOM TO LET.

She heard his footstep on the stairs, and pulled away from the window. She forced herself to stop shivering. That was not going to help. She went to the mirror to straighten herself out. She had lost comb, hair clips, and a lipstick in the satchel, and that did not help, either. Luckily, she had left a few things on the basin—her other lipstick, mascara, and a hairbrush.

Everything else she had was in her duffel bag, which stood at the end of her bed. It was an old habit of hers to live out of a suitcase, never to put anything in drawers or in cupboards. It took too long to pack, if you needed to leave quickly. This way, all she had to do was grab the bag and run.

She used the cosmetics to put some color in her face. Then she brushed her hair and pulled her clothes straight. She practiced some smiles in the mirror, memorizing the warmest one. She slipped on the sneakers, took a couple of deep breaths, and went out.

She knocked on Stefan's door. There was a long pause before she heard him call, "Who is it?"

She prided herself on having learned excellent English—she was a gifted linguist—but they conversed in French. "*C'est moi.* Sakura. Can I come in?"

"Yes."

His apartment had two rooms, both with large, north-facing windows, which she supposed was good for his work. The smell of oil paint and turpentine was intoxicating. Canvases were stacked everywhere. This was where Stefan did his real work, which was startlingly different from the photographic likenesses he churned out in the park. It was very hot. Stefan had stripped to his vest, and was brewing some coffee over a portable gas burner. He glanced at her with dark, opaque eyes. He was not a bad-looking man, though he was twenty years older than she was, and his face was scarred down one cheek. He was a taciturn, contained person who did not waste words.

"Hi," she said brightly, trying to remember the warm smile.

"Something is wrong," he said flatly.

She let the smile go. "Yes, something is wrong, Stefan. I lost my purse today, and I have no money."

"Ah-hah," he said.

"I can't pay your rent," she said quietly. "I can't even buy any food. I was wondering if we could come to an arrangement."

"What kind of arrangement?"

"I could do some work around here. Cook for you. Wash your clothes. Clean the place up. It's pretty filthy. It could do with cleaning."

His sallow face did not change. "If the place is so dirty, why don't you leave?"

"I have nowhere to go," she said, anxiously aware that she had offended him. "I don't mean to insult your house. I'm glad to be here, believe me."

"I don't want anything cleaned. I don't need my food cooked for me."

She felt despair wash away her tiny sand castle of hope. "I'm a very good cook. I know how to make terrific food really cheap. Oriental, Western, whatever you like."

"I'm not interested in food." He poured boiling water carefully over the coffee grounds, and the bitter smell mingled with the turpentine and linseed oil aroma. "But you could do something else for me."

She swallowed. "What?"

He studied the coffee without looking at her. "Take off your clothes."

She felt sick. She had been raped, and had survived that. But she had never willingly sold her body for money. She had probably done far worse things, in the eyes of whatever gods were watching her, but that was an inner barrier she had never wanted to cross. Right now, however, she was at the end of all her resources. After Stefan lay the street. She would rather beg than whore. But she had seen the beggars of New York, and she did not want that. They were what she had dreaded becoming all her life.

"I didn't mean that kind of arrangement," she said in a low voice.

"What?" He was a strange man, and he seemed to have forgotten what they were talking about.

"I said, I didn't mean that kind of arrangement. I'm not a prostitute."

He stared at her. "I never said you were. What's your name, again?"

"Sakura."

"I'm not talking about sex, Sakura. I'm talking about painting you."

"You want me to model?"

"If you're right. Take your clothes off."

She did not trust him, any more than she trusted any other human creature. But there was no other way, right now. She had to think of the money, and what it would buy. If he came after her, there was a bunch of palette knives in a jar within reach. Slowly, she undressed. Stefan stood swirling the coffee in the pot, watching her step out of her skirt.

"The underwear, too," he said.

Her face flamed. She took off her bra and panties, driving her shame to a small, hot place inside her. "Okay?"

"Turn around," he commanded. She obeyed, facing the peeling door. "Turn back to face me." Again, she obeyed. Stefan was studying her through half-closed eyes, a man trying to decide whether a piece was real or forged. "Lift your arms." She did so, waiting for him to say something, do something. At last he nodded. "You can put your clothes back on, now," he said, and turned away dismissively.

Humiliated and disappointed, yet also relieved, she dressed herself quickly. "You don't want to paint me?" she asked in a low voice, zipping up her dress.

"I'll pay you four dollars an hour to pose. Three hours at a time. It's not a permanent job," he said, as he saw the light in her eyes. "I can only paint you so many times. Maybe for a week. After that, it's finished. I lose interest. But while you pose for me, you don't have to pay rent. Okay?"

"Okay, Stefan," she said, her voice trembling.

"When you cease to interest me, you either start paying rent, or you get out of the room. Understood?"

"Understood, Stefan. Thank you."

He had made two cups of coffee, and he held one out to her now. "You want?"

"Yes, please." She took the coffee and drank gratefully. Stefan never seemed to smile. Perhaps, like her, he had suffered, because although she knew how to smile on the outside, on the inside she never smiled, either.

Francine studied the photographs of Sakura Ueda obsessively.

There was a dependable system, Clay Munro had informed her, that could determine whether photographs of an adult and a child were of the same person, by comparing the relative proportions of the faces. But she had no childhood pictures of Ruth. Everything she'd carried with her had been lost along the way. Everything. And when she'd finally gotten back to the house she'd shared with Abe in Perak, it was to find that it had been incinerated years before, the blackened wreckage already half-swallowed by the jungle. She had raked through the compacted ash, looking for something, anything, that might recall the life she had lost. All she had found were a few spoons twisted by the heat.

All she had were memories.

They were vivid enough. The years had not faded them. But her memories were of a child. The photograph she held in her hands was of a grown woman who, if she was who she claimed to be, would now be past thirty years old. There was a similarity, yes. But the Ueda woman wore some makeup, and even a little color, skillfully applied, could emphasize or minimize a similarity.

Between this grainy black-and-white image and the one in her mind lay a void so great that she could not fill it with her imagination. So many stages had been lost: girlhood, adolescence, the flowering of womanhood. All had passed by without her seeing them.

Once she had Sakura Ueda in her possession, she would arrange blood tests. Those, at least, could give an "impossible" or "possible" verdict. Nothing more; right now, no technology existed to unquestionably confirm that one human being was another's child.

She would also scrub the Ueda woman, scour off her makeup, strip her, and see if the similarity stood up when she had nothing more to hide behind.

More importantly, she would find out whether the Ueda woman had photographs of herself as a child, or as a teenager, closer to the age Ruth had been. Such photographs, if they existed, could fill in the gaps in a way that nothing else could.

Whatever story the woman told of herself would be colorful and probably pathetic, but would count for little. Not, at least, until Francine had some harder evidence. Pathetic stories were easy to dream up. The girl had already twisted Cecilia Tan around her little finger. She was probably a consummate actress. In a sense, Francine did not want to meet the woman, or even see her, for fear she might get sucked in, too. Perhaps, once they got their hands on her, Francine would ask Clay Munro to hold her in some secure place, and get an intermediary to do the interrogation. That way, they could make decent progress before she had to face the woman in the flesh. Yes, that was probably best.

Francine got up and made herself a pot of jasmine tea. Her balcony doors were open, and the constant noise of Park Avenue traffic filtered in. Since the intrusion of the Ueda girl, she had decided to get herself a dog. The result was diligently chewing one of her slippers on the balcony, a golden bundle of fluff she had christened Mr. Wu. He was a chow chow, a member of that breed the Chinese called Lion Dogs, famous for their devotion to their owners and their distrust of strangers. Francine expected Mr. Wu to have sharper instincts than Julia Lo, the elderly housekeeper who took care of the apartment for her.

She went out to check on him. At her arrival, the puppy rolled onto his back and beamed up at her adoringly, his blue-black tongue lolling. She bestowed on him one of her rare smiles.

Someone had once told her that dogs saw only in black and white. That had seemed logical to her. Dogs were not easy to fool. That was what she liked about them. Dogs knew by instinct whether people were good or bad. They were not taken in by charm or a sweet smile or a plausible story. They could give you an instant yes or no, and they did not change their minds.

She reached down and tickled the puppy's silky stomach. "Good boy," she murmured. She already felt fonder of him than she was of most people she knew. "Good boy."

Clay Munro walked into the public library. The place was swarming with kids from a neighborhood school doing some project. For once, the building hummed with life, its echoing spaces filled with chattering voices.

He crossed the atrium and went to the counter. He leaned over. "Anybody home?"

His sister Vivian looked up from a filing cabinet and smiled. "Hi. I got your books."

"Great." Vivian was the closest of his sisters in age, only two years older than he, and maybe for that reason had been the only sister who hadn't routinely whacked him as a kid. Maybe that was also why she was now his favorite.

"I asked Central to send me everything they had, Clay. You probably won't need all of them. Pick the ones you want."

He hoisted the leaden pile onto the counter. Vivian had got him at least two dozen books on the Ibans of Borneo, mostly heavyweight anthropology tomes. He flicked through them, looking for photographs. "You're an angel, Viv."

"I absolutely am. How's it going?"

"Okay. You?"

"Yeah, never better." He looked up to smile at her. It was a smile Munro gave nobody else, warm and real. Vivian was going through a tough time. Her marriage had broken up, and she'd been left with three children to support on her own. She fiercely fought all his attempts at financial help, but he knew she was finding it hard to manage on a librarian's wage. "I mean it," she said. "I'm happy in the Lord."

He nodded. She'd got hooked up with a local church and was going through a religious phase. Munro didn't care so long as they gave her support. He also hoped she would meet a decent man there. She was a sweet-faced woman with a heart as big as a house, and he hoped she wouldn't be alone for long.

"You dating anybody?" she asked. With the racket the school kids were making, for once they could talk in normal voices. He hated the creepy silence that hung over libraries.

"No."

"You prefer meaningless sex with loose women."

"All I can get."

"That's so disgusting."

"Yes, ma'am."

"You're wasting the best years of your life, Clay," she said earnestly. "You don't know what you're missing. There's no love in what you do."

"No complications, either."

"Marriages are never perfect. But having children is what life is all about."

"Not my life, sis."

"I think you could make a woman very happy, Clay."

"I try to make a lot of women very happy. Ain't that better in the Lord's eyes?"

"Don't blaspheme. I wish you would come to my church this Sunday. I could introduce you to some wonderful girls."

"Amen, sister." He grinned. "I don't go for those hats with the plastic flowers in the brim."

"You'd be very surprised," she said.

"So would they." He had picked the three books that contained the most illustrations. "I'll take these. The rest can go back."

She stacked the books. "It's Mom and Pop's golden wedding anniversary next month. The fourteenth."

"I hadn't forgotten," he lied.

"We're buying them a silver dinner service."

"You don't think Mom's cleaned enough forks in her life?" Their mother had worked in a restaurant kitchen for forty years, and had needed a double hip operation as a result. Vivian ignored him.

"It's really beautiful. King's pattern, in a velvet-lined box. It works out at fifty dollars each."

Munro took out his wallet and passed her a hundred-dollar bill over. "Here."

"I'll send you change," she said.

"Don't want change."

"I'll mail it to you."

"Vivian," he said firmly, "buy your kids a present from me. Please."

She put the money away reluctantly. "You're going to be there, aren't you?" she demanded.

"Sure."

"This is their *golden wedding anniversary,* Clay. I'll call you the day before," she said meaningfully. He had been known to miss family occasions before, preferring to field the furious comments of his sisters the next day than spend an evening with his father.

"Okay." He blew her a kiss. "Gotta go. Thanks for the books."

His office was not far away, and he walked there fast. The operation to find Sakura Ueda was becoming very expensive. He had built a good team specifically for the job. But looking for a needle in a haystack was nothing compared to locating an individual in greater New York, especially an individual who had shown such a marked aversion to being located. Munro didn't even know if she was in the city. By now she could be in Chicago, for all anyone knew. Or in Tokyo.

His best immediate hope lay in the venal instincts of others. Munro had placed ads in the *News*, the *Times*, the *Post*, and *The Village Voice*. He had also put ads in a dozen smaller papers and publications. He was lucky enough to get the second or third page in some. The announcement was the same in all cases. It read, "SAKURA UEDA: Would she, or anyone knowing her whereabouts, please contact this number immediately." The office switchboard number followed. The second line simply read, in bold characters, "LARGE REWARD."

He had debated adding a photograph, maybe mentioning the tattoo. But that risked driving the girl even farther underground. He wanted somebody to turn her in, somebody she bought drugs from, someone she rented a room from, a boyfriend. If no helpful Judas turned up in the next couple of days, he was left with the prospect of a mass hunt, a costly operation that could last months and still fail.

He went into his office and sat at his desk. He had some of the surveillance shots that showed Sakura's tattoo, and he spread them out to compare them with the photographs in the books Vivian had found him.

Borneo had always seemed a dreamlike place to him, somewhere that only existed in wild stories, so it was a surprise to see in the photographs that it was a real place that looked a lot like Vietnam.

The Ibans were, he learned, a warlike and aggressive tribe. At the time these books had been published, they were still in the brutal practice of head-hunting. Head-hunting had only been stopped in the 1930s. It had been revived in the last year of the Second World War, when the Allies had enlisted the Ibans to help them drive the Japanese out of Borneo. He wondered how they had managed to get them to stop the custom after the war.

The photographs of the Ibans showed extraordinarily handsome, wild-looking people. In most cases, the women went bare-breasted, the men just about buck-naked. Their perfect physiques had not been stunted or bloated by any modern disease. The men were often heavily tattooed, mainly on the chest, forearms, and thighs. He found a passage that explained, in painful detail, how the tattoos were done, by piercing the skin with a bamboo punch and a hammer. The whole thing apparently hurt like hell. Getting the tattoos was a manly ordeal, so he learned, as well as an adornment. It didn't sound like something that would be popular with women.

And he could not find a single photograph showing a tattooed Iban woman. Francine Lawrence had been absolutely right about that.

He picked up one of the photographs of Sakura Ueda. The girl was beautiful. That was one incontrovertible fact. Francine Lawrence was a handsome woman, too. Could this really be her daughter, come back from the dead?

Francine Lawrence was right to be skeptical. She was worth millions. She would be crazy to let some gutter kid fool her, live high on the hog at her expense for a couple of months, then clean out the wall-safe when her back was turned. Munro respected few people, but in the time he had worked for Francine, he had come to respect her. He liked her hardness, her courage. He liked the fact that she was half-Chinese. She didn't think the way white people thought. She could think in reverse, the way he could. She looked in the shadows as well as the bright places. She could see the shapes of things that weren't there.

That was something it had taken Vietnam to teach him, how to see what wasn't there and hear what wasn't said. It was sometimes the most important observation of all.

He stared at Sakura Ueda's image now, wondering what he was missing, what he wasn't seeing, what wasn't there.

Sakura was tired. She felt pared to the bone. Her deep muscles had started to shake, and it was getting difficult to hold the pose Stefan had put her in. If only she didn't feel so terribly weak inside, if only the coughing would stop. The stifling warmth of his room made her skin prickle. She had suffered equatorial heat without sweating, but now she could feel it beading her eyelids and her upper lip. Another bout of coughing shook her.

"Can I smoke?" she asked hoarsely.

"With that cough?" he said, concentrating on his canvas.

She swallowed, her tongue stiff as a piece of leather. "I need a break, Stefan."

"In a while." He changed brushes. "Don't move your arms."

"You haven't even looked up for the past half hour."

"Don't move."

"I need to rest." Her voice was shaking. She sometimes wondered why he wanted her at all. She thought his photographic stuff was remarkable, but his oil studies of her were very different, not recognizable at all. He cut her body into pieces, like a chicken carcass in a market, a breast here, a hip there. "I need to rest, Stefan."

He tossed his fistful of brushes down irritably. "Very well. Rest."

"Thanks." She had to stay polite, keep pleasing him. He was her bread and butter. She was in pain as she got off the chair. She stretched her arms upward, trying to get some air into her lungs. Stefan's eyes were on the rise of her breasts.

"You want to fuck?" he offered quietly.

At once she was wary. "I told you. That was not the arrangement."

"It might help us both relax."

Sakura tried not to show her anger and disdain. After all, he could not see her suffering, or sense her spirit. "No. I want a cigarette, please."

Stefan walked toward her. Instantly, she tensed, her weight riding on her back foot. Stefan stopped short. Naked as she was, she looked as though she was ready to rip him open. The way she crouched made him think of some dangerous animal with razor claws. He held up one hand in a placatory gesture. Then he drew the blue pack of Gauloises from his pocket and offered her one. Warily, she took it and lit up. "You want coffee?" he said.

He meant the cold, black dregs of what he had brewed that morning, and she shook her head. "No."

"How long do you need?" he asked.

"Five minutes."

"Five minutes, no more."

Sakura pulled on the stained gown and wrapped it around her body. She walked to the window, sucking on the cigarette hungrily. The strong, acrid smoke sank into her lungs, making her cough violently. Tiny, luminous stars swam in front of her eyes. She waited for the dizziness to recede.

She smoked and coughed, her mind far away. Stefan was sitting with a cup of coffee, reading the *New York Post*. He never bought newspapers, usually managing to pick up a discarded one in the street. "Your French has a strange accent," he said laconically, flipping the pages. "Where did you learn it?"

"Vientiane," she replied absently.

"Vientiane?" He seemed unsurprised. "Is that an interesting place?"

It was his only term of judgment. Things were either interesting or not to Stefan. No other distinction seemed to matter. "Yes," she replied, "Vientiane is interesting."

"Really? I would have thought the opposite. It must be a poor and miserable country, Laos."

She did not bother to contradict him. "It's a poor country," she replied neutrally.

"Is that where you got those tattoos, in Vientiane?"

"No. They were done when I was a child."

"They are strange. But I don't paint them. I'm not interested in the skin. Only in the bone, the muscle. That is why I wanted you. You are very strong, very agile. You're a *métis*, aren't you?"

"Yes," she said.

"That is why you have such a remarkable body. The mixture of races is always interesting. You can achieve things with such a body."

She dragged on the Gauloises, coughing some more. "Like what?"

He looked at her over his newspaper, his black eyes unfathomable. "Anything you choose. You're a child of the dust?"

She felt a momentary flicker of anger. But that was the logical thing for her to be. Any other answer would raise too many questions. "Yes," she agreed. "I am a child of the dust."

"I thought so. There is no shame. At least you were conceived in pleasure. Are you ready to work again?"

"Not yet." Uninvited, she reached for the cigarettes, which he had left on a table, and lit a fresh one.

He grunted in annoyance, opening his mouth to argue or complain. Then something in the newspaper seemed to catch his attention. He bent forward to study it intently.

Sakura turned back to the window. A plane thundered overhead from La Guardia, its shadow momentarily throwing a huge black cross into the room. Her imagination snatched at it desperately, so that for a moment she was almost aboard the plane, surging up into the clear skies. If only she could fly out of here, back to Louis. She had been here too long already. The whole voyage, the whole idea of approaching Francine Lawrence, had been an insane gamble. She had expended her last resources, material and spiritual, in doing it. She had failed, and now she was stranded, like a beached fish, gasping, dying.

"You can go."

She turned back to Stefan. "What?"

"You can go," he said shortly. "I'm done."

"I thought you wanted to paint some more?"

"I just remembered that I have to go out." He rose, carefully folding the newspaper. He reached in his pocket, and pulled out some money. He peeled off twelve dollars and gave them to her. She had posed for no more than an hour, but she took the money, not about to argue with his sudden change of mood. "You're going to be here tonight?" he asked.

She shrugged. "Where else would I be?"

He peeled off another ten dollars and gave them to her. "You said you could make cheap meals. Go buy something for tonight."

She took the money cautiously. He had changed in some indefinable way. "You want me to cook for you?"

"Isn't that what I just said?"

"Well, okay. What do you want to eat? Fish? Chicken? Meat?"

"I don't care."

"Do you eat pork? Pork is cheap."

"I don't care," he repeated.

"Tell me what you like," she said, puzzled by his altered manner.

"Anything," he snapped. "Anything. We'll eat together. Whatever's left over from the ten, you can keep, okay?" He opened the door for her, still clutching the newspaper under his arm. But his eyes did not meet hers. She knew that something was wrong, but she could not guess what. Her mind hunted for the hidden danger.

"Cooking a meal doesn't mean I'm ready to play house," she warned him bleakly.

He rattled the doorknob. "I'm in a hurry. Go."

"Whatever you say."

"Be here by six," he said. "I don't like to eat late."

"Okay, Stefan."

As she left, she caught sight of the canvas he had been painting, parts of her body, butchered like a chicken on a market stall.

He reached Francine at her office. She ordered the clerk out, and gave the telephone call her full attention.

"I just had a contact," Clay Munro said. "The guy is foreign. Greek or Turkish, I think. He says his name is Stefan Giorgieu. He says he's Sakura Ueda's landlord."

Her heart jumped. "Is he genuine?"

"He described her accurately. Right down to the tattoos on both arms. He also claims she has other tattoos. A star on each hip."

"Is he sleeping with her?"

"He says she's been posing in the nude for him. He's an artist."

She snorted audibly. "Where is this place?"

"In the South Bronx. He claims Sakura Ueda has been renting a room in his apartment for the past couple of weeks. He said he wanted a thousand dollars. We settled on five hundred. That all right with you?"

"I'll bring the money," she said. If five hundred dollars was all she had to pay, then she would have got off cheaply. "Is the girl there now?"

"She'll be there at six o'clock tonight. I'm going to get her."

"Pick me up at the office, Clay. I want to come with you."

"I wouldn't advise that," he drawled.

"Why not?"

"She's shown desperation before. She could put up a fight. I'm going to ask two off-duty cops to come along as backup."

"No police," she said bluntly. "You were too heavy-handed last time."

"I was, huh?"

"You scared her. That's why she ran. It's time we tried the gentle approach."

"The gentle approach? She's gonna dive through the nearest window, Mrs. Lawrence."

"She won't run this time. I just want to talk to her. Nothing more. I'll bring Cecilia."

"You, me, and Cecilia Tan?"

"Yes. She has no reason to run away this time, Clay. If she does, you will stop her."

She hung up. She had brought Mr. Wu into the office with her. He was lying under her desk. When she had hung up the telephone, she reached down to touch his golden fur. "Now we'll see," she whispered to the dog. "Now we'll see what's real and what's not." She pressed the intercom and summoned Cecilia Tan.

Cecilia came in. "Mem?"

"Clay has found the girl. We're going to pick her up tonight."

It was raining heavily, thunder rolling around overhead. Munro got out of the car and popped his umbrella. He went to meet Francine Lawrence and Cecilia Tan, who were emerging from the building. He ushered them into the elegant new car he had just bought for the firm, a blue Cadillac.

"There's still time to call the cops," he said as they stepped into the car. "I told them to stand by."

"There's no question of that," Francine said shortly.

Munro asked himself dryly why he wasn't surprised at that answer. "Okay."

"Have you spoken to Giorgieu?"

"Yeah. He lives in a second-floor apartment. He says she'll be cooking a meal when we get there. He'll leave the door unlatched. She doesn't suspect anything. All we have to do is go in quietly and confront her."

"Then let's go."

He lifted a large hand. "One thing. You let me go in first, Mrs. Lawrence. She might get excited when we first get there. I don't want you exposed to any danger. Okay?"

"There won't be any danger," Francine said. But his eyes stayed on hers like two yellow moons until she shrugged impatiently. "All right, Clay. Whatever you say."

"Okay, let's go."

They turned onto the FDR Drive and up into the Bronx. Cecilia Tan was visibly nervous, her hands shaking.

They drove into even heavier rain. The clouds had drooped so low that they were bellying onto the tops of the taller buildings. The rain had snarled the traffic, and Munro used his own aggression and the car's intimidating bulk to forge a path through the tangle.

They found Giorgieu's address, a drab building on a shabby street, within sight of the skyscrapers of Manhattan, but in a different world. There was a railway bridge nearby, and a train crossed it as they cruised by, making a hellish racket. Munro drove by the front without stopping, and went on around the block, investigating. The back of the row was a spider's maze of rusting fire escapes descending to a narrow alley that contained rows of overflowing, dented garbage cans, all but blocking the road. Munro had trouble squeezing the Cadillac past, inwardly cursing as one of the huge rear fins scraped on something.

He had been counting off houses, and he stopped the car. "This is the back of Giorgieu's place," he said. Another train clattered across the bridge, making a rhythmic, melancholy tumult. Immediately afterward, an airliner thundered overhead, invisible above the clouds, rattling such garbage cans as still had lids. Rents here were low, and you could see why. He himself had grown up in an alley just like this one, on Jamaica Bay. In a backstreet like this one he had learned to fight and flee.

The fire escapes looked as though nobody had inspected them for years.

The sash windows were steamed up. Probably nailed shut against the hood-lums.

"Okay," he said, setting the car in motion again, "let's go in."

He parked the sedan out front, wondering if he would still have hub-caps when he returned. They walked two flights of stairs, nobody speaking. At the door of Giorgieu's apartment, he glanced at the women. Francine nodded briefly. He pushed the door open, and went in first, entering a steamy miasma of oil-paint fumes and cooking.

Giorgieu's apartment was no more than two rooms, both crowded with canvases. A sallow man wearing a dingy vest was working at an easel. In the next room, a young woman was stirring a large pot on a portable gas burner.

Suddenly, Francine grasped Munro's arm. "Let me go first, Clay," she whispered. Before Munro could argue, she stepped past him. "Sakura Ueda?" she called.

The young woman turned. Her long brown hair was hanging over her eyes, and Munro did not get a clear glimpse of her face. She wore jeans and a white shirt. Against the white material, her bare arms were golden.

Francine began to say something else, but Munro did not catch the words. He saw Sakura's hands grab the handles of the big pot, and he was already jumping forward, knowing what she intended. He grabbed Francine's arm and jerked her aside violently. He was just in time. The boil-ing contents of the pot hissed through the air, spattering one wall. Munro felt some of it scald his hands.

She threw the pot after the stew, this time aiming at Munro's head. As he ducked, Munro had time to admire the incredible speed with which she moved. Then she had vanished, and Munro heard a door opening and slam-ming.

Leaving Francine still crouching and stunned, he took off after her. She had left through a tiny laundry area. He vaulted the ironing table she had overturned on her way out, and opened the door at the far end. He was in the corridor again. He hesitated, cursing. Then a door at the far end opened, and Sakura ran out. She was carrying a duffel bag. She gave him a desperate look, then took off down the stairs.

He sprinted after her, calling her name. Christ, she moved fast! He took the stairs four at a time, but was only just in time to see her cross the hall, heading for the back exit. The heavy bag was slowing her down, but not much.

He ran after her into the alley. He was damning Francine Lawrence for having turned down his offer of police backup.

In the alley, with exultation, he saw he'd lucked out. The girl had collided with some garbage cans, and was stumbling over her own bag. He could have brought her down with a football tackle, but he was afraid he might break that delicate back.

He grabbed her arms tightly. Her flesh was warm.

"Hey," he said, "it's okay. Don't be frightened." Without letting her escape, he turned her to face him. "It's okay," he repeated. "Nobody wants to hurt you."

Then he was looking into her face. She was more beautiful than he'd realized. Her eyes were almond-shaped, but the irises were a clear gray. They stared into his, and he saw the naked terror in them.

"Sakura," he said, "relax, it's okay."

The duffel bag dropped from her nerveless fingers. She went limp in his arms, her eyes half-closing, her full mouth opening. Alarmed, Munro let one arm go to support her body, his hands going around her slim waist.

Under his palms, he felt the muscles tighten, and knew he had made a mistake. She wrenched herself free of him. Her hand lashed at his face. In the last millisecond, he saw the wide-bladed knife in her fist. The razor edge whipped past his eyes.

"Jesus," he said. "Take it easy!" As he grabbed for her again, she swung her hip and shoulder back. She kicked the way karate fighters did, using the whole weight of her body to drive her heel forward.

The blow landed square on the place where the shrapnel had gone in. He felt the air burst from his lips, saw the world go black. The pain was unbelievable. He went down backward. The wet sidewalk struck him in the back, cracking his head.

He knew she was gone, and he did not bother trying to get up in any hurry.

How had she known? Clay Munro had not the slightest doubt that in the few seconds she had been in his arms, the woman had felt out his weak place, and had deliberately struck there. What intuition had guided her?

Coughing hollowly, he got onto all fours. Francine came running out and helped him to his feet. "Where is she?" she demanded, panting.

"Long gone."

"Clay, I'm sorry. So sorry. I should have listened to you."

"Yeah, you should," he said in a tight voice.

They made a somber group. Somewhere out there, the girl was running, coatless and bareheaded, in the driving rain. Francine doubted she would ever see her again. Not in this life. And Clay Munro had rightly told her that she had interfered with his arrangements and directly contributed to the disaster.

They sat in Giorgieu's stinking room, the rain beating at the window. The artist had demanded his five hundred dollars anyhow, saying he had done his part. It had been Francine's instinct to refuse, but she wanted him to tell her everything he knew about the woman, and she needed Giorgieu's cooperation.

Clay Munro was breathing raggedly, and holding his chest. But he was playing the hero, refusing to call a doctor, saying he would be fine in a while.

Cecilia Tan sat by the sink, periodically wetting the cloth she held to her cheek. Cecilia's thick overcoat had protected her, and the burn on her cheek was painful, but not serious. Thanks to Clay's quick-witted intervention, the boiling stew had not struck them full in the face, as Sakura had intended.

It had been a frightening demonstration. Francine's father had hunted tigers in Malaya, before the war, and she recalled his stories of how one in a hundred of the trapped beasts would turn on the closing ring of beaters, and claw his way out, leaving a path of blood and ruin in his wake. She had been reminded of those stories today.

None of them had tried to chase the girl. Only Munro would have had a chance of catching her, and he had been lying stunned in the alley.

If they could only learn why this young woman kept running, why she wanted to meet, but only on her own terms, why she reacted so violently. By now, Francine knew that she had made a terrible mistake in not following Cecilia's advice, right at the beginning. She had underestimated Sakura Ueda in a hundred ways.

"Tell me about the tattoos," she commanded Giorgieu. "Draw them for me, if you can."

The Albanian picked up a sketch pad and a stick of graphite. He leaned forward, elbows on his knees, and traced out the hourglass shape of a woman's body. "A bracelet on each arm, here and here. And here, on the point of each hipbone, a flaming star. All done with black dye." He sketched in the tattoos carefully.

"Did you ask her where she got them?"

"I asked her if she had got them in Vientiane, and she said no. That was all."

"Vientiane?"

"She said she had been born there."

Francine frowned. "She said she had been born in Vientiane? You're sure of that?"

He shrugged. "Maybe she just lived there." He was intent on his drawing, shading in the triangle of pubic hair. "She said she was a child of the dust."

"What's a child of the dust?" Cecilia asked.

Giorgieu smiled, showing bad teeth. "You don't know?"

Clay Munro spoke. "It's a French phrase. You hear it a lot in Vietnam. It means the child of a white man and a local hooker."

Francine focused on the Albanian. "But she said she didn't get the tattoos in Laos?"

"That's what she said. She said she got them as a child."

"She didn't say where?"

"I already told you. No."

"What did she do while she was staying here?"

"She went out every day. I didn't ask what she did. I didn't pay her any attention. Then one day she said she had lost her bag and all her money. She wanted to do some housework to pay the rent. I asked her to pose instead. She had an interesting body."

"Did she sleep with you?" Francine asked.

"Is she your daughter?" he asked, black eyes meeting Francine's.

"No," she said automatically.

"Then you have no right to ask this question." He finished the drawing, tore it off the pad, and passed it to Francine. "But I'll tell you anyhow. No. She did not pay me that compliment. But she was a good model."

Francine looked at the sketch. Giorgieu had a quick, photographic skill. The body he had drawn was perfect, though he had not given it a head.

"What else?" she asked.

"What else?" Giorgieu repeated. He looked at the chaos on the floor regretfully. "She said she was a good cook, and it looks like she was telling the truth. Also, she smoked a lot, and she had a bad cough. Like she was sick, or something."

"Seriously sick?"

Giorgieu shrugged. "Yes, I guess so."

Francine knew there was nothing more to be got from Giorgieu, but she kept pressing him for a long time, making him go over it, in case anything he had said earlier had been a lie.

They went to her room. Francine hadn't expected to find anything, and there was nothing to find. The shelves and drawers were bare. Apart from a comb and some cheap makeup in the sink, the room was as bare as if nobody had been living in it at all. The woman had been ready to leave at any moment. She had simply snatched up her duffel bag and taken off. Francine had to admire the fierce simplicity of that. She had once lived that way herself long ago.

As they left, Giorgieu offered to sell her one of his canvases. She refused. "If you had done a portrait of her, I might have bought that," she told him. "These are just figure studies."

"I do portraits in the park," he said contemptuously. "Here I paint."

She shrugged. "You haven't tried to paint her face or her character, only her body. That doesn't interest me."

"Her body was exceptional."

"But there was more to her than that."

"Of course. The mixture of races is always interesting. That is what I told her." He laughed silently, looking her up and down. "You are two of a kind, you and Sakura. I wish you good hunting."

Munro stared at the paintings all around. Giorgieu had seen Sakura Ueda as an arrangement of bone and flesh, not as a person. These were not portraits, but everywhere in them were to be seen Sakura's taut lines, Sakura's coiled strength, Sakura's animal beauty.

They walked out of the building. Cecilia Tan was crying, whether from the pain or the shock, Munro did not know.

"I told you," she threw at Francine. "Why won't you ever listen, Francine? Why are you so arrogant?"

That last look, just as she'd fled, plagued Francine like a ghost. Could it be possible? Could there be such things in the strange pattern of life? She could not bring herself to believe it. This girl with the haunting eyes, this stranger, this huckster: Could she be what had become of Ruth?

Francine turned to Munro. "What now, Clay?" she said in a strained voice.

He opened the door of the car for them. He did not speak until he was behind the wheel. "This is my fault, Mrs. Lawrence. But I'm going to find her. I promise you that." He reached for the ignition.

Francine's cluttered life was suddenly empty, and she had become desperate for distractions to take her mind off the overwhelming problem of Sakura Ueda.

That morning, one arrived in the form of news from Tai Po that workers at her main electronics factory had not come to work for the second day running. As they'd already done a few weeks earlier, they had joined in the latest bout of violent rioting that was bringing the whole colony of Hong Kong to a halt yet again.

Further tales had been emerging of the excesses being committed in the throes of what had been dubbed the Cultural Revolution in the People's Republic of China. The rifle butt was still smashing down on anything and anyone that smacked of deviation. China was still turning her back on the West.

The shock wave had spread through Hong Kong as a matter of course, the demonstrations temporarily paralyzing the economy. Francine, like other traders, was losing a lot of money. Soon, she knew, everything would settle down again. The concerns would go underground, the factories would be busy once more, the terror would recede.

But it would never go away completely.

In less than thirty years, Hong Kong was due to be returned to China, under the terms of the lease of 1898. Nobody could forget that. To Westerners, thirty years was a long time. She had heard more than one gwailo dismiss the whole issue with a laughing "Oh, we'll all be dead by then."

But to anyone with a Chinese cast of mind, thirty years was but a moment in time. Francine knew perfectly well that she would still be alive in 1997. Of course, she would be in her seventies, a pug-faced dowager whom nobody loved. *The world will have changed by then,* she thought. *Everything will be different. But it would still hurt to see what I have built up there torn down by Red Guards in khaki tunics.*

She got on the telephone, trying to get hold of one of her managers. The important thing was to know when the workers would be back on their assembly lines and benches. After half an hour on the telephone, she managed to locate Freddy Chong, one of her assistant managers.

The man was stuttering with alarm and consternation. He, like so many others, seemed to be under the impression that the Red Guards were at the gates of Hong Kong. She had to inject a steely note into her voice.

"This has been going on for three years," she told him brusquely. "Like every other half-senile old man, all Mao thinks of are teenage girls. Between concubines, some slurred curse against the foreign devils must have dribbled out of his mouth, and ten thousand sixteen-year-old cadres grabbed their rifles. But that does not mean we have to abandon our posts."

"The workforce are frightened," the manager stammered. "Half of them came here on a basketball, you know that."

He meant that they were I.I.'s, illegal immigrants from the Communist mainland, some of whom had made the hazardous crossing across shark-infested water, clutching a basketball for flotation. They dreaded what would happen to them and their families when the Communists took over.

"I know that," she said impatiently. "You have to reassure them." In her view, the Cultural Revolution was no more than the foul belch of a man who had already eaten and digested the meal. It was a sign that a major assimilation had already taken place. China was turning her back on the Russians. They were eager to modernize. "As soon as Mao dies, Freddy, all the xenophobia will be over. They need us. They need our skill, our ability to make money. Why should they hurt us?"

"You should be here, Mem," Chong said unhappily.

"I can't come right now," she replied. "I'm busy with something of vital importance to me in New York. I'll be back as soon as I can. Tell them."

"Yes, Mem."

"When the Communists take over, we'll all make more money than ever," she assured the man as she ended the call. "I have no fears for the future."

She meant that. Soon, she knew, the fistful of skyscrapers in the Central district would proliferate and girdle the island, like joss sticks around a golden Buddha on some prosperous festival day. After the stagnation of the postwar years, the colony was industrializing at a dizzying rate. The new man-made fibers and newly designed machinery had transformed Hong Kong's traditional mainstay, the textile and garment industries. Electronic advances had revolutionized her own main business, consumer electronics. Tiny portable radios, selling for a few dollars and blasting tinnily into teen-aged ears from New York to Vienna, had made many people millionaires overnight. There were few controls or restrictions upon greed in Hong Kong. Visibly, the sleepy colonial trading port was turning into a global hub. Francine was one of those who had made this happen. She shared the guilt, and the credit, in whatever proportion the gods chose to mete them out.

Francine smiled tightly to herself. For fully five minutes, she had not thought about Ruth or Sakura. *That is progress,* she thought. *Money is truly magical stuff. Perhaps a gold coin on each of my eyelids will make me sleep to-night.*

Munro groped for the telephone. He'd fallen asleep in his chair with a hand clasped to his side, like the gory print of Jesus with doubting Thomas that his mother had chosen to hang over the supper table. He'd had people in the Bronx searching for a trace of Sakura for four days, and he was half-afraid they had tracked her down, beaten him to the kill. "Yeah?"

"Hey, man. It's me. Randolph."

"Yeah," he said, straightening in his chair. "Got something for me?"

"I sure have, baby."

He grunted. His snitches had been calling him for days. The scent of money was in the air, but not a single one of them had been able to describe Sakura accurately. "Well, don't keep me in suspense."

Randolph's soft giggle floated down the line. "What's it worth?"

He bit back his impatience. "A hundred bucks."

"What? Two-fifty, man. At *least.*"

"We'll see," Munro said harshly. "What have you got?"

"A half-Chinese girl, running wild, sleeping rough? Tattoos on her arms? That what you want to hear about?"

His heart jolted. "Yeah."

"You know where to find me," Randolph said. "I'll be waiting."

He hung up.

Munro cursed and stared at the photocopy of Giorgieu's drawing, which lay on his blotter. The two flaming stars framed the pubic triangle provocatively. Giorgieu had drawn the breasts high and youthful. He recalled the feel of her body in his arms, the combination of suppleness and strength. Next time he held her, he promised himself again, there would be a different conclusion.

He unlocked the drawer of his desk, and stared down at the .38 automatic that lay inside. He looked at the gun for a long time. The scenario played through his head with a grim inevitability. If he drew on her, she would call his bluff. And then, he would have to either shoot her or toss the gun away.

He closed the drawer again and relocked it.

As he walked out, his secretary called after him. "What time are you coming back, Mr. Munro?"

He did not turn. "When I've found her."

Clay Munro looked up at the Vietcong flag. It was a full-size one, covering one wall of the shabby little shop. The whole place was dedicated to protesting the war. Its stock-in-trade was posters of Ho Chi Minh, books printed on cheap brown paper detailing American atrocities, NLF flags, cheap "Vietnamese" kites, and other artifacts, just about everything actually made in Thailand. He peered in the back. Randolph Pruneda was drinking beer with half a dozen others, mostly blacks, with one or two white faces. He knew most all of them from VA: the ones who had come back and organized marches, painted placards, made speeches. He felt ambivalent toward them, the way he'd felt toward civil-rights demonstrators in the sixties. He knew where they hurt, and he believed in what they were doing. But he felt as though he lived in a different world from them, and he knew he could never do what they did.

He edged in among the crowd, smelling the weed on the air, until he reached Randolph. He put his hand on Randolph's shoulder. "Hi, Randy."

Randolph swung on his crutches. "There you are."

"In person."

Randolph had lost a foot at Khe San. They'd made him an artificial one, but he'd never got the hang of it, and preferred the aluminum crutches. He was more than a little stoned, and his eyes were bloodshot. "Hey, there's a joint going around. You want some?"

Munro shook his head. "Uh-uh."

"We could go upstairs. I got a private supply. We could get a little high, talk about old times."

"I got no time, Randy. Tell me about the girl."

Randolph held out his hand, rubbing his finger and thumb together. "Gimme."

Munro gave him the $250 he had asked for. A speculative look entered Randolph's stoned eyes. "Cash on demand, huh?"

He smiled emptily. "Just tell me what you heard, okay?"

"Hey, what's your hurry?"

"My hurry is, I'm working."

"On a girl?" Randolph grinned. "You must be losing it if you have to pay for it."

"What you got, Randolph?"

Weed and beer had got Randolph's brain cells working. "If you'll pay two-fifty, you'll pay five hundred. Right?"

Munro's patience ran out with frightening suddenness. His fingers closed around Randolph's arm. Randolph's body jolted. Pain darkened his eyes. "Hey, man!" he gasped.

One or two people looked up. A silence fell, but nobody said anything.

Munro forced himself to let go of Randolph's skinny arm. "Tell me what you heard," he rasped.

"The Cross Bronx and the Bruckner," Randolph said sullenly. "There are some condemned tenements where winos hang out. Somebody said a half-Chinese girl was flopping there, hiding out from something. She's got tats on her arms."

The rage monster had subsided. Randolph was rubbing his arm. Munro felt bad, but it was too late for apologies now. He pulled out another fifty-dollar bill. "Thanks, Randy."

He walked out of the place, but not before he heard Randolph mutter, "Fuck you, man," behind his back.

He got in his car and drove toward the East River.

He could not stop running into that alleyway in his mind, recalling his own overconfidence, reliving the hard little heel that crunched into his chest. Clay Munro, Purple Heart, private dick—laid low in an alley by a hundred-pound girl with Chinese eyes.

Now he would flatten her like the alley cat she was. He thought of her, alone and penniless, fighting off winos. It was still raining hard. Good, he thought grimly. All of it would soften her up. He parked the car in front of a hardware store and walked.

Buildings were older here, windows broken or boarded up, razor wire or broken glass atop walls covered in graffiti. He was irresistibly reminded of Vietnam as he walked through the drizzle, of countless times he had waded through paddy fields or trudged through jungle in just this way, eyes searching for the tiny signs that might warn of minefields, ambushes, enemy forces. Every road, every village and field, could hide violent death. So many times, they hadn't even known what they were looking for. The information they'd been given was wrong, the maps were inaccurate, the weather forecasts were unreliable. The only thing that was always there was the sickening fear.

He reached the end of the street. Ahead of him lay an expanse of foggy marshland that went down to the Bronx River. The developers were at work here. Three blocks had been leveled and reduced to slag. A tall signboard explained, with plans, what they were doing, but he did not even glance at it. The first yellow machines had arrived, and were parked in a row, a lone watchman guarding them from inside a shed. Munro kept going, passing the first big square plain of rubble and wet earth.

She would have had a plan, he knew that. Someone who lived with her suitcase packed and ready to take off in three seconds flat would always have a plan telling her where to go next, even if the plan was a desperate one. Before she even moved into Giorgieu's apartment, she would have marked down her next hideout.

The cold was biting into his chest. The next plot had a huge depression in the center, which had filled with rainwater, like a bomb crater. Reflected from the far shore of the river, the city skyline quivered upside down in the water.

On the third plot, a lone three-story building stood, looking as though it were ready to fall down at any moment, now that the support of its neighbors had been knocked away. The vandals had already been through it, and not a window remained. But as Munro approached it, his nostrils caught the smell of woodsmoke and human excrement. The Bruckner Expressway swept overhead. There was no question that this was the place.

He walked around the building, studying it. Where the buildings on either side had been demolished, pipes and beams spilled out, like organs from a ripped carcass. There were no signs of life. The tenants had long since been cleared out. But that smell was unmistakable. There was only one door, and when Munro tried it, he found it locked.

Munro rammed his shoulder against it. It splintered open at the first attempt and he stumbled inside. Unexpectedly, a wave of heat swept into his face, carrying the stink of unwashed, alcohol-sodden human bodies.

Though the original tenants had gone, others had populated this place.

A woodstove was burning in the center. Around it, a dozen or more vaguely human shapes were curled up in sleeping bags or piles of discarded garments. Human derelicts had drifted into the derelict building and had made it their home. On this cold day, all were sleeping. Two or three disheveled figures raised their heads at his intrusion.

"Wha' the fuck you want?" someone asked hoarsely, his voice somewhere between fear and anger.

"Sakura Ueda," he called. "Where is she?"

"Ain't no Sakura here, man," the hoarse voice growled. Munro made his way toward the far door. The way was crowded with tables and sleeping forms, and the floor was littered with filth of all kinds. He stumbled on a bundle of rags that might have been somebody's bed and felt limbs flail in protest.

Several of the sleepers had started to rouse. Someone shouted in alarm. "They smashed the door," a voice said. "Who is it?"

"Who you?" A hand clutched at Munro's coat, dragging at him. "You a cop? Whadda fuck you want?"

He tore himself free. "Where's the Chinese girl?"

"Ain't no girls here. Gedda fuck outta here."

All around him, figures were shuffling restlessly in the lairs they had made. A bearlike man got up, and kicked the broken door. "What you do this for, man?" he growled. "We gonna freeze our asses."

"I'm looking for a girl. Chinese-looking."

"I'm gonna cut your throat." Angry eyes burned in a face that seemed mostly gray beard. There was a jagged bottle in his hand now. Munro stood still and just watched the bearlike man until the light in the wild eyes burned out. The bear tossed the broken bottleneck aside and fumbled back to his bed again.

Munro passed into the next room. The smell in here was truly terrible. It was the communal kitchen. Food stolen or scavenged from Dumpsters lay rotting everywhere. Several large rats slunk off as Munro entered. He did not envy the cops who would soon be brought in here to evict this colony of vagrants.

He emerged into a hallway. Stairs led upward, littered with debris and thick with dust. But there were footprints in the dust. He stooped. Some of the footprints were small enough to be hers.

He started climbing the staircase, looking upward cautiously. He reached the next landing, which was piled high with broken toilets, basins, and baths. This level seemed deserted. It was icy-cold up here, rain sweeping in through the broken windows. The rest of the inhabitants had huddled downstairs for warmth.

"Devil," a mad voice suddenly screamed in his ear.

Munro sprang away, the shock clenching his heart.

"Git outta here, you devil!" the voice yelled.

Munro backed away from the mad voice. The man was crouching in a corner, bundled in rags. His eyes gleamed like coals above a snarl of black beard. He had drawn something like a star on his own forehead with charcoal. He pointed a skinny finger at Munro. "Black devil!"

"Is she up here? The girl? Is she here?"

"Git back to hell!" the man screamed.

Munro backed away slowly, not wanting to turn his back on the man. He explored the other rooms. All were empty but for rubbish. The madman kept screaming that he was a devil and telling him to go back to hell. There was no trace of Sakura. But when he checked the steps that led up to the next floor, he saw only one set of prints in the dust, small ones.

"Git outta here, you black devil," the madman shrieked.

"Will you shut up, for Christ's sake?" Munro snapped at him.

The man scuttled away, falling silent. He curled himself in a taut knot in the corner and buried his head under a pile of rags.

Munro's breath was clouding around his face in the icy air. He started to ascend, very cautiously, aware that whoever was up there could easily crack his skull with a brick.

"Don't come up any farther."

He stopped dead, peering up. There was no sign of her. The voice had been low, but it had carried perfectly. He had no doubt it was her. "Come down, Sakura." He started climbing again, stealthily. "It's over. Don't make me hurt you."

There was no reply.

"You have nowhere else to run. You might as well realize that."

"Stop." She appeared at the top of the stairs. Her hair was streaked with dust, her cheeks gaunt. She must have been half-frozen up here. And half-starved. "Stop there, or I'll kill you." Her breath clouded at her mouth. Her accent had Asian intonations.

"You're not going to kill me, Sakura. You got me by surprise last time. That won't happen again. I know you have the knife there."

She had her hands behind her back, and now she brought them forward. She held the knife, point upward, in her left hand. It was wide-bladed, razor-edged. She held it in a way that told him, without any shadow of doubt, that she knew how to use it. He smiled bleakly. "You think I'm going to back off? Think again." He kept on coming up, slowly and cautiously.

She didn't reply, melting away from him as he came up, the knife pointing toward him. He was probably strong enough and skilled enough to take it away from her, but she could open a couple of arteries first. He didn't want to bleed to death in this filth-hole.

He reached the top. Most of the partition walls up here had been broken down. It was colder than ever. She was wearing the same clothes as at

Giorgieu's place, with a couple of sweaters pulled over the shirt, not nearly enough to keep out the chill. She looked as dirty and deranged as the others in this place.

"Don't come any closer," she told him, crouching lower. The point of the knife traced restless circles in the air. It was a knife-fighter's trick, to distract. He kept his eyes on hers.

"You might scratch me a little with that thing, but I'll break both your arms and drag you out of here screaming your head off."

The knife kept weaving, the blade gleaming in the dull light. He could not help noticing how graceful she was in her every movement. Every turn of her hands or limbs expressed a vibrant animal confidence. But he was afraid of her.

"For Christ's sake," he said tersely. "I'm not gonna hurt you."

"I know who you are."

"You do, huh?"

"Jai Han sent you."

"Who the fuck's Jai Han? I'm the guy you knocked down in the alley behind Giorgieu's place. My name is Clay Munro. I work for Francine Lawrence."

"You're lying."

"I never lie, Sakura." Trying to look and sound relaxed, he edged away from the top of the stairs. "I'm sorry about the way we busted in on you. But you have to come with me now."

Her eyes did not seem to blink. He knew she was waiting for him to make his move, waiting for him to try and charge her down. If he did, she would drive the blade up under his ribs, reaching for a vital organ.

He made an effort to soften his tone. "Look, why don't we get out of this dump? I'll take you somewhere to eat, freshen up. When you're ready, we'll go see Mrs. Lawrence. In your own time. Okay?"

"I saw your Ray-Bans."

"*What?*"

"It was you in the subway."

"Sure, it was me in the subway."

"I saw your Ray-Bans."

"That's right." She was truly crazy, he thought. "I wore Ray-Bans. You must be hungry, right? Have you eaten anything in four days?"

"I will never let you take me back to them."

"Back to who? Listen, the only person I work for is Francine Lawrence. I'm here all alone. To tell you the truth, I was wounded in Vietnam, and you kicked me right in the wound. My chest hurts like hell. I don't mean you any harm. So put the blade away, okay?"

"I can kill you as easily with or without the knife," she said.

"Jesus, you're a piece of work," he said. "You couldn't kill me with a bazooka. All you could do is hurt me a little. And I'd hurt you a lot."

The words did not sound as confident as he'd expected them to. He took a breath and moved closer to her, his hands raised to grab or parry. His heart was beating faster. If she knew her business, he was in for a very nasty couple of minutes. The closer he got, the dirtier she was. It covered her like a film. Beneath the grime, though, that vivid beauty still burned.

He heard a sound behind him, and turned quickly. The madman had crept up the stairs and was watching them, eyes gleaming from his thicket of hair.

"Go back where you came from," Munro commanded him, horribly trapped between these two crazy people.

"Youse go back where youse came from," the man hissed. "The black devil down to hell, the white angel up to heaven." He saw the knife in Sakura's hand, and cackled. "She's gonna stick you good, devil!"

Munro scooped up a piece of rotten plaster and hurled it at the madman. It splattered on the man's chest, startling him. He scuttled back down the stairs, muttering to himself.

He whirled back to face Sakura, half-expecting to find the knife buried in his sternum at any moment. "Your neighbor's kind of eccentric, isn't he?" he said. He was as close to her as he dared go, almost within stab or slash range. Her lashes were thick, and very long. The skin of her mouth reminded him of some jungle flower, an orchid maybe. He had been pursuing her with grim determination for days, yet now he felt a strange sense of privilege in being permitted to get so close to her, as though he were in the presence of some rare animal. And, despite the knife, he was also starting to feel pity for her. He could see now that her whole body was shaking. "Look. This is the end of the road, Sakura. If I want, I could go down and call for reinforcements. You understand? You can't keep running."

"Go away now."

The point of the knife stopped moving. In two seconds he would be fighting for his life. "Listen, Sakura," he said urgently, "the truth is, I'm the only one who can help you right now. You haven't a dime, you have nowhere to go, and you're afraid of just about everything. You can't stay here. The bulldozers will be here anytime, if those good folk downstairs haven't eaten you alive before that. You really have no choice but to trust me."

The knife flicked out at him like a steel tongue. "Go!"

He backed cautiously away. Maybe she had been in some kind of combat area, he thought suddenly. He had seen kids behave like this after coming back from the boonies. Maybe it was a kind of battle fatigue. "I want you to come with me, Sakura. I want to help you."

Suddenly, she sprang at him. She moved faster than he could have believed. Acting with blind instinct, he grabbed the belt of her jeans and swung her into a rough hip-throw. He felt the blade whistle past his ear as he lifted her slim body. He spun her away from him, too afraid of the knife to make it a good throw, one that would land her heavily on her back. She rolled away from him without losing her balance—or her grip on the knife.

At least he was out of range, and his throat was still intact. His knees were weak. "Okay," he gasped, "that's enough, Sakura. Next time, I'm gonna really hurt you. You got one chance, and that's to come with me. You can't stay here. You'll get pneumonia. You're resourceful and tough, but you're only human. A derelict building in the Bronx isn't the place for you. Come with me, and I swear you'll get a fair deal. You got no other choice. Face it. Unless you're crazy."

The truth was that Sakura was hardly in her right mind. The fever had affected her thoughts. Sleeping in this freezing ruin had made her worse. And now, at this critical point, the visions were coming.

For as the black devil yelled at her, Roger climbed up the stairs behind him. He grinned at her over the black devil's shoulder, and she was terrified, because in another part of her mind, she knew that Roger was long, long dead. She saw that he wasn't walking at all, that his head was mounted on a serpent's body made of fire, and that his eyes were made of stone. She whimpered and shook her head to make him go away.

But who else did she have?

You have me, Roger hissed at her side. She sprang away from him, but he coiled fiery serpent trails around her. His dead stone eyes laughed into hers. *You will always have me.* She stumbled back.

Kill him, little one, Roger hissed. He laughed in a voice of fire. *Kill him with the knife I gave you. I will look after you. I'll be at your side.*

She was not in New York at all, but back in Laos, on the Plain of Jars. It was dry and cold, the hills crisp in the light. Any moment now the B-52s would come, raining destruction, and the earth would jerk and flop like a man being beaten.

Terror flooded her. She could not stay here, in this dreadful place, to die. She had to launch out, as she had done so many times before, into the void.

She aimed the knife at the black devil's heart. "You are a Ray-Ban," she told him.

"The hell I am," the black devil said. "I don't know what you're afraid of, but you're going to have to trust me, Sakura."

She closed her eyes to shut out Roger. "Leave me alone," she whispered to Roger. "Please."

"You look terrible. Give me the knife, Sakura."

Her body moved automatically, without her volition. She could not feel her legs, though they carried her to the black devil. She thrust Roger's knife at him, but her body was weak now. He grasped her wrist, and wrenched the knife out of her fingers. His arm clamped around her throat, choking her. She opened her eyes. Roger was still there. Now his face had become a serpent's face, enveloped in flames, but he kept smiling at her. At his side, other flaming creatures were gathering. She could hear the roar of the flames, louder as they fluttered in the wind. She cried out in a choked voice.

His hand touched her brow. "Jesus. You're burning up with fever."

She tore her gaze away from the flaming creatures and looked into the black devil's face. She had seen few black men in her life. His face was a polished mask, carved by a savage. His eyes were amber, dark and deep. She discovered that so long as she stared into his eyes, the noise of the flames stayed in the background.

Without looking away from his eyes, she groped for his hand. Her fingers crept through his and clamped tight. "Are you a Ray-Ban?"

"No, Sakura," he said. He had a deep voice. "Whatever a Ray-Ban is, I'm not it."

"I'm afraid."

"It's okay, Sakura," he said. "We're getting out of here."

But she could not walk any farther. Her mouth had filled with something warm and salty. She knew what it was. She choked and spat.

Blood spooled out of her mouth in a brilliant scarlet ribbon that seemed to have no end. It spattered on her chest, splashed onto the ground.

She saw the black devil's mouth and eyes open wide.

Then her legs were crumbling, and she was falling into darkness, the light closing above her.

Francine was thinking about Clive Napier.

She had been nearly the same age as Sakura Ueda was now when she had discarded what was left of her emotions. The loss of Ruth, and the other suffering she had undergone, had left her remote from other people, disconnected from ordinary things. Her love for Clive, the last thing that had anchored her to a woman's feelings, had died and burned out during the exhausting postwar years.

The only hope had been of somehow finding Ruth alive again. But that hope had never borne fruit, and in the end, she had come to see that hope was a torturing disease that never let its victims go until they were gray ash. In order to protect herself, she had blotted out her feelings and relinquished hope. That meant accepting that Ruth was dead. It meant driving Clive away from her.

Since then, she had bestowed her attention on inanimate things—money, possessions, work. She was even prepared to cherish Mr. Wu the puppy, precisely because he was not a human being. She had become nuhuang, empress, a woman to be feared and obeyed, but never understood, never loved. She had doomed herself to live in a place the Iban called Sabayon, the land of the dead.

Now she was being recalled from Sabayon. Maybe the question was not simply whether Sakura was really her daughter or not, but whether she could bear the reawakening.

She had felt guilty about Clive for all these years. Together, they had sailed from Singapore to Borneo. Together, they had crossed Borneo on foot. After the war, he had wanted to be at her side. In a sense, she had used him. When she'd needed him most, he'd been there. Without him, she would not have survived. Then she had discarded him. Had it just been cold practicality? Or had she always loved him? Just as she'd never stopped loving Ruth?

There was a knock at the door, and Julia Lo ushered Clay Munro into the apartment.

Francine rose to her feet. "Clay?"

"I found her," he said.

"Where is she?" she demanded. He looked exhausted. Her eyes suddenly dropped to the bloodstains all over his jacket. Her heart shrank into a hard ball. "Oh, my God, Clay—is she dead?"

"No," he said. "She's not hurt. She's sick. She has tuberculosis."

She touched her throat. "Tuberculosis?"

"She was coughing up blood when I found her. The doctor wants to put her in the hospital right away. I wanted you to see her first."

Francine drew a shaky breath. "Where is she?"

"Asleep at my apartment. The doctor gave her something to bring the fever down. It knocked her out cold. One of my sisters is with her. Mrs. Lawrence? Are you okay?"

She nodded. "Yes. Can you take me to her?" she asked in a whisper.

"That's what I'm here for."

She sat in silence while Munro drove her through the rainy streets. He gave her a brief account of how he had looked for Sakura over four days, finally lucking out in a derelict building, where he'd found her half-frozen and delirious with fever. He told her how she had threatened him with a knife, then had suddenly begun to cough blood, and had collapsed at his feet.

By the time he'd gotten her to his apartment, she had been raving about Laos, bombs, fiery serpents, about a man called Jai Han, saying the Ray-Bans were coming for her.

When the doctor had arrived, she had quieted. The doctor had questioned her, and she had told him exactly what was wrong with her. Pulmonary tuberculosis.

"You've done an extraordinary job," Francine told him mechanically. "I won't forget this, Clay."

They arrived at Munro's apartment. He led her up. A pretty black woman, Munro's sister, let them in.

"You don't have to be quiet," she told them. "The doc says she won't surface for hours."

But they all fell silent as they approached her bed.

A small light burned by the bed. Sakura Ueda lay on her back. Her tangled hair was spread out across the pillows. Her skin was covered with a sheen of sweat.

Slowly, Francine walked to the bed, and looked down into her face.

THREE

RAIN

1954

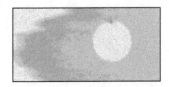

SARAWAK, BORNEO

The winter monsoon had come early. The year had not yet ended, and the heavy rains were already driving across Southeast Asia, from Indonesia to the Philippines. They would beat down for weeks yet.

Clive Napier, huddled under the corrugated-iron roof of the shelter, stared out at the runway of the Kuching airport. It was a vista of water in all its most frenzied manifestations—lashing down in curtains and exploding on the tarmac, driven up, down, and sideways by the wind, pouring from the ramshackle buildings in waterfalls, slashing muddy torrents in the disintegrating earth. Beyond the tarmac, the jungle trees flailed wildly. Palm fronds and branches had broken off, and littered the runway. A team of men, blinded by wind and rain, struggled to clear away the debris. It did not seem possible that a small plane could land in this weather.

Yet suddenly, the Beechcraft lurched out of the maelstrom, no more than two hundred feet above the thrashing trees. Buffeted by the crosswinds, it swung perilously from side to side. Clive's chest tightened in fear. Then the Beechcraft dropped like a stone onto the runway. A foot-deep river of water was sluicing the tarmac. The rubber tires could find no grip, and the little plane slewed violently to port.

Inside the plane, the debris that had spilled into the aisle during the dreadful flight from Singapore now hurtled pell-mell toward the cockpit. The flimsy cockpit door had long since burst open. Clinging to her seat with white-knuckled hands, Francine saw the pilot wrestling with the yoke and stamping on the rudder in an effort to stop the Beechcraft from overshooting the runway and plunging into the wet green jungle. At last, the plane skittered to a stop. Gingerly, the pilot steered toward the terminal building. The passengers began to talk in low voices. With a shuddering sigh, Francine sagged back in her seat.

She had flown all over Asia, and this had been one of the most terrifying flights she had ever made. All the way from Singapore, lightning had flickered around them as though it had wanted to catch them in its claws. The turbulence had been savage, shaking the passengers like dolls, jarring open lockers. For a while, one of the engines had cut out, making the Beechcraft stagger like a storm-broken bird. When it had restarted, yellow flames had fluttered from the cowling. She wondered whether it was some kind of omen.

The Beechcraft ground to a halt within fifty yards of the terminal. The steward flung open the door and dropped the ladder onto the tarmac. There was no bus to take them to the terminal. As she filed on shaky legs with the others to the exit, Francine saw the pilot slumped in exhaustion over the controls.

The rain, driven by winds that were alternately hot and cold, was a ferocious assault on all the senses. She was drenched to the skin within the first minute of leaving the plane. She blundered, gasping, toward the terminal, her sodden hair plastered around her face, her expensive clothes and shoes already ruined, her new attaché case dripping dye like violet blood.

A tall figure loomed toward her, carrying an umbrella.

"Clive," she spluttered.

The shelter of his big body wrapped around her. He kissed her wet face ardently. "Thank God you're safe. Welcome to Borneo. Come on."

They hurried on. Rain was coming down in huge curtains. Above the lashing jungle fronds, the thunder carried a primeval menace. In the shelter of the shabby airport lounge, they stopped and looked at each other. It had been eight months since they had last met, their longest separation since the war.

"You're so beautiful," Clive said, and she heard the catch in his voice. She turned away distractedly without acknowledging the compliment.

"I have another suitcase. A sort of carpetbag. There it is."

Clive went to the pile of luggage that was accumulating in a wet pool as the handlers brought it in from the storm, and hoisted her bag.

"My clothes are in there," she said with displeasure, seeing that the floral fabric was soaked dark.

He inspected it. "It's good quality. It should have held up. Come on, I have a taxi waiting."

The road into Kuching was not so much a road as a shallow river. The ancient Wolseley made heavy progress, lurching in the thick mud. She said nothing to Clive, though he tried to make conversation.

"Everything all right?" he asked at last, touching her hand.

"Yes," she said tonelessly.

"You must be tired," he said, as though needing to explain her silence to them both.

She nodded and stared out of the window without replying.

"We've had bad luck with the weather," Clive remarked. "I thought we'd get two clear weeks before the rains came."

Her nerves felt as though they were stretched tight under her skin. The flight had been an ordeal. Being with Clive was a horrible strain. Being in Borneo again was almost unbearable. It was an effort to address the subject that had brought them here. "Who is this woman?" she asked with an inner struggle.

"Ah, yes. The woman. I'm informed that her name is Annah. She lives in a Kayan village, but she's an Iban. They say she was one of Nendak's people. They say she was bayoneted during the Japanese attack, but that she survived by pretending to be dead. When the Japanese left, she crawled away and found help."

"We've met all the survivors," she said, her voice thin and flat. "We've been told a hundred times that nobody else came through."

"I know. But it's a possibility that we can't afford to ignore. If she was there, she may have seen something. She may know something."

Francine put her arms around herself and shuddered. The story of another possible survivor had brought her here as surely as a hook in the belly of a fish brings it to shore. But the pain of that hook sickened her.

Despite the monsoon, life was going on, and the streets were crowded. The daily market was in progress, the fruit and vegetables washed shiny by the rain. A few merchants crouched under makeshift shelters. Everybody else simply accepted the downpour. She felt crushed by the endless rain, the jungle, the oppression of it all. She longed for Hong Kong, for the hard certainties of her life there.

"Apparently she had relatives among the Kayans," Clive went on. "She went to stay with them, deep in the jungle. Nobody knew she was there until recently. I think it's a very exciting possibility, Francine."

"Exciting?" she repeated bitterly.

"Interesting," he amended, glancing at her set profile.

I have had enough of this, she thought. *Enough, enough, enough.*

"I presume business must be going well, if your new style is anything to go by," he said gently.

"What?"

"You've been tarting yourself up."

"What do you mean by that?" she demanded sharply.

He smiled. "Well, even under these conditions, my sweet, it's obvious that you've been on a spending spree. Italian shoes, French luggage." He flicked his damp hair back from his brow as he studied her. His face was very tanned. "Expensive jewelry. A salon hairdo. Hardly your usual style, is it?"

"What's my usual style, Clive?" she snapped. "Rags and a coolie hat?"

He raised an eyebrow. "You look wonderful, darling, I didn't mean anything except that. Don't be angry."

"What makes me angry is your arrogance," she retorted. "You're insufferable. You think you can say what you please."

He refused to respond to her militancy. "You're tired."

"In any case," she said in a low voice, "this is the style I am having to adopt. It is not of my choosing."

He touched her hand. "You're absolutely lovely," he said in an altered voice, "and I apologize if I offended you."

She glanced at his hand, strong and brown, covering hers. She pushed it away. "You think because you have seen me in rags that I am presumptuous to aspire to fashion."

"I told you—you look wonderful," he said.

"European style does not go well on me. I am a squat Chinese, and I look ridiculous. That has not escaped me, Clive."

"From the violent to the maudlin so quickly? Darling, you are not Chinese, and you are certainly not squat."

"I am not European, and I am not tall."

"As always, the truth lies somewhere between."

They said no more. The taxi meandered through the traffic to the bungalow they always rented, near Pangkalan Batu jetty. It was convenient to be close to the river. The river was the artery that would take them deep into the jungle. Deeper into the obsession that she increasingly felt was a process of self-destruction.

Since 1945, when the war ended, she had returned to Sarawak many times, sometimes for weeks at a time, traveling from village to village, from longhouse to longhouse, asking about Nendak's people. Asking about Ruth.

Everywhere, the answer was the same. The Japanese had come with bayonet and bullet. No more than a handful had survived, and those few had been scattered to the winds. Painfully, they had tracked down each last survivor. None of them had any memory of Ruth escaping. The children, she was told, had been among the easiest to kill: Lacking the understanding to run, they had crouched beside their dying parents, and been slaughtered wholesale. There had been no other survivors. There could have been no other survivors. Increasingly, Francine's only hope had been to find word that Ruth had died of dysentery before the Japanese had come.

In the first few years after the war, Clive had not always been able to join her. She had searched the jungle alone. She had sent agents to inquire in the deepest forest, on the highest mountains. Often, she had risked her life as she entered wild places where the Communist insurgents held sway. When the Emergency had been declared in 1948, restrictions had been imposed on civilian movement, and exploration had become almost impossible. She had continued her search through the Red Cross and a dozen other refugee organizations. There had been no Ruth. It was almost the end of 1954, and there had been no Ruth. *I will never find Ruth,* she told herself. *I must accept that she is gone, or this thing will destroy me.*

She had made some sound without intending to, because Clive turned to her in concern. "Francine? Are you all right? Darling, don't cry!" He held her close. "You must have had a terrifying flight from Singapore."

"I can't stand this much longer," she said shakily. "It's been over ten years, Clive."

"Maybe this time we'll get to the truth, darling," he said quietly.

She thrust him away. "The truth has been obvious for years. Why do we keep doing this, Clive? What for?"

"I've never given up hope," he said.

"You think we're going to find her?" she spat at him. "Suckled by wolves in the forest? Swinging from the trees with flowers in her hair?"

"Don't," he said. "Don't give up hope."

"Hope is a torturer," she replied. "You will never understand that, Clive. For you, this has become an interesting hobby. For me, it is something very different."

"I don't think *hobby* is quite the word I would have chosen."

"It is your way of keeping your hook in me."

"My hook?"

"So you can keep reeling me in." She stared at him with burning eyes. "So you can keep me attached to you, whether I want it or not. But it is all a lie, Clive. I know it, and so do you."

"You think I've invented the story of this woman, Annah?" he asked in a quiet voice.

"I think there will always be something. A survivor, a grave, a story, a sighting, a legend. Always. Every year some new horror will stir in the jungle, Clive, and you and I will have to go and dig it up. And so you will keep feasting on me. On my flesh. Until I stop this once and for all."

His expression had changed. "I had no idea you felt like that."

"Didn't you?"

"Of course not. I still believe we can find out the truth of what happened to Ruth. I thought you did, too." She turned away, and he gripped her arm. "I love you, Francine, and I always will. But I don't drag you to Borneo so I can impose myself on you. If you don't want to see me anymore . . ."

"This is the only place we meet any longer, Clive. Had that escaped you?"

He was silent, remembering a visit to Hong Kong the year before. He had tried to see Francine at her office. He had been kept waiting for an hour and a half, and then been told that her appointment book was full. When he'd tried to call her at home, polite staff had informed him that she was unavailable. The next day he'd been told that she had flown to Bangkok on business and was not expected back for days. He had returned to Australia, humiliated.

"It's always better to be open," he said at last. "You should have told me."

"I have been telling you for years, but you do not listen."

He sighed, and turned away from her. "I've been very obtuse, it seems."

"I feel that I'm being torn in half." She fought with her tears. "I can't be two people. I can only be one."

She did not know whether he understood her or not. "Here we are," he said, peering out of the window with dark eyes.

The bungalow was handsome but dilapidated, a relic of the colonial time of the White Rajahs. It stood behind the Square Tower, overlooking the boat jetty and the Sungei Sarawak, the wide green river. The house had been prepared as best it could for their visit, but the monsoon was already taking its toll. Green mold was appearing where the ceilings leaked, and the smell of rotting plaster nauseated Francine as they walked in. The atmosphere of the place brought back smothering memories of all the previous times they had come here, all the previous horror.

For the past few occasions, they had used separate bedrooms—her choice, not Clive's. As always, she took the front room, with a balcony overlooking the river. Clive took the back room, on the other side of the house, overlooking the lush garden. She unpacked, finding all her clothes, as she had expected, damp or ruined. The hold of the Beechcraft must have been awash all the way from Singapore. It hardly mattered; from now on, they would never be dry. She changed into a plain white dress and washed the makeup from her face.

A meal was waiting for them in the dining room, under a sluggishly revolving fan. Despite the suffocating heat, a fire had been lit in the grate, a valiant attempt to combat the humidity. The smell of smoldering, wet firewood revolted Francine. In any case, she would have had little appetite for the curry and rice that congealed on her plate. She and Clive sat opposite each other, picking at the food. Conversation between them had ground to a halt. Even though both of them were well used to monsoon weather, the heat and the humidity were choking, robbing the lungs of breath, covering the skin with clammy sweat.

After they'd eaten, they sat in the salon. It stretched the length of the house, a vast room whose high ceiling was supported by plaster columns. It had barely changed since the last century, ancient electrical fittings emerging from flaking plaster, a haphazard collection of sofas and rattan chairs scattered around. Venetian blinds had been drawn to keep out the worst of the monsoon, and the interior swam with a submarine light, as if everything and everyone were floating in tepid tropical waters. And, as though to complete the image, there was that sense of being unable to breathe the thick air.

"How are you feeling?" Clive asked Francine at last. His tone had been formal ever since she had said those savage things to him in the taxi. She was lying on a sofa, her white dress hanging limply around her.

"I'm all right," she said. She was covering her eyes with her arm, to keep out the light. Her eyeballs hurt. Her heart ached. Wearily, she lifted her arm away from her face and looked at Clive. He was surveying a map of Sarawak, spread out on his knee. "How far is it to this place?" she asked.

"If I've got the right village, two days up the river. If we're out of luck, we'll just have to keep going and asking for directions. The place is called Rumah Bulan."

"Does Bata know these people?"

"He's heard of them. They're in a remote side-stretch of the river, and don't have much contact with the outside."

"The rivers will be impossible after this rain."

"Bata says most of the rapids are still passable." He glanced at her. "You don't want to go?"

"No," she replied flatly. "I don't want to go."

"You're exhausted," he said, as though he needed to make an excuse for her. "You've been working far too hard in Hong Kong."

"I'm fine." She lay back on the faded chaise longue. Up in the vaulted ceiling, two fans chopped at the air, one very slow, the other with rickety speed. Geckos stalked insects on the walls. Thunder muttered overhead.

Clive went on in the same detached way. "You gave me a shock today. When you came in from the rain. You looked like another woman."

"I was half-drowned."

"It wasn't that. It wasn't just the clothes, either. It was the way you moved, the look on your face. You're gathering purpose, Francine. Your attention is turning in a different direction."

"To the future," she said quietly. "My eyes are turning to the future, Clive. I can't look into the past anymore."

"I understand that," he said. "And of course, your future doesn't include me. You made that clear this morning."

Something like pity touched her at his tone. "You'll always be a part of me."

"A part of your past."

"Yes," she said, meeting his eyes. "A part of my past."

"I hear your businesses are going well," he said.

"They're going well."

"You're growing rich."

"So are you, Clive, but I do not point it out in that accusatory tone."

"I am not accusing," he replied dryly. "Why shouldn't you like money?"

"I am interested in more than money."

"You're still expanding?"

"I am building a factory," she said, after a pause.

"Your own factory?" He did not hide his surprise. "Is that necessary?"

"It is not enough to simply distribute. I need to produce."

He was staring at her with questioning eyes. "Building a factory is a tremendous commitment, Francine. How are you raising the capital?"

"That is none of your business," she retorted.

"Why didn't you come to me?"

"I did not need you," she replied flatly.

"You have backers?"

"People trust me."

He frowned. "You're not involved with the tongs, are you?"

She gave him a withering glance. "I'm not a fool. I went to the HK and S, if you must know."

"Then you are doing well, if you persuaded the Hong Kong and Shanghai Bank to back you," he commented. "Where are you going to be located?"

"Tsim Sha Tsui," she said briefly.

"You've bought land?"

"I've had my name down on a land-reclamation project for two years. It's mine, at last. I've broken ground already. Construction will take seven months."

"Seven months!"

"A small electronics factory does not require a Versailles." She glanced at him. He was frowning. "Why do you look like that?"

"I'm just wondering if you're getting out of your depth," he replied.

"My depth?" She was truly angry now, so angry that she did not show it, either in her expression or in her voice. "The trouble with you, Clive," she said quietly, "is that you have never known my depth."

Her heart had contracted to a hard ball. She felt as though he were a stranger to her. It was a process that had been under way for some years. Now, the process seemed to be complete. *You're not involved with the tongs, are you?* He still thought of her as the country girl from Ipoh, ignorant, primitive. He could not see how she had changed, how she was changing. Even when she clawed at his smug face, he simply mopped away the blood and smiled indulgently.

He was silent for a long while. "Perhaps you're right," he said at last in an absent voice. "I only knew how to love you. I thought that was enough."

"It is not enough." Her tone was hard.

He turned back to his map without replying. Francine lay back on the sofa, feeling empty. Thunder rolled from one quarter of the sky to the other.

In the afternoon, they met with Bata, the boatman who would guide them up the river. He was a stocky, heavily tattooed Kayan in his early fifties, who had taken them on many such river trips. Once they left Kuching, they would depend utterly on him, not only to steer them through rapids and swamps, but also to provide them with food. The only provisions they would take were rice and salt; Bata would hunt for whatever he could to supplement the rice. As ever, he was stolidly reassuring, saying the rivers were not yet high enough to be dangerous, nodding over Clive's map, saying he thought he knew the area.

The rain poured down all afternoon. The evening meal was a repeat of the midday one. She and Clive picked listlessly at the savory but palate-scalding curry, an uncertain Iban servant in attendance.

After dinner, they prepared for the next day's journey. She would leave her Hong Kong clothes and jewels here: Theft was unknown in Kuching. She would travel with a light canvas bag containing three changes of cotton clothing, a medicine kit, and little else.

Clive knocked at her door. "Come in," she commanded.

He entered with a little white packet in his hand. "Did you remember your quinine this time?"

"No. I forgot again."

"I got an extra packet for you. Keep it."

Nodding her thanks, she took the packet to the sink and swallowed one of the powerfully bitter little pills. Malaria was a constant threat in the jungle, but somehow she always forgot the quinine.

Clive met her eyes in the mirror. "You should not give up hope, Francine," he said in a soft voice. "Even if hope is a torturer, as you say. There should always be hope."

"I am her mother," she said in an equally quiet voice. "You will never understand how I feel. How could you? She wasn't your child."

"I loved her, too, Francine. I feel as though she were my daughter, too."

She shook her head. "That's just a figure of speech."

"Not to me," he said sharply. "I would have died for her, Francine. I would have died for you."

"I know that," she said wearily. "I'm not sneering at your feelings, or what you did for us during the war. But it's different. Very different. For you, her death was sad. Even a tragedy, perhaps. You've spent years trying to find out what happened to her. But you've got on with your life. For me, it was more than a tragedy. It killed something inside me. It left me with only half a personality."

"You could have other children. Another family."

She put the quinine pills in her kit. "No, Clive. Not with you, not with anybody. That part of my life is dead."

"And your Hong Kong life makes up for what you've lost?"

"I'm trying to build a life for myself."

"A great step forward." There was unmistakable irony in his deep voice. "Building factories, making money, turning yourself into an empress—that fills the gap, does it?"

She turned and met his eyes. "I wake up each morning and remember Ruth. She is the last thought in my mind before I sleep. She is in my dreams. Nothing will ever fill the gap."

He raised a hand. "I apologize. That was inane."

"I have accepted her death, Clive. That is the great step forward that I have taken. If I don't accept her death, then I am doomed. You don't have to accept that she's dead. You can afford to keep on with this charade, because it doesn't tear you apart. You go back to Australia and slip happily back into your life there. But for me, each time I come back here is like losing her all over again. I can't keep doing it. I can't."

"I see," he said.

"I hope you do."

Clive nodded, and turned to go. "Sleep well, Francine."

She went to her bed and prayed for deliverance, that when they got back to this house in a few days' time she would have the courage to fulfill her brave words, and tell herself that Ruth was finally dead.

Francine was awakened very early the next morning by thunder. She arose, and went to the balcony. The yeasty green river swept in a curve past the bungalow. Already, though it was just after dawn, the river traffic was building up, sampans and barges drifting through the sheets of rain.

Lightning glared, and thunder crashed overhead. She wrapped a sarong around herself and went out of her room. Clive, too, was awake, and trying to make coffee in the kitchen.

"Damned matches won't light," he said in disgust. "Too damp."

She found the flint in the drawer, and used it to spark the gas burner into flame.

"Nice day for it, at any rate," Clive said, nodding at the weather.

"We should go."

"Right now?"

"Bata will be ready."

He shrugged, turning away. "All right, then. Let's get going."

She knew that he was both very angry and very hurt by the things she had said to him last night. For her own part, she felt a profound relief that they were finally in the open. He would never know what it had cost her to say them. Despite everything, she had loved him deeply. Too deeply. Over the twelve years that had passed since Singapore, she, Clive, and the ghost of Ruth had been locked in a death-embrace that had dragged her to depths she had never thought she would escape.

She had finally learned how to free herself from those leaden chains. Her businesses in Hong Kong, her projects there, had offered her a new life. She had discovered a talent for making money, but money was only a by-product of her salvation.

A week earlier, she had watched the yellow bulldozers cutting into the red earth, the red earth that was hers, that she had sacrificed so much to possess. Soon, her own factory would stand on that site. Soon, the fascinating game would take on a new dimension: There would be new rungs to climb, rungs that would take her farther out of this darkness.

"This is the last time, Clive," she said.

He stared at her. "The last time? The last time for what?"

"The last time between you and me."

His eyes darkened as he took in her meaning. "Jesus, you can be a coldhearted bitch sometimes," he said, showing one of his rare flashes of anger. "How can you talk to me like that, after all we've been through together?"

"Please," she said, her tone quiet, but cutting through like a knife nevertheless. "I know what we've been through together. You don't need to remind me."

"Money is destroying you, Francine. You've forgotten who you are!" He turned away and began to throw some last things into his bag, obviously furious.

"I know who I am. But I am not who you think I am."

"You think I don't understand you?" He looked up from his packing, his eyes black and hot. "You think I haven't seen you stripped to the bone? Francine, I understand you better than you will ever know."

"That's how you've always wanted me," she said evenly. "Stripped. A poor little Eurasian girl who needed you, depended on you for everything. You never wanted me to be anything else. You hated it when I started my own business. You hate seeing me grow."

"I hate seeing you turn your back on Ruth," he said brutally. "I hate hearing you say you're too busy making money in Hong Kong to bother trying to find out what happened to your daughter."

"My daughter is dead," she said in a shaking voice. "But you keep digging up her body and presenting me with it, like a stupid, vicious dog. I let you persuade me to leave her in that village. If I had listened to my own heart, and taken her with me, she would be alive today."

He flinched as though she had struck him. "She would have died within days!"

"Then at least she would have died in my arms," she replied. "And she and I would both be at rest now." She gestured at the bungalow around them, the monsoon that battered at the walls. "This is hell, Clive. This is the hell I have tried to escape from, and that you keep dragging me back to. But no more. No more, I promise you. This is the last time."

Bata had cut the outboard motor sometime earlier, and had lifted the propeller clear of the water. This reach of the river was broad enough, but the water was shallow, and treacherous with rocks. He and Clive had been paddling steadily for the past hour, against the swift current. From her place in the narrow, cluttered prow, Francine had been peering anxiously at the banks.

Now at last she saw something, and pointed. "Look!"

The two men paused. Standing on a shoal on the bank was a group of four children clinging to lianas. They stared with wide eyes at the strangers, completely silent.

Bata raised his paddle in greeting. He called out a question to them. One replied in a shrill voice, flinging out an arm to point upstream. Then all four children melted back into the forest, giggling.

"They say the village is around the next bend," Bata translated.

Francine nodded wearily. Clive picked up his paddle, and got back to work. Since they'd left Kuching, she and Clive had barely spoken to each other. It had rained steadily for six days, and that was almost the only sound any of them had heard.

Their journey had taken so long partly because they had encountered rapids made unusually treacherous by the swollen river. They had had to carry the boat for some distance through the jungle, and Bata had refused to put the boat back in the water until he had placated the demons of the rapids with a sacrifice. They had lost two full days while he chanted and laid out food in the pouring rain.

Francine wore a sarong knotted above her breasts, her slim brown arms and shoulders bare beneath the constant drizzle. If they could see her now, those bankers of Hong Kong, who had been so dazzled with her vision and her daring; if they could see her now, those financiers who had been so impressed with her sophistication, sitting half-naked in a longboat, gliding down a river in the heart of Borneo, what would they say? She hardly felt that she was the same person. The never-ending rain that beat down on her skin seemed to her to be slowly washing away everything she was, everything she had built up, reducing her to anonymous mud. She loathed that feeling. She was forcing herself to endure, not to lose what it had cost her so much to create in herself.

They rounded the bend in the river and suddenly the village swam into view. It was small, no more than two longhouses straggling along the bank, a scattering of boats drawn up on the shingle. The children they had seen earlier were running along the shore, calling out the news that strangers had come. A few adults appeared from the longhouses, staring wide-eyed at the new arrivals.

They paddled in to shore. Francine looked around. Rumah Bulan was a remote place, well hidden. It was easy to see how news from this settlement might take years to percolate to the outside world.

A group of Kayans had come down to meet them, the men helping them beach the boat and haul it up out of the water. They chattered eagerly to Bata in Kayan. She and Clive stood silently while the boatman passed around tobacco and talked for ten minutes. At last he turned to them.

"She is here," he said.

"The woman named Annah?"

He nodded. "She lives here." He gestured at one of the men who had come to greet them. "This man's name is Ismael. He is her brother-in-law."

The man called Ismael, naked but for a dark red loincloth, smiled at them shyly. "Annah is in the longhouse with her baby," he told them in Malay. "I will tell her you have come."

Francine felt her stomach tighten in a wrenching twist. She glanced at Clive.

Clive presented Ismael with a packet of tobacco. "The Annah we are looking for was an Iban," he said. "She was of Nendak's people, in the time of the Japanese war."

The man called Ismael, delighted with the gift, nodded. "Annah was of Nendak's people before she came to us," he said. "She still carries the scar the Japanese gave her at Rumah Nendak."

Francine's mouth was suddenly dry. It had not been a misunderstanding, a mistake. It had been true all along. For the first time since leaving Hong

Kong, the reality came home to her: They were about to meet one of the survivors of the massacre, one of the handful of witnesses who might testify as to Ruth's fate. It had been years since they had found a survivor. Instinctively she gripped Clive's arm. "She's here," she said in a shaky voice.

He nodded. "Yes. She's here."

Her legs were weak. "Let's go to her!"

"Wait." He held her back. "Let them speak to her first. And we should pay a visit to the headman before we see her. It would be courteous."

She tried to fight down the wild fluttering in her breast. "You're right. But let's go quickly, Clive. Please."

It was late afternoon, and still raining hard, before they were permitted to enter the *bilik* where the woman was shut in with her baby. Before that, they had to sit with Bulan, the elderly headman, drinking rice beer and talking on the ruai, surrounded by an inquisitive group of onlookers. Francine endured it with as much patience as she could. These were not people who understood haste. And it might be months before the next outsider came to this faraway longhouse. In other villages over the past few days, they had seen evidence of "civilization"—people wearing watches and other baubles, boys with Elvis Presley hairstyles, girls in brassieres. Here there were no such signs of contact with the outside world. She and Clive were a rare treat for these people, to be savored and appreciated.

The rain thundered on the atap roof endlessly, its roar almost drowning the talk of Kuching, of the rivers, of the rice crop. The hours stretched out agonizingly. But at last the chief's head began to nod with the long talk and the rice wine, and he slumped into the sudden doze of old age. Bata leaned forward.

"You may go to her now," he murmured. "Her brother-in-law will show you."

They followed Ismael into the bilik, the private family apartment where the woman lived. Stooping to enter the low doorway, Francine felt woodsmoke burn her eyes. The woman was sitting beside her fireplace. With one hand, she was stirring a pot. In the crook of her other arm nestled a very tiny baby, obviously born no more than a few days earlier, suckling at her breast.

Her heart pounding, Francine pressed her hands together in greeting and sat cross-legged. Clive joined her on the rush mat. The woman smiled shyly at them. She was in her mid-twenties, Francine estimated, and even if the rest of her features had not marked her as an Iban, her small, neat ears would have done so; the Kayan women of this community all had earlobes stretched into saucer-wide hoops by heavy brass earrings. The process had to begin in infancy, and it had been too late for Annah to start when she had come to Rumah Bulan. She was handsome, with large, serious eyes and a full mouth. Still livid across her neck and throat was the scar they had been told of. The slashing blow had been intended to sever the carotid and windpipe, and she must have escaped death by some miracle.

"The baby is beautiful," Francine whispered in Malay, her voice unsteady. "What is his name?"

"Kana," she replied, stroking the child's head.

"May he live long, and grow to be a great man."

Annah's smile was fleeting. "May it be so."

"We've brought some small gifts," Clive said, opening the bag he had brought into the bilik. He passed over some things they had bought in a bazaar: enamel plates and cups, a pretty cotton sarong, a carton of cigarettes. The woman's fine black eyes glistened with pleasure. The simple gifts were acceptable.

"Do you remember us, Annah?" Francine asked, still unable to raise her voice above a dry rustle.

Annah's eyes flickered from her to Clive. "Yes," she said.

"You know who we are?"

Annah nodded once. "You are the tuans who came to Rumah Nendak. The tuans who left the child behind."

Francine swallowed, trying to force her tight throat to open. Others they had interviewed had barely recalled their visit; amid the turbulence of the war, it had made little impact, and the subsequent catastrophe had blotted out vague memories. But this woman's intelligent, retentive mind shone from her face. "You remember the child?"

Annah's arm tightened slightly around her own infant. "I remember how she screamed, the day you left. I remember how she ran after you, screaming for you. I saw your face. I saw what you felt. That is something I have never forgotten."

"You remember!"

The Iban woman's eyes had turned inward. "I remember how we had to run after her," she went on, after a pause. "One of the men took her, and tried to stop her from crying. But she was like a wild thing. He had to put his hand over her mouth. The sound she made was too much to bear. She screamed for many days after you left. She would try to run into the jungle to follow after you, and we had to shut her in a bilik. She would not eat or drink. And she was already weak. We thought she would die. Then one day she stopped screaming. She took some water. After that, she started to eat a little." Annah rocked her child for a while. "I was fourteen or fifteen, and had no children of my own. I was one of the ones who fed her and tried to comfort her."

Tears were spilling hotly down Francine's cheeks now. She made a jerky attempt to wipe them away, but her arm did not seem to obey her. She swallowed convulsively. "I never saw my child again, Annah," she said. "That is why I have come to you now. To ask you to tell me what became of her."

Annah's eyes widened. "You don't know?"

Francine shook her head. "I've never known."

The Iban woman's calm seemed shattered. Agitated, she plucked the baby from her nipple, and began to wrap him in a cloth. He protested with a thin, fierce cry. "How can you not know?" she demanded, looking from Clive to Francine with her big, glistening eyes. "They must have told you!"

"Only a handful escaped, Annah," Clive said quietly. "And most of those were very old people whom the Japanese spared because they respected white hair. They had no recollection of us or our child."

"I do not understand," Annah said in a troubled way. "Why didn't you come back?"

"We came back many, many times," Clive said. "Nothing was left of your village. The people were scattered. We tried to find every one of them, but it was not easy, and none of them could tell us anything. We only heard of your name in the past few weeks. We did not know for sure that you even existed until we arrived this morning. This place is very remote from the outside."

She touched the scar on her throat. "I never want to see the outside again," she said quietly. "That is why I stay here." Her child was still fretting, and she comforted him.

Francine leaned forward. "Please," she whispered hoarsely. "Tell me what became of my child."

Annah was silent for a long while, avoiding Francine's burning eyes. At last she began to speak in a gentle, almost diffident voice. "It was a moon or perhaps two moons after you left. They came early in the morning, in a patrol boat. There were many of them, perhaps thirty. They made everybody come out of the longhouses and stand on the sand. Their leader shouted at us for a long while in Japanese. Nobody understood him, and some of the young men began to laugh. But I was very afraid, because I knew that a sentry had been killed, and that they had come to punish us. They made all the young men stand in a group. Suddenly, they started firing at the men. They killed them all very quickly. Then they turned on the rest of us, but they did not fire any more bullets. They used their swords and bayonets." She had lifted her hand, and was absently stroking the livid scar on her neck, her eyes shining with tears. "We were helpless. There was nobody left to defend us. The men were all dead. I saw them kill my mother and my two sisters. One of the officers struck me with his sword, here on my throat. I pretended that I was dead. I lay still while they killed everybody. I was afraid that I would bleed to death before they left. But they set fire to the longhouses, and at last they went away again. I was very weak. I managed to drag myself to the river, and I let the current carry me downstream. A few miles away, some men who were fishing saw me and rescued me. That was how I survived."

"And our child?" Clive asked quietly.

"They killed her. I saw it. A soldier thrust his bayonet into her breast. I saw it come out of her back. She could not have survived."

Francine's pain was too terrible to contain. She leaned forward with a jagged cry and began to sob. Clive put his arms around her and held her tightly. But she was oblivious to him or to anything else at that moment. Days earlier, she had prayed to hear this, to end her agony. But now that the words had been spoken, the anguish was as fresh and as dreadful as if she had just witnessed Ruth's death with her own eyes. Her child had been torn from her with a pain as great as childbirth, but as final as death.

Annah, frightened by Francine's grief, clutched her own baby tightly, rocking to and fro in silence.

"Francine!" Clive said in anguish. "Darling!"

But she felt as though her lungs were being crushed, as though she could expel breath to cry, but not take it in. Blackness swam around her. She fought for air, but her body would not respond. Her life was pouring out of her. In a strange hallucination, she saw Ruth standing before her. Her skin was bathed in light and on her face was an unearthly smile. Francine would have reached out to her child, but she had no arms, no body to command. Then the vision was gone, and Francine yielded to the blackness.

They carried her out onto the ruai and laid her on a mat. Her body was so limp that Clive was truly afraid. He pressed his ear to her chest to make sure that her heart was still beating. The pulse seemed so faint to him that he panicked, and tried to rouse her, shaking her and calling her name.

The Kayans stopped him. "You will damage her spirit," one of the men said earnestly. "If you wake her now, she may die. Leave her."

"She will sleep for a night and a day," one of the women said. "That is the way."

"Do not touch her." They pulled Clive away from Francine, gently but firmly. He watched helplessly as the women wrapped Francine in a woven blanket and carried her into one of the biliks.

Ismael squatted beside him. "They will watch over her," he said. "They know what to do."

"I need to get her to a doctor," Clive said stupidly.

Bata, the boatman, put his hand on Clive's shoulder. "She cannot travel like that," Bata said. "They are right—she would die."

"She's had a terrible blow," Clive said. He felt sick and shaken, both at the explicit description Annah had given them of Ruth's death, and by Francine's utter devastation. In all the years he had known her, during all they had been through, he had never seen her break down in that shocking way.

Ismael rolled himself a cigarette with the tobacco they had given him. "When she has slept, she will be better. In the meantime, you should rest, too, tuan. My people will give you food. Tonight there will be dancing and drinking."

The men left him there, and he sat staring out at the rain and the jungle, thinking. They had traveled a long and tortuous road to hear these words, in this far-flung place. He felt a sense of terrible finality now, in the nauseous aftermath; not just that they had reached the end of Ruth, but that he was also at the end of Francine.

There had been a brutal core of truth in the things she had said to him in Kuching. The search for Ruth was the only thing that kept them together anymore. And he had, as she had said, been unwilling to let that ghost rest, partly because doing so would mean losing her. Unwittingly, he had been torturing her for his own selfish motives.

You've played your cards badly, old boy, he told himself with sad realization.

He had harped on the past, on what was dead and gone. He had not understood that she needed a future. That she needed to move on.

He had regarded the things she was doing in Hong Kong as a threat. He had not wanted her to establish herself there, she had been right about that.

Secretly, perhaps he had even hoped she would fail, lose money, lose face, so that she would come running back to him, and resign herself to becoming his wife.

Resign herself. That phrase echoed through Clive's mind like a leaden bell.

If he had bet on Francine's future, and not on her past, he might be a winner now, and not a loser. He should have supported her more when she'd first gone into business, in her shabby little office, years ago. He should have known that there was a driving force in Francine that would always impel her forward, that would never allow her to rest.

That she would never fail. Would never lose money, lose face. Would never come back to him.

Night was falling already. Thunder boomed in the darkness and rain lashed at the roof of the longhouse. Clive Napier had never felt so sad or so alone.

Francine lay in the farthest corner of the bilik. The dim light of very early morning filtered through the opening above the fireplace. The two other women were already awake, one quietly weaving a straw mat, the other stirring a bowl of rice.

Francine's eyes drifted in a glazed way, taking in the humble furnishings, the two large clay jars that held rice, the few Chinese ceramic plates, the wicker utensils. She was very weak. Somewhere in her mind were echoes of her own voice crying, images of herself raging, but this morning, all that was no more than the dim recollection of a nightmare. She felt completely emptied. Even her grief had ebbed away. She was hollow, void. The whirlwind had passed through her world, and had razed everything that had stood there.

She moved her head. The women saw she was awake, and greeted her in murmurs. Their skin was the color of caramel in this soft light. The weaver was old, with a sunken face and flattened breasts. The other was very young, a teenager with conical breasts and an unlined face. The girl held out a bowl of glutinous rice. Francine shook her head. But the girl came to sit at her side, and with the animal grace of youth, leaned forward to put morsels of food in Francine's mouth.

The rice had no taste to her. It was merely a warm presence in her mouth. She swallowed obediently, allowing the girl to feed her as though she were a sick child.

The old woman's fingers worked swiftly, weaving the straw into complex patterns. "You will get better now," she said in Malay. She had no teeth. "It is over."

"Where is the tuan?" Francine whispered.

"Outside."

"Is he asleep?"

"Asleep!" The old woman cackled softly. "Wah! He can drink, that one! He does not sleep. He just drinks *tuak*. He has put our men to shame."

She found strength to push the next handful of rice away. She sat up slowly. Her body was weak and trembling. "Has it stopped raining?"

"It is the monsoon," the old woman said simply. "It never stops raining."

"Has the river risen?"

"Two palms."

"No more?"

"No more," the old woman said.

The girl tried to give Francine more rice, but she shook her head. "I want to go outside." She gathered her sarong around her and started trying to get to her feet. She was conscious of an emotion, at last, an anxiety that they should not be marooned here for the duration of the monsoon. She had to find Clive.

She had seriously overestimated her strength. She staggered and almost fell into the fire. The Kayan girl grabbed her arms and steadied her. With the girl's help, she managed to stumble out of the bilik. Rain was sweeping down from low clouds and there was a suffocating miasma of decay in the moist air.

She stared at the river. The water had indeed risen since they'd arrived here. Brown and frothy, it swept past the longhouses with formidable speed. The journey back would be dangerous, but it was still possible. Tomorrow or the next day, it would not be.

She could hear Annah's voice, somewhere in her mind, repeating the story of Ruth's death. She clamped her palms to her ears, shutting it out. She did not want to hear about Ruth. She did not want to see Ruth.

She turned to the girl. "Where is the tuan?"

"I will take you."

The girl led her carefully down the ladder. The earth was a sea of mud. The longhouse was raised on stilts, and beneath it was the only relatively dry place outside. Here the pigs, dogs, and chickens of the village had gathered for shelter. The girl steered Francine into the stinking shadows, one hand around Francine's arm to stop her from falling again.

"There he is," she said.

Francine stared into the gloom. Clive was slumped against an ironwood post, a bamboo jar clasped between his splayed thighs. Next to him lay a recumbent figure, snoring in a fetal ball. Francine recognized the red loincloth and tattooed buttocks of Ismael, Annah's brother-in-law. She peered at Clive. His face was the ghastly mask of a corpse.

"Clive!" she said, alarmed that he might truly have died in some prolonged drinking bout.

He opened bloodshot eyes. "Ah," he croaked. "There you are."

She stared down at him, lying among the excrement and the mud. "You look terrible," she said.

"You're no oil painting," he retorted.

"Have you finished drinking?"

"If you've finished crying." He groped for the jar of rice beer and peered into it. "Empty," he said. "They didn't brew enough. I must speak to the barman."

"I've finished crying, Clive," she said. "We have to go, before the river rises any more."

"What's your hurry, my sweet?" Clive reached out and slapped Ismael's back. "Barman!" The man did not stir. "Barman! The tuak has run dry."

"I'm going," she said in a still, clear voice. "If you want to stay here until the end of the monsoon, do so. But I'm leaving with Bata today."

She turned and walked away. Clive shouted something after her, but she did not stop.

The rain beat down on Kuching. Clive stared at the runway, reflecting, as he had done two weeks earlier, that it seemed impossible any small aircraft could fly in this weather. The Beechcraft was no more than a dim shape in the rain. But he could hear the engines running, and he knew that the Beechcraft would fly, despite the weather. In a few moments, she would be gone.

He turned to look at her. She was talking into the public phone, raising her voice to be heard on the poor line to Hong Kong. She was speaking Mandarin, but he caught a few words he understood: *factory, schedule, architect.* Her face was intent. She had lost a lot of weight in two weeks, and her elegant clothes were bedraggled. But purpose radiated from her, as though she were a neon sign, flashing messages.

A frown creased her smooth brow for a moment, and she hung up. She walked quickly back to him, putting her notebook in her bag.

"Everything all right?" he asked.

"They're still on schedule," she said.

He marveled at her. It was hard to believe she was the same woman he'd seen break apart in the longhouse. "That's good."

"Well." She looked up into his face. There were dark shadows under her eyes. She had tried to cover them with makeup, but they showed through nevertheless. She looked drawn. But the expression on her face was hard and tight. They were strangers now. It was as though they had never been anything but strangers. Since they'd left Rumah Bulan, she hadn't even been cruel to him. He wished she had: It would have shown that she still cared enough to want to hurt him. But she did not. "Thank you for everything, Clive."

He found the words with an effort. "I know this is the last time I'll see you," he said. His voice sounded strange in his own ears.

"Come and visit me in Hong Kong," she replied, as though he hadn't spoken. "I'll show you my factory."

"While you were lying in the bilik, I spoke to Annah some more," he said. He saw her face stiffen, and held up a hand to stop her from interrupting. "Wait, Francine. I only want to say one last thing. She saw a child bayoneted. She saw the blade come out of the child's back. So she did not see the child's face. When I asked her directly whether she had seen Ruth's face in death, she said no."

Her mouth was a tight line. "Clive—"

"Hush, my sweet." He leaned forward and kissed her cursorily. "Go. Fly away."

For a moment he thought she would say something to him, some bitter blow to poison his last memory of her. But she just turned and walked away from him, her head held high, her back straight.

A porter hurried after her, carrying her bag. She appeared not to notice as the man joined her, opening an umbrella over her head. They went out into the rain. She was the last to board. Clive watched her dim figure enter the white plane, saw the door thump closed.

A minute later, the Beechcraft's engines rose in pitch and the plane taxied onto the runway. It was raining so hard that he did not see it take off, but he heard the engines droning into the sky.

"Good-bye, Francine," he whispered, and turned to go.

FOUR

SAKURA

1970

NEW YORK

"When can I talk to her?"

Dr. Parsons frowned. She had been asking the same question for forty-eight hours, and for forty-eight hours he had been trying to hold her off. "You must understand, Mrs. Lawrence, that the patient is infectious. We'll be able to take her out of isolation in a week or so. The antibiotic works very quickly. After that, sensible precautions will be enough and you can—"

Francine cut through. "I cannot wait a week. Is she strong enough to talk this morning?"

Parsons glanced at Francine's glittering green eyes. He was a successful specialist, used to deference from patients and their families. "The fever is down from yesterday. But this disease has been wearing away at her for years. She needs extensive rest."

"Is she awake now?"

"Yes. Mrs. Lawrence, I would like to explain some details of her condition to you."

"I don't wish to be rude, Doctor. But can that wait until I have spoken to her?"

Parsons sighed his capitulation. He glanced at his watch. "You may have a quarter of an hour with her now. After that, I'll ask one of the nurses to call for you. It's imperative you wear a surgical mask. And I would ask you not to touch her."

Francine nodded curtly. "Thank you, I don't intend to touch her. Now take me to her, please."

The surgical mask covered Francine's nose and mouth. She followed the orderly down the corridor to the isolation ward. There was only one entrance, protected by double doors. As they passed through, Francine felt fans blow on her back. Air was allowed into this place, but not out.

She felt tight. Sakura Ueda had played a heartless game with her. But now there was nowhere left for Sakura to run. Now she wanted answers.

The orderly pushed the door open and Francine walked in.

Sakura was sitting up in bed. A nurse, masked and gowned, was taking her blood pressure. The rubber cuff had been fastened just above the black tattoo that circled Sakura's left arm. Francine's gaze flicked from the tattoo to Sakura's eyes. They had the untamed light of a trapped animal's. Francine offered no greeting, nor did Sakura.

"You have no right to do this to me," Sakura said in a fierce tone.

"What am I doing to you?" Francine asked.

"You hunted me down, and now you're keeping me a prisoner in this place."

"A prisoner?" Francine said darkly, reflecting on what the clinic was costing her each day.

"They've pumped me full of drugs. Injected me. They want to cut my hair. You have no right."

It was the first time Francine had heard Sakura's voice, and she was listening intently to the slight accent, the normally soft tonality that anger or fear had made harsh.

"They are trying to save your life."

"I've had this thing for years. I'm stronger than it is."

"No," Francine replied evenly. "You're not. It will kill you. But I require some answers from you before it does. So I intend to keep you alive until you tell me what I want to know."

Sakura's face, the fine lines pared by exhaustion, tightened at Francine's reply. "What right have you to interrogate me? Let me go!"

"Tell me the truth," Francine retorted, "and I assure you, you will be free to go out and die in the nearest gutter."

She had meant it to sound harsh, and it did. The nurse who was taking Sakura's blood pressure flinched. She unwrapped the cuff and gathered her instruments. "I'll come back to take your pressure again shortly," she said. She left the room, looking glad to be leaving.

When the door had closed, Francine took the miniature tape recorder out of her shoulder bag and put it on the table next to Sakura's bed. She switched it on to record. Then she reached up and undid the tape that fastened the surgical mask around her mouth and nose.

Sakura looked up. "What are you doing?"

"I don't think we need masks."

"Is that meant to be ironic? The mask is for your benefit, not mine."

"I doubt whether you'll infect me. I'm resistant to most kinds of infection. Let's not waste each other's time more than necessary. Are you well enough to talk?"

"I am perfectly well," Sakura said, her strained face belying the answer. "What do you want to know?"

"Tell me who you are."

"I'm Sakura Ueda. Who are you?"

"You know who I am," Francine said flatly. "You've been studying me for a long time. Haven't you? How long?"

For a moment, Sakura just stared at her. Francine returned the younger woman's gaze without flinching. Sakura was almost as pale as the white shift she wore, or the white sheets of her bed. Francine was wearing a black suit. *We are like two queens on a chessboard,* Francine thought, *ready to fight and slay.*

"I've been studying you," Sakura said, repeating the cadence of Francine's words exactly, "for five years."

Francine felt a bitter, slashing moment of triumph. "Then you admit you are an impostor!"

"Anything that will make you happy."

The mockery angered Francine. "Who are your accomplices?"

"I have no accomplices."

"Then who put you up to this five years ago?"

"Nobody. I read about you in a newspaper article in Hong Kong."

"And you dreamed up the whole scheme then?"

"Scheme. Accomplices. What a strange mind you have, Mrs. Lawrence."

Francine walked to the window. The only view was of the building opposite, another part of the clinic. Snow had been falling for two days and was still falling, ethereal in the air, turning to spiteful slush as soon as it reached the pavement. "You claim you lived in a village in Borneo as a child?"

"Yes. That's my claim."

"Describe the village."

"There is nothing to describe," Sakura replied. "It was a village like all the others. There were longhouses by the river, rice paddies on the mountainside."

"Who was the headman?"

"I remember nothing about the people."

"Who took you there?"

"I don't remember."

"Do you claim to remember me from your childhood?"

"No," Sakura said flatly. "Do you remember me?"

The question jolted Francine. "No," she said without hesitation. "There is nothing familiar about you." She saw a strange expression twist Sakura's face. "Does that surprise you? Did you expect I would welcome you with open arms?"

"I expected nothing," Sakura replied quietly.

"Do you remember your father?"

"No," Sakura replied.

"Did you get those tattoos as part of your strategy?"

"Strategy." Sakura was adept at mocking Francine's tone. "No. They weren't part of any strategy. They were done when I was a child."

"The Ibans do not tattoo girls," Francine said sharply.

"I was not tattooed by Ibans."

"Who, then?"

"By Penans who adopted me."

"What do you mean, adopted?"

Sakura was composed, her hands motionless on the sheet. "The Japanese came one day, and started to kill everybody. A Penan couple rescued me. They were called Manu and Wai."

"The Japanese?"

"Soldiers. I remember the shooting. The screaming. I remember how they forced everybody into a group, and then began killing them with bayonets. I escaped because I was small enough to duck under their arms. I ran into the trees. Manu and Wai were there, watching the whole thing. They picked me up, and carried me away. They ran for a whole day, carrying me between them. They didn't stop until we were deep in the forest." She looked up at Francine. "That's what I remember. That was my birth."

Francine kept her face expressionless, though her heart was pounding. "Why did they take you?"

"To save me." She paused. "They couldn't have children of their own. They wanted to keep me. So later they tattooed me with their own special designs." Involuntarily, Francine's eyes dropped to the black bracelets.

"They did it with a bamboo needle, using soot scraped from the bottom of a cooking pot."

"What was the name of the village the Penans took you to?"

Sakura's lip curled. "You are ignorant. The Penans have no villages. They live deep in the forest. They speak the language of the birds and the wild animals. They leave no trace. Nobody can find them who isn't also a Penan."

"Then how did you come to Japan?"

"A Japanese officer took me away from Manu and Wai."

"Why did he do that?"

"He recognized that I wasn't a Dayak. I lived in his compound in Kuching for a while. There were other war children there. He'd found them, like me, living wild. He gathered them up and sent them to other places."

"What other places?"

She shrugged. "Places they would be cared for."

"Orphanages?"

"I suppose so. The Japanese were not all monsters."

"What was this man called?"

"His name was Tomoyuki Ueda."

"Ueda? You took his name?" Francine said, unable to hide her incredulity.

"He gave it. I took it. What difference does it make?"

Francine tried to read Sakura's expression. "What was Ueda's interest in you?"

"He said I was special." Sakura's voice had lowered. "He sent all the others away, but he brought me with him to Tokyo. He called me Sakura, because it was the spring, and all the cherries were in blossom. He gave me his surname."

"What month of what year was this?"

"I don't know."

"Do you remember Hiroshima and Nagasaki?"

"Oh, yes," Sakura said quietly. "Everybody remembers the atomic bombs."

"Well, how long after you arrived in Tokyo did the bombs fall?"

"A year, I think."

"And where is Tomoyuki Ueda now?"

"He's dead," she replied. "After the war, the Americans took him away. He was sentenced to death for war crimes. I remember that year. It was 1947."

"How old were you?"

"I don't know. Around ten, I guess."

"How did you live after Ueda died?"

"I worked," Sakura said. "I swept and cleaned. I cooked. I did whatever I could to get food and shelter. Ueda's family were kind to me for a while. Sometimes I even went to school. But everyone wanted to forget everything connected with Tomoyuki."

"How long did you live in Tokyo?"

"I left Japan when I was eighteen or nineteen. I never went back. There was nothing there for me."

Francine heard movement outside, and knew that she would be asked to leave in a moment. She returned to the crucial question, the question upon which everything hinged. "What do you remember of your life before the Japanese attacked your village?"

"Nothing."

"No sound, no place, no smell?"

"I told you," Sakura replied. "My life began that day on the river. I remember nothing before that. No people, no places, no events. I have no memories before that day. Nothing." She paused. "I've tried many techniques—meditation, hypnosis, even drugs. There's nothing there."

"That is very convenient."

Sakura's eyes lifted to meet hers. "Or very inconvenient. It depends on your point of view."

"We will find what has been lost," Francine said quietly, but with great determination. "I promise you that." The door opened, and two nurses came in. The interview, unsatisfactory as it had been, was over. Francine nodded a curt good-bye, and left.

Sakura Ueda's chest X rays were clipped to the viewer. Dr. Parsons tapped the images with his pencil. "These are the active lesions, which caused the hemorrhage. Apart from these, there are old scars in the upper and posterior parts of both lungs. Here, and here. It will keep happening until her chest is fatally weakened." He perched on his desk and looked down at Francine. "This disease has to be cured, Mrs. Lawrence. Otherwise, she will die."

"I understand that."

"She's made progress. We're treating her with daily intramuscular injections of streptomycin, and two oral drugs, PAS and isoniazid. I've also prescribed corticosteroids to fight any toxemia that lingers on."

Francine nodded. The hospital accountants had already told her what this was going to cost. "How long before she's discharged?"

"If the fever stays down, and there are no further hemorrhages, in two weeks. The important issue is a permanent cure. Sakura is very willful. I would even say rebellious. She's led a rough life, and she's got a tough shell. You might consider getting some psychological help with her, to draw her out. We don't want a repetition of Macao."

"Macao?"

"She told me she had her first hemorrhage eight years ago, in Macao. She was working in a casino. Eighteen-hour shifts, in a confined, smoky environment. She coughed up a mass of blood one morning. But she left Macao without any treatment. She couldn't afford the medication. You didn't know?"

"No." Francine had told the staff that Sakura was a distant relation, without elaborating. She smiled stiffly. "I'm afraid I know very little about her."

"From what she told me, she's lived a pretty up-and-down sort of life all over the Far East. She's lived in the jungle for spells, as well as in urban slums, and both are ideal places to breed lung diseases. She's so strong that her symptoms disappeared after a while, in any case. She's an astonishingly strong young woman. What one might call a natural survivor. But she isn't going to make it without the right treatment." He cocked his head at her. "The family resemblance between you and Sakura is strong, Mrs. Lawrence."

"Is it?" she said flatly.

"Oh, yes. You say it's been many years since you saw her?"

She knew he wondered about her "distant relation" story, and was probing for more details. "Yes, many years."

"So you're not close?"

"Not exactly."

He leaned forward. "I'm asking all this, Mrs. Lawrence, because I want to emphasize something. She will have to take drugs for another year. But equally important, her lifestyle has to change, permanently. She has to rest, breathe clean air, follow a healthy diet. She needs bright surroundings and a cheerful atmosphere. There's no question of her working, not for many months. She shouldn't go back to Laos at all until she's cured. The ideal thing would be a sanatorium, but diligent home care with a nurse would be almost as good."

"I see," Francine said dryly.

"Of course, all this will cost a lot of money."

"And you're asking me if I will provide it?"

"Her life depends on the follow-up treatment," he said bluntly. He met her eyes directly. "Someone has to provide it."

Francine's mouth tightened. "Dr. Parsons, when I said that Miss Ueda is a relation, I wasn't being strictly accurate. She claims to be a relation. I haven't been able to check her story yet. Until I do, I can't commit myself in that way. I'll pay for her treatment while she's in this clinic, but what happens to her after that depends on whether her claim has any truth in it."

Parsons showed no surprise. "Okay. That leads us down another avenue. If she stopped the treatment early, the results would be disastrous. The tuberculosis organisms would develop resistance to the drugs. It would become impossible to treat her ever again. And she would become a carrier of resistant organisms. I would have to report that to the health authorities. They would quarantine her and deport her right back to Laos." He smiled at Francine. "Where she would be free to go and die in the nearest gutter."

The nurse had evidently reported Francine's brutal comment to Parsons, and Francine flushed.

"There's another thing, Mrs. Lawrence."

"What is it?"

"There are two armed men sitting outside Sakura's ward. They say they are guards with Mr. Munro's security agency."

"That's right."

"I'm going to have to ask you to tell Mr. Munro to withdraw them."

"Why?"

"It's hospital policy. We do not allow outside security agencies to operate within these walls. Especially not carrying weapons."

"They are there to watch over Sakura," she said stiffly.

"You mean, to stop her from escaping?"

"To protect her."

"From what?"

"I don't know."

"We have our own very good security officers," Parsons replied. "Rest assured, they will take care of Sakura. Those men must be gone within an hour, or I'll have them thrown out." Parsons checked his watch. "I'm due to operate. I have to scrub up. Let me know as soon as possible what you decide, Mrs. Lawrence." He ushered her out.

She had arranged for Clay Munro to pick her up from the hospital, and he was waiting for her in the lobby. He put away his *Time* magazine and rose as she approached.

"They want your men out of the hospital," she told him.

"Why?"

"Parsons says it's against hospital policy."

"I can't give you any guarantees if I can't have at least two people on the spot, Mrs. Lawrence."

She shrugged. "We'll have to do without them."

"Have you spoken to her?" he asked.

"Yes."

"Get anything out of her?"

"She's toying with me," Francine said. "She's trying to confuse me, play with my mind."

"But did she tell you where she came from?" Munro asked.

"She has a story ready, of course. A story full of ambiguities and loopholes. Parts of it are probably even true." Francine was grim-faced as they emerged from the clinic.

"Are you okay?" Munro asked as he opened the umbrella to keep the sleet off her head. "Did she upset you?"

"She tried hard."

"Maybe you should let me speak to her."

"We'll both speak to her again in a couple of days."

"Okay." Munro pulled up his collar against the bad weather. They plowed through the slush toward the car. Francine got in. Munro turned on the motor and switched the heat up to full. He went around the car, scraping snow off all the windows. His big shadow loomed against the light, and she watched his intent face as he worked. He was an intimidating man, and she was glad to have him with her. Perhaps his massive presence would help cow Sakura Ueda's insolence.

When Munro got back in the car, she passed him the tape she had made. "Her story is plausible. But it carefully avoids details. Wartime events in remote places, twenty years and more ago. How could it ever be confirmed? She knows it can't. She knows very well how to float her story between what's possible, what's plausible, and what's uncheckable. Trying to nail down the details will be like swatting gnats with a sledgehammer, Clay."

"I'll do my best."

"Focus on the reference to the Japanese officer. There must be records, though they may be hard to find."

"I'll find them." He put the tape in his pocket.

She put her hand on his arm. "She knows things about Ruth," she said quietly. "About me. She claims she first heard about me in a newspaper article five years ago. But maybe it goes back farther than that. I want to know who she is. I want to know who's behind her."

Sakura Ueda waited until the nurses had left her, then pushed the blanket away from her legs. She looked down at her own body. She had lost weight in the past weeks. Her life was ebbing out of her. Not just in the blood she spat; it was being sucked out of her by this place. While she'd been on her feet, she'd been able to fight. In this white room, she felt like a cornered animal, frantic, doomed.

She had always known that she would have to face interrogation from Francine Lawrence. And she had always known it would be difficult to get through that interrogation.

Francine was more elegant than Sakura had expected, and younger looking. She had anticipated someone dowdier and plainer. What Sakura had not anticipated, either, was the steel-spring aggression that she carried, like a fencer's foil, always ready to parry or thrust. She was an adversary to fear and respect.

Sakura drove the thoughts of Francine from her mind. They were a distraction.

She sat cross-legged on the bed, her open hands resting, palms upward, on her knees. She breathed deeply and slowly for a time, feeling her forces concentrate and settle. Then she closed her eyes. The lines of tension slipped out of her face, like ripples dying on the still surface of a pond.

She sat like that, breathing steadily, for several minutes. She was like a statue, only her slow, deep breaths lifting her breasts.

Then her fingers began to twitch. She frowned.

Her body began to sway to and fro. The muscles of her abdomen fluttered. Her jaw clenched. Some color had crept into her cheeks while she'd been relaxed, but now it drained away, leaving her skin white and cold.

She was too deep in her trance to scream out loud, but small sounds crept past her shut throat and gritted teeth, small whimpers and moans. Her hands were no longer open, but had clenched into fists.

And then she exploded from her inner world. Her eyes rolled white, and she cried out, as if in agony.

Her skin was crawling with the horror of it, her muscles quivering, her lungs gasping for oxygen. She stared around herself blindly, as if she did not know where she was. When she recognized her surroundings, she moaned.

Like an exhausted animal, she burrowed into her bed, pulling the sheets over her head.

When Francine Lawrence returned, she brought the black devil, Clay Munro.

Munro studied Sakura. His amber eyes were unfriendly. "How are you doing?"

She shrugged. She knew why Munro had been brought along. It was much easier for two interrogators to trip you, catch you out in small mistakes that could be worried and torn until huge holes appeared.

He sat opposite her, elbows on knees, his massive fingers interlaced. He had a face to frighten children. But she wasn't a child.

"Are you able to talk?" Francine demanded.

"Yes," Sakura replied. "What do you want?"

"Some answers."

"What are the questions?"

Francine switched on her tape recorder. "Why did you wait so long before coming to me, Sakura?"

"I don't understand the question," she said warily.

Francine's eyes were narrow. "Why didn't you come to me as soon as you read the article? Or any time in the past five years?"

"You make it sound so simple," Sakura retorted. "The article just said that you had lost a child in Borneo. I played a kind of game, putting it all together, seeing how it fit. That I was the right age, that I was in the right place at the right time, that I was Eurasian. It was a fantasy. I didn't for one moment imagine it might be true."

"Why not?"

"You were the highest of the high," Sakura said bitterly, "and I was the lowest of the low. Can you imagine what would have happened if I'd come to you with a story like that?"

"Yet you've come to me now."

Sakura was silent.

"Sakura," Francine went on, "do you have any idea how long I looked for my daughter? I combed Sarawak. I sent people into the deepest forests. I saw hundreds of lost children. I didn't stop until my heart was broken, and I felt in my soul that my child was dead—" She broke off, showing a sudden moment of emotion.

Sakura felt a tightening in her own throat as she watched Francine struggle with her feelings. But there was nothing she could say that would not be misinterpreted. In any case, she did not believe that she was capable of giving comfort, or that Francine was capable of receiving it. They were like two islands, separated by the sea. "I know that."

"It's hard for me to believe you could have been so indifferent to such an important issue."

"It wasn't like that for me," Sakura said in a remote voice. "I had no memory of my real parents. I loved Manu and Wai. They were gentle and kind with me. But I lost them, too. I have lost everyone I ever loved, all through my life. When I read that article, it was only a fantasy. Something to dream about. It wasn't until much later that I started to think it might really be true. And by then, I was in a place I couldn't escape from. So it was still no more than a dream. I never thought of simply walking up to you and introducing myself."

"What were you doing in Hong Kong?" Munro demanded.

"Working."

"As what?"

"A shipping clerk."

"You also worked in a casino in Macao? You get around."

"I've worked in Tokyo, Singapore, Macao, Bangkok, Saigon, Vientiane. I don't even remember all the things I've done, the places I've been."

"Yeah," Munro grunted. "I bet you don't. If these jungle people were so skilled at hiding," he asked harshly, "how did this Jap officer come across you?"

"He was different from the other Japanese soldiers. Most of them were afraid of the jungle, afraid of head-hunters. Ueda took pleasure in the jungle. He would go in deep, alone, living like the Penans. He was a reconnaissance expert. That's how he found me."

"And you just went with him?"

Sakura gave Munro an old-fashioned look. "I had learned to just go with whoever took me," she replied. "The most important thing was surviving. Besides, he was a Japanese officer with a gun and a sword. And his kindness didn't extend to adults. He would have killed Manu and Wai if they'd resisted."

"You say Ueda helped many children," Francine cut in. "Did you meet any of the others?"

"Some of them."

"In Borneo?"

"Yes. Sarawak was filled with displaced children. The ones who survived."

"They were in Ueda's care?"

"Yes. He had a walled compound with servants and fruit trees. We could eat all the bananas and rambutans we wanted. We were taken care of, fed, clothed. He would interview us one by one, give us puzzles to solve."

"Puzzles?"

"Tests he had made up. He believed intelligence could be measured by puzzles."

"He liked children, right?" Munro asked.

"Yes."

"And he liked you specially?" Munro went on, his eyes never leaving hers. They made her think of two jungle moons, yellow and sultry.

"I think so."

"You must have been one of the intelligent ones?"

"Yes."

"The most intelligent one?"

"That's what he said." She did not add that Tomoyuki Ueda's special regard for her had kept her alive, a source of heat in a life that had been largely empty of love.

Francine took over. "Were there other Eurasian children in this place?" she demanded.

"A couple, I think."

"Girls of your age?"

"No," Sakura said. "No girls of my own age."

Francine was watching Sakura intently. "You're certain?"

"Quite certain."

"No little girl called Ruth Lawrence? A little girl you talked to? A little girl who told you about her mother and father?"

"No," Sakura said, tense now.

"A little girl you saw die," Francine pressed, "and whom you remembered years later, when you needed money?"

"That is not what happened," Sakura replied fiercely. "And you must be sick in your mind to even think of such a thing!"

"Sakura," Francine said in a hard voice, "I have no doubt that you are very clever. But I want you to have no doubt that I will uncover each lie you tell me. And for each lie, I will make you pay."

Sakura's tension flared into sudden, incandescent heat. "You will make me pay?" Her eyes, brilliant with fever, blazed open. "What do you imagine you can do to me that hasn't been done already? Do you think you have the power to make me suffer an inch more than I've already suffered? What sort of life do you think I've lived? What sort of road do you think I've walked? You speak of making me pay! Which one of us has paid, Francine? Which one of us should pay now?"

Taken aback, Francine tried to retort. "Don't bluster. That will achieve nothing."

"Fuck you," Sakura spat. "Fuck you and your threats."

Munro growled, "Watch your mouth, sister."

"Who do you think you are? Who do you think I am? If I was the cheapest swindler God ever put breath in, you would have no right to speak to me like that."

The VDO needles on the tape recorder were fluttering into the red. With a flash of panic, Francine felt that Sakura was about to rise and stagger out of here. "Calm down. There's nothing to gain by this."

"Don't ever tell me you'll make me pay," Sakura said. She had lifted herself in her passion. "Don't ever threaten me again, Francine." She broke off, coughing. She could taste the warm salt in her mouth. She groped for a towel, and pressed it to her lips, choking. Red dots spattered the white cotton of the towel.

The nurse came in swiftly. She sat beside Sakura, putting an arm around her shoulders and holding the towel to her mouth. "Sit forward, honey," she said.

Sakura coughed more blood. The nurse looked up at Francine and Munro. "I'm going to have to ask you to leave," she said. "She needs rest."

Her face set, Francine rose and picked up the tape recorder. She and Munro walked out, once again leaving Sakura with the last word.

Clay Munro watched Sakura through the one-way mirror. He didn't think she'd figured out that she could be observed through it.

She was walking around the room like a panther in a cage, her hands clasped in front of her, whispering to herself. He'd have given a great deal to understand the words she said. Maybe she was half-crazy. She arched her neck and looked up at the ceiling. Munro could suddenly see the sheen of tears in her eyes. He frowned. The tears spilled down her cheeks. She buried her face in her hands like somebody on the verge of desperation. For a moment, her whole strong body sagged. He held his breath. What the hell was wrong with her? What was she so afraid of?

Then she turned the gesture of despair into one of wiping away her tears. She folded her arms tight, as though holding herself in, and stared at the window, biting her lower lip.

Just tell us the truth, Munro thought. *Make life easier for everybody.*

Her face set, Sakura turned, and walked over to the sink. The one-way mirror was between them, but she was physically no more than two feet from Munro as she washed her hands. Munro felt himself tense at her proximity. He could see the curve of her breasts under the thin gown, the nipples dark. Her hair hung, thick and tangled, down to her shoulders. There was something about her that made his hackles rise. And other parts of his body. He cursed himself silently as he felt his dick stir and harden.

Abruptly, she looked up, and her eyes seemed to lock on his. He held his breath, his pulse accelerating. That extraordinary face was pale and taut. The full mouth was compressed, the nostrils of the slightly snub nose arched. It was the face she wore when they gave her the injection, which he knew hurt like hell. She was beautiful, despite the TB, despite everything. And now, as the big gray eyes held his, he was truly aroused, his pulse pounding through what felt like a foot-long erection.

You're a fucking Peeping Tom, man, he told himself.

She looked closer at the mirror, frowning. He had a sharp moment of unease. If she guessed this was a spy mirror, she was capable of putting a chair through it in a flash. But she only seemed to have seen that her hair was dirty, because she tossed it forward, stooped, and started wetting it in the sink. He heard the door open, and Francine came in. He turned, trying to look nonchalant, and not like a steamed-up pervert.

"Hello," she whispered, shutting the door silently behind her. "What have you got for me?"

"Tomoyuki Ueda existed."

Francine looked up at Munro steadily. "You're sure?"

He passed her a folder of photocopied sheets. "I got these from the war museum. They're transcipts of Tomoyuki Ueda's war-crimes trial in Tokyo."

She took the folder and flipped it open. The observation room was always dimly lit, to avoid revealing that the mirror was transparent, and she could hardly read the sheets. The file was thick and closely typed, but Munro had inserted yellow markers in a couple of places. There were two blurred photographs, their quality further reduced by the photocopying, showing a harsh-faced Japanese officer in wartime uniform. "So he's real," she said quietly.

"Yeah, he's real. Or was. He served in Borneo. And he was found guilty by the tribunal, just as Sakura said. I've read through the transcripts, and marked the stuff that might be interesting. He was one of those crazy Japanese types, a martial-arts fanatic, but also a poet. He never married, but he liked children. And Sakura was right about something else: He had theories about measuring children's intelligence. He worked out a kind of early IQ test—that's what Sakura must mean by his 'puzzles.' But his theories were mixed up with a lot of racial stuff."

"Racial stuff?"

"He thought the Nazis had it right, except he talked about an Asian super-race. Who knows, that may be why he picked Sakura, because he thought she was bright, and would be good breeding stock later on?"

"Perhaps."

"Anyway, he was no respecter of human life," Munro went on. They were talking in low murmurs. "He iced dozens of prisoners in Kuching. Cut off their heads with his samurai sword. But while he was cracking the parents' skulls, he grabbed the kids. Said he was making sure they were taken care of. His lawyer tried to use that in his defense, showing how Ueda had been kind to war orphans. Kind of thin, right? He claimed Ueda also sent certain children back to Japan, and sponsored their keep and education."

Her eyes widened. "Are any names given?"

"No," Clay Munro replied. "It's a very brief reference. The lawyer wanted to call one of the children, an older boy, to testify, but the judges turned him down. It wasn't relevant. The evidence all came from witnesses from the camp in Kuching. They'd seen him hacking off heads every day for months, so basically he didn't have a defense. He was sentenced to death by hanging. No appeal. It was what you'd call rough justice."

Sakura was drying her hair in a towel now, walking listlessly away from the mirror.

Francine watched her, touching her mouth with her fingertips. "So that much is true."

"Yeah. I got in touch with a Japanese agency in Tokyo to see if Ueda has any surviving family in Tokyo. There's an outside chance someone kept family photographs from the period. It's going to take time. And money. We may have to take out newspaper ads all over Japan."

"We'll do what's necessary," Francine vowed.

Now Sakura was changing her clothes. Her back was to them as she dressed. She had a beautiful back, muscled and lean. Her buttocks were hard and strong. It was no problem for the nurses to get the needle into the muscle for the streptomycin injection. But it wasn't like a boy's butt. It was definitely a woman's butt. He was acutely aware of Francine's presence beside him.

Sakura pulled on pants and turned. Her breasts were perfect, heavy enough to have a rhythm of their own as she leaned forward to get clean clothes. He cleared his throat awkwardly.

"Do you think she is beautiful?" Francine asked quietly.

His dick did, and was doing his best to get out and prove it, but he couldn't say that. "Yes, she's very pretty."

"But what is she inside?"

"Uh-huh." He was half-relieved, half-disappointed when she put on a shirt. "She looks better today," Munro said.

"She's making progress," Francine said shortly. "But I doubt whether Parsons will let us speak to her for a couple of days. He thinks I have a bad effect on her."

"We should go easy with her, Mrs. Lawrence," Munro advised. "She may be scamming you, but her sickness is real. You don't want her spitting up any more blood. How long is she going to stay in this place?"

"A couple of weeks."

"And then?"

"There's time," she replied curtly. "We'll get to the bottom of her story before she's discharged."

"And if she doesn't check out?" Munro asked.

She glanced at him, her eyes hard. "If she doesn't check out, that's her problem."

"You'll wash your hands of her?"

"Of course."

"She'll die," Munro said.

"She would have died in any case."

"Uh-huh."

"What does that grunt mean, Clay? You think I should send her to a sanatorium in the Swiss Alps for a year?"

He raised his hands. "I didn't say a thing."

"Don't go soft on her, Clay," Francine said warningly.

"I'm never soft on anybody," Munro said, beautiful teeth showing in a tiger's smile.

"The drugs are making me worse," Sakura said, her eyes hostile.

"That may be the way it seems now, Sakura," Dr. Parsons replied, "but I assure you, you're getting better every day. What I'm trying to avoid is a repetition of yesterday."

"I didn't intend it to happen."

"Your lungs are healing. But any exertion could start the bleeding again. No shouting. No emotion. Or I will forbid you to talk to Mrs. Lawrence again."

"You'd be doing me a favor," she said with bitterness in her voice.

He studied her. "Are you her daughter?" he asked bluntly.

Her eyes met the doctor's. "I never said that," she retorted.

"Look, it's none of my business, Sakura. But why not tell her the truth about yourself, whatever that is?" He patted her arm, and left her.

The darkness in Sakura's chest came welling up in her throat, choking her. In her own mind, the blood did not come from any illness. It came from the heart-wound they had given her in Laos. It was her pain that came into her mouth, salty and hot.

She reached for the towel and pressed it to her lips, rocking her body to and fro, thinking of Parsons's words. *Tell her the truth about yourself, whatever that is.*

As if that were going to help now.

She clambered painfully out of bed, and went to the set of drawers. The few clothes she'd brought with her into the clinic had been laundered and pressed, and were stored here. She had no bag to carry spares, so she pulled on as much as she could wear: three shirts, two pairs of jeans, two pairs of socks under her sneakers. Bulked up with clothing, she was already hot, which was good: She was going to have to bundle the rest of her things in her denim jacket.

The haul from the lockers was pathetic, but it was all she had. She zipped it into the pocket of the jacket.

She went to the window. It was locked, but she had long since observed that the key was left on top of the pelmet, a poor hiding place. She stretched, took the key, and opened the window. Icy air blew into her face. She stared up at the dark sky for a moment. Then she pushed the window wide, gathered the bundle of clothes to her chest, and climbed out.

Clay Munro walked out of his building into a moderate snowstorm. It whirled around his ears, making him hunch into his parka. His car was wearing a foot of snow. He was already prepared with a plastic shovel to scrape the windshield clear.

"Captain Munro?"

The use of his old army rank surprised Munro. He turned. The man was gaunt, around fifty.

"Yeah?"

One of the man's hands came out of the pocket of his gabardine coat. Munro found himself looking at a plastic card announcing that the bearer was Major Christopher McFadden of Army Intelligence Corps. "Munro, we need to talk."

"What about?" Munro said. As he spoke, he sensed a second presence behind him. He turned and faced a burly man with a brown Asian face, his bullet head cropped, his muscular jaw masticating gum. He jostled Munro against the wall, patting him down for weapons.

Munro raised his hands to thrust the man away. Then he saw the Colt automatic pointing at his chest.

"This is my colleague," the American said, "Sergeant Thuong."

The brown man dug in Munro's pockets, groped his crotch. "No gun," he grunted.

"Okay. Let's go, Captain."

Munro's heart was pounding. The brown man thrust Munro into the back of a car parked at the curb. The other man got behind the wheel and set the car in motion.

"Let me see that ID again," Munro demanded.

"This our ID." The Asian held the pistol against Munro's abdomen. He chewed gum, his eyes mocking and hot. He had the pitiless face of a Vietnamese noncom.

Munro froze into immobility, staring at the gun. "Watch that fucking thing."

"How is the Ueda girl doing?" the gaunt man asked.

"What business do you have with her?" Munro asked, hearing the tension in his own voice.

The gaunt man's eyes met Munro's in the rearview mirror. "We've just come all the way from Laos, Captain, and we're tired. So don't fuck us around. That's an early warning, okay? Now answer the question. How is the girl?"

"She's sick," Munro said.

"What's wrong with her?"

"She has TB."

"She going die?" the Vietnamese asked.

"Not if she's treated."

The white man grunted. "How much is that fancy clinic costing Mrs. Lawrence?"

"I don't know."

Clogged with falling snow, the streets were heavily crowded. They had been creeping through the dense traffic along Tenth Avenue. Now they turned down West 42nd, where things were even worse. "Ueda claims to be Francine Lawrence's child, right?"

Munro shrugged. "I wouldn't know about that."

Thuong's gun dug into Munro's belly. "Is she Francine Lawrence's child?" McFadden asked patiently.

"I don't know," Munro repeated, focusing on the gun carefully. "Nobody knows."

"Lawrence thinks this kid is her daughter, doesn't she?"

"I don't know what she thinks."

"Don't jerk me around."

"I don't know what she thinks," Munro repeated.

"You dumb nigger bastard," Thuong said.

McFadden's dead gaze met Munro's in the mirror again. "Thuong is right," he told Munro. "You're a dumb nigger bastard. We could take you to a quiet place and rip out your fingernails. Or we could fix it so you lost your job, your grubby little license, and every pathetic shred of dignity you cling to."

"What do you want?" Munro asked quietly.

"We want back what Sakura stole."

"What did she steal?" Munro asked.

"Why the fuck you think she's come to Lawrence? Tell her time's running out, Captain. If she wants to see him alive, she has to give back what she took. Can you tell her that for us?"

"See who alive?"

"Just tell her. We'll kill him, and if that doesn't work, we'll start on her. Nobody can hide from us. We're the eagle's eyes. We see everything. You understand?"

"I'm trying."

"Tell Sakura we're waiting."

Munro realized they were driving down Second Avenue, approaching the clinic. Maybe he wasn't going to get shot after all. "Okay," he said.

The black car pulled up outside the clinic entrance. McFadden reached back and pushed a card into Munro's pocket. "My number's on that. Call me. Don't make me call you. Now get the fuck out of my car." Thuong opened the door. Munro got out. The black car pulled away and vanished into the billowing sheets of snow.

The license plate was covered in slush. Munro took a deep breath and walked into the clinic. He was going to get some damned answers out of her.

He pushed open the door of Sakura's room. It was empty. Sakura was gone.

His heart pounding, Munro turned furiously on an orderly passing by. "Where'd she go?" he rasped, grabbing the man by the lapels.

"She hasn't been out of her room all morning," the man stuttered, peering blankly into Sakura's room.

Munro raced down the corridor to the nurses' station. "Where's Sakura?"

The two women rose in alarm. "Isn't she in her room?"

"No."

"She didn't pass this way, Mr. Munro."

"The window!" He ran back to her room, feeling sick.

The window in her room was unlatched. He yanked it wide. It gave onto a narrow ledge, unprotected by railings. She had made her way forty yards along the ledge, and was trying to reach a second ledge that led to a fire escape. Between the two parapets was a gap of six feet. Beneath that, nothing but air and the street far below. She was a very small figure against the face of the building.

He was terrified that she would jump, right in front of his eyes.

"Sakura!" he shouted, his voice tight, "don't try it!"

She turned her head briefly. She saw him and turned back, crouching to jump.

"No!" he yelled.

She jumped.

He saw her land awkwardly, saw her sneakers slip in the frozen snow. She was clutching something to her chest, a denim jacket wrapped around some clothes. The bundle hampered her. For a moment, she slithered, right at the very edge.

"Sakura!" he screamed.

She teetered, righted herself, reached out her free hand to grasp at the brickwork. She shot him another glance over her shoulder, then kept going, her feet slipping in the slush, dark hair blowing in the wind.

"Oh, fuck it," Munro groaned. He turned, and ran back into the corridor. People scattered at the sight of his six-foot-two frame hurtling toward them. If she reached the fire escape, she would be down in the street in thirty seconds, and gone in forty.

A bridge linked the two wings, walls of glass affording views of the clinic's small garden. Through the glass, he caught sight of Sakura outside, clambering over the railing of the fire escape. Someone pointed and called out.

Munro sprinted around the corner, pounded down another corridor to the fire doors at the end.

He burst through the doors. Immediately, a fire alarm clanged into urgent life.

He was face-to-face with Sakura on the fire escape. She stared at him like a cornered puma, hunching, hissing at him angrily.

"You crazy little fool," he rasped.

"Get away from me."

She turned and ran back up the stairs, the ironwork booming hollowly under her feet.

"Sakura!"

He sprang after her. She turned and hurled her bundle at him. He ducked instinctively. It gave her the moment she needed to clamber back onto the ledge.

Two of the hospital security guards hammered up the stairs behind him. He turned and thrust them away. He didn't want these goons knocking Sakura seven stories onto the sidewalk. "Hold it," he snapped. "I'll deal with this."

Sakura was scrambling back along the parapet. He had no choice but to follow her.

The fire alarm shrilled insanely. Munro tried to be careful. The ledge was horribly narrow and horribly slippery with snow. He shuffled after her. She was as agile as a cat, and as fearless.

"Sakura!" he yelled after her, fury roughening his voice.

She glanced at him over her shoulder. "Leave me alone." She spat the words. She reached the corner, rounded it, and was gone.

Clinging to the bare bricks with his fingertips, Munro scraped after her.

He turned the corner, glancing down at the nauseating drop below his feet. He was filled with a grim premonition that they were both going to end up lying in a pool of blood on the sidewalk.

He looked up ahead. He'd had a stroke of luck. Sakura had reached the bulky column of a chimney shaft. This time the jump was too much for even her feline skills. She was trapped.

He shuffled toward her. He saw that she was crying now, tears of rage or frustration. He was surprised the tears weren't freezing to her cheeks.

"Don't move," he commanded.

"I'll jump!"

"Listen to me."

"Go back. I'll jump."

She poised herself as if to leap out into nothingness.

"The men from Vientiane are here," he said. He did not know whether the words would push her over the edge, and for a moment his pounding heart seemed to stall as he watched her. She turned her head very slowly to look at him.

"What?"

"The men from Laos. They're here. Right now, you only have me to help you."

She stared at him.

He edged forward, reached out to her. "We have to talk. Grab my hand." Crumbling plaster made the parapet slippery. City sounds drifted up from the street below. As he reached her, she seemed to lean forward into the void, like a gull about to take flight. He grabbed hold of her arm. For a moment they tottered there, high above the street. Then Munro slammed her back against the wall, so hard the breath burst out of her lungs.

"Jesus," he muttered, pinning her there. "You fucking crazy woman."

Sakura's skin was frigid. Her cheek was like marble against his. She moved faintly in his arms.

"Hold still," he growled, "or I'll break your worthless little neck."

He shuffled with her slowly back to the window, trying not to look down at the drop beneath his feet. The soles of his shoes slipped on the snow. Sakura's body was solid and heavy against his.

He reached the open window of her room. Several people were leaning out, calling to them.

He scrabbled at the ledge, grunting with the effort. Hands reached out to take her from him, dragging her inside. And at last he was climbing back into the room.

Sakura did not try to resist while the nurses pulled her layers of clothing off. Their silence, and the looks in their eyes, said more than any scolding could. They thought she was an animal, a madwoman.

"That window was locked," the orderly kept saying in a panicky voice.

"Well, she found the key," Munro panted. He looked as angry as he felt. He brushed snow off himself with shaking hands. "I want that fucking window secured. Get it welded shut, right now."

"I'll go get the handyman."

The man was there in ten minutes. Munro supervised the job. While Parsons arrived and checked her over, the man welded the window. It did not take long. A few bursts of brilliant blue light, the buzzing of a giant wasp, the acrid smell of burned metal.

The milling crowd in the room dwindled away after Parsons had rebuked her severely and walked out in majesty. A security guard came in with her denim jacket and the bundle of clothes she'd thrown at Munro.

"This was on the fire escape."

"Leave it there," Munro commanded.

The man glared at Sakura and left. And then she was alone with Clay Munro.

She opened her mouth to spit some insult at him, but he reached her in two strides and grasped her wrist. He spun her around in one brutal movement and wrenched her arm up behind her back.

"Next time you run away from me," he growled, his breath hot against her ear, "I'll just plain shoot you."

Pain seared through her tearing muscles and she had to bite hard not to scream out loud. "Please," she gasped. "You're breaking my arm."

He slammed her down on the bed. He loomed over her, one massive hand knotting in her hair. She was as helpless in his power as a leaf on the sea. She was suddenly really afraid of him, of the rage she could feel throbbing in his huge body. She had defied him on other occasions, but right now, she knew he was capable of tearing her heart out.

"*Don't*," she said in a high, shaky voice. "Please don't hurt me."

His eyes were amber, the eyes of a night-hunting predator. His teeth showed in a snarl, white against his dark skin. For a moment, he glared down at her. Then she saw the fury start to fade. He released her, and she sagged in reaction. She had not felt a second of fear out there on the ledge. But in these past thirty seconds, her heart had been pounding.

He sat on the bed, beside her. "You're crazy," he said quietly to her. "Where the hell were you going?"

"Back to Laos," she said shortly.

"Oh yeah? And how were you going to pay your way?"

Wearily she stretched out her hand for the denim jacket. "Pass it to me."

Munro gave her the jacket. She unzipped the inner pocket, and pulled out the tangle of metal inside. She dropped it on the bed.

"Well, I'll be." Munro poked through the collection: watches, rings, necklaces. "Now where did all this bullion come from, Sakura?"

"I found the nurses' lockers."

"You opened the lockers?" he said, looking at her speculatively. "How?"

"With a barrette. It was easy."

"Easy?" he repeated, staring at her.

"I know it was wrong, but I was desperate. Tell them I'm sorry."

"They'll probably piss in your oatmeal from now on. I would. Anything else up your sleeve?" he asked.

Sakura glanced at the window. Six silvery slugs of metal now held the steel window permanently closed. No way out, and no way in.

At first, she had referred to Clay Munro in her mind by an impolite Japanese word meaning a stupid man, but she had learned that he was neither stupid nor slow. She had learned that he was like those opponents at the dojo who fooled you because they were so big you thought they would be clumsy, until they skewered you on the mat.

"You said the men from Vientiane were here," Sakura said. "Who did you mean?"

"Two guys, a Major Christopher McFadden and an Asian called Thuong, who's probably Laotian. They claim you stole something from them. They want it back. Or they say they'll hurt somebody you know."

Sakura's head dropped forward. Her long brown hair tumbled around her face. She said nothing.

"Who are they?" Munro demanded.

"Jai Han sent them." She tried to keep the tears out of her eyes.

"Tell me who these people are."

"They're Ray-Bans."

"Ray-Bans? *Those* guys are the Ray-Bans?"

"That's what we call them," she said. "They don't wear uniforms. But you can tell them by their Ray-Bans."

"What did you steal from them?" Munro asked.

"Money."

"How much?"

"A lot."

"And who is this person they threaten to kill?"

She swallowed, her heavy eyes raising to meet Munro's. "My child."

Munro stared at her in silence. Then he rose. "I'm going to call Mrs. Lawrence. Don't go anywhere."

Running through Francine's mind, beyond the initial, shocked reaction, was the question, Was this the second act of an elaborate play designed to defraud her?

"Start at the beginning," she said quietly.

Sakura was tight-faced. "I worked for a Chinese businessman in Vientiane called Li Hua."

"What kind of businessman?"

"He traded with the hill tribes."

"You mean opium?" Munro asked.

"It was not what you think."

"Not what I think? What was it, then?"

"It was a legitimate business."

"But it was opium, right?"

"Yes." Munro and Francine exchanged glances. "Everybody respected Li Hua. He was a gentle old man who treated me like his daughter. I was happy working for him. I had a lover named Roger Ricard. He was a pilot with a small charter business, flying from the north into Vientiane. Roger gave me a child we called Louis. When my baby came, I thought I had finally found my life. I thought I was going to be happy. But nobody knew the war would grow like that, that the GIs would come. The GIs wanted heroin. And Li Hua was killed."

"Who killed him?" Francine asked.

"Jai Han's soldiers. General Jai Han is the commander of the Meo. They are a hill tribe, opium farmers, warriors. They hate the Communists. Jai Han turned the Meo into an anti-Communist army. To keep Jai Han loyal, the Ray-Bans fly the Meo opium in their cargo planes. All part of the 'win their hearts and minds' policy. Jai Han took over the opium business, and so I had to work for him."

"And McFadden? He's in the heroin business with Jai Han?"

"McFadden is CIA."

Munro and Francine glanced at each other swiftly. "CIA?" Francine repeated incredulously.

"He helps train the Meo for Jai Han. Teaches them to use weapons. But war and heroin are the same thing."

"What do you mean, the same thing?"

"While McFadden shows the men how to fight, the women are growing opium in the villages. The American planes carry rice and guns to the hills, and bring the opium base back to Vientiane."

"And then?"

"And then it is turned into heroin."

"By McFadden?"

"No. By the princes, and the generals, and the gangsters. Vientiane stinks of vinegar so you can hardly breathe. It's the acetic anhydride the chemists use to dissolve the morphine out. Then they fly the refined heroin to Saigon."

"And that is why McFadden is here, Sakura? On behalf of a heroin cartel?"

"Yes. Thuong is one of Jai Han's brothers-in-law. They're both dangerous, but they don't care about the heroin. They only care about the money. The Ray-Bans never have enough. They need it to buy guns for their armies."

"So all this time you've been talking about the Ray-Bans," Munro said, "you've been talking about the CIA?"

"Yes."

"Sakura," Francine said, "nobody is going to believe that the American government is sponsoring the heroin trade in Laos."

"Somebody is," Munro said in a quiet voice. "Saigon is full of heroin. We had instructions to locate every drug user in our outfit and ship them to a detox center, but there's no way we could have done that. We'd have been left with nobody. You can buy it in every village, from every child. We were always told it was the Communists behind it."

"It is not the Communists," Sakura said. "The Communist tribes grow food, not opium. Meo hill farmers have been cultivating opium for centuries. But they never refined opium. Westerners did that. They turned opium into something deadly. The ultimate capitalist crop," she said bitterly. "Some is sold to GIs. The rest is sent to America and Europe. The Ray-Bans sell it to the Corsicans, and the Corsicans sell it to the dealers."

Francine watched Sakura's face. In her mind, a still voice was asking, *Are you my daughter? Are you what has become of Ruth?* "You knew this was evil."

"Yes. Of course I knew it was evil."

"Why didn't you get out?"

Sakura's face twisted. "I would have. But they took my beautiful little boy from me."

"Who did?"

"Roger took him first." Her eyes were heavy with tears again. "Roger lost his airline. The Ray-Bans put the local charters out of business. Roger grew very bitter. He started drinking and became violent. I saw what he was really like. And I hated the heroin trade. I wanted to get out of Laos. I wanted to make a better life for us, find somewhere where I could bring up my child far from war, away from heroin. I tried to leave Vientiane, but Roger found out, and stopped me. He took Louis away from me. Louis was only two years old. Roger only let me be with Louis on weekends, in his house. But I couldn't get Louis away from him. Roger had a plan. He wanted me to help him steal from Jai Han. I told him it was crazy, but he was obsessed with the idea. He had Louis. He made me agree."

"You swindled Jai Han?" Munro asked.

She nodded. "Yes."

"How?"

"I knew how Jai Han worked. He sends all his money to a bank in Thailand. We used to take it to the airport in a car and put it on a Royal Air Lao flight to Bangkok. I told Roger the route we would take one morning. They stopped our car and grabbed the bags. Nobody was hurt. It was so simple. But it was much, much more than I ever imagined it would be. It came to almost seven hundred thousand American dollars."

Francine gasped softly. "Seven hundred thousand?"

Sakura nodded. "Six hundred and eighty thousand. Jai Han was in a rage. I had to run. Everyone was looking for us, the police, the Meo, the Ray-Bans. Even the Corsicans, because they were afraid this would finish them off in Laos. They betrayed Roger, so Jai Han found him and killed him. Roger's partner got away. They found Louis, and they took him. They searched for me, but I went to the hills and hid in a cave with the Vietcong, where they couldn't reach me. Eventually I crossed the border into Thailand. But Jai Han sent me a message. He wants his money back, or he will kill my child." Sakura crushed her fingers together. "But I don't have the money. Roger's partner took it out of the country, and he's vanished. The money is gone."

Nobody said anything for a long time. "Is that why you came to me at last?" Francine asked quietly.

"Yes."

"You thought I would help you?"

"I thought you might help me."

"Why did you run from me at first?"

"When you had me followed, I thought you must have told the Ray-Bans about me." She was trying to control her voice. "They've been looking for me since Vientiane. They don't just want Jai Han's money. When I ran, they thought I would speak to the journalists. I know what happens in Laos. I know about the arrangements between Jai Han and the Ray-Bans. Thousands of American soldiers in Vietnam are addicts already, everyone knows that. And the heroin is making more addicts here in America. They want to close my mouth."

Francine rose. She looked down at Sakura. "So you didn't come to me because you wanted to know me. You came to me because you hoped I would get you out of trouble."

Sakura swallowed. Francine saw the slender throat pulse. "I have no one else. I came to you because I hoped you could save my child."

For a moment, Francine stared into the girl's eyes. But she was looking through Sakura, into some other reality. Then, without another word, she turned and walked out of the room.

Francine had arranged to meet Munro in the big, featureless hotel that stood opposite Sakura's clinic. Her cab dropped her off in the slush of Midtown. She pushed through the revolving door and headed for the bar. The warmth and soft lighting enfolded her.

Munro was already sitting at the bar, waiting for her. The place was crowded, but there was a space around Clay Munro. There was always a space around Clay; whether it was his bulk, his blackness, or the harsh planes of his face, Francine did not know. Perhaps all three.

"What can I get you, ma'am?" the man behind the bar asked.

"Whiskey," she said.

"Scotch, Irish, American, malt, straight up, on the rocks?"

"I don't care."

"Make it two malts on the rocks," Munro said.

Francine sat on the bar stool beside Munro. She ran her hands through her hair, shuddering at the cold. "What have you got?" she asked him.

"I had a team search the news archives for stories on Southeast Asia printed in the last ten years. Christopher McFadden's name came up in several references. This was the most significant." He passed her a photocopy. She saw that it was from a three-year-old *Time* magazine article about Laos. Munro had marked the relevant lines with yellow highlight. She read intently.

Christopher McFadden was mentioned, not as a CIA operative, of course, but as a veteran member of an American-funded aid organization called International Voluntary Assistance. The mention was brief but glowing, describing McFadden as a rural vocational-skills teacher, and praising his life's work of helping Asian farmers grow more rice than ever before. "It is men like McFadden who are winning the hearts and minds of Laos," the article concluded. There was a photograph of a middle-aged man with his arm around the shoulders of a grinning Laotian peasant in black pajamas.

"That's McFadden," Munro confirmed.

"It says he's an aid worker."

"Spooks are always aid workers. That's the one sure thing about them." He tapped the picture with a huge forefinger. "I think McFadden's exactly what Sakura told us he is. A CIA field officer. The background is kind of interesting. Since 1957, the U.S. has been spending more on foreign aid per capita in Laos than in any other nation. But it ain't going on rice and beans."

When the whiskey was served, Francine drank, feeling it burn her throat. She stared at her own reflection in the pink-tinted mirror behind the bar. Her face was hard.

"You know what I thought?" Francine said bitterly to Munro. "I thought the whole thing was probably just about the TB, and nothing more. She couldn't afford the treatment, so she claimed to be Ruth. So I would pay the bills. You understand?"

Munro nodded.

"But it's not about the TB."

"No," Munro said. "It's not about the TB."

"If only it were. It's like a nightmare that just keeps getting worse. Now we see who is really behind her."

"You still think she's lying about her past?" he asked.

"I've lived a little longer than you," she replied. "Seven hundred thousand dollars is a great deal of money. My mother had a lot of old Chinese sayings. One of them was that to get a lie accepted as truth, it needs to be repeated by three people. Sakura was the first. Now McFadden. Who will be next, I wonder?"

"This thing is very messy to be a conspiracy," Munro replied.

"You think she is telling the truth?"

"I think she's half-crazy, and the other half is crooked as cat shit." Munro hesitated. "But she's in danger. We're gonna have to do something, or they will cut her down right in front of our eyes." He signaled the bartender. "Two more."

"I know influential people," Francine said. "I'll speak to somebody in Washington."

Munro shook his head. "Uh-uh."

"Why not?"

"Because nobody in Washington will talk to you about the CIA. Not as far as the war in Asia is concerned. And especially not about the CIA trafficking in heroin."

"They must know."

"Mrs. Lawrence, I was in the army for ten years, in Vietnam for four. Believe me, nobody in America has any idea of what really happens on the ground. Not the Senate, not Congress, nobody."

"Then we'll deal directly with Langley."

"Maybe not even anybody at Langley knows. It would take weeks to get anywhere with them, and by then it would be too late. You can't talk to anybody about this."

"McFadden must be under somebody's control."

"Yeah, but you'll never find out whose. You can't do this through any official channels."

"So what rules do we play by?"

"These guys, the Meo, they're like the montagnards in Vietnam. They collect enemy ears. One time, we said we'd pay ten bucks for every VC ear they brought. They started cutting off their wives' and children's ears. We had ears an inch long coming into the base. We had to stop that one right away. These are the people you're dealing with. People who would cut off their own children's ears for ten dollars. Sakura's life, or yours, or mine, would mean nothing to Jai Han."

She gave him a mechanical smile in the mirror. "Thank you for that analysis, Clay."

"I'm always here," Munro said gently. "I ain't going anywhere."

She studied Munro's polished, ruthless features. She was thanking God for his calm strength, his loyalty, the sureness of his movements. "You were never married, were you, Clay?"

"No."

"No children?"

He let one of his rare smiles show. "None that I know of."

She drained her glass. "Take my advice. Don't have any. Let's go and see Sakura now."

Sakura had been drifting in a dark sleep. She awoke with a start, and jerked herself upright.

Francine Lawrence was standing at the foot of her bed, watching her in silence. For a long while, they looked into each other's eyes without speaking.

"Now you know the truth," Sakura said at last.

"I know what you wanted me to know."

"Let me go back to Laos," Sakura said. "If I let them kill me, they may spare Louis."

"Was that your plan, when you climbed out of the window?"

Sakura nodded. "Yes."

"You hadn't even told me about your child."

Sakura shrugged. "I knew it would be useless. I could tell by your attitude to me. The way you questioned me. You don't believe a word I say. I wasted my time coming to you. I have no other option open. I have to go back to them, and let them do what they want to me."

"They would torture you," Francine said sharply.

"There is always death at the end of torture," Sakura said quietly.

"And then what would happen to your child? If they killed you, they'd probably kill him, too."

"Then perhaps that would be best," Sakura said in a still voice.

Francine walked to the window. Her suit was a pastel green, setting off her skin and enhancing the Burmese jade bangle and earrings she wore. "I could pay, Sakura. But you don't know whether you are my daughter. I don't know whether I am your mother. I don't even know whether this money would save you or your child."

Sakura's eyes were heavy. "Why didn't you give your child a mark?" she asked in a harsh voice.

"I don't understand."

"When you left your child with the Ibans, you must have known it might be a long time before you saw her again. In your place, I would have marked my child in some way, so I'd know her again, even after years. A scar under the arm, or on the scalp, under the hair."

"Like branding a cow? I'm afraid I'm not as practical as you, Sakura. That didn't occur to me. Did you mark Louis?"

"No. But I didn't know I was going to lose him."

"I did not know I would lose my daughter."

"Will you pay?"

Francine shrugged. "Sakura, people everywhere know that I've accumulated wealth. Every day I get letters from all over the world. People who say their child will die if I do not send them money to pay the doctors. Men who say they will commit suicide if I do not pay their debts. People in prison, people dying, people whose whole families will be exterminated if I do not send a hundred dollars, a thousand, ten thousand. Some of these letters are even genuine."

"And do you help?" Sakura demanded.

"Sometimes."

Sakura's jaw tightened. "Then why not me?"

"For one thing, perhaps your manner of asking leaves something to be desired," Francine replied dryly.

"Is that it? You want me to go on my knees and beg?"

"I didn't say I wanted that."

"I have never lied to you, Francine. I could have claimed to remember your face, your voice. I could have held out my arms and called you Mama. I could have put on a show that would have melted your heart."

"Then why didn't you?"

"I've been many things, but never a liar."

"Not even to save your child?" Francine asked.

"I do not know how to lie. I know you suspect that I'm a wonderful actress, that I'm faking everything. I'm not an actress. I am what I am. There is nothing more."

"If only you'd come to me before this happened," Francine said heavily. "If you had come of your own accord, not asking for money, not up to your neck in trouble, it might have been very different."

"If this hadn't happened, I would never have come to you."

Francine grimaced. "That's honest, at least."

"When I started to realize that you might really be my mother," Sakura said, "I suddenly knew why my life had turned out the way it had. Why I was the child brought up by wolves. My first reaction wasn't to love you. It was to despise you."

Francine drew a breath. "And you think telling me this will make me want to help you?"

"If you help me, I will try and put my anger aside. I'll start again with you, from zero. And I'll let you know Louis."

"How generous," Francine said with cold irony.

Sakura did not hesitate. "I told you, Francine. I cannot lie to you, and I never will. You say you want the truth, and I'm giving it to you."

"Your truth."

"And yours. I see into your heart, even if you can't or won't see into mine. I see that you've been dying for years. Seven hundred thousand dollars will buy back your life. Is that so expensive?"

Francine answered with a twisted smile. "I didn't know you were so clever with words."

"Your life has been much better than mine. I have had to do things that hurt me, that made me ashamed, that almost killed me. You have lived for money. To accumulate wealth, as you so daintily put it. I thought of you as the mother who abandoned me as a baby in the jungle so you could save yourself."

"That is not how it was, Sakura," Francine said in a strained voice.

"I didn't come to you before. But I've come now." She swallowed, her throat raw. "Louis is an innocent child, Francine, and his life is in your hands. You have the power to save him."

"And what if, when this is all over, it turns out that you are not my daughter after all, Sakura?"

"I will pay you back. Every penny."

"How?"

"I'll work. I can do anything. Anything. You don't know me. You don't know what I can achieve." Her fingers clenched the coverlet. "I'll be your slave, if that's what you want. For the rest of my life."

"I'm not in the slave business."

Sakura threw the coverlet aside, and pulled herself out of bed. She walked to Francine with flaming eyes, her face white and set. "I have the only thing you want. What do you care for money? You have more than enough. The truth is that you're empty inside. What lies ahead, Francine? Despair and loneliness. You will shrivel up until your own bitterness devours you."

"That is the fate of all humanity, Sakura," Francine said in a strained voice.

"No!" Sakura grasped Francine's arms. Her fingers were feverish claws. "You pretend to despise me, but I offer you the only hope you've got. The only possibility that your child might be alive, after all. You can't turn your back on me. You might as well kill yourself right now, because there would be nothing left for you."

"Let me go," Francine said, trying to pull free from Sakura's hot grip.

"You cannot take that chance," Sakura said, her eyes burning into Francine's. "Can you? You know that if you don't help me, I'll disappear. You'll never see me again. And for the rest of your life, you'll be haunted by the thought that your daughter came back from the dead, and that you let her die again. You let her die, and you let her child die. Can you face that? What will you tell the devils in hell when they ask you why you killed your child twice?"

Francine managed to pry Sakura's fingers loose at last. She was struggling to stay calm. "You little bitch," she said unsteadily.

"Is that why you're rejecting me? Because I'm a little bitch? Trash? A woman who floated around the world like human garbage? What did you expect, Francine? I've done what I could to survive. That I'm here at all is a miracle. You cannot know the number of times I was almost nothing, or worse than nothing. I survived. And now everything has come full circle, and everything depends on you. Just as it did all those years ago, in the jungle. Now what are you going to do? Walk away again?"

"You understand nothing," Francine whispered.

"I will tell you what I understand, Francine. When I look into your face, I see my face. When I look in your eyes, I see my eyes. And when I see myself in you, I hate you."

Sakura's burning eyes made Francine afraid, as though they really spat out a vision of endless hell. "Hate?"

"Oh, yes," Sakura said fiercely. "My hate for you is the one thing that makes me certain you are the mother who left me in the jungle all those years ago."

Francine turned blindly and walked out of the room.

She was sitting on the bed, hugging her knees, her head turned to one side. She did not look at him, but she sensed it was Munro.

"How're you doing?" he asked.

She made no response.

He pulled the chair up to the bed, and sat on it, his elbows on his knees, deliberately entering her field of vision. Still, she did not look at him. Her eyes were somehow veiled, as though she were looking into a different space.

"Sakura, what do you expect?" he asked. "Do you really think you're going to get anywhere like this?"

She showed no sign that she had even heard him.

"Did you think you could come to her with insults, yelling at her, blaming her for everything that went wrong in your life and still expect her to help you?"

"I no longer need her help," Sakura said. "I'm going back to get Louis."

"So they can cut you up? That won't save your kid."

"She won't save him, either."

"She might. If you tell her the truth."

"She cannot face the truth," Sakura said. "She thought she was free of me when she left me in the jungle. But I came back. Now she's trying to shake free of me again. Well, let her, and let her rot."

Munro met her eyes. There was a silvery light in the irises, almost a luminescence. "You really believe you are her daughter," he said quietly.

"Yes," she said shortly.

"You said you didn't know. How can you be sure now?"

"Because I feel it," she said grimly. She touched her breast. "When I'm with her, I feel it, in here. I know she is my mother."

"Why don't you tell her that?"

"I have told her."

"And she doesn't believe you?"

"She doesn't want to believe me." She smiled bleakly at him. "She cannot accept that I despise her."

"You told her that you despise her?"

"Yes."

He shook his head. "That's good going, Sakura. Nice work."

"I told you," she replied, "I won't lie to her or lick her boots."

"But you want her to pay out six hundred and eighty thousand bucks for you?"

"For her grandson," Sakura retorted.

"Wake up, Sakura," he said roughly. "You're sitting here full of tuberculosis. The Ray-Bans are gonna kill your child if you don't come up with a whole shitload of money. Go back, and they'll kill you both. There's only one person on earth who might possibly help you, and you spit in her face. What gives you the right to judge what she did? She didn't abandon her child so she could save herself. She left the child to save its life. How come you can't understand what it took to do that? You did the same."

"I didn't leave Louis," she said fiercely. "He was taken from me!"

"He was taken, you left him, what's the difference?"

"There is a difference! I would never have willingly left my child! I would never have been so selfish! Or so fainthearted! I would have taken him with me, whatever the price."

"The price would have been the child's life." His amber eyes glowed at her. "You know what she did? She walked across Borneo. On foot, across three hundred miles of tropical jungle and mountain. It took four months, and when she got to the other side, she weighed seventy-two pounds. That's about what a skeleton weighs. No child would have survived that. She left her little girl with the Ibans because the child had dysentery, and was already weak. If you're her daughter, Sakura, then the only reason you're alive today is because she left you with the Ibans. Otherwise you would be a heap of bones in the jungle."

Her eyes dropped. She turned away from him, her mouth a tight line.

"Now listen to me," he went on, lowering his voice. "You've got to grow up, fast. You're no fucking angel, Sakura. The reason you're so deep in shit right now is all your own fault. Not Francine's, not anybody else's. You got mixed up with a lot of bad things and a lot of bad people, and now you need help." He rose, towering over her like a dark mountain. "This is make-or-break. She's about got to the end of her rope with you, and she's ready to turn her back and let you take your chances with McFadden."

He walked to the door. His hand was on the handle when he heard her speak.

"You think I don't know?"

He turned. "What?"

"You think I don't know it's my fault?" He was surprised to see that her eyes were shining with tears now.

"Then don't put all the blame on her."

"She hurts me. More than you can imagine."

She was crying properly, her shoulders shaking. He stared at her. Was she just a wonderful actress, a chameleon knowing instinctively how to change her skin, how to react to each new situation? He went back to her and sat beside her on the bed. "You want to know what I think, Sakura? I think she would help you, given half a chance. But you won't even give her that half a chance. You're too dumb and you're too proud."

Unexpectedly, she put her arms around him and laid her head on his shoulder. "Speak to her for me," she whispered.

"That's not my job," he said, trying to push her away. Her breasts were soft against him. Her body was unlike other women's bodies. Under his fingers, there was strength as well as softness, a supple power in the muscles. Making love with her, it occurred to him, would be an interesting experience. With the thought came a mighty surge of arousal at his loins. He managed to untwine her arms from his neck. "You speak to her," he said roughly. "Tell her the truth."

She looked at him with bloodshot eyes. "You despise me, don't you?" she said in a low voice.

No, he thought, *despising you isn't my problem. What I feel for you is something a lot more difficult to deal with.* "My feelings aren't relevant. Get your act together, Sakura."

Taking a serious risk with his fly, he rose and walked out.

He found Francine in the observation room. "You heard that?" he asked.

"I want to speak to him, Clay," she said.

"Speak to who?"

"McFadden. You have his number."

He considered. "These people are dangerous."

"I know that."

"What do you want to say?"

"It may be possible to reason with them."

"I very much doubt that."

She looked at him steadily. "Set it up."

Munro opened his mouth as if to object further. Then he shut it. "Okay. I'll set it up."

The park was bleak and cold. Beyond the leafless trees, Fifth Avenue glimmered with an icy light, glints of capitalist gold capping mercantile granite.

Francine held on to Munro's arm as they walked along the jogging path. The cold wind off the lake had cleared away all but the most determined runners, a handful of burly men, muffled in hooded tracksuits, who trotted along the shore. The joggers were Munro's backup men, their tracksuits weighted down with iron, and they never strayed far from the thin figure sitting on the bench at the end of the path.

"McFadden," Munro said. He felt Francine's fingers grip tighter on his arm. "Thuong isn't with him."

Munro had no idea what Francine intended to say to this man, but he had set up the meeting nonetheless. He had known that McFadden would not consent to come to his office, and he had no intention of letting Francine get into McFadden's car, so the park had been a compromise, despite the unusually bitter weather. He had brought in muscle, of course, and had instructed the men to be highly visible. He wanted to let McFadden know that any rough stuff would meet with an armed response.

They walked toward McFadden. He was smoking a cheroot, legs crossed. He exhaled a plume of smoke upward by way of greeting, and did not bother to rise. "It's kind of fun watching a bunch of goons pretending to jog with thirty-eights banging against their balls. Where'd you get these clowns, Munro? Must be the dregs of your 'Nam outfit, huh?"

"A couple of them. Where's Thuong?"

"Busy," McFadden said laconically. "Take a seat."

Francine and Munro sat on the bench. McFadden swiveled to face them, his flat brown gaze finding Francine's. "Mrs. Lawrence. Tell me you brought a nice fat check."

"No," she replied.

"You spoke to Sakura," he said, not making it a question.

"Yes."

"You know the score."

"Sakura was pressured into doing what she did," Francine replied, her voice quiet. "Her child was taken away from her by the father. She had no choice but to go along with what he wanted. The Frenchman planned the whole thing. He also got the money, and he passed it on to his confederates. It's gone. She doesn't have the money. She never did have. It's useless to hurt her or the child. That won't get a cent back."

McFadden puffed on his cheroot, studying Francine. "I ain't asking you for money. Your daughter is."

"She's not my daughter."

"She told Ricard she was your daughter."

"Her delusions are not my business."

"It's possible, isn't it?"

"No."

"Nothing's impossible, Mrs. Lawrence." He cocked his head at her. "You must have done blood tests."

"Yes," Francine said reluctantly.

"Don't keep me in suspense."

"She's the right blood group."

McFadden chuckled. "Well, hey, hey, whaddaya know." His tone was satisfied.

"But she's O-positive," Francine added. "That's the most common group. It's not proof."

"Sakura must remember you from her childhood."

"She doesn't remember anything," Francine replied. "She has no memories of her parents. She doesn't know who she is."

"There are effective techniques for stimulating the memory," McFadden said. "Want me to help her?"

"She does not remember anything, Major, because there is nothing to remember. She is not my child. It's that simple."

"Oh, it's not that simple, Mrs. Lawrence," McFadden said softly. "Believe me, it isn't. Why are you paying for the clinic? Why have you got Munro investigating her? Why are you so concerned that we don't hurt her? You know you can't let go. You can't take that chance."

"I have not accepted Sakura as my daughter," Francine said inflexibly.

McFadden rolled his cigar between his fingers, squinting reflectively through the smoke. "You're still shocked, aren't you? Not exactly a pleasant surprise to find your long-lost daughter is a heroin dealer, a thief, a liar. But that's the way it turned out, huh?" McFadden reached into his pocket, gripping the cigar between his teeth. "By the way, I brought you a snapshot of the kid to give her."

He handed it to Francine. The black-and-white photograph showed the corpse of a small child. It had been badly burned with napalm, blistered stumps of limbs protruding from a bloated torso.

Francine felt a wave of black nausea.

"You're sick," Munro said quietly.

McFadden smiled thinly. "Oh, my, I'm sorry. That's the wrong picture. I meant to give you this one."

He tossed another photograph onto Francine's lap. She forced herself to turn it over. This picture showed a small boy with a mop of dark hair. He was sitting on the ground, looking up at the photographer with haunted eyes. The legs of a soldier in camouflage were included in the shot, army boots astride, framing the small figure.

"You can show her both shots, come to think of it," McFadden drawled. "Kind of before and after."

Munro spoke in a deep drawl. "Those boots in that photo. Yours, right?"

"Yeah, mine." McFadden's eyes mocked Munro.

Francine looked at McFadden with disgust. "Is this the way the CIA does things, Major?"

"She stole from my colleagues. You're responsible."

"How can I possibly be involved in your criminal activities?"

McFadden seemed amused. "Your kid stole from the U.S. war effort in Southeast Asia. The money she stole was going to fight Communism. Now that's a crime."

"Hey, McFadden," Munro purred, "spare us the patriotic bullshit, okay?"

McFadden's eyes settled on Munro. "All you spades think patriotism is bullshit."

Munro smiled coldly. "It was drug money."

"Don't be a fool, Munro. Nobody gives a flying fuck how the money was raised. What matters is where it was going." McFadden nodded toward the trotting figures of Munro's backup men. "You and your kind just fill the trenches. Half a million men, ten billion dollars' worth of matériel, a whole corps of generals, and you've been losing the war from the start. I'm doing the job you couldn't do."

Munro's eyes were contemptuous. "You're losing, too, McFadden. Don't kid yourself."

McFadden turned to Francine. "Get me the money, Mrs. Lawrence."

Francine's voice was steady. "I have seen war and death, just as you have. I am not a child to be bullied and frightened."

McFadden leaned forward. "Listen to me," he said. "Sakura only has one chance of saving herself and the kid. And that's if you pay Sakura's debt. Put it another way, the only chance you have of finding out whether Sakura is your daughter or not is to pay up. You're not gonna find out anything after we rip her throat out."

"And you will not get a penny of your money if Sakura or her child is harmed," Francine said icily. "Your threats are wearisome."

McFadden spat out a shred of tobacco. He smiled. "Wearisome, huh? You can't keep her safe, Mrs. Lawrence. Not from me."

A shivering wind rushed off the lake. Munro had been watching McFadden from under hooded eyes. Suddenly, he knew what that smile meant. "Oh, shit," he said quietly. "Sakura!"

Francine put her hand on Munro's arm. "What is it?" she asked in dread.

"We have to go." He pulled her to her feet, his heart thudding.

McFadden was still smiling. "We'll talk again later. Stay in touch, okay?"

Munro's men moved forward, sealing off the avenue, so McFadden could make no attempt to follow.

They ran out of the park onto the avenue.

Sakura sat cross-legged on her bed, her palms resting on her knees. She breathed steadily, with each breath trying to expel her anger and her fear. She waited until all the negative emotions had drained away, leaving her empty. Then she closed her eyes, and began the long walk through the forest to the river.

It was a form of meditation that Tomoyuki Ueda had taught her, when she'd been no more than five or six years old, in a garden in Tokyo. Over the years, other *sensei* had helped her understand the technique with the mind of an adult, not a child.

Each time, she started the journey with the same hope of reaching her destination. But she had never reached it in all the hundreds of times she had tried.

It was a long way to the river: The forest was thick and dark, and peopled with so many shadows. Some were kind, many were cruel. But each one who had touched her, in pleasure or in pain, for good or for evil, was there. Each one had his place along the path.

Some stood out from the others, rimmed with fire: especially her dead fathers. The first father she met was Li Hua, the most recent of all. Stroking his white beard, as in life, he smiled gently on her as she passed. Beyond him were a host of lesser shadows, soldiers and others. Roger was among them, no longer a fiery serpent, but handsome and laughing, as he had been when she'd last seen him. In his arms he held the bright baby that was Louis, and Sakura wanted to cry out to him; but her journey lay past them. She had to force herself to walk onward.

A long, long walk through the crowded forest. A legion of people, a world of places.

In time, she reached Tomoyuki Ueda himself. He, too, was as he had been in life, feet planted wide apart in the samurai stance, eyes glaring. But she knew those black eyes were not angry with her, only with a world that did not understand his complex nature. She saw him raise his hands in banzai. She knew he was urging her on, urging her toward the river.

The river was close now. She could hear it roaring beyond the trees. From here, her journey would become ever more difficult, even impossible. Now each yard taken was a deadly effort, and the path lost itself at each step.

Her earthly body, which had been relaxed and still, was now rigid. She had to force her mind onward, to stop it from fleeing to the outer world.

She was not yet lost. Here, in the darkest and most shadowy place of all, were Manu and Wai. They greeted her with joy. They spoke no word. She felt their fluttering hands on her, stroking her, touching her to see that all was well with her. Their eyes, dark and liquid, gleamed in the dim jungle light. She remained with them for a long while, drinking in their calm. Small and almost frail, they were like animals of the forest.

At last she gathered her strength to leave Manu and Wai, and to make the final, most perilous part of her journey. Now terror started to seize her in earnest.

Her faltering feet took her toward the river. The water roared and thundered beyond the trees. In the tumult were other sounds. As she emerged from the trees, onto the bank, she saw what she knew she would see, what she always saw: the terror.

The men in khaki swarmed through the river, shouting to one another. In their hands they carried rifles, bayonets, swords. The other people, her people, stood naked and motionless, waiting to receive them.

And then the killing began.

So much blood: There was enough of it to stain the mud of the bank red, to pour into the river and darken its flow. The steel sank into human flesh, drawing out more blood.

She had to force herself to creep through the murderous and dying ghosts, force herself to approach the river. She kept her eyes on the ground, so as not to see the terror. The blood stained her naked feet. The screams deafened her. She compelled herself to keep moving, to pierce the secrets.

At last she was at the river. The water was ice-cold. It lapped at her feet, chilling her bones. Slowly, she lifted her head. Around her, a whole village was dying. But she tried to concentrate her gaze on what lay across the river. She knew that on the far bank, figures stood: the figures of those who had brought her to this place.

For a trembling instant, she could almost perceive them. And then, her soul burst out of the trance. The images were torn from her eyes, leaving only darkness behind.

Shuddering, she forced her body out of the lotus position. She was drained. She had done this so many times, so many times hoping to see the truth. But she had failed, as she always failed. She could not get to that place, could not see those figures. She could not see beyond her own birth.

She heard the door open, and turned her head wearily.

Then her heart jolted as though an electric current had passed through her chest.

She recognized Thuong immediately, despite the white coat he had obtained from somewhere. His black eyes were hot. He closed the door behind him and walked to her bed.

"How did you get in here?" she stammered.

"You bitch-whore. You piece of shit, you motherless trash." He spoke to her in Lao, the glottals gurgling deep in his throat. "You think you can hide from us?"

She shrank away from him. The bell was set in the wall behind her bed. If she could reach it and press it, a nurse would come. "What do you want?"

"You know what we want." She saw the long knife in his hand, and knew at once that he was going to hurt her. "Why will the woman not pay?" he demanded.

"She does not believe that I am her daughter," Sakura said, her mouth dry as bone.

"You must make her believe."

"I can't. She wants proof."

"Give her proof."

"There is no proof, Thuong."

Thuong moved between her and the bell. "If she does not pay, you know what will happen to your bastard child."

"There is no proof," she repeated desperately.

"You are only alive so that you can get the money from her. Otherwise I will butcher you, little sow. Piece by piece." Moving too fast for her to escape, Thuong grabbed her left ear, jerking her head brutally forward.

Suddenly, agony tore through Sakura, burning like fire. Thuong was slashing with the knife. Hot blood sprayed down the side of her face.

"No," Sakura screamed as she groped for the blade, trying to wrench it out of Thuong's hand.

"I will cut your fingers off," Thuong rasped. "Look at me, whore."

Thuong jerked Sakura upright. She clutched at the side of her head, feeling her neck wet with blood. The ear was hanging loose, but not severed completely. Thuong was grinning, showing his gold tooth. He wiped the switchblade carefully on Sakura's bed, then poised the needle tip an inch from her face.

"Shall I cut the nose, too?" he asked.

"No," Sakura said in a strangled voice, her body rigid. In some part of her brain, she wondered whether she would lose the ear. The pain was crushing. "Don't."

"Get the money from her."

"I will try," she gasped, her whole being focused on the knife aimed at her eyes, and on the thick fingers holding it.

"Do more than try. What I do to you, I will also do to your child, Sakura."

"Give me time," she whispered.

"Twenty-four hours," he said. "After that, no more time. You understand?"

She nodded, clutching at her ear. Blood seeped between her fingers.

Thuong snapped the blade shut. "We can reach you anywhere. Any time." He leaned forward and, almost casually, spat into her face. She made no attempt to wipe the spittle from her cheek.

Thuong walked quickly out of the room, closing the door behind him.

She dragged herself off the bed. Her legs were almost too weak to support her, and she stumbled. She had to lean against the door, gathering strength. Blood was pouring down her face, soaking into her gown. She groped at the handle, and fell out into the corridor.

Francine stared down at Sakura's unconscious form. She had been sedated after they'd put thirty stitches in her ear and administered a tetanus shot. She lay, somehow crumpled, one half-closed hand pressed to her forehead. Her skin seemed transparent in its paleness.

"I did this to her," Francine said in a dead voice.

"No," Clay Munro said. "I did."

"She came to me for help, and I held her off." She looked up at Munro, and he saw the terrible pain in her eyes. "I can't deal with this." She looked back down at Sakura. "A slash of a knife can be an effective way of separating what matters from what does not."

Munro was very still. He was remembering McFadden's smile in the park. "He won't get away with this," he said quietly.

"No, Clay. We can't fight the CIA." She reached out, and touched

Sakura's slack fingertips with her own. "She is too important to risk. Whoever she is. After everything else is gone, she will be the part that remains. She will be the part I have to live with."

Munro, too, looked at Sakura. "It could have been part of the plan. Done with her consent."

"Do you really think that?" she asked quietly.

"No. But it's possible."

"And it's possible that this is Ruth." In the pause, Sakura moaned something in a language neither of them understood, then fell silent. "It's more than possible," Francine went on, her voice dropping so Munro had to strain to hear her. "I can't shut my eyes or my ears any longer. I have to face the truth."

Her eyes were shimmering now. Munro had never seen her cry before, and he put his arm around her. She wept briefly, untidily, the tears of a woman unused to release.

Outside, there was a bustle of activity and fervid consultation. The hospital security people were still trying to work out how Thuong had managed to get himself into Sakura's room. Munro knew that it had been all too easy, and he cursed himself for having allowed Parsons to bully him into withdrawing his own people.

Right now, one of his best men was sitting outside, armed. Four others were positioned around the entrance to the ward. This time, Parsons had made no objections.

"They won't try anything in here again," he said. "But the minute Sakura steps out of this hospital, they're going to grab her. They'll hold her till they get their money from you. Then they'll kill her."

Francine nodded. Her eyes were dark after weeping. "Yes."

"We have to get her somewhere safe. And we don't have much time. You want me to set up a safe house somewhere out of state?"

"We need to go farther than that," she replied. Her moment of emotion seemed to have cleared her mind, and she was once again controlled. "We'll take her to Hong Kong."

"Hong Kong? They'll find out you have a house there. They'll track us there in twenty-four hours."

"I have other properties in Hong Kong, Clay." She smiled tautly at him. "Properties that are not common knowledge. Only I know who owns them. We'll have time, at least, to work out what to do next. I know that traveling to Hong Kong is beyond your sphere of operations, Clay. I will adjust your pay scale accordingly."

He shrugged. "Don't worry about my sphere of operations. I meant it when I said I wouldn't let you face this alone."

She looked into his face for a moment. Then she leaned forward and kissed his cheek. Her lips were cool. "Thank you, Clay."

"No problem, Mrs. Lawrence."

"My name is Francine," she said.

"Okay."

A nurse entered noiselessly. "The police have asked to speak to you and Mr. Munro, Mrs. Lawrence," she whispered.

"What are we going to tell them?" Munro asked.

"We'll stall them," Francine said. "By tomorrow she'll be gone. I want to move her tonight."

"Tonight? She's still sedated."

"The risk is far greater if she stays here another day. Moving fast and unexpectedly is our only hope of outdistancing them. It's the one thing they won't be expecting."

He stared at her with his lion's eyes. "Maybe not."

"We'll take a private jet. I use a company that is very discreet about passenger manifests."

"Think she can stand a long flight?"

"I think she can stand a great deal," Francine replied coolly.

She was her old, formidable self again, Munro realized, and he nodded. "You want to take a nurse with us?"

"No. No nurse. No extra help. Just you, me, and Sakura. We'll take a supply of her drugs with us, and you and I will administer them until we can get medical help in Hong Kong. I want maximum security, Clay. Nobody must know she's leaving the hospital. Nobody must know what we're planning. We'll transfer her straight to the airport and get right on that flight."

They walked down the corridor together.

"And if McFadden contacts me today?" Munro asked.

Francine's eyes glowed. "Tell him I will be in touch."

High above the dark Pacific, Clay Munro was glad to awake from a brief, tortured sleep. He'd dreamed of Vietnam, of the death of friends, and the images remained in his eyes for a few moments as he stared out the black window. There was a streak of blood in the night, the first sign of the rising sun.

He shook off his blanket, and looked around. Francine's papers and calculator lay on her seat, but she was not in her place. She was at the back, checking on Sakura. He rose and got two cups of coffee from the machine. There were no attendants on this flight.

He took the cups to the back of the plane. He had never traveled on a private jet before. The Lear had been designed to carry twelve or more passengers, and with only three of them on board, the softly lit spaces were empty. They had decided to take no one with them, to keep their movements as compact and as fast as possible.

Francine was sitting beside Sakura, who was lying on a bunk, covered with blankets. "Is she still asleep?" he asked.

"Yes. But she looks better," Francine said. Sakura had only surfaced two or three times during their journey, and had seemed only dimly aware of what was happening to her. She took the coffee from him. "Thanks. This is very welcome."

"I'll spell you, if you want. You should sleep."

"I don't need much sleep. I worked for a while, but I can't concentrate. I was just sitting here, thinking."

He sat down beside her. "What were you thinking about?"

A strange expression crossed her face for a moment. "About hope."

"Hope?"

"Hope is a torturer, Clay. Many years ago, I forced myself to accept that my daughter was dead. If I hadn't done that, I would have gone mad. I would still have been there in the jungle, looking for her. The only way I could rebuild my life was to accept that she no longer existed. That's how I survived. You can understand that, can't you?"

"Yes," he said quietly.

"And then this happened." She nodded at Sakura. "This hungry ghost."

"Hungry ghost?"

She smiled. "Sakura came to me on the Festival of the Hungry Ghosts. Chinese believe that if a person dies without the proper ceremonies, their ghost goes hungry in the underworld. It comes back to haunt the living during the seventh moon. They burn paper money and possessions to appease the dispossessed. And here was this half-wild woman, nearly thirty years later, telling me she might be Ruth. I couldn't accept that it wasn't a hoax. I didn't want to be tortured anymore. The possibility of a miracle was so small, so very small. I tried to keep my balance. I was cautious with her. I felt that I had to be. And when all the rest emerged, the drugs, the corruption, war, violence . . ." She met his eyes. "I'm trying to explain why I seemed to be so hostile to her at first."

"You don't have to explain anything."

"I have to explain my own stupidity."

"You really think she might be your daughter?"

"I think the tiny possibility that she is Ruth far, far outweighs the large possibility that she is not. Up until they cut her face, I worked on the opposite assumption."

"And now?"

"And now, I have to behave as though she is Ruth. Until the opposite is proven."

"You're thinking of paying," he said, not making it a question.

"Rather than see her killed, or her child killed—yes, I would pay."

"You've got that kind of money available?"

"I'll make it available, if necessary."

"Won't that hurt your finances?"

"It will hurt. It won't cripple."

"And what if she vanishes into thin air the minute you pay?"

"Then I'll have been swindled. But at least I'll be able to live with myself."

He glanced from her face to Sakura's. "For what it's worth, she looks an awful lot like you."

"Does she?"

"She's like you in other ways, too."

"Such as?"

"Sakura has your strength. She's . . ." He hesitated. "She's special."

"Yes, she's special."

"She burns. As though there's a flame inside her."

"That flame sometimes burns in people who've suffered early on in life. What was it she said? 'I have lost everyone I ever loved, all through my life.' "

"Yeah. That's one of the saddest things I ever heard. You also lost those you loved, Francine. You burn, too. In the same way."

"Perhaps that's the only link between us."

"Maybe. It's going to be hard, Francine. You lost a little girl who clung to you and did everything you told her, and now you've found a big, bad woman who's done big, bad things. Sakura lost a loving mother who was all the world to her, and now she's found an unfriendly stranger. Happens to all parents and all children, I guess. Just that, in normal lives, the process is a lot less violent."

"Yes." Francine touched her eyes. "I feel tired."

"I'll sit with her," Munro offered, "if you want to get some rest."

"Yes," Francine said. "Perhaps I will sleep now, after all."

Sakura lay in a jumble of bodies: other children and the dogs of the village. It was the bite of a flea, which she had scratched raw, that had woken her. She was reluctant to leave the warm tangle of limbs, but curiosity was tugging at her. Now was her only chance, before anyone awoke, to look at the treasure.

The other children had told her about the treasure of the tribe, hidden in the forbidden room at the end of the longhouse. She had been bursting to look in there all day, but it was not allowed. It was not a place for children.

But now, while they all slept, she could creep there, and peek inside, and see what it was they guarded so jealously. Her mind pictured golden crowns, piles of precious stones.

She disentangled herself from the slumbering pile, and crawled on her hands and knees onto the outside platform. Thick mist hung over the river. Below the longhouse, pigs were rooting, and a dog scratched, but the sun had not yet risen.

She hesitated for a moment, looking around. Nobody was stirring.

She walked slowly along the platform, the loose bamboo poles twisting under her bare feet. They creaked and rattled, and at every moment she expected to hear an adult shouting at her. But nobody stopped her.

The room at the end of the corridor was closed with nothing more than a thick atap flap. No lock was needed to secure the treasure room: What kept intruders out was the power of the sacred law. But she was not of the tribe, and she did not fear the prohibition of sacred law.

She pushed the flap aside and went in.

Her eyes had to accustom themselves to the darkness. But to her intense disappointment, there was no gold, no silver, no rubies, no emeralds. The room was small and dusty and piled with sheaves of straw, old fish-traps, worn-out mats, and other junk.

In a corner was a large sack. She unfastened it and looked inside hopefully. It was filled with seed rice. This was riches of a kind, the promise of next year's harvest, and the next year's. But it was not the treasure she was looking for. She plunged her hands into the rice, groping among the husky grains, but her fingers found nothing.

She lifted her eyes. Hanging from the roof beam was a cluster of grayish, gourdlike objects. Her heart, already racing with the wickedness of what she was doing, started to pound. Perhaps this was the treasure! Perhaps the gourds were filled with jewels and gold!

She clambered onto a sheaf of straw and looked closer. They were not gourds.

They were human skulls.

There were at least a hundred of them, perhaps twice that number. Most had lost their lower jaws. The eye sockets were empty. Some still had a parchment covering of skin and dusty locks of hair. Generations of spiders had woven webs around them, thick and white. They hung like hideous fruit, laconically stored in this dusty little chamber, the treasure of the tribe.

One of the skulls was fresh. It had been smoked, and the brown skin had shrunk tight around the bones. The yellow teeth, some with steel caps, were bared in a grimace of astonishment. The hair had been cropped close. It was unmistakably the head of a Japanese soldier. The dull, withered fruit of the dead eyes glared at her.

Terror seized her, and she fell off the sheaf of straw, her hands clawing for support. But her fingers were meshed in the cobwebs the spiders had woven. She was choking on her own bile.

Sakura surged into wakefulness. She tore aside the mosquito net that hung over her. She was in a small, featureless room that she did not recognize. *Where am I?* she thought in panic. Then dim memories returned, of leaving the clinic, of being in an airplane. Her skin was chilled by air-conditioning, but she sensed it was hot outside. A row of chick blinds covered one wall of the small room. She pulled one up, and opened the door onto a narrow terrace.

Francine Lawrence was sitting outside, wearing dark glasses, reading a newspaper. She rose as Sakura came out.

"Sakura?"

The day was swelteringly hot, the noise of the city loud in her ears. Mountains of white cloud hung overhead, towering into a sky the color of a duck's egg. Tall buildings shut off the view, but Sakura saw the Chinese script on the neon signs, and knew where she was.

"Hong Kong," she said.

Francine nodded. "Kowloonside. You're safe. How do you feel?"

"Dazed," Sakura said. Under the greenish sky, everything had a strange unreality. The stitches in her half-severed ear hurt dreadfully. "Can I look at my face?"

Francine nodded. She led Sakura inside to a bathroom. The apartment was small, clean, anonymous. "Nobody knows I own this flat," she told

Sakura. "They won't trace you here. Clay Munro is with us. He went out to buy food. He'll be back soon."

Sakura looked at her face in the mirror. There were shadows under her eyes. She peeled the bandage away from her skin. The wound around her ear was ugly and black, the antlike stitches glued in place with dried blood. Getting them out was not going to be pleasant.

"I asked them to be very careful with the stitches," Francine said. "They say there will be a scar. But your hair will cover it."

"Why the kindness, Francine? I didn't think you'd turn squeamish at the sight of a little blood."

"I'm not squeamish," Francine assured her. "I am simply trying to be practical."

"Why have you brought me here?"

"To protect you."

"You can't protect me."

"I doubt whether you know what I can and cannot do," Francine said dryly.

Sakura met Francine's eyes in the mirror. "Are you going to help Louis?" she asked quietly.

"I'm going to see what I can do," Francine said coolly.

Sakura swallowed hard. "You don't need to bother protecting me, Francine. But save him. Please."

"I told you. I'll see what I can do." She touched Sakura's shoulder lightly. "You've slept for eighteen hours solid."

Sakura stooped and splashed water on her face. "I was dreaming about the longhouse," she told Francine. "About the time I found where they kept the skulls."

"What skulls?"

"They were head-hunters. One of the men had killed a Japanese sentry, and cut off his head, and brought it back to the longhouse. The heads were their treasure. The heads the warriors cut off their enemies."

Francine's expression had changed. "You remember all this?"

"It was something I'd forgotten. I remembered it in my dream."

"Why do you think this came back to you?"

"I don't know. Maybe the sedative they gave me. It was all so real. So vivid. I remembered how I slept, with a lot of other children, and dogs, too. It was so clear in my mind." She glanced at the tiny shower cubicle. "I haven't washed in days. Could I shower?"

"Of course. But I have to give you your injection first." Sakura watched as Francine got the streptomycin injection ready. "Which side is it?" Francine asked.

"I can't remember," Sakura said. "It doesn't matter." She lifted her nightgown for the injection, showing the scattering of dark bruises high on her buttocks. Francine gave the injection briskly. Sakura winced.

"I'll get you some towels," Francine said, disposing of the syringe. "I bought you some clothes, but I don't know how well they'll fit. They're in your room. We'll buy you some more, when you feel well enough to go out."

Sakura nodded. "Thank you, Francine," she said in a quiet voice. She took off her gown and got into the shower.

When she got out of the shower, she dressed in the clothes Francine had left for her, white slacks and a cotton shirt in a neutral tan color. The sizes were almost perfect, and the clothes were cool for the climate.

Clay Munro had returned, and was setting out some food on the table, foil cartons of take-out rice and duck. Sakura's head was exploding, and the thirty microstitches in her ear were thirty points of agony.

"Hungry?" Munro asked.

The antibiotics made her nauseous, and the smell of the Chinese food was enough to make her gorge rise. "I'll just have some fruit," she said.

They sat down together. Sakura took a slice of papaw and a mango. Munro and Francine sat opposite her. "Tell Clay about your dream," Francine commanded.

She lifted her eyes to Clay's briefly. "I dreamed of the longhouse. Of finding a Japanese soldier's skull hanging in a room."

He nodded. "Uh-huh. What else do you remember?"

"I don't know. Tiny things. Things I haven't thought of in years. About the way we slept in the longhouse—all the children and the dogs, in a big pile."

Munro smiled briefly. "A big pile of fleas."

"Yes," she said, "I remembered the fleas in my dream, too. I remember scratching till I bled."

His eyes were hooded, as so often when he listened to her. "You often dream of that time?"

"Never," she said. "I've never had a dream like that before."

"And why do you think you had it now?"

"I don't know. You think I'm lying to you?"

"I didn't say that."

"Your face says it for you."

"Cool it, Sakura. Nobody's hassling you."

"You said you could remember nothing before the massacre," Francine said quietly. She was eating with chopsticks, expertly. "But this memory is from before the massacre."

Sakura nodded. "Yes. It came back from the dark time."

"The dark time?"

She struggled for words. "It's as if there's a dark room, and a window has opened, and a little bit of light has come in."

"Is that what you feel? That there's a dark room inside your mind?"

She nodded. "Something like that."

"So, if this window opens farther, you'll remember more?"

"Maybe. I went to a hypnotist in Singapore once, to try and remember. He couldn't help me. Another time, in Saigon, a psychologist gave me drugs. LSD, I think."

"A psychologist gave you acid?" Munro asked.

"He said it would bring back my memory. But nothing came back, only frightening dreams. He said that I had selective amnesia, that the experience of seeing the Japanese kill all those people had been so terrible that it made me forget who I was."

"I'm not a shrink," Munro said. "But you remember the attack clearly, don't you?"

"Yes."

"You said you remembered the killing, the bayonets, the blood?"

She touched the bruised, swollen left side of her face. "Yes."

"So how come you remember the bad things, Sakura? If your shrink was right, those memories would have been wiped out."

She tightened her mouth. "I'm telling the truth."

"But if the massacre wiped out your memories, then surely you wouldn't be able to remember anything about the massacre? It doesn't make sense."

"I'm telling the truth," Sakura repeated, her eyes blazing. "Fuck you, Clay! Don't play clever cross-examination games with me!"

"I'm just trying to get things straight," he replied.

"I know what you're trying to do!"

Francine laid her chopsticks next to her bowl. "Now that Sakura is her old self again," she said dryly, "I think it's time we called in a doctor to take a look at her."

The apartment was in Kowloon City, near the harbor, in a residential district that was not rich, nor poor, nor frequented by tourists. Francine had bought the apartment, and several more like it, as investments over the years. It was not registered in her name, but in the name of one of her anonymous companies, and she doubted whether it would be easy for anyone to track them to that address.

Nevertheless, she was cautious about taking Sakura out of the apartment the next day, even after the doctor had agreed that she would benefit from some outside air. Sakura needed new clothes, so Francine took her to a shopping mall nearby, choosing the busy midafternoon, when the unusual combination of a black man and two Eurasian women would not be noticed.

Sakura took little interest in the clothing, so Francine bought what seemed practical and useful in her own judgment. They walked back to the apartment, carrying the packages. It had rained overnight. Between the clouds, the sun gave splendid visions of Victoria Peak. The greenery was dense around the slopes, a snatch of wilderness among the swathes of skyscraper and apartment block.

Near the apartment, they passed a small park where children were playing. Sakura stopped.

"Can we sit here?" she asked. "I'm tired."

"We're nearly home," Munro said.

The slash in her ear felt as though it were on fire. "I need to rest," Sakura snapped at him. "Is that a crime?"

"No, it's not a crime," he said patiently. "I just don't want you to be noticed."

"Who will notice me here?"

"They'll surely notice *me*." Munro took her arm. "Let's get back to the apartment," he advised. "It doesn't make sense to be out here."

She threw his hand off. "Don't grab me!"

"Let her stay here for a moment," Francine conceded. "The air will do her good. I'll go back to the apartment. There's a call I want to make."

"Okay," he agreed reluctantly.

Munro followed Sakura into the park while Francine went back to the apartment. They sat on a wall in one corner. The playground was crowded, children swarming on the swings and slides, the benches filled with parents, grandparents, and a sprinkling of Filipino nannies. Munro glanced at Sakura, and saw the way she was watching the children play, her face tense, her fists clenched.

"How old is your kid?" he asked carefully.

"He's almost two and a half."

"Does he talk much?"

"He speaks English, French, and Lao. He—" Sakura swallowed the hot lump in her throat, unable to continue.

"Did you love this guy?" he asked.

"Yes."

"But you must have known he was a bad boy."

"He was beautiful."

"That made it okay?"

"I didn't see what he was until it was too late. Women never do," she added bitterly. She touched her chest with her fingertips. "This thing inside me stopped my periods for years. I thought I was sterile, so I didn't take precautions. I was a fool."

"You didn't want Louis?"

"I didn't plan Louis. When he came, he was the greatest gift of my life. He made up for everything else."

"Made up for what?"

"Not being anybody. Not having anywhere to go. I used to hold him in my arms when the B-52s came over."

"The B-52s?"

"You never see them or hear them. The bombs just fall. The high explosives tear up the land. They pour poison from the sky to kill the trees. It is in the water, and nobody can drink it anymore. Babies are born dead or deformed. The animals die. Crops fail."

"I saw that kind of stuff in 'Nam," Munro said. "How come you settled on Vientiane, after all the places you went through?"

"It was so peaceful. After Tokyo, Bangkok, Singapore, places like that, Vientiane was like a return to my childhood."

"What do you mean?"

"I sometimes used to think that my earliest years—before Sarawak, I mean—must have been spent in a place something like Vientiane."

"Have you told Francine this?"

"No."

"Why not?"

"She doesn't want shadows. She wants hard facts. And I don't have any. I can't find words to explain anything to her."

"You're explaining it to me."

She glanced at him. "You're different."

"I'm just the hired help."

"I trust you, Clay."

Her eyes were on him, but Munro was silent, watching the children.

"Do you think Francine will pay the debt?" she asked.

Munro shrugged. "She'll work something out."

"She would pay it if she believed I was her daughter."

"Yeah."

"Since she learned what I am and what I've done, it's worse. Everything I tell her makes it worse."

"She understands you more than you think."

"And you, Clay? Do you try to understand me?"

He glanced at her at last. "Come on. Let's go."

She laid her hand on his. "I could have done so many other things, been so many other people. I never had much of a chance, Clay."

"Maybe your chance has come now, Sakura," he said quietly. "You better take it while it's here."

"I will," she said. "I promise you, I will."

He nodded. "Okay. Let's go."

Since 1954, Francine had called Clive Napier no more than three times.

He had made his life in Australia after the war, and was now a partner in one of the country's biggest companies, with affiliates across the Southeast Asian business world. Though their paths might have crossed on several occasions, Francine had taken care that they should not meet. She would have found such a meeting unacceptably painful. It would have opened the wounds it had cost her so much to heal. But now it had become essential that she speak to Clive.

She had to give her name to be sure the call would not be intercepted by a secretary, and when Clive's voice came on the line, the first thing he said was, "Francine, is that really you?"

"Hello, Clive."

"My God, Francine," he said. "It's wonderful to hear your voice. Are you all right?"

"Yes, I'm fine. And you?"

"Never fitter," he said.

"I hope this isn't a bad time to call."

"I'm at my desk," he replied, "looking across the harbor. Matter of fact, I have your picture in front of me right now."

"My picture?"

"There was an article about you in the *Straits Times* a couple of months ago. I got a copy of the photo. You look wonderful."

"It was probably taken ten years ago."

He laughed. "Maybe so."

She braced herself. "I'm calling you because I've been approached by a woman who claims to be Ruth."

Clive's voice changed. "She claims what?"

"Her name is Sakura Ueda."

"That's a Japanese name."

"She's Eurasian, around thirty. She claims she doesn't know where she was born, but says her earliest memories are of living in an Iban village as a small child during the war. The village was destroyed by Japanese soldiers. She was the only survivor. She was rescued by a Penan couple who took her into the jungle for a time. They put tattoos on her forearms. Black, Dayak-style tattoos. Are you still there?"

"Yes," he said quietly. "I'm still here. Go on."

"She was picked up by a Japanese officer, who brought her back to Japan, probably in 1944. He was executed for war crimes in 1947. After that, she was on her own. She's grown up wild, wandering all over Southeast Asia. And now she's in desperate trouble. That's why she's come to me."

"What kind of trouble?" Clive demanded.

"She got herself mixed up with the heroin trade in Laos. She and her boyfriend stole nearly seven hundred thousand dollars from a cartel run by the CIA on behalf of a right-wing warlord named Jai Han. Now they want their money back. They sent two men after her, violent men. One is CIA. The other is married to one of Jai Han's sisters. They have her child in Vientiane, a boy of two. They say they'll kill him if she doesn't pay."

"You mean if you don't pay," Clive said grimly.

"I told them I wouldn't deal with them. She has tuberculosis, Clive, and I had to put her in hospital. They attacked her in her room. They almost severed her ear."

"Jesus, Francine," he said in a shocked voice. "Where are you now?"

"In Hong Kong. I needed to get her out of New York as fast as possible."

"Is she all right?"

"She can cope."

Clive grunted. "And she can't or won't speak of her life before Borneo?"

"She says the memories were wiped out by the trauma."

"So she wants you to pay seven hundred thousand dollars on the strength that she might be Ruth, with not the slightest shred of evidence?"

"She is desperate to save her child."

"Desperate people tell desperate lies."

"I know that," she said wearily. "But I have no time to patiently sift for the truth."

"What do you mean, 'no time'? You're not thinking of paying, are you?"

"I have to do something, Clive."

"Francine," he said curtly, "why do you think all the pressure is being put on you? Precisely so you don't have time to patiently sift through the truth. So you don't see through the charade."

"I know that's possible. But what if it's all true?"

"Jesus, Francine," he said, his voice tightening. "How could it possibly be true? Think! Think of the odds!"

"I know about the odds," she said quietly. "She has the same blood group as Ruth."

"You're sure?"

"Yes, O-positive."

"Millions of people have O-positive blood, Francine. Remember all those orphans we saw? She could be any one of them. Does she look like she could be Ruth?"

"Her eyes are different from Ruth's, darker, and her hair is not the same color. But Ruth was a little girl, and Sakura is a grown woman. Children change so much. Who can tell how Ruth would have turned out? When they attacked her with the knife, I looked at her, and I thought, *She is Ruth.* I nearly broke down. And then, an hour later, I swung full circle, and thought, *She can't be. It isn't possible.* I go like that from day to day."

Clive's voice was urgent. "I want to meet this woman, Francine."

"Yes. I want you to meet her, too."

"I can be there in twenty-four hours," he said.

"Can they spare you on such short notice?"

"They don't have any choice."

"Then I'd appreciate your coming, Clive. I'd like your opinion."

"You can have whatever you want. We've been through fire together before now."

"Yes," she said. "I remember."

She put the phone down.

Darkness fell. The rhythm of the city changed. Neon exploded in the darkness, and the smell of food drifted on the humid air.

They ate, Sakura barely tasting her food. Afterward, they went out onto the small terrace. The roar of evening traffic rose up to them. But there was a kind of peace up here. Other families were taking the air on other terraces around them, tiny aeries high up in the night, spilling voices, laughter, the sound of cooking.

"We're getting a visitor," Francine told them.

"Who?" Munro asked warily.

"My husband died during the war. He was captured, and he died in a prisoner-of-war camp. But there was someone else. Clive Napier, the British officer I escaped from Singapore with. He's my oldest friend. He's coming out from Australia."

"To check me over?" Sakura asked, from her place in the darkness.

Francine glanced at her dim outline. "I value his judgment. He might be able to help us."

"When does he arrive?" Munro asked.

"Tomorrow," Francine replied.

"Another test for me to pass," Sakura said dryly.

"If you are my daughter," Francine said in a neutral tone, "then Clive Napier is the closest thing to a father you ever had."

"The closest thing to a father I ever had," Sakura said tightly, "was Tomoyuki Ueda."

"Yeah, but they hanged him," Munro said brutally.

"They did not hang him."

Her reply had been very quiet, and Francine barely caught it. "I thought he was executed?"

"No."

"You mean he's still alive?" she said blankly.

"Of course not."

"So what happened to him?" Munro demanded.

Sakura was quiet for a long while. "He was sentenced late in the afternoon," she said at last. "Execution was put forward to the next morning. They were going to hang him. That would have been a terrible disgrace for him. He was samurai. You know what that means, don't you?"

"Yes," Francine said. "I understand that."

"He asked to see me, so they brought me to the prison where he was held. Some of his family and some brother officers took me. We went into his cell to say good-bye to him, one by one. Just before I went in, they put something inside my shirt."

Francine listened to Sakura's low voice, feeling a mounting unease. "What was it?" she asked.

"A knife. It was small, with a bamboo handle, but it was very sharp."

Francine and Munro glanced at each other.

"When samurai commit seppuku, they use two blades, the little dagger and the big sword. They could never have taken a sword past the sentries, so he had to use only the little dagger. They didn't search me properly, just looked in my pockets. I was only a girl. The knife was against my belly. They didn't find it."

Francine sighed. "Oh, Sakura."

"When I went in to Tomoyuki, he embraced me. He put his hand inside my shirt, and took the knife. He thanked me. He made me sit down so he could talk to me one last time." Sakura smiled at Francine, but it was a fractured smile. "He was a very special man. He taught me some of the most important lessons I ever learned. I suppose I was around nine or ten by then. He explained to me that he could not face what the executioners had planned for him. He told me that there was always another option. Self-destruction. I realized what he was going to do with the knife, and I started to cry. He made me stop. He told me that when disgrace was too much to bear, or when there was too much pain, this was a gift I could give myself. He told me to study hard and be a good girl. Then he said good-bye. They took me out. In the night, he cut open his belly in his cell. He made no sound. He just bled away. When they checked on him at dawn, he was dead. There was no more Tomoyuki."

"Poor Sakura," Francine whispered. "Poor little girl." She watched the green and red lights reflected in the thick waves of Sakura's hair. She thought how many tragic things were locked in that head. Yet out of that horror had grown a fierce pride, a defiance of life's unfairness. Those jagged defenses were all she had seen at first. She had understood very little about Sakura, had made very few allowances.

"It's time for your injection. And then you must sleep. Come, Sakura."

They went to Sakura's room, leaving Munro sitting in the darkness with his own reflections.

"I haven't been what you hoped for, have I?" Francine said quietly as she filled the syringe.

"You look at me with such contempt," Sakura said. "Your eyes are so cold."

"Sakura, in your eyes I see the same coldness."

Sakura looked up with a haunted expression. "If there were only some proof, Francine. I used to dream that there was some special sign on my skin. That there was something secret about me you would recognize."

"Only in fairy tales, Sakura."

"I shouldn't have said those things to you in New York." Sakura touched Francine's hand. Tonight, she was very different from the "big, bad woman who had done big, bad things" who had shocked Francine. "At first, I thought you had told the CIA about me, and that they were trying to kill me. I was hardly in my right mind. I was burning up with fever, hallucinating."

"You don't need to apologize."

"And . . ."

"And?"

Sakura's voice dropped. "And I was very hurt."

"So was I."

Francine stooped without thinking, and kissed Sakura's temple. The younger woman's skin was like satin. She walked out quickly before she could give way to emotion.

Francine went to Kai Tak alone to meet Clive.

She stood in the milling concourse, thinking about the last time they had been together, in Sarawak, long ago.

That day, they had listened to the story Annah had told them. She had believed it to be true, and it had marked the end of the first half of her life, and the beginning of the second part. Clive, she knew, had not believed it.

Had he been right? Had she been wrong? Standing among the turmoil of Kai Tak like a stone in the river, Francine wondered whether she was once again at a turning point in her life. Was everything coming back to her? Were the ghosts forming once again out of the mist?

And then she saw him, a tall, solid figure, head and shoulders taller than the Asian passengers around him. She waved.

"Clive!"

He saw her, and made for her. The saturnine face was more lined, and the thick hair carried streaks of gray, but otherwise he was the same Clive, piratical and dark. He stopped short before reaching her, as though he had hit some kind of invisible barrier between them.

"Hello, Clive."

"Francine, darling." He half-reached out to her, as though he wanted to break down that invisible barrier and take her in his arms. Francine touched his hand. She felt a hot lump in her gullet, tears pricking her eyes. "You haven't changed."

"Nor have you." He leaned forward and kissed her cheek gently. The memory of their brutal separation years earlier was painful between them.

"Come, let's go," she said in a voice that was meant to sound business-like. "I want you to meet her."

In the taxi, he began to recover his poise. He looked at her with apprais-ing eyes. "You look wonderful," he said. "Are you on monkey gland, or something?"

"Ginseng tea," she said, and smiled. She could see that time had been kind to him. His face was a little craggier, and his eyebrows were shaggier than she remembered. But he looked fit and strong. The Australian climate was probably perfect for him. He had a tennis-court tan and clear eyes. His graying hair had been expertly cut, and he wore a gold watch on his left wrist, but no wedding band. He carried a different kind of authority now, not the arrogance of youth and military rank, but the poise of maturity. "I'm so glad you came, Clive," she said.

"I didn't have much choice. Does Sakura know who I am?"

"I explained briefly."

"You shouldn't have done that."

"Why not?"

"It gives her a chance to prepare."

"She's not an actress, Clive."

"Of course it doesn't seem that way to you."

"You haven't even met her."

"Let's get one thing straight," he said, laughing. "I'm not here to rescue Sakura Ueda. I'm here to rescue you."

"From what?"

"From your spell of moonlight madness."

She tapped his knee. "Let's get another thing straight," she said shortly.

"I don't need rescuing, by you, or anyone else. If you've come here to play the white knight, you can get right back on the return flight to Sydney."

"What?"

"If you can help, then help. But don't push me, Clive. I have enough on my plate without you playing the fatherly old fart."

He held up his hands, laughing. "All right, all right."

"As long as we've got that straight."

"We've got it straight. Now, tell me about her."

"Well, she's at a low ebb, physically. The TB has been wearing her down for years, and the knife attack was traumatic. But she's as tough and re-sourceful as anyone you've ever met. She is . . . unusual."

He studied her expression. "Unusual because you feel an affinity with her, or unusual because of the way she looks?"

"Unusual because of what she is. It's hard to describe. Clay says she burns, and it's true. As though there's a flame inside her. You'll see."

"She's ingratiating, I take it?"

"God, no. Just the opposite. She's very antagonistic. She's had a rough life, and she blames me for it."

He quirked a dark eyebrow. "I see. Nice touch."

"She can be hostile. She's only just starting to open up, and some of the stories she tells are horrifying."

"Hard-luck stories?"

"Very-hard-luck stories."

"One thing puzzles me. What did this Japanese officer want with her in the first place?"

"According to her, he liked children."

"In what way?"

Francine picked up the nuance. "She didn't say he did anything to her. But she's buried so many memories that she may have buried that, too. He was interested in intelligence, and he recognized that she was very bright. She helped him commit suicide in jail."

"That's preposterous," Clive scoffed. "This reads like a bad TV script, Francine."

"When you hear her tell it, it rings true."

"What does she say happened to her after Ueda's death?"

"She cleaned and worked in kitchens, and picked up some kind of edu-cation along the way. Eventually, Ueda's relations either cut her off, or she cut herself off, because she left Japan in her late teens, and hasn't lived there for years. It'll take months to learn about her life, Clive. She's worked in Singapore, Macao, Bangkok, Saigon, Vientiane, and God knows where else. I don't think even she can remember all the things she's done or all the places she's been."

"And how did she make the connection with you?"

"She says she saw an article about me five years ago, and filled in the blanks."

"But she didn't come to you until now?"

"No."

"Yet now she claims to be Ruth?"

"Not directly."

Clive smiled grimly. "She's leaving you to fill in the blanks, too? And she can remember nothing before the Japanese attacked the village?"

"I think that was such a terrible experience that it's wiped out her earlier memories."

Clive shook his head slowly. "That's so convenient. It's so very easy to make up a story like that to fit the facts."

"You don't need to tell me that."

"Francine," Clive said carefully, "isn't it significant that you didn't instinctively recognize her when you first saw her? That makes me think she can't be Ruth."

She was silent for a while before replying. "There wasn't any mystical mother-feeling that told me this was definitely Ruth. If I'd given in to that kind of fantasy, I'd have been crazy. But when I first saw her, there was . . . something. And it's been growing. It gets stronger every day."

"Oh, Jesus." Clive sighed.

"Everything is ambiguous, everything is shot through with paradoxes and coincidences. But what if she is Ruth? How can I ignore that possibility?"

"You can't ignore it. But you have to get right to the bottom of this before you make any decisions. Especially about paying hundreds of thousands of dollars."

"There is no time. They will kill her child. A little boy who may be my grandson, Clive."

"He probably doesn't even exist."

"But what if he does?" She had been forcing her voice to sound calm, but her emotion was now audible in every word. "How can I take a chance on that? How can I?"

Clive's face darkened. "Francine, what better ploy could this girl use than picking up some brat and telling you it was your grandchild?"

"I know that. I know that, Clive. But that doesn't help."

Clive sighed again, looking out of the window at the sunlit skyscrapers. "Well, you'd better fill me in on all the details."

They arrived at the apartment block, and went up in the elevator. Francine knocked at the door, and Munro opened.

"This is Clay Munro," Francine said, "my security consultant. Clay, this is Clive Napier."

The two men shook hands.

"Where's Sakura?"

"On the terrace," Clay said. "I think she's sleeping."

They walked out onto the cramped terrace. Sakura was lying in a chair, sunglasses covering her eyes. She turned her head slowly, and then rose to her feet to meet them.

"Clive," Francine said, "this is Sakura Ueda. Sakura, Clive Napier."

There was a moment of silence. A jet rolled overhead from Kai Tak. Sakura took off her dark glasses. She and Clive looked into each other's faces for a moment. Francine saw Sakura's face blanch to the color of bone. Her eyes seemed to go blind. Clive, too, was suddenly pale.

"Hello, Chicken-Licken," he said quietly. He reached out to her. Sakura was frozen for a second. Then, with a sob, she was in his arms, her face buried against his shoulder. Francine could not see Clive's face, but the hand that stroked Sakura's dark hair was trembling.

When Clive tried to let go of Sakura to say something to her, she sagged, and almost fell. Munro grabbed her. Her head lolled on her neck like a snapped flower. "She's been sick this morning," Munro said warningly.

"I don't feel so good," Sakura muttered. "Sorry." Her eyes were white slits between fluttering lids.

"Let's get her to bed," Francine said. "Maybe I'll call the doctor."

Between them, they helped Sakura to her room.

Clive sat beside her and smoothed the hair away from her brow. "My God," he said in a low voice as he studied Sakura's face.

Sakura sprawled back on the bed. Her dazed eyes half-opened and looked into Clive's.

"I know you," she whispered.

"Do you?" he said.

"You were there."

"Where?"

"At the longhouse. You were there. Weren't you?"

Clive reached out and touched her cheek. "Yes, I was there."

"And before."

"And before."

"I know you were," she replied, staring up at him. Shivers were running along her body. She could not take her eyes from him. "Clive," she whispered. "Clive."

Clive looked up at Francine. Francine saw there were now tears in his eyes. "Can I be alone with her for a moment?" he asked.

Francine nodded, and walked out.

Clive turned back to Sakura. "Are you so sure you know me, Sakura?"

She nodded. "Yes. I feel as though I'm dreaming."

"What do you remember about me?"

"You used to call me Chicken-Licken."

"What else?"

She was so certain she knew this middle-aged man that it made shivers run down her spine. But there were no memories to back up that knowledge, nothing in the brain. It was something that lurked in the marrow of her bones. "You remind me of a pirate. From a childhood book."

"Francine tells me you worked in a casino in Macao, eight years ago."

"Yes."

"I used to do business in Macao. Gambled in all the casinos. You probably took a few thousand pataca off me in your time. Maybe that's why you remember me."

She shook her head decisively. "No. I remember you from another time."

"What time?"

"From the longhouse."

His eyes were formidably intelligent. It would be very hard to lie to those eyes. "Francine tells me you dreamed of the longhouse a few days ago," he said.

She nodded.

"Tell me about it," he commanded.

"I dreamed of finding a bunch of skulls hanging in a room."

He nodded. "Enough to give a little girl hysterics, I should think."

"I was shocked, but I didn't have hysterics." Her voice slowed. "It was . . . important."

"In what way?"

"There was a Japanese soldier's skull there."

"Why was that important?"

"It was the reason the Japanese came back," she said without thinking.

His eyes narrowed. "What do you mean?"

She spoke in a dreamy voice. "The Japanese killed some of the people in the village first. I don't know why. So the young men went to the Japanese camp and killed a sentry. They brought his head back."

"How do you know all this, Sakura?"

"Everybody was talking about it in the longhouse. But the Japanese came looking for the head, and when they found it, they killed everyone."

He studied her. "Except you."

She nodded. "Except me." She looked up at him, her lids now heavy with exhaustion. "Are you Francine's lover?"

"Oh, no. Today is the first time I've seen Francine for many years. I lost Francine after the war. When she accepted that Ruth was gone, it was as though something inside her stopped living. Unfortunately for me, that part of her was also the part that loved me. So I lost her." His eyes were serious. "I loved Ruth very much, you know. She was a part of me. Her going left a hole inside me, too."

Sakura was shaking. Something was trying to burst out of her heart. "You know who I am."

"I think so," he agreed.

"Who am I?" she whispered.

He paused a long time before replying. "You're Sakura Ueda," he said gravely. "Whatever happened at that longhouse, Ruth is gone. She will never come back. But Sakura is alive. And Sakura is beautiful and vibrant. You have to understand that. So does Francine. So do I."

"But I don't know who Sakura Ueda is!"

He touched her face with his fingers. "Even though I believe you were once Ruth Lawrence, it doesn't solve that particular problem, Chicken-Licken. Not knowing who you are is part of the human condition."

"I want to know who I am!"

"A tiger can hide in a patch of sunlight, Sakura," he said gently. "Sometimes we can't see the thing we're looking at, only the things around it." He kissed her brow. "Sleep."

Her lips formed other words, inaudible. Then her lids closed, and she sighed. Her breathing grew deep and regular.

Clive rose slowly to his feet. He covered Sakura with the sheet, then walked out of the door. Outside Sakura's room, Francine was waiting for him. His eyes met hers.

"She's alive, Francine. After all these years. I can hardly believe it."

She felt her stomach muscles jolt. "How can you be so sure?"

Clive's face was awed. "She's you, Francine. As you were, when I fell in love with you, twenty-eight years ago."

She had anticipated many reactions from Clive, but not this incontrovertible, lightning recognition. It shook her. "Come on," she said, taking his arm. "Let's get a drink."

They sat on the terrace, the sun setting behind the tall buildings and flooding the sky with red.

"I can't believe it," Clive repeated. "It's a miracle. She's exactly like you. Look at this. I brought it with me."

He held something out. Francine took it. It was an old black-and-white photograph of herself with Clive, taken in Raffles Hotel. She remembered the occasion vividly—New Year's Eve, 1941. She stared at her own youthful face, and suddenly saw Sakura's mouth, Sakura's eyes. A kind of hot pain seared through her heart. She passed the photograph to Munro, without comment.

Munro looked at it. His eyes widened. "Jesus."

"You kept that all these years?" she asked Clive softly.

"I have other pictures. But that's the way you were when I first met you. That's how Sakura is now. Francine, I came here a skeptic. But I'm like Paul on the road to Damascus. She told me about her dream, about the skulls. She said the soldier's head had been the reason the Japanese had come back and destroyed the village. That's not too much for a child of four to have understood. The important thing is that the sequence of events she describes fits in exactly with what we know." He counted off on his fingers. "One, the Japanese punished the village for some minor offense by killing a handful of the villagers. Two, in revenge, the warriors went to the Japanese camp and killed a sentry, bringing his head back as a trophy. Three, the Japanese came looking for the head, found it, and slaughtered every living soul. Except little Sakura." Clive's dark eyes were intense. "It's what we know happened, Francine."

"Yes."

"Remember when we first reached Nendak's village, after the *Lotus Flower* sank? Remember how we found four or five corpses, hanged or bayoneted?"

"I remember."

"Then, when we went back to Nendak's village, after the war, they told us the Japanese had exterminated them all because the Ibans had killed a sentry. That fits correctly with what Sakura just said. The young warriors decapitated a sentry to avenge the murder of their relations. And the Japanese came back with a platoon. Francine, it probably happened within weeks or even days of our leaving her there."

Francine's voice was tight. "She could have read that. She could have imagined or invented the dream to fit the facts."

"She doesn't know any facts," Clive said forcefully. "Yes, there have been articles about you, and what happened in Sarawak. But none of them ever went into any details. None of those journalists wrote about the dead sentry, the reason why the Japs destroyed Nendak's village, or anything else. All they said was that you had left Ruth with some Ibans, and that she had vanished."

"How do you know?" she asked.

"Because I've collected every word that has ever been published about you since 1954," he said, his voice gentling. "I pay cutting agencies in a dozen countries."

"Why should you do that?"

"You would not speak to me or write to me," he replied. "In the absence of any communication from you, I was forced to follow your life through newspaper articles."

"Oh, Clive."

"I don't think this is some facile invention by Sakura. I think this is a real memory. Francine, do you really have doubts that this is Ruth?"

"I will never be completely free of doubts," she said quietly.

"But you're capable of accepting an overwhelming probability? Francine, an angel from heaven will never come down and tell you this is your daughter. But she is the right age, the right blood group. She was in the right place at the right time. She has your voice, your face. She even, God help her, has your stubborn nature."

She smiled wryly at him. "You came here thinking you would make the scales fall from my eyes, Clive, but it seems the scales have fallen from yours."

"By God, yes. I'm not as rich as you, but if you have any problems raising the capital, I'll help."

"The capital?" Francine asked.

"We need to raise six hundred and eighty thousand dollars."

"The money has nothing to do with you," she said firmly.

"Ruth has a lot to do with me. I can manage to raise four hundred thousand dollars cash."

"Your retirement pension," she guessed.

"I'll work a couple more years." He shrugged.

"Dear Clive," she said dryly, "wait until your jet lag wears off."

"I'm not jet-lagged. You intend to pay. I want to help."

"With your pension?"

"Look. I'm over fifty. I only loved one woman in my life, and she left me. I only loved one child, and I lost her. I didn't have anything to look forward to. Retirement, and another twenty or thirty years of watching the sun go down. That's not exactly a thrilling prospect. And then, like a comet out of the sunset, this. All the wasted years suddenly don't matter. Through some miracle that I do not intend to question, I have a chance to set right the mistakes. To reclaim what is lost. What does money matter?"

Francine poured three more whiskeys. They sat in silence for a while, listening to the rumble of traffic.

"I don't want your money, Clive," Francine said at last. "But thank you for the offer." She glanced at Clay, who had said nothing. "Clay, do you think I could deal directly with General Jai Han?"

He shifted in his chair. "Jai Han? Jai Han might be very hard to reach."

"It would cut through all the bullshit, wouldn't it?"

Munro nodded. "Yeah, it would sure cut through all the bullshit."

"That's my speciality," Francine said. "When Sakura wakes up, I'll ask her how to contact him."

Francine sat on Sakura's bed, preparing the syringe. She jabbed it into Sakura's buttock, adding another black flower to the collection. "Sakura," she said, withdrawing the needle, "I need to contact Jai Han."

Sakura turned to look at Francine. "Why?"

"I want to speak directly to him. I need to see what can be done."

Sakura's voice tightened and rose, like a girl's. "You will pay the money?"

"I didn't say that," Francine replied quietly. "But I want to speak to him."

"Dealing with Jai Han is not easy."

"Nothing in this affair is easy," she agreed. "How can I contact him?"

"When he's in Vientiane, he stays at a place called the Vieng Chang Hotel. He owns it, or part of it. People leave messages for him there."

"Then I will call him there."

Francine rose to go out. Sakura grasped her hand. "Francine, thank you," she whispered.

"I have done nothing yet."

"All I want is Louis back. I don't want him to die!"

"He won't," Francine said. Hesitantly, she touched Sakura's hair. Sakura clung to her. It was almost the first physical contact they had ever had. Sakura's body was slim and taut, shaking with emotion as it pressed against hers. "Be strong."

Sakura looked up at Francine. "I would have brought Louis to you when he was born," she said, speaking low and fast. "I have never lied to you, and that is the truth. I felt I could face you at last. I felt I had finally done something wonderful. Do you understand?"

Francine nodded.

"But they wouldn't let me take him. Roger kept him, so I would do what he wanted. I know I have been a fool, I know it. But Louis is innocent. If you save my child, I will do everything, be everything I should have been."

"Oh, Sakura," Francine said gently. She kissed Sakura's cheek, and went to the telephone.

The call to Vientiane had to be made through the exchange, and took some time. It was almost five minutes before the connection was made, and the telephone at the other end began to ring. It was answered by a lazy female voice. She gave her name and asked for General Jai Han. The receiver was put down with a clatter. In the background, she could hear tinny music, male laughter.

At last the telephone was picked up. A deep male voice demanded, "Yes?"

"General Jai Han?"

"Yes."

"This is Francine Lawrence."

"Francine Lawrence! Why you leave New York like a ghost, Francine Lawrence? You say nothing to my friends. You make them look like fools. Make them lose face. Now they very angry." The accent was pidgin American, the torrent of English staccato. "You in Hong Kong, ha?"

There was no point in denying it. "Yes, I'm in Hong Kong."

"Sakura with you?"

"Yes, she's with me."

"I will speak with her."

"I'm sorry. She's very sick. She can't speak to anybody."

"Too sick to speak to General Jai Han?"

"Yes. I'm sorry."

"Too ashamed, perhaps." She heard him drink something. "Sakura is a bad girl. Your daughter?"

Francine hesitated. "She may be."

He laughed boisterously. "Maybe, ha? I got maybe children, too. Lots of maybe children. You know what she did to me? She stole from me. Six hundred eighty thousand dollars." The voice grew rough. "I trust that girl, and she betray me big-time. What can I do to punish her? Ha?"

"I am more interested in what can be done to solve this problem," Francine said, before he could go any farther down that line.

"You pay six hundred eighty thousand dollars for a maybe child?"

"I do not have that kind of money."

She heard him drink again. "You very rich, Mrs. Lawrence. Everybody in Asia know your name. You nuhuang. You very clever businesswoman. Too clever to throw away so much money for a maybe child? But listen, Nuhuang. I got many maybe children. You only got one. Only one. Different for a woman." Francine was silent, not knowing what to answer. He spoke in Lao to someone standing by, and she heard other men laugh in the background. She guessed they were in the midst of a drinking session.

"Reports of my wealth tend to be greatly exaggerated, General."

"So why you call me, ah?"

She gathered herself. "I'm calling you to ask you to release Sakura's child."

"Sakura's child? My family looking after him. My wives like aunties to him."

"He should be with his mother, General."

"You think Jai Han is a barbarian?" The jagged voice was suddenly dangerous. "Think he would hurt a little baby boy? Maybe burn him? Maybe let dogs eat him?"

"I know that Jai Han is too great a man to hurt a child," Francine said, keeping her voice level. "If you release the child, I am prepared to discuss the money."

Jai Han grunted. "Discuss?"

"General Jai Han, I am a businesswoman. I do not cheat. I do not lie. But I do not bargain under duress, either."

"You not like duress? Duress even harder for a child, Nuhuang."

"The child must not be hurt," she said sharply. "And Sakura must not be hurt, either. There must be no more punishment of her, General. I know that she has angered you, and she is very sorry. But she has suffered greatly for what she did. I offer to negotiate on the understanding that she will be allowed to live in peace after this."

"Not negotiate. Not discuss. You pay everything." He was clearly angry now. "You pay everything, or I kill them both. You understand?"

"General—"

"Why you waste my time? You think you can bargain with me? Get a discount? You think like a woman, Nuhuang. Time to think like a man! Now, you pay, or not pay?"

In the silence, distant voices speaking Thai and Lao drifted along the line, a tenuous electric impulse reaching out through the Asian night. "I will pay," she heard herself say.

"How you pay?"

"I suggest you send representatives, with the child, to Thailand. I have some infrastructure in Bangkok. And I believe your bank is there. When I have seen the child, I will authorize a bank transfer for the full amount. As soon as your bankers confirm receipt of the funds, the child can be released."

"Wait, Nuhuang."

With a clatter, the telephone was put down. She heard an energetic conversation being conducted between several male voices.

She had just told Jai Han she would pay him six hundred and eighty thousand dollars. Words on the telephone. But she knew that she had taken a step that was irrevocable. If she did not comply, blood would be shed, and the blood would be on her hands.

A woman screamed briefly, and there was a blast of music as a door opened and was closed again. Francine tried to imagine the scene, some tawdry hotel filled with soldiers and whores.

At last the receiver clattered again as Jai Han picked it up.

"Nuhuang?"

"I'm here."

"Bank transfer not acceptable. Sakura steal cash. You pay cash."

Her heart sank. "That is much more difficult. And more dangerous."

The harsh voice was threatening again. "Not possible?"

"Yes, it is possible. But delivering large amounts of cash is not easy, and not safe. You know that."

He was indifferent to her objection. "You bring American dollars. Not smaller than fifty-dollar bills. You give us the money, we give you the child."

"Where?"

"Here, Nuhuang, here. In Vieng Chang Hotel, Vientiane."

"You want me to come to Vientiane with the money in a suitcase?" she said dizzily.

"You come. And Sakura come, too."

"Sakura? I told you, General, she is very sick."

"Sakura must apologize to me," he said harshly. "She must look in my eyes and apologize. I must hear it in her own words. My people must hear it, too. Otherwise she never see her child. And maybe dogs eat him."

Francine tried to stay calm. Everything was slipping out of her control. "General Jai Han, with all respect, I believe my suggestion is a good one. For us all to come to Vientiane would be taking unnecessary risks—"

"You don't trust Jai Han?"

"I do not trust the situation to be safe."

He grunted. "Too bad. Jai Han trusted Sakura, and Sakura betrayed him big-time. Now you got to trust Jai Han."

"But General Jai Han—"

"*Assez*," he said with sudden violence. "You come to Vientiane with cash money and Sakura." The barked commands were savage. There was no longer any laughter in the background. "How long you take to get to Vientiane?"

"I don't know," she said breathlessly. "It will take a little time to organize—"

"I am busy man, Nuhuang. I do not like to wait."

"I'll be as quick as I can."

"You call me here tomorrow. Same time. You tell me you got the money. You tell me when you come to Vientiane with Sakura. You understand?"

Francine took a deep breath. "Yes. I understand. I will call you again tomorrow."

He grunted, and the line clicked dead in her ear.

Her hand was shaking as she replaced the receiver. She looked at Clive and Munro. "He insists I come to Vientiane with the money. And he wants Sakura there, too."

"What for?"

"He wants her to apologize to him in front of his men."

"And then he'll blow her brains out," Munro said.

She stared at the two men. "What are we going to do?"

"Let me go to Laos alone," Munro said flatly. "I'll take him the money."

"He said he would not give back the child unless Sakura came, too."

"What did he say about the kid?"

"He said his wives were looking after Louis. But he made veiled threats. He said he would mutilate the boy, or feed him to the dogs."

"He'll send us the boy's fingers, one by one, if he thinks you're stalling," Munro said.

"But, Clay, seven hundred thousand dollars in a suitcase?"

"Maybe he's changed his plans for the money," Munro said. "Maybe he wants the money for himself now."

"Things are not going well for Jai Han."

They all turned at Sakura's voice. She was standing in the doorway, pale and tense.

"He's losing the fighting?" Francine asked.

"Not just that. Vientiane was the biggest gold entrepôt in Southeast Asia. But there are too many Communists, up in the hills, and now in Vietnam. The Tet offensive frightened the traders. Now Singapore has established a gold market. Singapore is safe. Vientiane will collapse, and there will be nothing worth fighting for. Even the Americans will go."

"You're saying he will lose everything?" Francine asked.

"Yes."

"Why can't we just send the money to Switzerland or Andorra?"

"Jai Han knows nothing about Switzerland or Andorra," Sakura replied. "He is a general, but he is only a Meo tribesman. I must go to Vientiane," she said in a low voice. "I insulted him in front of his men, and he needs me to apologize to him."

"What if he wants more than that?" Clive asked.

"He can have what he wants," Sakura said.

"Even your life?"

"If I do not go, he will never release Louis. I cannot ask him to spare me. I have to accept whatever he wants."

"What if he wants to hurt you physically?" Francine said. "Even kill you?"

"I don't know."

"What does he do to Pathet Lao prisoners?" Munro asked.

Sakura thought. "Sometimes he shoots them. Other times, he puts them in gasoline drums and buries them in a pit."

"That gives you a pretty good idea," Munro said shortly.

"I have not come this far in order to lose you now, Sakura," Francine said. "If necessary, I will pay Jai Han more."

Sakura shook her head briefly. "He won't accept, Francine. You don't understand his nature. If I do not go, he will kill Louis."

"We all have to go," Munro said. "The problem isn't just with Jai Han. It's with McFadden and his crew. Sakura knows too much. It'll be harder to kill her in front of three foreign witnesses."

"Sakura's knowledge is also a weapon," Clive said. "She can write a statement, explaining the opium connection between the CIA and Jai Han. We can leave that statement with a lawyer. And if she, or any of us, fails to return from Laos, the lawyer will publish the record, together with details of our disappearance. All that can be explained to Jai Han in advance, so it has time to sink in before we get there."

There was a silence. Francine closed her eyes for a moment. Fate was catching them all, snaring them in a web from which she doubted they could all emerge intact. For these past weeks, it had been as though she had been watching a movie of herself, seeing herself do things, say things, that she had never known were in her. "Very well," she said. "So be it. We all go."

Clay Munro awoke like a cat, fully awake in an instant. He rolled his big body out of bed and padded silently out onto the balcony. He'd sensed her presence there, and his instincts hadn't failed him. He could see Sakura's slim figure at the railing.

He went to her. "What the hell are you doing?" he asked quietly.

"Just looking." She was staring down at the weaving ribbons of light far below. An ambulance or a police car raced down the street, lights flashing, siren howling its two-tone message of bad news. "What time is it?"

"Five A.M. What are you doing out here?"

"I couldn't sleep. They're still talking."

"Francine and Clive?"

"They've talked all night."

"Old friends, old lovers. They have a lot to say."

"I'll never be like that with anybody," she said. "I wouldn't have enough to say to fill ten minutes."

"Baby, you could talk about your life for a year and not repeat yourself."

She shook her head. "I can't talk about myself the way other people do. Sometimes I want to tell things that happened to me, things that hurt me. But I can't."

Munro took her arm. "Come away from the edge, Sakura."

"Why?"

"The railing's too low."

"You're afraid I will jump." She smiled slightly. "You thought I was going to jump that day in the hospital."

"Were you?" he asked.

"Maybe."

"Then come away from the edge." His fingers tightened around her arm. She put her hand over his.

"You love Francine, don't you, Clay?"

He was taken aback. "You're way off base, honey."

"I don't mean sex. You love her for what she is."

"She pays my bills."

"No. You love her. She knows that. So do I."

Munro was silent for a moment. "She's special."

"I am special, too, Clay."

"Yeah," he said. "I guess you are."

"Are you on my side?" she asked.

"I've always been on your side."

"No. You've always been on Francine's side."

"If you're asking me to move my loyalty from Francine to you, the answer is no," he said brusquely. "But she wants to help you, and that means I want to help you, too."

"For her sake? Not for mine?"

He was uncomfortable enough to feel his skin heat up. "What do you want from me, Sakura?" he asked in frustration.

"I want to know if you feel what I feel."

"About what?" he demanded. But he knew.

"Sometimes your eyes are amber, like a lion's," she said. "You stare at me, and I think you could swallow me up."

"I stare at you because I never know what you're going to do next."

"Isn't that a good thing?" In the soft light, she looked like a child. It occurred to him that when this was all over, Francine would enclose Sakura in a forbidden city of wealth and gilded privilege, and he would probably never see her again.

"You should go back to bed," he said.

"Don't you like being out here in the dark with me?"

"We could all get another couple of hours of sleep."

She laughed quietly. "You're afraid of me."

"I'm not afraid of you, Sakura."

"Yes, you are. You were afraid of me in that tenement, when I had the knife." Her eyes glinted. "You knew I would cut you. You thought you would beat me, but you knew I would leave you bleeding. Isn't that true?"

He smiled slightly. "That's true."

"Now I have no knife. But you're still afraid of me. Why?"

"I'm afraid you'll hurt yourself."

"By jumping?"

"And in other ways."

"I carried Tomoyuki's death inside me for years," Sakura said dreamily, watching the street beneath. "It was like this sickness inside me, weeping black tears. All my life I thought about destroying myself. Of becoming nothing. Like Tomoyuki."

"You're a survivor, Sakura," Munro said, keeping close to her.

"Does it seem that way?" Sakura's full mouth twisted. "Once, a really bad thing happened to me, in Saigon. I thought I would kill myself then. I thought I would use what Tomoyuki taught me."

"Why didn't you?"

"I got ready to. I talked to Tomoyuki for a long time. In my mind, I mean. All night long. I said good-bye to him then. And you're right; I'll never think about killing myself again. Unless it would save my son. So don't be afraid of me anymore."

"We'll save him. You don't have to die."

"Do you despise me?" she asked.

"No," he said. "Why should I despise you?"

"You shouldn't," she said seriously. "You and I are alike, Clay."

"We are, huh?"

"Bad things have happened to you, too. In Vietnam."

"Bad things happen to everybody in Vietnam."

"But to *you*." Unexpectedly, she laid her hand on his chest. The small palm seemed to burn his skin like fire. "To Clay Munro, the person you are. Vietnam changed you."

"How do you know?"

"I feel it." She did not take her hand away. "They did evil things to you, and you did evil things."

"Right," he said in a rough voice. "That's war."

"You can't carry it inside you forever. You have to empty yourself. Like I did."

"Yeah. Thanks for the psych talk." He took her hand away from his chest, finding it a distraction. Her fingers twined around his, locking tight.

"Look. You can't let go of my hand. Try."

He pulled his fingers out of hers. But she had learned some kind of hand wrestling, and she was as quick as a snake. Her hand clamped around his wrist, locking tight again. She smiled. "I used to play this game with other children in Tokyo. Nobody ever beat me."

Irritated, he jerked his hand the other way. She had anticipated his move, and though he was strong enough to break her grip, her supple fingers snaked around to imprison him again.

"That mirror in my room, at the hospital," she said. "You could see through it, couldn't you?"

He hesitated. "Yeah," he said. "It was one-way glass. An observation mirror."

"And you used to *observe* me through it?"

"That was my job."

"You saw me undress?"

He tried to get his hand free of hers, but she was very fast, and there was extraordinary strength in her slim hands. The only way to escape would be to hurt her. "No," he said impatiently. "I didn't."

"Didn't you see me naked?"

"No."

She smiled wickedly. "Did you see my breasts?" she asked.

"I didn't look."

"You're lying. I felt your eyes on me. I felt you. You enjoyed watching me."

"Bullshit."

"Do you want to know what happened to me in Saigon that time?" she asked.

"If you want to tell me."

She was silent for a moment. "Five GIs took me for a whore. They didn't believe me when I said I wasn't. They raped me and beat me."

Munro said nothing. But he stopped trying to free his hand from hers.

"I could have fought one, maybe even two. But not five. I know how to fight a man. You know that."

"Yeah, I know."

"I did judo, karate, and jujitsu. I was good."

"I know you were."

"But I was never a whore. That was one thing I never did. So, after the GIs, I felt they'd taken the last thing I had. You understand?"

His mind full of visions he did not want to see, Munro nodded.

"I went to the river and sat on the edge of the wharf all night, watching the lights dance in the water. I wanted to go and dance with them. But I didn't. I would not let them crush me." She glanced up at him. "I've upset you. You see? That's why I never talk about myself."

"You didn't upset me."

"I've never told anyone else before."

"Not even Roger?"

"He would have laughed. You are the first person I've wanted to tell."

"I'm sorry," he said. "That shouldn't have happened."

"I seem hard, Clay. But I'm only hard on the outside. On the inside, I am gentle." Her face was a glowing oval in the dark, her mouth a shadow. He was thinking of a girl, sitting in despair by the edge of dark water, wondering whether to end it all in that liquid night. She reached up and touched his face with her fingertips. "You're so big, so strong," she whispered. "Everyone is afraid of you. But your skin is like velvet. And now, when you touch me, I feel your gentleness, too."

Munro had desired many women, and had never been denied what he wanted. He had always been the powerful one, and after the conquest, his interest had always faded fast. But Sakura was different. It wasn't just that she was desirable. She fascinated him. He wanted to find out all about her. He wanted to know each pain she had suffered, the whole rocky road she had trodden.

But there was danger and treachery in her. Sakura was a whirlpool, and once he got inside, he might never come out. He cursed himself for the fuse that was running along his blood.

"We weren't made for each other, Sakura," he said quietly.

"Yes, we were!" she said in a whisper. "This was the way we had to meet. This is the way it has to happen." She pressed close to him. Her body was supple and warm. Immediately, he felt desire surge through his loins. She felt him rampant against her body.

"You want me," she said quietly.

"That isn't enough," he said.

She reached her slender arms up around his neck, lifting her face. His head suddenly swimming, Munro stooped to kiss that orchid mouth.

Her lips were so soft, clinging to his. She kissed him like a child, her eyes closed, her tongue not stirring.

"You see what I'm really like," she whispered against his mouth.

He looked down at Sakura's face, thinking about the first time he had seen her, as he'd followed her, pale and exhausted, from Francine's office into the subway. Without knowing it, he had been wounded by her beauty, even then. By the strangeness of her. He thought of her now as the perfect point between East and West, a face he had been looking for all his life.

He stroked her hair. It was thick and heavy, and smelled of jasmine. They had wanted to cut it in the hospital in New York, saying short hair was easier to keep sterile, but she had reacted so fiercely that they had abandoned the idea. He was glad. If they ever made love, he wanted her to spread it around him the first time, like the dark wings of a dark angel.

"I've been bad, Clay," she said dreamily. "But I'll be good with you. If you give me the chance."

He laughed softly at her. She felt as light in his arms as a cloud. But he pushed her away from him. "No lovey-dovey, Sakura," he said. "And no promises you can't keep."

"I only promise what's inevitable," she said quietly.

The sun was starting to rise. In the pink light, the sky was tender. He studied her with brooding eyes. "I'm from a different world," he said. "There's such a gulf between us. Bridging it would take a lifetime."

"Then let's take a lifetime."

He shook his head. "How am I supposed to trust you? You're a crazy woman."

She winced, as though something had cut her. "*Kichigai.* That is what they called me."

"What's kichigai?"

"It's Japanese for a crazy person. I have been crazy, yes. But now I am sane."

"And if the TB doesn't kill you, Jai Han or the Ray-Bans will. You're not what I'd call a safe bet."

"You will protect me," she said simply. "You can protect me from anything."

He laughed softly. "Is that why you want me?"

"No. Most people are children, Clay, but you are an adult. So I will speak to you as an adult. You must face the ugly things about me. You must trust me when I say that they are over." She touched her breasts. "There is sickness in here, yes. But there is also great treasure. I promise you, Clay, I have so much for you. I can make you very happy."

"You're kichigai," he said dryly.

"And you are *baka*," she said to him, smiling.

"What does that mean?"

"It's a very rude Japanese word meaning a stupid person." She turned to the sunrise and started tying back her hair. Her beautiful breasts lifted in peaks beneath her shirt, and his eyes were drawn irresistibly to them. "I think you could love me," she said.

"Time to stop dreaming," he said. "I'll go fix some breakfast." He shook his head and walked away.

Clive and Francine watched Sakura's silhouette on the terrace.

"What's going to happen between those two?" Clive asked.

"They'll break each other's hearts," Francine replied.

"He is tougher than I was. Even when I first met you, Francine, when you were a sweet, naive child from the backwoods, you had that steel core inside you. You knew what you wanted and where you were going. I'll never forget the sight of you walking away from me in Sarawak, your head high, your back straight."

"I'm sorry I hurt you," she said. "I never meant to. I was just trying to protect myself."

He was silent for a moment. "We'd given so much, lost so much. We nearly died so many times. It was unbearably hard." He smiled. "Do you remember Raffles?" he said. "God, when I think of the way we danced, while the Japs bombed our world to bits. We had no idea."

"By Popiah Street we had a better idea," she said.

"Oh, yes," Clive agreed softly. "Much better."

Francine glanced at him. He was thinking of the first time they had made love, on her narrow bed in Union Mansions. Or perhaps of other times, under the stars, on the cool balcony, listening to music. The memories filled her own veins with a warmth she had not known in years.

"I go to Singapore often," he said. "Lee Kuan Yew has cleaned up the town. Arab Street, Death Street, Bugis Street, the brothels. All vanished. Just skyscrapers and parks. I liked the old Singapore."

Francine thought of Battling Bertha, dead in the road outside the Golden Slipper after a raid. She had not thought or spoken of these things for half a lifetime. Yet the recollections were as hot and brilliant in her mind's eye as though it had been yesterday. The thought came to her: *Clive is the only person on earth with whom I can share these things.*

"Are you going to do to me what you did in 1942?" he asked.

"What do you mean?"

"You could take care of yourself and Ruth in just about any situation. But with the Japanese at the gates, you needed a protector. A loyal male to help get you to safety. So you tolerated me until we got to Australia. After that, you had no further use for me."

She was shocked. "You cannot believe that!"

His mouth wore the ghost of a smile. "Isn't that the way it was?"

"You know it was not," she spat at him. "That is a loathsome thing to say, after all these years."

"So you really loved me in Singapore?"

"Of course I loved you!"

His lids drooped over his dark eyes. He drew in a slow breath, as though inhaling the bouquet of some rare vintage. Then he sighed. "Isn't it sad? A fifty-year-old man badgering a fifty-year-old woman into a twenty-five-year-old admission of love?"

"I am not fifty," she said in a razor-edged tone. "I am forty-eight years old. And you are fifty-two."

"You're such a beautiful woman," Clive said, smiling again. "Lightning flashes from those eyes, my sweet."

"Take back what you said about me."

"I can't. I think you made a devil's compact with me in Singapore, all those years ago. You promised yourself to me, if I would help you and Ruth get to safety. But we lost Ruth. And my punishment was to lose you."

She stared at him. "Is that why you are so keen to prove that Sakura is Ruth? Because you imagine it will bring us together again?"

"At least we're in the same city for the first time since 1954," he said. "That's a start."

"A start to what?"

He shrugged. "You tell me. I know one thing, Francine. Some men love many times. Or maybe they never love at all. They just go from one woman to another, saying the same things, feeling the same feelings. But I'm not like that. There was never anything like you before in my life. And there was never anything like you afterward."

She was silent, her anger ebbing away swiftly. "You never loved again?"

"I never stopped loving, Francine. I never stopped loving you."

FIVE

JAI HAN

1970

VIENTIANE, LAOS

The flight from Bangkok had taken them across northeast Thailand, a scrubby perspective of rippling hills and endless rice paddies. As they crossed into Laotian airspace, they craned their necks to look down at the Mekong, winding like a fat brown snake between jungled hills.

The DC-40, painted in cheerful colors, but showing its age in sprung rivets along gaping seams, was full, mostly with Asian males in civilian clothes. They slept from takeoff to landing, in the mouth-open sleep of people with severe hangovers.

They emerged from the DC-40 into suffocating tropical heat. Wattay Airport was primitive, the peeling signs written in French and Lao. Munro, carrying a bag containing over six hundred thousand dollars in cash, was keyed up, his heart pounding. But the airport was all but deserted.

Sakura had assured them there would be no problem with customs, and she was right. The customs hall contained only one dozing official, and they carried the money right past him without disturbing him. He looked to Munro as though he was sleeping off an opium pipe.

A handful of very old Peugeot taxis awaited them, the paint on the bulbous 1950s shapes worn away to the metal. For safety, they took two taxis, Munro getting in the first one with Francine, Clive following with Sakura.

"Hôtel Diplomatique," Francine told the driver.

He grinned at them amiably, showing a row of gold teeth, and set off. Munro checked behind them, and saw Sakura and Clive's car following. Their taxi was so slow among the throngs of bicycles that barefoot children were able to trot alongside, shouting, "Farang, farang!"

Buildings were shabby and unpainted, people lounged in the shade of patched awnings. Even the palm trees were tilted at lazy angles, like idlers too slothful to stand straight.

They passed a large Buddhist temple, orange-robed monks wandering in the coconut-grove garden, their shaved heads gleaming. Then they were driving out of Vientiane.

Francine had chosen the only four-star hotel, the Diplomatique, on Sakura's advice that it was where diplomatic and company visitors stayed. The Diplomatique was a twenty-minute drive from the town, through a landscape of jungle and paddy fields, dotted with primitive huts. There was no agricultural machinery in the fields, no vehicles on the road, not even a bicycle. Now and then they passed a bullock cart or a family group of peasants knee-deep in the paddy.

"It's like going back four hundred years," Munro commented.

The hotel was set in a palm grove, and consisted of a series of thatched bungalows almost at the river's edge, with colorful gardens in between. It seemed almost completely empty; diplomatic and company traffic in Vientiane was moving slowly. The two taxis pulled up outside the peak-roofed reception building.

"L'Hôtel Diplomatique," the driver announced.

They got out, Munro still cautious and watchful. They were deep in the country, and there was no noise, just the distant buzz of a boat on the Mekong, and a gurgling of doves in the palms.

The receptionist was a pretty young woman who curtsied to them with palms pressed together in the traditional Lao greeting called a *wai*. They had decided that the safest accommodation arrangement would be adjoining twin-bedded bungalows. Clive would share with Francine, Sakura with Munro.

The bungalows were primitive but spacious, each with a rudimentary bathroom, a Japanese television set, and a pretty view of the river. The beds were narrow, but when Munro tested them, they seemed to be new and comfortable.

"We should get the money to a bank," Munro said.

Sakura shook her head. "There's only one big bank in Vientiane, La Banque d'Indochine on Thanon Samsenthai. Those are the people Roger stole from. The manager and Jai Han are close friends. The other banks are very small, and cannot be trusted."

"Aren't there any other banks?" Francine asked.

"There are Thai banks across the river at Nong Khai. They are reliable.

But we'll have to get a ferry each time we go, and we'll need multiple-entry visas."

"What are we going to do with it, then?" Munro demanded.

"Sit on it, by the look of things," Clive growled.

"And when we have to go out?"

"This hotel has a strong room," Sakura said. "It's probably the safest place. There are always international diplomats staying here. Not even Jai Han would try to force his way in here."

Munro put the bag containing the money into the flimsy pressboard cupboard, and locked the door, knowing it was a pathetic precaution.

Clive and Francine left the room.

Sakura was washing her face in the bathroom. Munro held out a towel.

"Where can I buy two handguns?"

She turned to him, her face beaded with water, her eyes anxious. "Why do you want to buy guns, Clay?"

"We can't carry hundreds of thousands of dollars around unarmed. I'm not talking about bazookas. Just two automatic pistols."

She dried her face. "You can buy anything you want in the *talàat*."

"The talàat?"

"In town, behind the police station."

"In Vientiane you buy your illegal handguns behind the police station?"

"Vientiane is the biggest gun-smuggling center for five hundred miles. But you are doing something stupid, Clay. A farang buying two guns will be noticed. Jai Han will hear about it in one hour."

"That's the general idea," Munro said. "I want everybody to know they can't just walk in here and grab the money."

She gave him one of her brief, twisted smiles, and touched his face with her fingertips. "This is not Saigon."

"I can see that."

"The Lao are very polite people. They do not react well to rudeness."

"I'm a rude boy, honey. Nothing to be done about that." He left.

Sakura stood at the window, watching the Mekong. The river had shrunk since the summer, winding sluggishly between huge sandbanks.

She wondered whether Louis had already been brought down from Long Chen, whether he was somewhere here in Vientiane. Jai Han had told

Francine his wives were caring for the child. That was, perhaps, a euphemism. Maybe everything they'd been told had been a lie.

She trusted Jai Han's word, despite what she had done to him. Jai Han was a simple, brutal man, a man who routinely buried his enemies alive, but a man who did not bother himself with small lies. To lie about a child would be a very small lie. Too small for a great man. That was what she had been telling herself, again and again.

Yet beneath that mantra ran a darker stream of thoughts, that there were others around and above Jai Han, others who lied by profession, others who were not great, but sucked blood to nourish their own evil. Those others terrified her in a way Jai Han did not, because they would lie to Jai Han as easily as they lied to her, or to anyone else.

There was a tap at her door, and Francine came in.

"Clay has gone to the market to buy guns," Sakura said. "I couldn't stop him."

"Men need guns when they're afraid." Francine was wearing her beautiful jade jewelry, and a dark blue silk suit. She looked rich and imperious. Sakura knew she had dressed like this for Jai Han, and admired Francine's understanding of the man's psychology. Jai Han was expecting a nuhuang. He would not be disappointed with Francine. Francine, at least, knew the way things worked here. Sakura had a lot more faith in the protective powers of Francine's silk suit than in Clay's gun. "Do you want to call Jai Han now, Sakura?"

Sakura nodded, steeling herself. She went to the telephone, and asked the operator to connect her to the Vieng Chang Hotel. Outside in the garden, a flock of starlings squabbled noisily among the palms. A lone sampan drifted on the river; the three teenage girls on board were throwing a net with lazy grace. Sakura was aware of the pressure in her blood, thudding in her ears.

Francine listened to Sakura's conversation. It was in English, but very short. She replaced the receiver after a while and turned to Francine. She was pale.

"We must go to the Vieng Chang at five this afternoon."

"Did you speak to Jai Han?"

"No. To an American who called himself O'Brien."

"Do you know him?"

"I've heard of him. He is a Ray-Ban, like McFadden."

"Did he say where Louis was?" Francine asked.

"No." She offered Francine a tight little smile. "And I didn't ask."

As they approached the Vieng Chang Hotel, weaving their hired Peugeot through the throngs of afternoon strollers, Francine sensed again the heavy languidness of the place. Vientiane floated in lethargy.

To Francine, there was something sinister about this air of universal indifference. It reminded her of Singapore in the weeks before the Japanese invasion. It seemed to her like the apathy of a town that had already surrendered to an enemy who hadn't even arrived yet.

The Vieng Chang was built on a sandbank, raised on stilts against the rise and fall of the water. Red paper lanterns hung in festoons along the eaves. They parked the Peugeot on the crumbling edge of the road, and the four of them walked up the rickety stairs into the hotel. Francine was gripping Sakura's hand tightly.

In her imagination, she had pictured this meeting taking place with theatrical formality in a barracks, Sakura making obeisance to a stern, uniformed Jai Han in a deathly silence.

The reality, as she realized at once, was going to be very different. The heat of the place rushed into their faces, carrying a greasy smell of cheap perfume and cheap cooking, undercut with the sickly whiff of opium smoke. A blast of Thai pop music assaulted the ears.

They were greeted by a small, wizened woman, who stared at Clay Munro's huge black bulk in amazement. All of her front teeth were metal, and gleamed dully in the dim light.

"Is General Jai Han here?" Francine demanded in French.

"You the nuhuang?"

"Yes," Francine said. "I'm the nuhuang."

The old woman laughed and grabbed Francine's arm. "Come, Nuhuang. Your table is waiting."

It was dark in the bar. By the light of oil lamps, Francine saw that the place was still half-empty, rowdy groups of soldiers sitting at large tables. Everybody turned to stare at Clay, and there were low exclamations of astonishment. The old woman pushed them to a corner table, still piled with empty beer bottles and full ashtrays from the last customers. She screeched something to the nearest waitress, then left them.

As Francine's eyes adjusted to the dark, she saw that the waitresses were all naked, wearing nothing but fixed smiles. She was growing angry at the humiliation of being brought to a place like this. Jai Han had evidently calculated the insult.

"I'm sorry," Sakura said to her, as though reading her thoughts.

"It doesn't matter. It will be over soon."

One of the naked waitresses sauntered over to their table, grinning at them. She put a bare foot on Clay Munro's thigh, and pushed herself up onto the table. She gyrated to the rhythm of the Thai pop music for a few beats, tossing her hair and pinching her own nipples briskly.

"Jesus," Clive muttered to Francine. "Where the hell is Jai Han?"

"I don't know. Be patient, Clive."

The waitress squatted suddenly. She produced a cigarette from behind her ear, and inserted it between her legs. She flicked a Zippo into flame. Rippling her abdominal muscles flamboyantly, she lit the cigarette. They watched in a blank silence as she puffed at the cigarette, using her internal muscles, sucking and expelling smoke neatly from her crotch. Grinning at them, she swiveled, so they could all see the trick.

It was Clay Munro who leaned forward, a ten-dollar bill in his hand. "*Merci bien,*" he told the girl. "*Très joli.*"

The girl took the money, looking pleased. She extracted the cigarette, and put it in Munro's mouth. "You want beer? I bring food."

She sauntered away, lean buttocks rolling. Munro took the cigarette out of his mouth. "This place reminds me of Saigon," he said. "Only cleaner."

"Are we in for any more cabaret?" Clive asked.

"They have all kinds of tricks," Sakura said quietly. "Don't be offended. The soldiers like it."

"Do you know any of these people?" Francine asked Sakura.

She glanced around and shook her head. "All the Meo come here. The girls know how to make their food, the things they like."

"And Jai Han owns this place? He's a good businessman."

The waitress returned with a piled tray. She shoveled bottles of beer and bowls of food onto their table. As a centerpiece, she put an opened bottle of J&B whiskey in the middle. The bowls gave off a smell of sour fish.

"What the hell is this?" Munro demanded. "Smells like something died in here."

"It's *pàa da-ek,*" Sakura said. "Fermented fish. But don't eat it. It can give you worms in the liver."

"Then, tempted as I am, I'll pass," Munro said, pushing the bowl away. He polished the neck of his beer bottle meticulously, and swigged. Neither Clive nor Francine touched the food or the drink in front of them.

The bar was filling up. Occasionally, men swaggered in, in groups of three or five. Most wore a half-uniform of olive blouse and pants. They were small, stocky men, for the most part, with the worn faces of peasants, lined by work rather than by age. There seemed to be an endless supply of naked waitresses to serve them.

"Hi there, folks." They all turned at the American voice. A burly man of around thirty had loomed suddenly over their table. He wore jeans and a loose khaki shirt. His hair was cropped in military style, but there was a week-old growth of stubble on his heavy jowls. "It's a real pleasure to see you all. My name's O'Brien. I work with Kit McFadden." He spoke with a slight Southern accent, perhaps Louisiana. He made a pistol out of his index finger and thumb and shot each of them in turn. "You're Mrs. Lawrence. You're Sakura Ueda. You have to be Munro." He paused at Clive. "Who's this?"

"Clive Napier," Francine said. "A friend."

"Pass, friend," O'Brien said. He pulled out a chair and sat. "Enjoying the food? How was the floor show?"

"We were told we would meet General Jai Han here," Munro said quietly. "Where is he?"

"More to the fucking point," O'Brien said, "where's the money?"

"We've brought the money."

"Where is it?"

"Waiting across the river in a Thai bank," Francine lied, not wanting to admit it was in the Diplomatique's strong room.

"In cash?"

"In cash."

O'Brien seemed to relax slightly. Francine could now see that he was very dirty, his hands blackened, his shirt soiled. "Diem will be here soon."

"Who is he?"

"Diem is Diem. You gonna eat that, big fella?" he asked, turning to Munro.

Munro pushed the bowl across to O'Brien. "*Bon appétit,*" he said in a flat voice.

"You don't like raw fish?"

"I was told it could give you worms," Munro said as the American began to eat.

"Not if you drink enough whiskey with it."

"Where is Jai Han?" Munro repeated.

"Up north," O'Brien replied.

Francine felt a rush of angry disappointment. "Isn't he coming?"

"No, he's not coming, Mrs. Lawrence."

A crash of boots on the wooden floor made them all turn. A slight, middle-aged Lao in ornate military uniform was making toward them. Stamping behind him were two ramrod-straight sergeants, all white braid and shiny boots. Every soldier in the room jumped to his feet, except O'Brien, who kept eating with the intentness of a very hungry man. "This is my colleague," he said laconically, "Colonel Diem."

Diem smiled placatingly, as though apologizing for the stir he had caused. "So pleased to make your acquaintance," he said in stilted English. He sat, but the two sergeants remained in rigid at-ease positions behind his chair.

O'Brien's jowls were lowered over the bowl. "You got to adjust to Lao cooking. It takes up where other cuisines leave off. They sauté the things we toss in the trash or shoot as varmints." He grasped the whiskey bottle and poured himself a glass. "Jai Han's wife Number Two cooked for me all this week. She made the same thing every day. Boiled pig guts, with the pig shit still inside. Must be a Meo specialty. Right, Colonel?"

Diem smiled. "The Meo are a colorful tribe. But they have been fierce fighters against the Pathet Lao." He seemed suddenly to notice that every male in the room was still standing to attention. He waved a slim hand, and the men took their seats again. The shouting and laughter resumed.

"Why didn't Jai Han come to meet us?" Francine asked.

"You think you're the big item on Jai Han's agenda?" O'Brien asked ironically.

Diem crossed his thin legs. "*Madame,* you may treat with us in perfect confidence," he said. "We are General Jai Han's close colleagues. The general is occupied on military business at this time. He finds it impossible to meet with you. He has asked us to represent him. I will take charge of the money, and I will see that it is given to Jai Han."

"Colonel Diem is convenor of the General Staff, chairman of the bank regulatory committee, and deputy minister of agriculture," O'Brien said. He belched. "He's also a prince. Right, Colonel?"

Diem bowed slightly. "Yes, that is correct."

"He's cousin to the king of Laos."

Diem smiled. He took out a cigarette and lit it with a solid-gold lighter.

"I cannot give the money to anybody but Jai Han," Francine said shortly.

"You got no choice," O'Brien said. He wiped his mouth and glanced from Clive to Clay Munro. "You two cowboys bought popguns in the talàat today. What do you think that's gonna achieve? You think Diem couldn't cut you to pieces any time he wanted?"

"My arrangement was with Jai Han."

O'Brien rubbed his eyes with thick, blackened fingers. "Jesus," he said quietly. "I've been in a chopper for the past eight hours. My head hurts." His eyelids were heavy and greasy, his lips swollen among the stubble. He jerked a thumb at Diem. "Colonel Diem is the Laotian government. And I'm the American government."

"You mean the CIA," Munro said.

"What's the difference?"

"Last time I heard, there was a small distinction."

O'Brien lowered his head on burly shoulders like a tired bull. "Colonel Diem is Jai Han's commanding officer, and I'm his supervisor. You understand, boy? You stole from Jai Han, you stole from us. You give back the money, you give it to us."

"Where is Louis?" Sakura asked tautly.

O'Brien turned dark, oily eyes on her. "You and your boyfriend threw a big fucking wrench in the works."

Diem leaned forward. "Ricard tried to shoot it out with us in Savannakhet." He smiled. "We counted twenty-six bullet holes in his body when we pulled him out of the car, and he was still alive. I conducted his interrogation myself, but he died very soon."

Sakura's face showed no emotion, whatever she was feeling inside. "Is my child alive, Colonel Diem?"

"But of course," Diem said, shrugging as though the question were an absurd one.

O'Brien seemed to notice his filthy hands for the first time, and wiped them on his shirt. "Yeah, the kid's alive. Crying all the time, though. Driving Jai Han's wives crazy."

"How will Louis be brought to us?" Francine asked.

"You will go to get him," Diem responded, "once we have settled the account."

There was a tight silence. It was broken by the chirrup of Diem's gold lighter as he lit himself another cigarette, leaving the first still half-finished in an ashtray.

"You want us to pay you the money here," Munro asked, "then travel up north to collect the boy?"

"You will be escorted in safety," Diem said in his mild way. He was turning the lighter in his fingers, polishing its buttery smoothness with his thumbs. "Our own people will take you there and back again."

"I think we should collect the boy first," Francine said, equally quietly, "and then pay you the money."

"You can think what you like," O'Brien said with a sour grin. "But it ain't gonna work like that. What the money buys you is a guided tour of the insurgency area. You pick up the little souvenir, pay your respects to J.H., then get the hell out of Laos. That's the way it's gonna work."

Diem murmured a command in Lao to the sergeants behind him. One of them marched off, heels thudding on the wood floor. "With your permission, he will fetch the pilot," Diem said with stilted politeness. "Your servant is a fine specimen, *madame*." He studied Munro. "Are all your people as big as you?"

"What do you mean by 'my people,' Colonel?"

"The black people," Diem said, inspecting Munro's massive shoulders with interest. "The Negroes. Are they all as big?"

"No, man," Munro said dryly. "Our babies are just itty-bitty things."

Diem smiled blankly.

The sergeant returned, leading a man by the arm. This man was older, with a lined face and sad, pouchy eyes. He wore a sloppy brown uniform, the logo of a flying company stitched on his breast.

"Poonsiri Krong," Diem said, presenting the man to them as though he were introducing a minister at court. "He is one of the best charter pilots in Vientiane. He will fly you up-country for a reasonable fee. How much, Krong?"

"Two hundred dollar," he said.

"You're a Thai, right?" Munro demanded of the man, who nodded. "What kind of charter you fly?"

Krong picked his nose. "Medical supply."

Munro turned to Diem. "He's an opium pilot."

"Krong is highly experienced," Diem said calmly. "He will take you all to see General Jai Han and to collect the child. He knows the routes, and he speaks English."

Munro looked at the pilot, seeing the ravages of opium addiction in the vacant eyes and cadaverous skin. "Jesus," he muttered bitterly. "Welcome to Dope Air."

"Tomorrow, we will take delivery of the money," Diem went on. His gold-rimmed glasses glittered as he looked at them all. "I will give you a paper for Jai Han. You may leave with Krong immediately afterward."

None of them replied.

"I believe the money is in safekeeping at your hotel," Diem went on, smiling blandly. "I will come for it at . . . shall we say eight-thirty? I apologize for the early hour, but you will wish to make an early start, in any case. Krong will wish to make the return flight during daylight." Diem gave them his polite smile. But Francine realized that the Lao prince's politeness was no more than a mannerism. Beneath it lay the calm certainty of a man who knew that he held all the cards, and was going to win all the tricks. "I trust this is acceptable," he said, rising. "Enjoy the evening. Until tomorrow." He turned and walked away, followed by Krong and his two sergeants.

O'Brien's weary eyes followed Diem. "They think we're so fucking stupid," he said quietly, almost to himself. "They sell the guns we give them to the Burmese. They fly their fucking heroin in our planes and tell us it's rice. They take our money and pay thousands of dollars to soldiers that don't exist. You think anybody can win a war like that?" He turned to Munro. "You think so, Munro?"

"No," Munro replied.

"No," O'Brien repeated, "I don't think so, either."

"Can I trust Diem?" Francine asked O'Brien quietly.

"You got no choice," O'Brien said. "Don't fuck around. The shit is really hitting the fan this time. Only thing that's gonna save them is the big rains. The Pathet Lao just keep pounding away. Our boys are either dead, or dead tired. Or they just ran away. The hills are full of people. Just running." He exhaled smoke at Munro. His speech was blurring, either with the alcohol, or with exhaustion. "We're taking a bad beating. Worse than last year. Say, it's nice to speak to some fellow Americans."

There were roars of laughter from an adjoining table. A waitress was squatting among the Beer-Lao bottles, performing the cigarette trick, or some other feat. O'Brien focused on Munro. "You a political thinker, Captain? Ever hear of the domino theory?"

"Thought that's what I was in Vietnam for."

"Yeah." O'Brien looked at whatever it was the waitress was doing at the next table. "One thing's for fucking sure, the fate of civilization isn't gonna be settled here. All this is gonna burn in a little while."

"How long?"

"Maybe tomorrow. Who knows? Listen, Nuhuang. Do yourselves a favor. Pay the money and get the kid out before something blows him to bits." O'Brien drained the glass of whiskey. "Understand? Don't think about it. Just do it."

"I don't see what choice we have," Francine said curtly.

They were back at their hotel. The ferocious heat of the afternoon was starting to fade. Sakura was pale and tightly strung. "If we give the money to Diem," she said, "he will keep it all. Jai Han will never get a dollar of it."

"You heard what O'Brien said, Sakura," Clive said gently. "Diem is the Laotian authority. Jai Han will have to accept the arrangement, the same as we do."

"He will cheat Jai Han," Sakura said in a still voice. "When Jai Han learns what we've done, he'll kill Louis."

"Diem has the plane," Munro said. "How else are we going to find Jai Han? You want to drive through Laos with the money in a suitcase, looking for him?"

"That would be better than giving it to Diem."

"We cannot do that, Sakura," Francine said wearily. "Diem knows the money is here. It's too late to try to take it across the river to Thailand. He will be here at eight-thirty tomorrow morning. We have no choice." Francine had changed out of the silk clothes of this afternoon, and was wearing a brown cotton pantsuit and sandals. Munro noticed that she had the neat little feet of a girl. The same feet as Sakura. Munro was filled with admiration for her, and even—Sakura was right about this—a kind of love. They had been through a lot together, and he had come to understand just what kind of person she was. She was very special, very strong, very resilient.

Sakura was gritting her teeth. "Please listen to me. I know what I'm talking about."

"But what can we do? We're in their power."

"We must find some other way!" she pleaded. "Everything Diem told us was a lie."

"How do you know?"

"I know!"

"If we try to stall Diem," Munro said, "he'll just take the money anyhow. You think that tin-pot little strong room would keep him out?"

"We must get the money and go now," Sakura said tautly. "We must make our own way to Jai Han."

"That wouldn't work," Munro replied. "We'd get hijacked in the first twenty kilometers."

Sakura covered her face with her hands. They all watched her in silence.

"Perhaps we should find McFadden," Clive suggested. "Maybe he's closer to Jai Han than to Diem."

"How are we going to find McFadden?" Munro shook his head. "I saw people like Diem in Vietnam. Spruce and sleek little guys, lighting their cigarettes with a gold Dunhill, grinning while they watched us eat shit with the peasants. This is Diem's country, and always will be. You could get around him, but there's always another Diem stepping forward with a big grin and a gold Dunhill. If we don't pay him, there'll be somebody worse behind him."

Francine nodded. "Yes. Besides, I understand people like Diem. They can be dealt with." She touched Sakura's shoulder. "Diem gave me the impression that we'd be doing the right thing, Sakura. We have to trust him."

"You cannot trust him," Sakura said in a low voice.

"I disagree," Francine replied, rising. "In any case, Sakura, we have no choice."

When Francine and Clive had gone to their own bungalow, Munro turned to Sakura. She was sitting in a chair, gripping the seat.

"You really think Diem will cheat Jai Han?" he asked.

"Diem will keep the money." Her lips were dry. "You were right. There is always a Diem. He will make promises to Jai Han, speak sweet words. But Diem is a prince, and Jai Han is a Meo tribesman. Jai Han will never get the money."

"Maybe he'll be happy with this paper Diem says he'll give us."

"He will know what it is worth."

"Diem is Jai Han's commander, isn't he? Then I just don't see what else we can do." He went to her, and kneaded her shoulders. She was very tense. "Try and relax."

Her face did not lose its intentness. "Clay, take me to my house."

"What house?"

"My house here in Vientiane. When I ran, I left things there, things I want to get."

"What if somebody's waiting for you there?"

"Nobody will be waiting."

He shook his head. "It's too big a chance to take."

She whipped around. Her eyes were haunted. "Please, Clay. These things are very important to me."

"And you're very important to me."

"I need you to drive me there, Clay. *Please.* I beg you."

He sighed, relenting despite himself. "Okay. Let's go."

Munro drove slowly. There was no other way to drive in Vientiane. The earth roads were crowded with pedestrians, oxcarts, and pedicabs.

In the twilight, the beauty of the city was starting to percolate through to Munro. They drove down an avenue of jacaranda trees in full bloom. The tiny lilac flowers had carpeted every inch of the road. In vivid contrast, a group of Meo women walked along in black pajamas cinched with magenta and lime-green scarves, heavy silver chains around their necks.

She was staring out the window. "That is where I worked," she said quietly. He followed her gaze to a red corrugated iron roof set among a lush garden of palms. Painted on the roof in white letters, designed to be visible from the air, was the sign AGENCE LI HUA. "They killed him in his office," she said. "Jai Han owns it now."

"Why did they kill him?"

"They said he traded with the Pathet Lao."

"And did he?"

"Of course. Everybody trades with the Pathet Lao. Everybody wants them to win. People are sick of the fighting, sick of the Americans."

"Sounds familiar," Munro said dryly. "Jai Han trusted you, even though he killed your boss?"

"Yes."

"Did he want to make you wife Number Three, or Four, or whatever?"

"He has three wives," she replied. "He doesn't need another."

"He seems to take what you did personally," Munro commented. "He's got his wives looking after Louis. He wants you to come to him in person. Maybe he wants to cut your throat with his own hands."

"Maybe," she said shortly.

"Kind of like an angry lover? A betrayed lover?"

"I had no relationship like that with Jai Han," she said, turning to look at him with a frown. "You have no need to be jealous."

"Oh, I'm not jealous," Munro said. But he knew he was lying. In fact he felt relief at Sakura's denial. That was one less man she'd slept with. Then he felt ashamed of the thought.

They had to stop for a file of young monks slowly crossing the road in vivid saffron robes. Little more than boys, they silently paused to pick up the bowls of rice that the devout kneeled to leave for them, ignoring the respect-ful wais that accompanied the offerings of food.

"That looks like a peaceful way to live," Munro said.

"Tomorrow they'll leave the temple and probably wind up fighting for the Pathet Lao," Sakura replied.

Munro leaned on the steering wheel, waiting for the monks to file past. "That guy O'Brien just got back from heavy fighting," he said. "He had that look. I know that look. That smell. If what he said is true, Laos is falling apart."

"Yes," she said. "The country is falling apart."

He grunted. "When are the big rains due?"

"Soon," she said. "The fighting is ruled by the seasons. Every dry season, the Communists win a little more territory. Then they dig in, trying to last out until the monsoons return. If they can do that, they're safe for the summer."

"Same as 'Nam. But this time, it's the government forces who are praying for rain, huh?"

"The Communists have overrun them." She was looking tense. "Vientiane has changed. I knew it the moment we got on the plane. Those people, those passengers, were Filipino and Chinese aircraft mechanics. You could see by their faces what they'd been through. Then, riding in the taxi from the airport, I saw a truckload of men I know are Pathet Lao. They should not have been within a hundred kilometers of Vientiane, let alone showing themselves arrogantly in the main street. Stop, Clay. This is where I lived."

Munro stopped the Peugeot. The dilapidated row of shop-houses ambled along the edge of a rambutan orchard. A rickety veranda gave shade to the fronts of the shops, most of which were closed. In the story up above, shutters had been thrown open to catch the evening breezes.

"Which one's yours?" he asked.

She indicated a blue-painted house above a rice merchant, the only shop that was open. "That one."

Munro checked up and down the street. A couple of slow women in sarongs were ambling in the middle of the road, a bullock cart loaded with melons was standing idle. A couple of kids trotted up, but they did not beg for money or candy, the way Vietnamese kids did. They seemed content to stare at the towering, midnight-skinned foreign devil.

"I have to speak to the shopkeeper."

"Be careful," he said sharply.

"There's no danger, Clay," Sakura said. "It's safe."

He followed her into the merchant's shop. It was dark and smelly. The shopkeeper was a little, wizened man with a few strands of hair slicked across a large bald head. When he saw Sakura, he ducked instinctively behind his barrels of rice and dried fish, as though expecting a hail of bullets to come after her.

Sakura pressed her palms together and made a wai, speaking soothingly.

The man answered in rapid Lao, eyes flickering in fear toward Munro.

"He thinks you're CIA," she said, turning to Munro.

Munro shook his head. "Uh-uh. No way, chief." He showed the man his cheap plastic sunglasses. "See? Not Ray-Bans."

The man grinned nervously. Sakura asked him something, he nodded his head vigorously, and disappeared into the back of the shop.

"He doesn't seem pleased to see you," Munro commented. He was feeling distinctly edgy about this whole episode.

"We are friends," Sakura said. "He repaired my door. He's gone to get the key."

"And maybe call the cops?"

"No. He will not do that."

The little bald man reappeared. He held a key out to Sakura, using both hands. She took it in the same way, and bowed, murmuring something Munro took to be thanks.

They climbed the stairs to her flat. When they reached the door, Munro stopped, pushing her behind him. "Let me go first."

"There's nobody here," she repeated. She gave him a tight smile, and unlocked the door. It sagged open on decrepit hinges. "You see?"

Munro was still cautious. But as they went in, his shoulders dropped. "Jesus," he said.

Sakura made no comment. The tiny apartment had been ransacked with venomous energy. Smashed furniture was piled on the bed. The mattress and the plain sofa had been slashed and disemboweled. Drawers had been ripped out and splintered. There was a smell of decay everywhere from food that had gone bad.

"This must have been a nice place once," he said flatly.

Sakura was not wasting time on grief. She was already hunting through the debris. "It was nice," she agreed evenly. "They were looking for the money. They must have known it could not be here."

Munro picked his way to a bookshelf that had been broken to pieces. The spine had been torn out of every book, the pages ripped. Not just a search: This had been an expression of rage. He picked up a mutilated volume: Baudelaire, *Les Fleurs du Mal.* She had made notes in the margin, but they were in French, and he could not read them. He put the book in his pocket and looked around. It was a world violated. Her records had been broken, her pretty little things crushed, her clothes rent and trampled on the floor.

She had found a linen shopping bag, and she was thrusting random things into it: torn photographs of her child, broken jewelry, an old cigar box.

"This is the stuff you wanted so badly?" he asked.

"They've taken a lot of things away." She raked through the debris, hunting intently, snatching up bits and pieces and throwing them in the bag. "My jewelry. My best clothes. All gone. I knew they would have done it." She looked up at him. Unexpectedly, she gave him a smile. Its beauty turned his heart over.

"That's it?" he asked in surprise.

"That's it."

"You don't want anything else?"

She shook her head. "I had to get it out of my system. I'm okay, now." She rose and lifted her face to him. "Thank you for bringing me here."

Munro put his arms around her. She drew his head down and kissed his lips. Her mouth was like a jungle flower, dewy petals clinging to his lips, tasting of nectar. He felt his head swim. Her tongue touched his, warm and moist. Their kiss deepened and unfolded into passion. Her body, slim and strong, molded to his, and he crushed her against him.

He had always been a lonely man, and had never wanted it any other way. But now he felt that he held something infinitely precious in his arms. Would this work? Wouldn't it be wonderful to have just one woman, to have her always, and to be hers? The strangeness of that idea filled him with wonder. To belong to Sakura, to have her belong to him. To spend the rest of his life with her. If they survived this. The amazing possibilities unveiled themselves, as though he had reached the peak of a mountain he had been climbing for years, and suddenly saw another world stretching out at his feet.

He was hard with desire, and Sakura pressed her belly against him, purring softly. She pulled her lips away from his. Her eyes were alight. "Let's go back and make love," she whispered, pulling him by the hand.

Bemused, he followed her, stepping over the broken pieces of her former life. She did not even look back, as though it meant nothing to her now.

It was dark by the time they got back to the Diplomatique. The humid air was throbbing with insect song. They checked in with Francine and Clive, then went to their bungalow.

Sakura sat on her bed, and began to sort through the haul she had brought back from her house.

"Let me see what it was you just couldn't live without," he said, smiling.

"They're personal things," she replied, closing the bag again.

His eyes narrowed. "You told me I could trust you, Sakura."

"I meant it," she said. She pushed the bag onto the floor, smiling at him. Then, in one fluid movement, she hauled off her T-shirt. Her skin was golden, her breasts perfect, pale orbs, centered with dark nipples. He took a breath.

"Don't you like to see me? Stefan told me my body was beautiful. He liked to paint me."

"I'd paint you, too, if I were an artist."

"You can paint me with your body," she said softly. She arched her hips and yanked off her jeans. With a hot shock, he recalled Stefan Giorgieu's sketch of her. On the point of each hip, a black star swirled, framing the dark triangle at her loins. Her hips were wider than her slender waist would have suggested, hips made for love, for bearing children.

Munro went to her as though sleepwalking, and sat beside her, looking down at her naked body. He could smell her, the jasmine she always wore, the darker scent of her skin, her sweat. He touched the tattooed stars with his fingertips. "Do you remember when they did this to you?"

"I remember the pain. They had to hold me down. They only do it to women. It draws attention to this." She touched her own pubic hair.

"Yeah," he said, his lips dry. "It does."

"Is it ugly?"

"No. It suits you."

"That's good," she said, smiling slightly. "It's permanent."

"Whoever made you," he said, "they made you beautiful." Fine golden hair glinted on her fine skin. At her loins, the triangle was thick and dark. He touched the curls. "Vietnamese girls have almost no hair here."

"How can you talk about the pubic hair of all Vietnamese women unless you've made love to every one of them?"

"I made love to all the ones I came across," he replied gravely.

She smiled. "They shave themselves. The prostitutes. Because they know that's what you round-eyes expect."

"I guess so." He stroked the flat plane of her belly. She shuddered at his touch.

"You see?" she whispered. "You are starting to paint me."

What you're doing is crazy, man, he told himself. *Walk away from this, Clay.* But she was too sweet; the whirlpool that was Sakura was too sweet and too strong. It drew him down, and he bent over her, touching her tender brown nipple with his lips.

Her fingers touched his neck. "Yes," she whispered. "You are mine. Mine."

Her nipple carried a fleeting hint of salt, of the oils of her skin, bitter and intoxicating. The satin skin wrinkled, the softness thrusting against his tongue with extraordinary strength. He sucked the erect flesh, and Sakura moaned quietly. Desire for her was crushing his brain against his skull, but he forced himself to be slow, and gentle. This was their first time, and there would be only one first time. And there might never be another time after this.

He looked down at her, his eyes heavy with desire. "When you kicked me in that alley, that time, you hit me right on the wound."

Her face wore a sheen of sweat, of the closeness of the night, of her arousal. "I felt it was there."

"How?"

"I always feel for an opponent's weak place."

"You could have gone for my balls. You took a chance, going higher."

"I felt that was a strong place." Her orchid mouth moved in a small smile. "I went for your heart, instead."

He bent again, and kissed the black stars on her hips. Close up, they were cloudy swirls just below the golden surface of the skin. She lifted her slender thighs slowly. Her sex was the flesh of a scallop, perfect and glistening in the curve of the shell. He touched her with his tongue. Like her nipples, the salt greeting was undercut with a deeper, darker taste, the taste of her body.

Sakura shuddered, her back arching. She knotted her fingers in his dark, springy hair. He slid his tongue into her, as far as it would go, where the taste was different, hotter and more narcotic. He heard her laugh unsteadily. "Where are you going with that tongue?" she whispered.

Within the soft petals, a pearl had grown. He took all of her in his mouth, drawing the melting flesh against his tongue, sucking the peak of her desire. She gasped, panicking. "Clay! It will end too soon!"

"Then we'll start again," he promised, smiling up at her.

Her eyes were huge and dark. "Nobody ever did this to me before."

"But you're a black belt in judo?"

"I know far more about that than about this!"

"Well, I'm glad there's something I can teach you, then." He turned back to her body, amused and touched by her innocence. In so much, she was hard and calloused. But in this, she was an innocent, despite all her bravado. He had just seen that in her eyes.

He clasped her hips in his strong arms so she could not escape. Using his mouth as expertly as he knew how. He felt the supple strength of her body as she strained off the bed, as though he had netted a dolphin. She came with an explosive burst of energy, crying out his name, her thighs clenching him. Against his tongue, he felt the spasm of her release, that strange power of woman's flesh.

He came to her, seeing her face covered with dew, her mouth and eyelids still swollen with pleasure. "Clay," she whispered.

He kissed her lips. Her tongue slid between his teeth. "I can taste myself in your mouth," she whispered.

"Me, too."

She giggled, unfastening his shirt. "Will you let me do that to you?"

"You can do what you like with me, honey."

She pulled his shirt off, and caressed the arching wings of his collarbones. She found the wound that had opened his chest, and touched it gently. "This is where I hurt you."

"Uh-huh."

"I could have killed you. Poor Clay," she said, her eyes full of tears. "Poor soldier."

"Yeah, poor soldier." He smiled.

She unfastened his jeans and pulled the zipper down. He was aching for her, and his manhood burst out like a jack-in-the-box. "God, you're wonderful," she said, taking him in her hands. "I'm glad I chose not to kick you here."

She bent over him and took him in her mouth. The hot, moist heat made him shudder. His head swam. "Hey," he said gently. "Maybe not too much of that. Next time, okay?"

She looked up at him. "Why? Am I doing it wrong?"

"You're doing it fine," he said, touching her face. "Just, I want you so much, I'm liable to go off like a rocket, right now."

"Then we have to hurry," she said gravely. She pushed him back onto the bed, and straddled him.

Munro looked up at her slender body. "You're so beautiful," he whispered. He cupped her small, firm breasts in his palms. "You're flawless, Sakura."

She smiled down at him, her eyes dark and mysterious. "Not flawless. I'm marked."

He stroked the tattooed bracelets on each arm, the black stars on each hip. "These aren't marks. They're you."

"I haven't had many men," she said to him. "But all the men I had have hated my marks."

"Not me."

She took his manhood in both hands and guided it between her thighs, her face intent. "You're very big. You must be careful not to hurt me."

"I'll never hurt you."

She sank down slowly. Munro felt his heart surge as he entered her, deep into the tight, hot center of her. She, too, was panting, biting her full lower lip, her eyes half-closed. "There," she whispered as her buttocks sank onto his thighs. "You fit inside me."

He was too afraid to move, lest he lose control. He wondered whether it would always be like this, whether he would always reach his peak so quickly with her.

"It feels as though you have entered my heart," she said to him. She touched his muscled stomach. "You are made like a lion, Clay. I've never seen a man as beautiful as you."

He reached for the place where they were joined, feeling the trunk of his own manhood entering her. He stroked the slippery flesh that held him prisoner. She moaned behind closed lips. He could feel her wetness spread around him hotly. When she moved again, she was exquisitely slippery. He whispered her name, and she moaned back, arching.

"Clay . . ."

She reached up, her breasts lifting. Her hair was tied back in a knot. She unfastened the knot now, and shook her lovely head. Her thick, dark tresses fell around her shoulders in rippling waves. As if in a dream, he reached for her. She stooped, sweeping her own hair around their faces, until they were lost in the scented darkness of it.

"How did you know?" he whispered.

"I knew."

She kissed him hard, her hips rocking, her lips crushing against his so he felt her teeth grate against his own. He thought he could taste the salt of blood on his tongue. He felt her soft breasts swing against his muscular chest.

He tried to push her over. "I want to be on top."

"*No*," she said fiercely. "You're *mine*."

She was panting as she made love to him. She cried out, longing and desire mingled in her wordless sob. He thrust up into her, touching her deep inwardness with his own solidity, his own heat. At first she was frantic, her nails scratching him, her hips thudding against his. She had been so mysterious to him, a closed world that he had never been able to penetrate. Now he was within her. He had not imagined, had not dreamed, that there was so much need in her. So much emptiness aching to be filled. So much sweetness waiting to be given. Then she gentled, sank into a movement that was more languorous, infinitely surer of purpose.

The narrow little bed rocked and creaked. Surging waves of emotion swelled in him. He felt her rising with him, and knew that it was perfect, that there was no greater oneness than this.

He felt the world tilt, then turn upside down. What was inside was revealed; what was manifest became mystery. He felt his love surge from deep within his body, deep into hers. He cried out her name in a hoarse voice, erupting into her.

When the shuddering slowed, he looked up at her. Two shining tracks glistened on her cheeks, where tears were sliding noiselessly down. They splashed onto his nipples, hot against his skin.

"I love you," he said helplessly.

She reached down and touched his lips with her fingertips. "Sweet Clay," she whispered. "Don't stop loving me."

"I won't, Sakura."

"No matter what I do?"

"No matter what you do."

"Because if you do stop . . ."

He pressed his lips to hers to stop her words. "I'll always love you."

She sank onto him as though sinking into a grave. He wrapped strong arms around and held her tight, tight.

I found her, he thought. *I found the one.*

Late in the night, Francine ran herself a cool bath, wanting to wash away the residue of the day. The bathroom was dilapidated, the ornate brass taps dull. A vine hung down over the window, the sharp smell of its tiny, starlike flowers strengthening with the night and the humidity.

She began to unwind slowly. In the water, her body was pale gold in color, matter-of-fact in its compactness. Her father's Celtic genes had mingled harmoniously with her mother's Cantonese ones. Yet she was recognizably a hybrid creature, and to Chinese she would always look Western, and to Westerners she would always look Chinese. That simple fact put a barrier between her and other people right at the very start, before you even began to consider the dizzying complexities of upbringing and experience. Sakura faced the same problem. *We stengahs are a unique breed,* she thought. *Each one of us comes into the world different and alone.*

Why did Clive still love her? Did he still see in her the girl she had been in Singapore, all those years ago?

She picked up the hand mirror and studied her own face dispassionately. But she did not think it was possible to guess her age. She had the porcelain skin and strong cheekbones that are the best defenses against time. She put the mirror down and looked at her hands. They were a girl's hands, smooth and unlined, the nails pearly pink and short. Yes, she appeared young. But she was no longer young. And within, the biological clock was ticking. She closed her fingers slowly on nothing.

She washed herself, dried her body, and put on her nightgown. She went to the window. There were no stars, but a fitful moon sailed among ragged clouds. Beyond the garden, the lights of Vientiane shimmered on the Mekong.

For a long time, she stood there, listening to the distant traffic, smelling the night air. Then she went to Clive.

He was poring over a map of Laos. As she walked slowly to him, he folded the map closed. Her heart was thudding as she sat beside him and reached out her hand. He took her hand in his, and drew it to his mouth. He opened her fingers, and she felt his warm lips kiss her palm. His eyes were smoky. He touched her hair, her face. "Do you remember Singapore, Francine?"

"I remember."

"Those were the happiest days of my life."

"Other happy days will come."

"Only if you are with me. I don't want you to leave me again. I don't want to lose you." His touch was light and warm. "When you left me, I thought that if I just waited, you would come back. But it's been a long time, Francine."

"Men are strange creatures," she told him. "You'll spend hours looking at a map of nowhere, and show complete ignorance of the geography of the human heart. You have to try to understand me, Clive. I know it's difficult. I am a difficult person."

"Yes. You are difficult, the way a Bach partita is difficult."

"Difficult, painful, impossible."

"Difficult, wonderful, worthwhile."

She shook her head. "How can there be anything left, after all these years?"

"Perhaps you don't want there to be anything left."

"It can't be the same feeling you had so long ago!"

He smiled. "We're both a little older. But for my own part, I love you more than ever." She felt his warm lips brush her knuckles. She shivered.

"Clive, I know I hurt you in Sarawak."

"Let's not talk about that."

"No, let's talk about it."

Seeing her expression, he nodded. "All right."

"I was half-crazy in those days. I was in pain almost all the time, and I blamed you. I wanted to punish you. I wasn't fair. It was the stupidest thing I did in my life."

"You did what you thought you had to do."

"I shouldn't have driven you away. I've never been good with words, Clive. I don't know how to express myself. But I'm so sorry, and I so much want you to know that."

"Francine, listen to me. You taught me something very important in Sarawak. That day in the longhouse, when Annah told us her story—that was the first time I'd ever seen you break down. It was the first time I really understood what you'd been through, how much you had suffered. Then later, when we parted, I saw something else I'd never seen before—your strength, the steel that was in you. I was so sure that I knew you, but I never had. Not really. I'd never understood either your weakness or your strength. It was as if I hadn't understood who you were until the moment I lost you. And then it was too late."

His words, gently spoken as they were, seemed to crush her heart. "We've lost all those years, Clive. They'll never come back. And I'm sorrier for that than I know how to say."

"We have the years that are still to come, Francine," he said seriously. "If we're wise enough to take them."

Her eyes were blurred. "I don't know how wise I am anymore. But I need you, Clive. Now and always."

"Then come to me."

His skin was hot. She felt his strength, her palms tracing the contours that they had almost forgotten, and yet were so familiar to her, so familiar. She leaned forward and kissed his lips.

"Oh, God, Francine," he whispered. "I've been patient for such a long time. But I've missed you so much . . ."

"I remember how we used to hurry," she said. "You used to tear my clothes, leave bruises on my arms. You've grown gentler."

"Only because I'm terrified this is a dream, and I'll wake up alone."

"With a cutting for your scrapbook?" She kissed his shoulder. "Do you keep a scrapbook about me, Clive? To preserve all those clippings?"

"I don't need to."

"Nor do I. I remember everything." She wanted to give him everything, make up for all the sorrow he had been through. With her body, she wanted to give him back everything he had lost. She wanted it to be as though the years had not passed, as though there had been no pain and no separation. As though there were nothing to make up for. "As it was in the beginning," she said dreamily.

"And tomorrow?" he asked, looking up into her face.

"Don't ask about tomorrow, Clive." She silenced him with her lips.

The four of them waited at Reception for Diem. The early-morning air was cool, but the heat would soon build up. They sat in a group, not talking much.

He was staying close to Sakura. She was strained this morning. Munro knew she had not slept. She had lain in his arms all night long. Now and then he had heard her whisper things to herself, though he could not make out the words. Since last night, his feelings for her had become frighteningly intense. He had never felt such love for any human being before, and it made him panic. The thought that something bad could happen to her was unbearable. He kept looking at her face, but she would not meet his eyes. She was locked back in that dark inner world.

"Here's Diem," Clive said.

Colonel Diem had arrived outside in an open jeep, wearing a dark Western suit. He had his two dapper little sergeants in tow. There was no sign of O'Brien. "Good morning," Diem greeted Francine politely, but didn't bother with the rest of them. "I trust you slept well?"

"Yes, thank you." Francine gestured courteously. "Shall we conduct our transaction?"

"I'll stay outside," Sakura said in a low voice to Munro. "I feel sick."

"What's the matter?" he demanded, taking her arm.

"Nothing. I just need air."

They went into the hotel, leaving Sakura looking very pale. The hotel manager gave Diem a deep wai, almost falling to his knees, and opened the strong room for them. Francine indicated the two suitcases. "Here they are, Colonel." There was no indication on her smooth, unlined face of how she felt at that moment.

"Do you want the cases back?" Diem asked Francine.

"No, thank you, Colonel. I don't need them."

"But they are excellent suitcases," Diem said seriously, inspecting them. "Haliburton Zeros, I believe. They are very expensive."

It was hard to tell with these people whether they were being sophisticated and mocking, or childish and polite. Francine smiled her Mona Lisa smile at Diem. "Then please accept them as a very small souvenir of our association, Colonel."

Diem looked delighted. He stroked the lustrous aluminum. "I shall take them with me when I next travel to Paris," he said. "I must be there on the twenty-sixth, for the start of the horse-racing season."

Munro glanced at Clive Napier and rolled his eyes. Clive shrugged infinitesimally.

"Don't you want to count the money?" Francine asked.

Diem looked at her in surprise. "How much is here?"

"Six hundred and eighty thousand dollars."

"Then there is no need to count it." He nodded to his sergeants. They picked up the two cases, and marched out, their bootheels ringing on the wooden floor.

Diem passed Francine a sheet of paper. It wore an impressive seal featuring the elephants and parasol of Laos. But she did not read Lao, and the looping script meant nothing to her. It might be a warrant for a firing squad for all she could tell.

"Show this document to Jai Han. Krong will be waiting at the military landing field," Diem told Francine, taking her arm in a courtly way as they filed out past the bowing hotel staff. "Sakura knows the way. Krong is an excellent pilot, and you will find the Helio Courier a remarkable aircraft. The landings and takeoffs are especially thrilling."

"Hey, Colonel," Munro said. "Are we going anywhere folks are likely to be shooting at us?"

Diem laughed politely. "No danger whatsoever. The child is kept safely away from the disturbances."

"So we can go with the women?" Munro pressed. "No problem?"

"No problem." Diem smiled.

"There better be no problem, man," Munro growled. Diem frowned, offended, and walked away.

They emerged from the hotel. Sakura was leaning against Diem's jeep, her face gray.

"You okay?" Munro asked in concern.

She nodded without replying. In the dazzling sunshine, Diem's sergeants loaded the cases into the back of the jeep. Munro hoped there wasn't another Roger Ricard waiting around the corner to snatch the money again.

"You will be flying over the Plaine de Jarres," Diem said, blinking amiably. "The Plain of Jars. Archaeologically, a most fascinating area, Mrs. Lawrence. Megalithic monuments weighing many tons, some as tall as a man. And the scenery is exceedingly beautiful. If you wish to see anything, tell Krong. He can land the Helio almost anywhere."

"You're very kind," Francine replied, with no trace of irony in her velvety voice.

"We will see each other when you return, perhaps tomorrow," Diem said. "Perhaps you will do me the honor of allowing me to offer you a meal?" He bowed over Francine's hand, saluted Clive briskly, and threw a nod toward Munro and Sakura. Then he was driving away in his jeep, his sergeants and his suitcases propped on the seat behind him.

"He's happier about the damned suitcases than about the money," Munro commented dryly.

Francine shrugged. "The money was going to be his anyway," she replied. "These suitcases are something extra, something for nothing. It sweetens the deal." She smiled at Sakura. "Sakura, I think everything is going to be all right now."

"We have to follow Diem's jeep," Sakura said tightly.

"What for?"

"We have to hurry!" She grabbed Clay Munro's arm and began dragging him to their own Peugeot. "Please, Clay. Come. Quickly."

He jerked her to a stop and pulled her to face him. "What, Sakura? What have you done?"

She stared at him with burning gray eyes, her mouth pressed into a white line. "Forgive me, Clay," she whispered.

"Oh, shit," he said, his stomach churning as the truth began to dawn on him.

"What is it, Clay?" Francine asked in a tense voice. "What's happening?"

"We've got to go after Diem," he said, breaking into a run. "Come on."

Diem's jeep was making unhurried progress along the dirt road, a cloud of dust billowing from its wheels into their faces as they followed.

"What the hell is going on?" Clive demanded curtly, leaning over Munro's shoulder.

"She's put something in Diem's jeep," Munro said in a brusque voice, concentrating on the road.

"What has she put in his jeep?" Francine asked in bewilderment.

"I don't know. A bomb, right Sakura? Ask her."

Francine turned blankly to Sakura. "That cannot be true, Sakura."

Sakura did not reply. Her eyes were fixed on Diem's jeep.

"That's why she waited outside the hotel," Munro said.

Clive shook Sakura roughly. "Is that true? What did you put in his jeep?"

"Some *plastique*," Sakura replied.

"Plastic explosive?"

She nodded.

"Where the hell did you get it from?" he asked, flabbergasted.

"From her house," Munro said. "That's why she insisted on going there yesterday." He remembered the way she had smiled at him there.

"You had explosives at your house?"

"It was Roger's," she said. "He showed me how to use it."

Francine felt her mind spinning dizzily. "You're insane! We'd come this far, and now *this*?"

"We'd come this far," Sakura repeated, "only to be robbed by Diem. Jai Han would have killed Louis. And then all of us."

"You don't know that!"

"I know!" She turned to Francine, her face fierce. "My child's life is at stake! I will not see him die now!"

"You told me I could trust you, Sakura," Munro said roughly. He had a flash of last night, of her magnificent, naked body sinking onto his. She had made a fool of him all over again.

"You can," she said in anguish. "You can! Trust me now, Clay! I've done the best thing!"

"How much, Sakura?" Munro demanded. "And where?"

"A quarter of a kilo," she replied. "On the rear axle."

"What kind of detonator?"

"A pencil fuse."

"What length?"

"Ten minutes."

"How much longer now?"

Sakura checked her watch, her hand shaking like a leaf. "One more minute. Maybe less."

"Sound the horn, Clay," Francine commanded urgently. "Stop them, warn them!"

"Too late," Munro said tersely. He braked hard, allowing the distance between the two vehicles to lengthen. "I hope you got the detonator right, Sakura. If they reach Vientiane, we're all fucked."

"They will not reach Vientiane."

Francine felt she was in some terrible nightmare. She could see the figures of Diem and his two sergeants. They were completely relaxed. They had not even turned to see that the Peugeot was behind them. To the right was jungle, to the left paddy fields, young shoots of rice spiking the shimmering water. "The money will all burn," she heard herself say.

"The suitcases are strong," Sakura replied.

Suddenly, Diem's jeep seemed to leap upward. A black cloud of dust and fragments jerked into the air, followed by a belch of black smoke. The shock wave spun the Peugeot in its tracks. Francine felt her eardrums compress agonizingly. A wheel came bounding down the road toward them, at the last moment veering off into the undergrowth.

"Oh, my God," Francine heard herself whispering, "Oh, my God."

Munro drove cautiously through the cloud of dust to the jeep. It was not burning, but it was upside down in the middle of the road, looking like a crushed beetle. One of the sergeants was facedown in the weeds beside the paddy field. The two others were lying in the road, motionless.

They got out of the Peugeot, their ears ringing. The quiet country road was deserted. There was no sound from either the jungle or the paddy field. The explosion had either been heard by nobody, or had driven any witnesses into cover.

"You should have told me," Munro said to Sakura.

"You would have stopped me." She crouched beside the overturned jeep and reached beneath it. She dragged out one of the aluminum suitcases, panting. It was dented, but intact. "Here's one. I can't see the other."

"Are they dead?" Francine asked, looking at the bodies.

Munro walked to the blackened figure of Diem. He inspected it briefly. "Doesn't look like he's breathing."

"I had almost a kilo of plastique," Sakura said. "I could have used it all. I didn't want to kill them."

Suddenly, the gasoline tank of the jeep erupted. The blast hurled them all back, and they staggered away, covering their faces. An orange fireball bloomed, swiftly swallowed by black smoke, which swirled furiously around the vehicle.

"The other case!" Sakura screamed at Munro. "Where is it?"

Shielding his face from the ferocious heat, Munro ran around the other side of the jeep. He saw the other Haliburton gleaming in a ditch. He hauled it out, the crackling flames at his back. There were deep gouges in the aluminum, but it had survived.

"This one's coming around," Clive called. He was crouched next to one of the sergeants, who was stirring aimlessly. He tugged the sergeant's revolver out of his holster and held it to the man's head.

"*No,* Clive!" Francine screamed over the roar of the flames.

Clive glanced up at her. "We're better off without them now."

"Please," she begged. She felt as though the ground beneath her feet were swinging wildly. "Don't."

He rose and tossed the revolver into a field. It landed with a splash.

Munro was loading the suitcases into the trunk of the Peugeot.

"What are we going to do now?" Francine asked.

"Go to the airfield as planned," Munro said briefly, "and hope Krong doesn't get to hear of this before we reach Jai Han."

"How can we take that risk?" Francine said breathlessly, staring at the thick column of black smoke that was spiraling into the air.

"We've got no choice," Clive said, grim-faced. "We're following Sakura's script now. Which way, Sakura?"

Sakura pointed back the way they had come.

"Okay. Let's move."

They got into the Peugeot. Munro spun the wheels making a turn, then drove back fast. "The whole world's gonna be here in ten minutes," he said.

Sakura was staring out of the back window. "They will say it was a Pathet Lao attack," she said.

"Somebody's bound to have seen us."

"Everyone in Vientiane hates Colonel Diem and his people. Nobody will say anything."

"Diem's probably dead, Sakura," Clive said.

"Nobody will mourn." She spoke matter-of-factly.

"I don't understand you, Sakura," Francine said. "You speak as though it's nothing to take a human life."

"He was going to steal your money, Francine." Sakura faced her. "He saw us coming, and he tried to hijack us. He would have watched all of us die, and laughed. So don't waste your time feeling sorry for him. Or those two butchers of his."

"What if Diem had reached Vientiane?" Munro asked, meeting Sakura's eyes in the rearview mirror. "What if your little bomb had gone off in a crowded street?"

"It's a twenty-minute drive," she said shortly. "I used a ten-minute fuse."

"And if they'd stopped to admire the view outside the hotel?"

"They didn't."

"We can't come back to Vientiane," Clive said practically. "Once we get the child, we'll have to make Krong take us into Thailand."

"There are many places to land in the paddy fields," Sakura said.

"If we don't get shot down by the Thais," Clay agreed.

Sakura touched Munro's arm. "I'm sorry," she said quietly. "I didn't lie to you, Clay. But I knew you would stop me. And this was the only way."

Francine stared at her, wordless with shock.

They reached the military landing field.

Francine looked around in dread. She expected at any minute to hear the screamed commands that would end their lives. But there was no hysterical posse of military police waiting for them, only Krong and his Helio Courier.

They carried the aluminum suitcases to the plane. Krong was coughing the opium addict's soft, persistent cough, his death-mask face hanging wearily on his skull. He helped them stow the now-battered Haliburtons behind the seats, making no comment. The cabin was cramped, the seats thin and hard. They fastened their safety harnesses.

Krong slowly checked the controls. The radio was crackling messages in Lao. Francine could understand nothing, but any one of those messages could spell their deaths.

Clive leaned close. "Relax, Francine," he murmured.

"She's insane," she hissed.

Clive gave her an ironic smile, dark eyes creasing. "I disagree. I think she's rather resourceful. But not insane."

Clay Munro grunted his agreement. "She's resourceful, all right. Aren't you, Sakura?"

"It was the only way," Sakura insisted.

"Did you fuck me to distract me from what you were doing?" he asked.

She met his eyes. "We made love because we had to." Her voice gentled. She put her hand on his arm. "You gave me courage to do what I had to do, Clay."

He shook her hand off brusquely. "Don't touch me, Sakura. That's over."

Her eyes darkened.

Krong smoked impassively while he waited for clearance. There seemed to be no hurry about this, just as there was no hurry about anything else in the Land of the Million Elephants and the White Parasol. "Oh, God, please," Francine heard herself whisper. Sitting in this airplane that felt so flimsy, swaying on its small wheels each time one of them moved, she felt as though her heart were bursting out of her throat.

A harsh message crackled out of the radio, making her start in panic.

Krong fired up the single motor. Everything in the cabin vibrated wildly in turn as the engine pitch rose through various harmonics.

The Helio taxied to the edge of the runway, then raced forward with climbing revs. In less than thirty meters, they were airborne, climbing almost vertically into the blue sky. Krong pulled on a faded red baseball cap, flicking switches with practiced dexterity.

Almost at once, the cabin began to fill with condensation, swirling whitely upward from their feet. Krong banked the plane steeply over Vientiane. Francine found herself staring down at rice fields, separated by muddy

THE SEVENTH MOON · 327

brown canals in which children were swimming with water buffaloes. The green tile roofs of temples swept by, set among the corrugated-iron patch-work of shanty houses; banana and coconut groves, streets with multicolored traffic, a glittering curve of the Mekong; and then the Helio straightened up, leveled off at a few thousand feet, and set a course north.

She had to crane her neck to see down now. Dirt roads snaked below them, winding between the crooked shapes of rice paddy and vegetable patch. Then, swiftly, the cultivation ended. The red roads crept for a little way farther into the thick, dark green forest. Then the meandering roads, too, ended, and there was nothing below them but primary jungle.

The little aircraft began climbing to clear the mountain ranges that were ris-ing beneath them. There was a mass of heavy cloud ahead of them, clotted darkly around the peaks of the mountains. Turbulence shook the Helio. Munro leaned forward to Krong.

"Is there good radio contact between Jai Han and Vientiane?"

"Very bad radio contact," Krong replied. He gestured. "Mountains too big."

"I figured that. It's something, anyhow." It was getting cold. Munro reached behind his seat for the cheap canvas bag he'd bought in the market, and pulled out his denim jacket. The others, too, were reaching for extra gar-ments.

The Helio gave a sudden lurch. Krong gestured for them to look down. Beneath them stretched a dry, undulating plateau, bordered on all sides by the mountains. Gray circles were scattered across the grassland, and it took Munro a moment to register that they were the mouths of huge stone urns. They were flying over the Plain of Jars.

They were so low that he could see how ancient the urns were, lichen covering the gray sandstone. Some were upright, others were tilted at drunken angles. Nobody really knew who had made them, or when, or what for. *Laos's definitive historical monument,* Munro thought. *A remote plain covered with stone jars of unknown purpose, provenance, or antiquity. That figured.*

Yet, looking down at the huge carved vessels beneath the Helio, he felt something else, a fleeting sense of the mystery of this country, the enigma of its heart.

Suddenly, he knew why Sakura had adopted this country as her own.

Because it's like her, he thought. *A beautiful orphan with no past and not much future.*

Then the Helio banked sharply, and something caught his eye outside. He turned to look. A heavy, black column of smoke was rising from the ground, tormented by the wind.

A small village was huddled against the mountainside. Or what was left of a small village. Something had hit it hard, artillery or planes. He could see craters and rubble. The thatch roofs were burning. There were no people in sight, no animals.

"What's that?" he shouted to Sakura above the roar of the engine.

"I think it is one of Jai Han's villages," she called back.

More smoke filled the air up ahead of them. The Plain of Jars, he knew from the map, was dotted with settlements, most sheltering among the low hills. There had been a lot of bombing, judging by the smoke. As far as he could tell in the murk, at least five separate targets were burning across a twenty-mile radius.

"Somebody's taking a bad beating," Munro said. "We're flying into the fucking war, man."

Sakura was staring out. This was not the way it was meant to look, her eyes said that. Krong kept banking the Helio to avoid the black, twisting columns of smoke.

Clive turned to glance at Munro. "I don't like this," he shouted.

"We gotta get in and out fast," Munro yelled back. "This is much, much bigger than I thought it would be."

Clive nodded his agreement. "It's a full-blown war."

"Yeah. We've been spun a lot of bullshit, Clive." Beneath them, people were moving along a winding earth road, hundreds of them. He couldn't see the end of the line. He saw the occasional tawny back of a buffalo flit beneath their wings. The people were carrying things: possessions, young children. They were heading south, he realized, toward Vientiane. He tried to make out who they were, and saw the black pajamas of the Meo. Then he saw olive-green, too. "Oh, fuck," he said to Clive. "Half those people are troops. You can see their uniforms."

"O'Brien wasn't kidding. This is a rout."

Munro's head swiveled, searching the skies. One enemy plane, one panicky antiaircraft gunner on the ground, and they were dead. He prayed that the weather would turn really bad. Right now, he would take his chances in monsoon turbulence, if it kept the gunships away.

He glanced at Sakura, huddled against the window. Despite himself, he reached out to her.

What has she done to us? Francine kept thinking, watching Sakura cling to Clay Munro's strong shoulders. *What has she done to me?*

It was as though her mind could not encompass Sakura's ruthlessness of purpose. She had known that Sakura would do many things to defend her child. But to put plastic explosive on the axle of Diem's car. To risk everything. To be prepared to kill or maim, to face being killed or maimed herself: Those things were beyond Francine's understanding.

Was I like that with Ruth? she wondered. *Perhaps if I had been like Sakura, I would never have lost her.*

Beneath them, the ground suddenly changed color. The dry grassland had given way to red earth, to some weird, desertlike geological formation.

Then Francine's eyes adjusted, and she knew she was looking at man-made desolation. This had not been done by the Pathet Lao. Only one country on earth could have done this.

The B-52s must have come over and over and over: big formations of the monstrous eight-engined bombers, flying so high they could be neither seen nor heard. Their cargo had disemboweled the earth, then disemboweled it again. Then again. Here and there, the black spike of a tree stump remained. There was nothing else left, just the huge craters dug by the high-explosive bombs. They stretched as far as the eye could see, devoid of life.

Francine stared out. *They aren't showing this on the evening news back home,* she thought grimly. The incredible devastation was proof of a vast operation that had been hidden from the American people, from the whole world. Nobody had been watching or reporting this secret war, so there had been no restrictions on what the army did. The remoteness of Laos, the poverty of communications, a willful conspiracy of silence, had all combined to keep a terrible secret hidden.

The devastation swept beneath them, on and on. To have been anywhere near this target area must have been unimaginably terrible. Tens of thousands of tons of bombs had been dropped by the Stratofortresses.

Whatever had lain beneath this rain of fire had been obliterated forever. Roads, fields, villages, living creatures, all had been churned into red earth. Nothing could cross this wasteland. Nothing could live on it, farm it, extract any profit from it. When the rains came, this would become an ocean of sterile mud, a gigantic obstacle that would force the enemy to make exhausting detours.

Francine looked at Sakura and Munro. He was talking in her ear, trying to comfort her. His whole being was focused on the woman in his arms. He had evidently forgiven her already.

They were a different generation, shaped by a different world, a different war. She and Clive were ignorant of their world, their horrors. Just as Sakura and Clay were ignorant of what had gone before. And yet, within the shock, Francine felt something like awe, almost a kind of satisfaction in what Sakura had done. She had blown up the man who had killed the father of her child. There was a brutal justice in that. And she had been right about one thing: Nobody would mourn the passing of Diem and his kind.

Clive went forward to speak to Krong. He came clambering back, looking worried. "He says Jai Han's at a place called Phou Vieng," he said. "Up north."

"How far up north?" Munro yelled at Krong.

Krong waved his hand languidly to indicate some unspecified but considerable distance.

Munro straightened his map, and tried to make out where they were, and where Phou Vieng was. The printing of the map was poor quality, the topography colors too bright, the place-names fuzzy. The outlandish spelling of the French legends didn't help.

At last he found Phou Vieng, right up at the far end of the plain, in the northern foothills. He saw Diem's polite smile in his mind. *No problem.* The little jerk. That was why they hadn't bothered to bring Louis back to Vientiane. He was stuck in the middle of a Communist attack. Even with this shitty little map, from what he had seen from the air, Munro knew there wasn't likely to be any retreat from Phou Vieng. No streams of plodding villagers, escorted by soldiers who'd turned tail. Phou Vieng was going to be captured. So were the villages around it.

And he knew that Krong wasn't going to take his shiny new plane into Phou Vieng, either.

Even now, the opium pilot was losing altitude and airspeed. They were bearing toward the splayed fingers of some low hills. Buried in the valley would be some safe village.

Anger clenched in his chest. He thought about getting out his Colt and shoving it against Krong's red baseball cap, making the little bastard fly them to Phou Vieng. But getting shot down by the Pathet Lao wouldn't help.

He checked the Colt anyway, and shoved it into the inside pocket of his denim jacket. He zipped the jacket up to his throat and reached for his bag. He started tossing stuff out. From here on, he only wanted to carry the essentials.

Francine clung to her seat as the Helio landed. The landing strip had been carved out of the scrub on a steep hillside, like a ski jump, and Krong had no more than a few yards to stall the plane and bring it to a halt.

The long wings flapped wildly as they jolted across the dirt. The Helio slewed sideways at the last moment, just before it shot off the end of the strip. It spun around, and taxied back down the hill, toward the little group of thatched huts.

They clambered out of the plane. Francine's head was ringing. She turned to Krong. "Where is the child?" she demanded.

He waved his hand. "You take jeep," he said laconically. "I wait."

Clay Munro thrust the map at the Thai. "Where are we?"

Krong pointed with his stained thumb. "Phou Fa."

"And Phou Vieng?"

Again, Krong indicated with his thumb. "Here."

"How come they're there?"

"Jai Han wife at Phou Vieng. Her village."

Munro studied the area for a moment. "Figures," he said grimly, folding the map open at that place.

"I don't understand," Francine said. "Where is the child?"

He showed her the map. Clive and Sakura came to look. "We're here. Phou Fa. Jai Han and the kid are up north, at Phou Vieng."

"A long way?" Clive asked tersely.

"Doesn't look that far on the map," Munro said. "Except, the map is kind of Mickey Mouse."

Francine turned angrily to the Thai opium pilot. "Colonel Diem told us you would take us directly to where the child was!"

"Too risky." Krong leaned against the Helio, his face impassive. "You take jeep," he repeated.

"He's right." Munro pointed to the map. "The Pathet Lao are attacking from here. The only way to Phou Vieng is to drive there and back, and hope we don't meet a patrol."

"No Pathet Lao on ground," Krong said stolidly. "Pathet Lao soldier too scare to come close. Just fire rocket from mountain."

"Just rocket, huh?" Munro said. "Well, that's a relief. How far to Phou Vieng, Krong? Twenty kilometers?"

"Maybe fifteen."

"This is madness," Francine said bitterly to the pilot. "Why can't you fly us there? It will take hours by jeep on the mountain roads, even if we don't get lost, or shot. You could fly us there in ten minutes!"

Krong shook his head. "Colonel Diem say, land here."

Francine looked around. The hills were deserted. There was no movement from the scrub, or from the huts. But in the distance, the rumble of artillery vibrated on the air. The black sky lowered overhead, shedding a few heavy spots of rain. "Diem lied to us," she said quietly.

"Yes, Diem lied," Clive agreed. "I'm starting to feel a lot better about that little surprise of Sakura's. Where's the jeep, Krong?"

Krong indicated the tattered huts. "I show."

The jeep was parked up behind one of the huts. It had been covered with branches in an attempt to camouflage it from the air. The village itself was completely deserted. It must have been abandoned days earlier, which was possibly why nobody had bothered to shell it.

Munro hauled branches off the vehicle. "It's not a jeep. What the hell is it?"

"It's a Citroën Méhari," Clive said.

"Has it got four-wheel drive?" Munro asked, looking at the boxy little vehicle in disgust.

"No," Clive said. "But they're tougher than they look."

"Jesus, it better be. There's only a quarter-tank of gas."

"Plenty for Méhari," Krong said indifferently. "You get there, easy."

Munro kicked the Citroën's skinny wheels, cursing. He got in the car and pushed the ignition. It chugged into life, spewing white smoke from the exhaust. He revved it up, listening to the engine. "What do you think?" he asked Clive.

"It'll probably do another fifty miles." He turned to Krong. "How long will you wait for us?"

Krong shrugged without replying.

Sakura whispered to Munro, "We can't leave Krong here."

"You want to take the bastard with us?" Munro asked Clive in an undertone.

"No room," Clive replied, glancing at the Citroën. "We have to take the suitcases. Can you cover him for me?"

"No problem." Munro eased the Colt out of his waistband and got out of the Citroën. Clive walked back to the Helio. He unfastened the engine cover and pulled it open, delving inside.

Krong uttered a shout of anger, and ran toward his plane. But Munro stepped in his way, holding the Colt in both hands, pointed at Krong's face. "You want to eat this?"

Krong stopped dead, raising his hands. "I tell Colonel Diem," he shouted. "You all be shot!"

"Yeah, tell him all about it when we get back," Munro said.

Clive was returning from the airplane, carrying something wrapped in a bundle of dirty rag. He had also appropriated Krong's binoculars, which he had slung around his neck. He opened the bundle and showed a greasy piece of machinery to the Thai. "Rotor arm. You got a spare?"

Krong glared at him, pouchy eyes furious. He had emerged temporarily from the languid depths of his addiction. The long grass whispered in the silence.

"Well, I sure hope you don't," Clay commented. "We're going to take it with us. Okay? You still think we should drive to Phou Vieng? Or you got some better advice, now?"

Krong looked from Munro to Clive. "You drive to Phou Vieng," he said abruptly. "Come back in three hour. Or no Helio. No Krong. All dead. Okay?"

Francine got into the Méhari. "Let's go," she said shortly.

The distance on the map didn't look like much. What bothered Munro were the concentric circles of color around Phou Vieng. The ink went from yellow to orange to brown. A steep climb would probably kill this jalopy.

He had been unbelievably stupid. He had allowed Diem's smooth bull-shit to fool him. He should have demanded that Diem issue them all with fragmentation-protective vests, helmets, proper weapons. He hadn't been thinking. Their two popguns, as O'Brien had called them, weren't worth shit. And they were merrily driving into combat in a canvas-topped vehicle with no gas and $680,000 in cash.

The sound of the bombardment up in the mountains was louder all the time. He didn't even know if they were coming into Phou Vieng from the right direction. He didn't want to think about the probability of crossing a minefield, or driving through an ambush laid by Jai Han's apprehensive warriors.

The Citroën bounced wildly on the rutted road. Clive drove well, not afraid to charge obstacles down. But when they turned a corner and reached a great swath of hillside blackened by fire, he stamped on the brake hard, bringing the Citroën to a slithering halt.

Sakura leaned forward. "It's okay," she said. "It's just where the Meo burn off the grass to plant rice."

"And that?" Munro demanded, gesturing to a bottle-shaped clearing on the slope of the next hill.

"The Meo made that, too. It's a place for snaring sparrows."

Munro turned briefly. "They eat sparrows?"

Clive crashed the Citroën into gear and shot forward again. The road was climbing steeply, winding endlessly around the hillsides. Munro divided his attention between the map and scanning the terrain up ahead. It was the most savage country he had ever seen, not lush, like Vietnam, but dry and jagged everywhere you looked.

This was a world indifferent to humans. But up ahead, black smoke swirled over the hilltops, where humans were busily slaughtering one another.

A few heavy drops of rain kept spattering the windshield, without ever turning into real rain. Real rain, as O'Brien had said back in Vientiane, was about the only thing that was going to save their asses now.

Francine kept staring at the columns of smoke in the distance. Black smoke, unmistakable, the same smoke she had seen so many times in Singapore.

Clive struggled to keep the lightweight Citroën on the road as they rounded a curve. Here the road had all but disintegrated. He slammed the box into a lower gear and revved hard. The slender tires scrabbled for grip. For a moment they were sliding sideways into the scrub. Then the rubber held somehow, and the Citroën hauled itself up the steep slope.

They breasted the peak. The track ahead descended in a long, snaking red ribbon down the rough hillside, until it disappeared among iron-gray scrub and slabs of rock. Beyond, a narrow valley opened up like the gaping jaws of a monster, deep and desolate. The mountains towered darkly over it, steep flanks bare, veined with undergrowth here and there.

They could see Phou Vieng now, or at least, where the high explosive was hitting Phou Vieng. Black smoke hung over the place, a man-made thunderstorm. Dense, low clouds prevented it from rising any higher.

The whole tableau was lit by a lurid, stark light that threw each detail into pitiless focus.

Clive stopped the Citroën, and they stared at the scene. They could hear the cracking and thudding clearly now, above the eerie moan of the wind among the rocks, the rustle of the dry grass all around.

The child is there, Francine thought, her heart in her throat. "Can we get in?"

"They're firing from the northeast," Munro commented, staring through Krong's binoculars. "Big damn rockets by the look of it."

He passed the field glasses to Clive, who scanned the vista, gnawing his lower lip. "It's a bloody mess," he commented.

"The road in is clear," Sakura said. "Let's go."

"Yes," Francine agreed.

Clive threw the Citroën into gear, and they rattled toward Phou Vieng. Sakura could not take her eyes from the black clouds that hid her child. Fire was raining down, but she knew that Louis would be safe. God would protect Louis, because Louis was innocent, and did not deserve to die.

The stony road twisted and dodged like a live thing. Here and there, craters gaped. In a poppy field, a woman crouched next to her hoe. Or perhaps she was dead. The opium was still in bloom, red and white and purple, livid in the dull light.

They reached the first people coming out of the village, a small family group, carrying sacks of rice, teenagers with their baby brothers and sisters piggyback, old people pushing handcarts. They moved at the trot of people who needed to go a long way. They edged off the road to let the Citroën past, staring with blank faces. Sakura twisted in her seat to look at the young children, to see if one of them might be Louis. But the faces were Meo, brown and stolid.

More craters along the road. More people, walking in ragged groups, the adults trotting, the children running to keep up.

How much time? The Meo would have waited until the last moment to leave their homes, everything they had. Not much time.

The *chop-chop-chop* of a helicopter drifted on the air. She wondered whether it was Jai Han, also leaving. She could not see the aircraft through the smoke.

They were at the outskirts of the village now. A dead bullock lay on the road, belly already bloated, legs sticking out stiffly. They had to drive into a rice field to avoid it. Here, buildings had been blown up, just rubble foundations and cremated beams.

Phou Vieng was on a steep road that went up a green hill for a way, then abruptly ended. Meo houses were clustered along it. On either side, opium fields, bright and irregular, twinkled. Half of the houses had been hit. Their flimsy materials—thatch, bamboo, atap—had burned out. Only the masonry groundwork remained.

Clive stopped the engine and wrenched on the hand brake against the steep incline.

"They got forward positions up there," she heard Munro say. "On the other side of the village. But they won't hold out much longer. We gotta get in and out, fast." He grabbed Sakura's hand. "Let's find Louis and get out of here."

Francine stared around. Every living soul seemed to have left.

To the right was a Quonset hut. It sagged to one side, sheets of metal twisted and buckled. But the red cross painted over the door was still visible.

"There," she called. The four of them ran to it. The door was hanging open. It had been a warehouse, but was now a field hospital. Two dozen bodies lay scattered across the floor. Francine ran from one to the next. All were men, most already dead, motionless humps under blood-soaked blankets. There was nobody else.

They kept moving along the street, peering into the houses. A hundred or so yards up ahead, machine guns were rattling in businesslike bursts. It was growing very dark, the heavy cloud and the pall of smoke together blotting out the light.

She heard Munro shout. A man had appeared in the road, a white man wearing bleached khaki fatigues and a slouch hat, carrying a recoilless rifle. It was Christopher McFadden.

"Get off the fucking road," McFadden yelled at them. They followed him into a banana grove, and crouched beneath the bunches of green fruit.

"Welcome to the end of the line." McFadden was filthy and gray-faced, squatting over his recoilless rifle. "Where the hell did you people drop from?"

"A Helio flew us to a place called Phou Fa. We left it there, and drove here by car."

"Man, you must be riding with Jesus. You brought the money?"

"We brought the money," Francine said.

"Nobody tried to bushwhack you in Vientiane?"

Francine wondered whether he had somehow heard about Diem on the radio yet. But he just kept staring at her. "We spoke to a Colonel Diem," she said cautiously.

"Diem? That figures. Who was with him?"

"An American named O'Brien. He said he was a colleague of yours."

McFadden grunted. "O'Brien's a supply man. Diem wanted the money, right?"

"Sakura persuaded Diem we would be better off giving the money directly to Jai Han."

"Persuaded?" McFadden showed his yellow teeth in a skull-like grin. "He's not dead, is he?"

"No, he's not dead," Francine said tightly.

"He's gotta be dead if he passed up six hundred and eighty thousand bucks."

Sakura spoke. "Jai Han would have killed us if we'd come to him with empty hands."

McFadden nodded. "Absolutely."

"So we did the right thing, bypassing Diem?" Munro demanded.

"Yeah, but I'd still like to know how you did it." A shell exploded beyond the village, and they all crouched instinctively. "Our own fucking T-28s bombed the shit out of us this morning," McFadden said. "Might have been an accident, but I have a feeling Souvanna Phouma and his cousins have decided to back the other horse. By nailing Jai Han for the Pathet Lao." He grinned, his face creasing into a thousand lines. "That's a bitch, ain't it? But basically, you could kill all the Diems you wanted and it wouldn't make a bit of difference. This country has about a week left." He jerked his head at where the firing was coming from. "These guys are gonna be in Vientiane in time for the rains."

"Where is Jai Han?" Munro demanded.

"Eating," McFadden said. "Wait until after lunch."

"We got no time, Major," Munro said. "We have to get back to our transport."

McFadden chuckled. "You think your Helio's gonna be there when you get back?"

"We disabled the plane. We took the rotor arm with us."

"You're a busy little bee, ain't you?"

"Where's my child?" Sakura demanded tightly.

McFadden gestured. "With wife Number Three in one of those huts."

"I want him!"

"I told you, kid, wait until Jai Han's eaten. He's easier to deal with when he's got some rice and beer in his gut."

"This place isn't going to hold out until Jai Han finishes lunch," Munro said grimly. "Take us to him, McFadden."

McFadden shrugged. "It's your funeral. Follow me."

This is Malaya, all over again, Francine thought as they waded through the banana grove. *This is the end of the world, all over again.*

They reached a small clearing, with a thatch hut in the middle. A trestle table had been set up outside the hut, and four uniformed men were seated around it. An old woman was kneading a huge ball of sticky rice in a bamboo container.

At the head of the table sat a stocky man in his early forties, wearing a slouch hat like McFadden's. He was holding a sheaf of maps in one hand. He looked up as they approached, and Francine knew she was in the presence of Jai Han.

This is what Genghis Khan must have looked like, she thought. A moon-faced, handsome man, with fierce slit eyes. And a hot smile, like those places on the earth where the rock opens and spits fire.

Jai Han looked at them, eyes leaping from one to the other. He raised a square fist, and dashed it down on the board in a gesture of satisfaction, or surprise, or anger, Francine could not tell which.

He rose from the table, tossing the maps down, and walked toward them. He was short, burly, his hair cropped close to the sides of his head in American military style. He stopped in front of them, legs straddled, hands clasped behind his back.

"Nuhuang," he barked, eyes on Francine's.

"General Jai Han." She pressed her palms together, and made a deep wai.

"You brought the money?"

"It is in our car, General."

"Where your car?"

"Next to the Red Cross hut."

Jai Han barked out an order, and two of his men ran off. He looked Francine up and down, grinning his tiger's grin. "You one beautiful lady. I thought you must be old, white hair." He waggled his fingers in front of his face to indicate wrinkles. "Ah?"

"I am not young anymore, General."

"You young," he said, roaring with laughter. He had not even glanced at Sakura. "You strong. Maybe you come fight Communists with Jai Han. Ah?"

"Jai Han needs no help from a woman," she said with a thin smile.

"You like Laos?"

"Laos is very beautiful," she replied.

He nodded. "Yes, very beautiful." He wore a general's stars on his shoulders, but the rest of his uniform and person were deceptively ordinary. "Laos will be a great nation when we break the Communists."

His men had returned, each one lugging one of the aluminum suitcases. He snapped a command. The men began to fumble with the cases, but the sophisticated catches defeated them.

"Let me," Munro offered. He opened both cases. Jai Han glanced at the thick bundles of money within. He jerked his cropped head down in a quick bow. "Okay. You clever woman, Nuhuang." He swiveled on his heels to face Sakura. "Now Sakura's turn to pay."

Munro had been watching Jai Han with fascination, a cocky little guy with a big smile, considering half the Vietcong army seemed to be just over the next hill. The man's charisma blazed out of him, an erratic, mercurial force of character.

He saw Jai Han turn now, and face Sakura. Sakura looked straight back at him, no expression in her eyes or on her mouth. His heart suddenly started to race.

He saw Jai Han draw back his hand, and slap Sakura with all his force across the face.

Munro's palm was on the butt of his Colt, inside his jacket, but a hand gripped his arm like a steel claw. It was McFadden. "Don't be an asshole," McFadden muttered. "You got this far by dumb luck."

The blow had staggered Sakura, and she had almost fallen. With a slow effort, she pulled herself upright, and faced Jai Han again.

"Bitch. Whore." Again, Jai Han's hand lashed out, hitting the other side of her face, knocking her to the other side. Blood was running from the half-healed wound around her ear, and her eyes were glazed.

Munro was frozen now. At the edges of his vision, he saw Francine try to move forward. But Clive grabbed her tight, stopping her. The three soldiers at the table were watching without expression. Only the old woman's spidery fingers kept moving, kneading, kneading the sticky rice.

Sakura steadied herself in front of Jai Han, breathing raggedly.

He struck her again, grunting with the effort. This time, Sakura crumpled to her knees. Her head lolled, her brown hair tumbling over her face. But with slow movements, she pushed herself to her feet again. She lifted her head, her eyes closed now. As if in a nightmare, Munro saw blood running freely from her nose and ear, spattering her shirt. There was a deep gash on her cheekbone. Jai Han wore a heavy gold ring, and it had torn a triangular hole in her flesh.

Jai Han struck her again, across the other side of her face. She spun like a rag doll and fell heavily. She had not made a sound, but she groaned quietly now as her fingers groped in the earth. Munro realized she was trying to pick herself up again. In a complete silence, they all watched as she lifted her hips, brought up her knees, forced herself into a crouched position. She tried to stand. Her blood puddled on the earth under her face.

Jai Han was rubbing his knuckles, twisting his gold ring, looking down at Sakura.

Please don't get up, Munro begged her in silent agony. *Please don't get up.* He did not know whether her obstinate refusal to lie down and grovel was impressing Jai Han, or inflaming him even more.

But Sakura was struggling, forcing her body to obey. She got to her knees, swaying. Jai Han reached out and grabbed her hair abruptly. He dragged her to her feet. Then he wagged his finger in her face, and yelled, "I trusted you! I trusted you!"

"I'm sorry," they all heard her whisper. Her mouth was full of blood. "I'm sorry."

"Sorry not enough." Jai Han snapped open the sheath clipped to the harness he wore. He jerked out a jungle knife. "Now you pay."

Munro's blood had turned to ice. His heart had stopped, his lungs were empty.

Suddenly, Francine walked forward. Before anyone could stop her, she stepped in front of Sakura, facing Jai Han's knife. "No," she said in a low voice.

Jai Han grinned fiercely. "I not kill her. You still get your daughter. But I mark her."

"No. You've hurt her enough already, General."

Jai Han's eyes flared in rage. "Get out of my way!"

"Go away, Francine." The thick voice was Sakura's. "Let him do what he wants. That's why I am here."

"Sorry not enough," Jai Han shouted. "I will write my name in her face now. She must remember, every time she look in mirror."

"I won't let you do that," Francine said quietly.

"Nobody tell me what I can do," Jai Han said in a fury. He struck Francine in the stomach. She crumpled to the earth.

Jai Han stepped over her and barked an order to his men. Two of them ran forward, grinning, and grabbed Sakura by the arms. They held her upright, immobile. Jai Han spun the knife in his fingers so the blade pointed down. He stepped forward, raising the point over Sakura's face. "You remember me," he rasped, "every time you look in mirror, every time a man look at you."

Sakura's eyes were closed now. Her head rolled back, her blank face offered to the steel blade.

Francine forced herself up. She reached out and grasped Jai Han's belt with shaky fingers. She hauled hard, dragging herself to her feet, making the stocky general stagger backward.

Munro suddenly saw that she had taken possession of Clive's Colt automatic. She held the heavy pistol in her slim hand. She lifted it, gasping for breath. She had to press the muzzle behind Jai Han's ear to stop it waving aimlessly. She cocked it with a hard click.

"Stop," she hissed.

Jai Han became very still. His eyes rolled back, searching for Francine, but he did not turn his head. "Nuhuang, you dead," he said quietly.

"No, you're dead," Francine whispered. "I'll pull the trigger, Jai Han. Drop the knife."

Jai Han's fingers opened. The knife dropped to the ground. The two men who were holding Sakura were staring, astounded.

Francine, still winded by the blow, had to keep grasping Jai Han's belt to stop herself from falling. "Tell them to let her go," she ordered tightly.

McFadden spoke in a dead voice. "Mrs. Lawrence, I thought you were smart. This is very dumb."

"You tell them to back off, McFadden. I mean it. I'll kill your cherished general right now." Her voice shook, but there was steel in it.

McFadden spoke a few words in Lao. The soldiers released Sakura and stepped back. Munro ran forward to grab Sakura. She sagged against him, her blurred eyes on Francine.

Francine kept the muzzle pressed behind Jai Han's ear. "Sakura has be-haved badly, Jai Han," Francine said, her voice unsteady. "The fault was not hers. She had no father. No mother. But she has a mother now."

There was silence. An aircraft engine shuddered on the wind, above the fleshy green banana leaves. Despite the pistol pressed to his skull, Jai Han moved his head to peer up through the thick green canopy.

McFadden, too, was looking up. A black, buglike shape swam into view through the smoke. The thud of a heavy machine gun exploded across the sky. McFadden crouched. "The T-28s are back," he yelled. "Grab some shel-ter, folks."

Jai Han ducked his cropped head, swung an elbow, and knocked Francine roughly aside. He sprinted toward the hut. He did not look behind him at any of them. His men ran after him.

"Move!" Munro yelled. He hustled Sakura forward.

"Jesus, Francine," Clive said in a tight voice. There was no time for any-thing further. He grasped her hand, and they ran after Munro and Sakura. The banana grove was full of other running figures, men hurrying away, grabbing helmets.

The T-28s were approaching swiftly, the thunder of their engines roll-ing overhead. They were horribly exposed, a long way from cover. Had they come so far to die now?

There was a blinding flash beyond the trees. A row of atap houses leaped into the air. Francine had a vague impression of the blast rushing through the banana grove toward her, a haze of white air uprooting trees, hurling human figures like matchsticks. It slammed her like a truck. She hit the ground and rolled for yards, coming to rest against the bleeding, wet trunk of a banana tree. She sat up stupidly, looked down at herself, saw her own body sticky with smashed green bananas. She tried to rise, gasping for breath. She felt as though she had been turned inside out. She managed only to get to her knees. She could get no further. She could not see Clive. She did not know if Clay had reached shelter with Sakura.

Another blast wrenched the sky. She saw a sheet of metal, bearing a painted red cross, whirl through the air. The Quonset hut had taken a direct hit. The sheet of metal smashed down among the banana trees. A man fell from the sky after it, thumping onto the red earth not far from her. Debris rained down. She dragged herself to a concrete wall and huddled in its mea-ger shelter. The man who had fallen from the sky had no head; blood pumped from the stump of a neck.

A third bomb erupted at the other end of the village. Again, she saw the blast wave rip through the air, plucking trees like daisies, tearing roofs and walls out of the buildings in its path. Shattered things showered from the sky or rolled in the alleys between the trees. The air was thick with the smell of high explosives and pulped green bananas.

The T-28s faded over the hill. She waited a few moments longer before emerging from her shelter. Her whole body felt battered. She forced herself into a limping run, searching numbly for the others among the smoke. Fire poured from the ruined Meo houses, growing into a pillar against the sky. She reached the street. It was littered with rubble and bodies. A Meo soldier marched briskly toward her, shouting meaningless words, blood jetting from a severed arm. As he reached her, he suddenly spun round and collapsed. He lay without moving.

Up ahead, the rattle of rifles and machine guns continued briskly. She knelt beside the Meo soldier, pulled off his belt, and tried to tie it in a tourniquet around the stump of his arm. The flow stopped. She could not tell whether he was dead or unconscious. She screamed for Clive, Sakura, Clay, hardly able to hear her own voice. The wounded Meo began to thrash around. Blood spurted from the stump of his arm again, spraying her brown pantsuit. She recoiled and staggered away. She had to find the others.

Then she heard Clay's voice shouting her name.

"I'm here!" she screamed, looking around.

He appeared from behind a hut, covered in red dirt, his eyes wild. "Francine? Are you okay?"

She grabbed his arm. "Where's Sakura?"

"With Clive. We thought you were dead." He peered at her, as though not quite believing his eyes.

"The child!" she yelled at him. "Louis! Where is he?"

"They're digging for him. Come."

He grabbed her hand and they ran across the street, in among the houses.

Soldiers and others had gathered around the ruins of a house. It had taken the indirect force of the blast. Its concrete foundation had been torn apart, and the bamboo superstructure had collapsed. It had not caught fire, but the people who had sheltered in it were buried in rubble. Foul green water was pouring across the ground from a burst water tank.

"He's in there," Munro said. "So's Jai Han's wife, and her sisters."

Francine saw Sakura and Clive tearing at the debris side by side. She ran forward and joined them. Clay followed. Christopher McFadden had found a triangular Meo hoe, and was hacking at the ruins, cursing in a steady monotone. Francine dug with her bare hands. She tore at the earth and shattered cement like an animal, her fingers scraping, her nails breaking.

They dragged out three Meo women first. All were dead. Beneath them lay two children of around twelve, their black pajamas soaked in blood. They, too, were dead.

In the remains of the next room, they saw the broad, naked back of a Meo man. He was alive, moving feebly.

"It's Thuong," McFadden said. "For Christ's sake, go easy."

Between them, he, Clive, and Clay Munro cleared rubble off the man. He lay on his stomach, his head turned to one side. His half-naked body was a welter of blood, the scarlet overprinting the tattoos on his back. His mouth was open and gasping, his eyes staring through a mask of dirt.

McFadden knelt beside his friend, calling his name. Francine saw that a two-foot-long splinter of wood had impaled him. It protruded from his side, quivering with the labored gasping of his lungs. Everything around was drenched with Thuong's blood.

They tried to roll him over. Thuong's body was heavy, his inert limbs trapped under concrete breeze-blocks. In silence, Francine and the others struggled to free him. At last they released him.

Francine heard Sakura scream, "Louis!" Sakura thrust forward and reached under Thuong's body. Thuong had been lying on a child. Deliberately or otherwise, he had protected the smaller body with his own. Francine caught a glimpse of black hair, glazed eyes, a small and bloodstained shirt.

Sakura and Clay lifted the boy out of the grave he had been lying in. His eyes and mouth were open. Moaning, Sakura crouched and cradled him in her arms. Numbly, Francine reached out to touch the child. The soft little body was warm and limp. Then they saw the child's lips move, his arms and legs stir. He began to cry, groping for Sakura, calling, "Mama, Mama."

Too shocked to speak or weep, Francine helped Sakura examine Louis for injuries. He appeared to have been miraculously unscathed. Thuong's burly body had sheltered him.

Sakura, her battered face blank, gathered the child in her arms and looked at Francine. "He's alive," she said in a hoarse voice.

At their feet, Thuong stopped breathing with a jolt. He was now clutching the wooden dagger that transfixed him, as though he wanted to pull it out. Francine looked down at him. His eyes stared into Francine's with extraordinary intensity for a moment, as though there were something overwhelmingly important that he wanted to communicate. Then the wild gleam began to glaze over. His eyes rolled upward. "What can we do for him?" she begged McFadden.

McFadden squatted, his hands hanging limply over his knees. "Nothing."

Thuong's spell of shivering jerked to a stop. He lolled into a perfect stillness.

"Ah, fuck it," McFadden said wearily. He looked up at Francine. "He was protecting the kid. You saw?"

"I saw," Francine said.

"That's what these little guys are like." McFadden's bloodshot eyes were wet. "You never know what the fuck they're going to do next. I have to go find Jai Han and tell him his wife and Thuong are dead. You better get out of here, Nuhuang. He'll kill you if he sees you again."

"Is Jai Han gonna send anybody else after us?" Munro demanded.

"Christ, I don't know. Just go."

"McFadden," Munro said quietly, "you got an M-16 for me? All we have are these pistols."

McFadden rose without a word, and unslung the carbine from his shoulder. He passed it to Munro. "Get out of here, okay?"

Francine nodded. "Let's go."

They began to limp away.

Francine realized she was barefoot. She had lost her sandals in the banana grove. One of her feet was hurt and bleeding. Clive put his arm around her to support her. She leaned on his strength.

They made their way through the huts onto the road. The roaring in Francine's ears had dwindled into a strange sound like distant funeral music, pounding of kettledrums and drone of brass. Exhaustion and shock had deadened her emotions. It did not matter, next to the miracle that the child was alive.

As they walked, she absorbed individual details—the way Sakura clung to the weeping boy in her arms; the sight of a bullock cart tumbled like a bug, dead animals upside down between the shafts; Meo soldiers hauling bodies from the rubble, laying them in rows on the earth. She trudged past the destruction and the carnage, holding on to Clive, wrapped in a gray cocoon of silence and shock. Above, the black pall of smoke swirled. Heavy drops of rain battered her face. The smell of burning was everywhere. They were going home.

Through the roaring in her ears, she was aware of shouting. She paid it no attention, until four Meo soldiers ran in front of them. All were carrying M-16 rifles. Their faces were angry. One of them jabbed at Francine with his rifle, pointing and shouting.

She stopped wearily. "What do you want?"

"You come to Jai Han," the man shouted.

"I already paid Jai Han. There is nothing more to say."

"You come!" the man screamed. "Come now!"

"She's not going," Clive said curtly.

One of the other Meo ran forward, swinging his rifle butt. It smashed into the side of Clive's head, knocking him to the ground. The leader grabbed Francine by the arms, dragging her away from Clay and Sakura. "Come now! Come now!"

"Leave her alone," Clay shouted, moving forward. All three of the other Meos raised their M-16s and aimed at Clay, crouching in readiness to fire.

"You go," the leader commanded, waving at Clay and Sakura. "You go back! Nuhuang come to Jai Han."

They dragged Francine away from the others, pulling her back toward the banana grove and the column of black smoke. "Go to the car," Francine shouted to them. "Don't wait for me." The Meo soldiers jerked her along. "Drive back to the plane," she called. "Go back to Vientiane. I'll see you there."

It was then Sakura screamed. It was a sound Francine had heard only once before in her life, a sound of unbearable desolation. She turned. In the face of the Meos' weapons, Sakura was running to her. The scream came tearing from her lungs as though her soul were leaving her body.

Francine could not, at first, make out what it was Sakura was screaming. And then she heard the words. And then she remembered what it was she had not wanted to remember, what it was Sakura had been unable to remember.

Because Ruth is running along the jungle track after her, screaming with the sound that a child makes when her heart is being torn out of her.

"Mama don't leave me, Mama don't leave me, Mama don't leave me."

Ruth has seen more of death than any child should ever see. But now she is seeing something worse than death: her mother, walking away from her. She runs, her little legs pounding, her arms reaching out.

Mama.

And Francine has to leave her, because there is no other way. She cannot hold her child any longer, cannot offer any more explanations, cannot
offer any more of what a mother offers. She has to turn her back, and walk
away, with Clive's arms around her. Her heart is being torn out of her, too.

And she has to listen to Ruth screaming, *"Mama don't leave me, please
don't leave me, please don't leave me,"* behind her, until the Ibans grab her
and lift her bodily off the ground.

Ruth feels herself swept into the air. She is still running, but now her
limbs just flail the air. The Iban warrior holds her tight, trying to console her.
But there is no consolation.

And still the screams follow Francine down the track. And Francine has
to tell herself that it is the child's life, and not this dreadful pain, that is at
stake. She has to repeat the formulas that everything will be all right, that
they will meet again in another life and in another time. That, and Clive, keep
her going.

But still the screams follow her. The screams pour out of Ruth, coming
from her entrails, from her very life. Until a hand, kind and brutal as death,
closes over Ruth's mouth and silence falls over the shocked jungle.

So that Francine can trudge forward into the land where the dead go,
the land called Sabayon, leaving all personal hope behind, praying that she
has done the right thing for her child, that the child will live while she dies.

And still, beneath the hand clamped over her open mouth, Ruth is
screaming and screaming. As she will scream for days to come. Until suddenly, the screaming stops, and becomes silent, because it has become an
internal scream, that nobody hears, not even that other child, called Sakura
Ueda, who will tread another path.

And everything that was beautiful between mother and child has been
torn asunder, and the hideous, brutish world has broken the spell, and nothing is as it was, and nothing can ever be as it was again.

And, in just the same way now, Sakura screamed after Francine, "Mama
don't leave me, please don't leave me."

The Meo were savage little men, their weapons cocked and ready. They
would kill without a moment's hesitation. Why should they hesitate, as their
village burned around them, as the enemy thrust down from China, as their
own king sent bombers to kill them and their women and their children?
What would the lives of a handful of farangs matter?

But this time, Francine stopped and turned. Her body would receive the bullets and the bayonets this time, if that was what was needed. She held out her arms, smiling that special smile.

And so Ruth was in her arms again. The years had changed her, made her tall and beautiful, a woman who in her turn had brought forth life. The little girl had long gone. But it was Ruth who clung to her, Ruth whose tears spilled onto her face.

The two women embraced, oblivious to everything else. The Meo were ready to fire. Clay Munro could see that, he saw their fingers curled around the triggers.

It was Clive who staggered to his feet, and put himself between the soldiers and the women who were clinging to each other. He raised his arms, as though with flesh and bone he could keep away the copper-jacketed hornets that would howl through the air.

It was a day of sacrifices.

There was nothing Clay could do but drop to the ground, clutching the child and curling himself around the small body. He shut his eyes.

"Fuck off, you assholes. Get back up the fucking hill."

Christopher McFadden trudged toward them wearily, covered in red dirt, like a scarecrow, or some kind of lunatic. "Get out of here. Go."

More rockets rushed over the village, exploding among the banana groves.

"Come on!" Munro said. They turned and ran toward the Méhari without looking back at McFadden or the Meo soldiers.

The leader of the Meo shouted something at McFadden.

McFadden spat something back at them in Lao. Clay Munro was still waiting for them to open fire. But they didn't. The hiss of rockets ripped through the air, and the scarlet poppy field behind them belched a fountain of earth and rocks.

The Meo were backing away now, still with their fingers around their triggers. Rocks and poppy flowers were raining down, and Francine felt something smash into her shoulder. She staggered against Sakura, who held her up.

Francine wondered whether the bullets would cut them down. But they reached the Citroën and clambered in. Clay Munro twisted the key, and the air-cooled motor wheezed into life. "Thank God," he said, slamming it into gear.

Then they were flying down the track, all four wheels leaving the ground at times, landing with a crash that jolted the bones and all but burst the tinny plates of the Citroën.

She and Sakura were clinging to each other, the limp boy between them. Sakura's battered face peered at her. "I remember," she said through torn lips.

"Yes," Francine whispered. "I remember, too."

"Oh, God. Oh, Mama."

She sobbed as though her heart had broken, as though she had never been able to cry until that moment, and now was pouring all her three decades of sorrow into it.

But Francine had no more tears. She was too afraid. Death had meant nothing to her until this moment, but now she was filled with a blind terror that she was going to lose Ruth all over again, lose everything she had regained. She held tight to Sakura's slim body, trying to protect her from the worst of the jolting, and stared fearfully at the wilderness around them, her eyes searching for danger in its harshness. She had never felt that she was so remote from anything she knew. These alien hills frightened her. Their vastness could swallow the human soul, leaving only what was bestial behind.

As the Citroën crashed along the appalling road, she thought, *The people who are most important to me are with me in this car. If we hit a mine, we will all go together, and that will be the end of the story.*

Away to their right, an aircraft had been shot down in a rice field, she could not tell what or whose. Olive-green fuselage blazed hotly, black smoke curling swiftly upward. The fire had charred the rice for half an acre downwind.

The smoke from the burning plane stung the eyes, burned the lungs. Through it, tattered caricatures of people filed along the road. These were the last refugees to leave, the old men and women, moving with stiff misery, their grizzled hair hanging in disheveled manes around bony shoulders.

They drove past the refugees into a torrent of rain. It lashed the little car, cutting visibility right down.

"Fuck," Munro growled, hauling on the wheel as the Citroën slid, "if we bog down now, we're dead." He glanced swiftly over his shoulder. "How is everybody?"

"I don't know," Francine whispered. Sakura was crooning, sometimes to her child, sometimes to Francine, her eyes wearing the glaze of concussion and shock. Clive lolled on the seat beside them, half-conscious and covered in his own blood.

"We're okay, Francine," Munro said.

"Yes, we're okay," she replied mechanically. She wondered if it was true.

Rain blew in under the canvas top, washing the dirt and the blood from their faces. Sakura and her mother held each other, Louis between them, their heads pressed together over the child that had come from their flesh.

They reached Phou Fa after nightfall. It had not stopped raining. Already, the road had become a shallow river of mud. By tomorrow, it would have disappeared. In the aftermath of shock and injury, all of them were moving like automatons.

The Helio was abandoned, the village empty. There was no sign of their pilot, Krong.

"Do you think he's run away?" Francine asked Munro.

"He's more likely smoked a couple of pipes and passed out somewhere." Munro cupped his hands around his mouth and screamed for Krong. His own voice mocked him, echoing back from the mountain. Rain thrashed the broken roofs of the huts, drumming on the fuselage of the Helio.

They wandered around, calling for Krong. No reply came, except the endless beating of the rain. Francine felt a bleak horror. Was this how it was going to end, here beside the Helio?

Then she heard Clive croak something. He was pointing with a shaky hand. Krong was peering at them from behind a hut.

"What the fuck are you doing, man?" Munro yelled at him.

"I think you Pathet Lao," Krong said, coming forward.

Munro tossed the rotor arm at him. "Let's go, chief."

They clambered into the Helio. The child, who had slept for the past hour, was awake and crying in Sakura's arms. Sakura was at the end of her strength, so Francine took the child from her, and comforted him. He stopped crying and looked up at her. In the darkness, his face was a ghostly echo of Sakura's.

Clay Munro had his Colt automatic in his hand. "There's a change to the flight plan, chief," he told Krong, as the Thai pilot checked his instruments. "We ain't flying back to Vientiane. You're gonna have to take us to Thailand."

"Thailand?" Krong asked, staring at Munro's pistol.

Munro shrugged. "What difference does it make? Nothing for you here anymore, is there?"

Krong stared at him. Then he nodded slowly, and fired up the Helio's engine.

Sakura slumped against Francine. "Mama," she whispered. "Mama."

Francine held her, and tried to say the name of her lost daughter. But Ruth had gone a long time ago. The woman beside her was Sakura, would always be Sakura. But there would be a new life now. A life that would start again, in some new, as yet unimaginable, but wonderful way.

They would have to talk about it, when there was a time and a place, about that jungle parting, that tear in the fabric of things that had thrown them into different worlds for so many years; that trauma that had robbed Sakura of her memory, and Francine of her ability to love.

Forgiveness had taken a long time to come, and had arrived at one minute to midnight.

Krong rushed the boxy little plane into the night sky. The poppy fields swept beneath their wings, the crimson and white petals already dissolving in the rain. Then there was only the night.

They flew through the darkness toward Thailand, a darkness shot through with the murderous flashes of night gunships hovering over the doomed villages of Laos, carrying with them what had been lost, what had been found.

ACKNOWLEDGMENTS

As always, I wish to thank Elizabeth Murray for her help with research material.

I especially thank my editor, Beverly Lewis, for her help during the long course of this novel's evolution.

Finally, I want to thank my wife, Linda, for patiently reading and correcting endless drafts of the manuscript.

ABOUT THE AUTHOR

MARIUS GABRIEL, author of *House of Many Rooms, The Mask of Time,* and *The Original Sin,* is a former Shakespearean student who left his academic pursuits to become a full-time writer. Mr. Gabriel is also an artist and a musician. He lives in Spain with his wife and three children.

Visit Marius Gabriel on the Web at www.mariusgabriel.com